THE Corpse WITH THE Granite Heart

CATHY ACE

FOUR TAILS PUBLISHING LTD.

PRAISE FOR THE CAIT MORGAN MYSTERIES

"In the finest tradition of Agatha Christie...Ace brings us the closed-room drama, with a dollop of romantic suspense and historical intrigue." – *Library Journal*

"...touches of Christie or Marsh but with a bouquet of Kinsey Millhone." – *The Globe and Mail*

"...a sparkling, well-plotted and quite devious mystery in the cozy tradition..." – *Hamilton Spectator*

"...If all of this suggests the school of Agatha Christie, it's no doubt what Cathy Ace intended. She is, as it fortunately happens, more than adept at the Christie thing." – *Toronto Star*

"Cait unravels the locked-tower mystery using her eidetic memory and her powers of deduction, which are worthy of Hercule Poirot." – *The Jury Box, Ellery Queen Mystery Magazine*

"This author always takes us on an adventure. She always makes us think. She always brings the setting to life. For those reasons this is one of my favorite series."
– *Escape With Dollycas Into A Good Book*

"...a testament to an author who knows how to tell a story and deliver it with great aplomb." – *Dru's Musings*

"...perfect for those that love travel, food, and/or murder (reading it, not committing it)." – *BOLO Books*

"...Ace is, well, an ace when it comes to plot and description."
– *The Globe and Mail*

The Cait Morgan Mysteries
The Corpse with the Silver Tongue
The Corpse with the Golden Nose
The Corpse with the Emerald Thumb
The Corpse with the Platinum Hair
The Corpse with the Sapphire Eyes
The Corpse with the Diamond Hand
The Corpse with the Garnet Face
The Corpse with the Ruby Lips
The Corpse with the Crystal Skull
The Corpse with the Iron Will

The WISE Enquiries Agency Mysteries
The Case of the Dotty Dowager
The Case of the Missing Morris Dancer
The Case of the Curious Cook
The Case of the Unsuitable Suitor

Standalone novels
The Wrong Boy

Short Stories/Novellas
Murder Keeps No Calendar: a collection of 12 short stories/novellas
Murder Knows No Season: a collection of four novellas
Steve's Story in "The Whole She-Bang 3"
The Trouble with the Turkey in "Cooked to Death Vol. 3: Hell for
the Holidays"

For all those who allowed me to discover and develop
my love of Shakespeare

MONDAY

"...all the world's a stage..."

The taxi journey from London's Heathrow airport to the Chelsea Embankment had been a trip down memory lane, seeing places I'd been familiar with when I'd lived in London decades ago. Sadly, my darling husband Bud didn't seem quite as enthralled, however he bucked up a bit when we headed through Earl's Court toward the Thames, understanding we were nearing our final destination – John Silver's home. The main purpose of our trip was to meet John's freshly minted fiancée, one Bella Quiller, to whom he'd recently become engaged...little more than six months after he'd endured a blisteringly acrimonious split from his then-girlfriend, Lottie, with whom we'd spent a difficult time in Jamaica, earlier in the year.

The cab came to a surprisingly silent halt; the new London taxis might look as though they're just a refreshed version of their old diesel-guzzling forebears, but their sleek metal shells hide a secret – they're powered by electricity, so no longer rattle and belch while you're getting out of them.

"Will we fit?" I asked as the cab eerily hissed away.

"How d'you mean?" Bud looked puzzled...tired, a bit grumpy, and puzzled. To be fair, I'd managed to sleep for at least eight of the nine and a half hours of our flight from Vancouver while he'd – apparently – managed no more than a catnap;

unusual for a man who swears his years in law enforcement allowed him to develop the ability to sleep on a pin, at will.

I replied, "I'd put money on Number 1, Thamesview Terrace, Pimlico – John's home, in other words – being no more than twelve feet wide. Where's he going to put us?"

Bud and I scanned the five houses which comprised the terrace – they were almost identical: the ground floor of each sported a window and front door; each upstairs floor was clad with slate, within which was set a pair of tall, narrow windows. The only distinctive feature of the dwellings was the color of the front doors – each was a different pastel shade. We were due to be John's houseguests for five nights, and I was imagining us being shoe-horned into something no bigger than a box room.

"We could have stayed at a hotel," I said, sounding as underwhelmed as I felt. "I know it would have cost a fair bit, but we could have afforded it."

"We're here as his guests, Cait. Besides, it's a great view," said Bud, turning and giving his attention to the Thames and the imposing sight of Battersea Power Station beyond it. He was right; the waters transformed the slate afternoon skies into an Impressionist's rendering of color and texture.

A bus swooshed past, and I scampered away from the threat of filthy, flying spray. "Come on, it looks like it's about to start snowing again." I began to drag my uncooperative suitcase toward the two steps leading up to the doorway.

"Stay there – I'll do it," said Bud, grappling with both our bags. "I texted John from the cab, he knows we're due."

As my husband raised his hand to the knocker, the door flew open and there stood John Silver, Bud's sometime-colleague in all manner of international intelligence-gathering activities, and our savior on a couple of occasions. He looked a great deal better than the last time I'd laid eyes on him: then he'd been haggard – looking older than his sixty-ish years – and coming to terms with a significant discovery about his own fallibility – so, not his best. Now? He looked happy, and in great shape; his long, lean body looked slightly fuller than usual around his midsection, and his smile? It could have illuminated the whole of Trafalgar Square.

"Bud! Cait! How wonderful. Come on in…"

John took Bud's suitcase, and Bud stepped down to take mine. Once both men, and both pieces of luggage, had disappeared through the door, I followed. John immediately enveloped me in his long arms, squashing my face into his chest. *Tall people never seem to realize they could easily suffocate a short person when they hug them.*

John eventually released me, then stepped back and told us how well he thought we were looking – considering we'd been on the road for pretty much twenty-four hours. Bud commented upon the size of John's smile. John patted his tummy, rolled his eyes in naughty-schoolboy fashion, and replied, "That's not all that's bigger these days – Bella's a dab hand in the kitchen."

"And we'll get to meet the lucky woman this evening, right?" asked Bud.

"Yes…yes, you will…" John was faffing – never a good sign.

"Anything we should know?" I couldn't help but ask.

John let go of the handle he was fiddling with and looked at his feet; another tell of his. "We're having dinner at her place. You'll meet her then, and her sister, and brother…and a few other close friends of the family, too."

I could tell by the redness creeping up John's neck there was something he wasn't sharing; for a secret service liaison he's worryingly transparent, on occasion.

"And?" I prompted.

Bud flashed a frown at me, but John finally made eye contact.

He swallowed. "It's not one of her spag bol specials. Rather, it's a dinner to mark what would have been Bella's late-father's eightieth birthday. He died a few weeks back."

"Sorry to hear it," said Bud. "Was he…? I mean, how did he…?" It's not often Bud's lost for words, so I decided he must have been as tired as he'd claimed.

John came to his old comrade's rescue. "Don't panic – no cause for alarm at all. I know what life's like for you two, having to unmask killers wherever you go. This was one of those 'blessed release' situations; poor chap had been ill for some time. Cancer. Pretty much riddled with it by the end. Only managed three days in palliative care. Bella's doing…not well, to be truthful. Maybe, considering the circumstances, that's understandable, but be assured those circumstances are absolutely *not* suspicious. While death appears to follow you wherever you go, on this occasion it beat your arrival quite handily, but with no reason for you two to become involved. You may stand down, sir, madam." He mugged a grin and saluted both Bud and me.

Bud seemed strangely relieved by John's assurances. "Like I said, sorry to hear of his loss, for Bella's sake, and her family. But, if what you say is true, at least we're not wading into muddy waters." *Yes, Husband, you're definitely tired.*

I thought it best to not pick up on John's comment that his fiancée wasn't doing well. Besides, I was in urgent need of a loo, so had no option but to break the mood of the moment to ask if our host could direct me to the nearest bathroom.

"Let's get you into your digs, then you can use your own," he said, seemingly pleased to have an end to the conversation. He opened a door leading off the hallway, and I was surprised to find myself looking into an exceptionally large bedroom.

"Oh, it's bigger on the inside!" I sounded as surprised as I felt.

Bud laughed. "That's a *Doctor Who* reference, I've learned."

John patted Bud on the shoulder. "No need to explain, old man. I grew up terrified of the Daleks too. And yes, it is, Cait. I dare say you've worked out by now that the front of the building I call home is no more than a façade. This terrace was built in the 1960s on the spot where two large Georgian homes had been bombed flat during the war. They built five little houses on the site, then a chap snapped up the whole lot in the mid-1980s and remodeled it like this, knocking four homes into one, leaving Number 5 as a separate dwelling. Vaseem and Vinnie live there – they look after this place when I'm away, and look after me when I'm here: shopping, laundry, cooking, driving, that sort of thing. I don't take any rent from them, of course. Quid pro quo. Great blokes. Don't know what I'd do without them."

"Sounds like an ideal arrangement all round," said Bud.

"It is," replied John, beaming. "This'll be your room for the duration, and your bathroom is through that door. I'm just along the hallway, at the back of the house. Everything else is upstairs – for the view to the river across the road, of course. I'll let you get yourselves sorted, then why not come up when you're ready? We'll need to head out of here in about an hour and a half. Smart casual is fine – it's nothing too formal this evening, just a small gathering, as I said. But, Bud, I suppose I should mention that smart casual here would suggest a jacket, if no tie, okay, old man?"

As Bud and John exchanged some friendly banter about John's use of the term "old man" when referring to Bud, who is his junior by a few years, I took the opportunity to survey our room – it was delightfully appointed in a neutral beige with exquisite taupe and grey accents. Restful, abstract art hung on the walls. It was all a bit too close to "hotel chic" to feel personal in any way, but it made an ideal guest suite.

"I do remember what it's like to move in London society, John," I remarked, possibly more snappily than I'd meant to…because I could now actually *see* the door to the bathroom that was calling my name. "Bud's brought one good multi-purpose jacket which should be suitable."

John smiled. "Of course, you used to live in London, Cait. Right-o, see you in a bit."

John left, and I dashed to the loo. When I emerged, Bud was coming into our room from the hallway with his suitcase; mine was already in front of the large built-in wardrobe.

"Nice room," he said, bouncing on the edge of the bed – which I judged to be a double. "Tiny bed, though. We'll have to cuddle."

I sat beside him. "Yes, Wife will be a lot closer tonight than she usually is at home…though Marty won't be between us, gradually wriggling himself into his preferred sideways position, with each of us hanging onto our edge of the mattress – so we'll probably have more room than normal, if you think about it that way."

"To be honest, I don't care how small it is, this bed looks like heaven at the moment." Bud actually stroked the duvet. "If we're due out of here in ninety minutes, do you think it would be rude of me to grab a nap for an hour? I don't know, maybe I'm getting too old for all this jetting around the world. I'm a bit wiped out." He looked at his watch. "Do you reckon it's too early back home to check with Jack and Sheila that Marty's settled in okay?"

I squeezed Bud's hand. "He'll be fine – you know he adores going to stay with them, probably because they always spoil him rotten. He always comes back to us an even tubbier black Lab than when they take him in."

"True," replied Bud, yawning.

"Look, I tell you what, you get out of those clothes and into bed. I'll pull out what we need for this evening, so the creases can ease in your clean shirt, then I'll text Sheila, and pop upstairs to catch up with John while you nap. I'll wake you in time for you to jump into what you'll see is a spectacular shower – with body-jets and so forth – then I'm sure you'll be your usual sparkling self over pre-dinner drinks."

Bud yawned again. "No argument from me. And it sounds as though we'll both need to be on form if we're at a birthday party for a dead man, *and* meeting John's fiancée. But at least this guy died a natural death, so I dare say we should be grateful for that, given our track record."

I knew what he meant. "Yes, poor thing. Horrible, but natural, as you say. And I'm dying to meet Bella."

"Not a joke, right?"

"Absolutely no joke intended," I replied.

Bud was already clambering between the sheets, his clothes tossed on an antique slipper chair in the corner of the room. I unpacked as quietly as I could, then went to hunt for John upstairs.

I found him in what turned out to be an enormous open-concept white box into which had been dropped black leather sofas, a glass-topped dining table – all accented with massive pieces of multi-colored abstract art on the walls – and an all-white kitchen with a vast marble-topped peninsula.

John was sitting on a chrome stool beside the countertop, his head on his arm, his free hand clutching a tumbler of amber liquid. His back heaved as he sobbed.

Oh dear...what now?

"…the course of true love…"

My tummy clenched, but I strode the length of the room until I could rub John's back. "What's up?" I asked.

John's face was puffy, his eyes rimmed with red. "Bella just phoned. She says the wedding's off."

I was taken aback. "Wedding? You only just got engaged. You'd already set a date for the wedding?" *News to me.*

"Chelsea Town Hall. This Friday at three thirty. Bella and I were going to ask you and Bud to be our witnesses when we were all together this evening. Now? Now I don't know…"

I didn't say anything. Sometimes I *am* capable of that…just about. I pulled a face to signify sympathy, and rubbed John's back a little harder.

"I love her so much, Cait. I don't know what I'd do without her."

All sorts of comments swirled in my head, most concerning the fact that he and Bella had known each other for only a few months, and hadn't he been head over heels for Lottie the last time I'd seen him? But I knew I shouldn't utter a word. I also knew that if I rubbed his back any harder, or longer, I might start to slough off his skin through his shirt, so I stood back and looked around to see if I could spot a kettle: a pot of tea was called for.

"I'm so sorry, John," was the most neutral and supportive statement I could muster as I scanned the cavernous kitchen. Not a kettle to be seen – neither electric, nor stovetop. How on earth did John boil water?

"Fancy a cuppa, instead of whatever's in that glass?" I was concerned I might have to cope alone with John trying to drown his sorrows until I had a chance to rouse Bud.

"I'll do it." John sounded defeated, and looked it, too. He stood, still towering over me despite an unusual stoop. "She's not been the same since her father died. She'd led me to believe they weren't terribly close, but his death has cast a tremendous pall over Bella and her sister. I've been hoping tonight's marking of her father's birthday would give them a chance to get past this...this...I don't know what to call it, really. They've both become extraordinarily maudlin since he died. Bella's not like that, as a rule. One of the reasons I love her is that she's always full of light, and hope. She's such a wonderful person, Cait – always positive. Upbeat. Sees the good in everyone, and every situation. Loves to be...well, I suppose spontaneous is the best word. Surprises me all the time. A little madcap, on occasion. But I enjoy indulging her; life's not been a bed of roses for poor Bella, not by a long chalk. Her sister...well, she was always the apple of their father's eye, and Bella always came second in his thoughts. Nowadays she's just dreadfully miserable all the time."

I weighed my response. "The death of a loved one can affect a person in the most unexpected ways, John. Maybe seeing her father suffer through a protracted illness ground her down, emotionally, then his death provided the release you mentioned earlier, but at the expense of her feeling some guilt."

"But she didn't see him suffer, that's the thing." John sounded as though he were talking to himself, not me. "She hadn't seen her father for years. He remained close to her sister, but Bella and he didn't even speak to each other, and she rarely spoke about him. Until he died, that is. Prior to his death I knew almost nothing about him...except for his public persona. And I'd done a bit of extra research into him and his background, of course, when I was...well, while I was doing a bit of digging around in Bella's history." He nibbled his lip. "After that mess with Lottie, you'd expect me to at least do that, right?"

I nodded. *Oh yes, at least that, John.* "You learned a great deal from that, I'm sure. And I know from personal experience that it's possible to pick entirely the wrong person before you find the right one. Just think of me and Angus; he was absolutely the worst thing that ever happened to me. Took me down to rock bottom. But now? Now there's Bud. See? It's possible to find good coming from bad. Though I'm sorry to hear you say Bella's not coping well with her father's death."

"Oh Cait, she's become obsessed by the man, and he's no longer here – he's dead and should be gone, but it's as though his shadow has lingered, and it's brought her to this point where she says she can't go through with the wedding."

I had no idea who Bella's father had been, nor why he had what John had called a "public persona", but I realized finding out wasn't a priority at that precise moment. "Did she give you a reason for wanting to postpone the wedding?"

John gulped from his glass. "Not postpone, *cancel.* She wants to call it off completely. She said she can't expect me to marry into such a family."

My face must have expressed the fact I didn't know how to respond.

John's voice was brittle when he replied. "Yes. I don't know what that means, either."

I plastered what I hoped was a sympathetic look onto my face. "Do you want to go to her home this evening, as planned, with Bud and me as reinforcements, to try to find out more? Or did she tell you, categorically, not to come tonight?"

John nibbled his top lip. Finally, his chin lifted, and he straightened his shoulders. His eyes flickered with defiance as he replied, "No, she didn't mention this evening, specifically. So, yes…yes, I do want to go."

"Very well then, Bud and I will do all we can to help."

"And you can pick up the pieces if she won't budge."

"Let's cross that bridge when we come to it, John…*if* we come to it." I reached up and hugged him. "As for now, what about a pot of tea? I could kill for a cuppa. How on earth do you manage without a kettle?"

"Ah, look at this." John's still-red eyes shone a little as he pulled open the door to a cupboard which held an assortment of coffee-making paraphernalia, as well as a kettle that looked as though it had been designed by someone who'd grown up watching 1950s sci-fi films and had developed a deep-seated love of chrome.

"Excellent."

As John set about making tea, I couldn't help but wonder what an evening celebrating the life of a dead man, whose demise seemed to have adversely affected at least two of his children, held for us. I also had no idea how Bud and I could possibly help John in his current situation. I'm a professor of criminal psychology, so I've always studied those whose psyches and actions deviate from the norm. However, I'm pretty hopeless when it comes to relationships…as witnessed by the fact I'd gone so far as to migrate to Canada well over a decade earlier to escape the hounding of the British tabloids which continued even after I'd been completely cleared of killing my abusive ex-boyfriend, Angus. I reminded myself I'd also spent many of the intervening years building a reputation as something of an expert in profiling victims of crime, as opposed to criminals. Was there anything in my arsenal that would be useful when dealing with a probably-grieving woman who was breaking the heart of someone I knew and respected a great deal? I felt a little at sea, and I can't swim, so that's never a good feeling for me.

"Tell me more about Bella – and her family," I said. It seemed to be the best thing to do.

John leaned on the counter. "She's wonderful, Cait."

I smiled. "So you said. *Really*, tell me about her, John. Clearly you have strong feelings for her – but tell me some facts. Who was her father, for example? What about her siblings? Go on – just the facts, sir, just the facts." I mugged an American accent, but John looked puzzled. I added, "Joe Friday? *Dragnet*? Nothing?"

John shook his head. "You've been away from here too long, Cait."

"In my defense, *Dragnet* was a hugely successful television series in the 1950s, well before my time, but the repeats ran here for years. You can't tell me you've never heard of it."

John turned to pour water into the teapot. "Well, I've heard of it, but don't know anything about it."

I realized there was little point pursuing the matter. "Never mind, just tell me all about Bella and her family."

"Biscuits? I've got some shortbread fingers."

I nodded. "Yes please. And facts…"

John managed a smile. "I give in! Okay – Bella is Bella Quiller. Izabel, on her birth certificate. Married – briefly, when she was quite young – to a chap named Brian Quiller, who's rather well-known as a designer of theatrical productions. She was Quiller when she started to make her mark in her own field, so – with his agreement – she's continued with her use of the name, even though they've been divorced for years. Her father was Oleg Asimov. Have you heard of him?"

I shook my head. "Nope. Fill me in."

"The Asimovs came to London in the early twentieth century with nothing. Literally nothing. Bella's great-grandfather settled in Spitalfields…you know, here in London…and set about making some sort of life for himself. By the time his first son was born, the Asimovs owned a boarding house; by the time his third son – Bella's grandfather – was born, they owned a dozen. From then on, the family grew its business of buying houses, doing them up, and renting them out. Bella's great-grandfather was – by her account – a juggernaut of a man, and he became known not just for his refusal to take no for an answer, but also as something of a wit, and raconteur. He began to move in some elevated circles, and was able to leverage his connections to his, and his family's, advantage. All three of his sons were bright, all won scholarships, and attended some of the best schools in the country. Bella's grandfather took over the running of the family business, and by the time Bella's father – an only child – was a young boy, the Asimovs were well placed to take full advantage of the post-war building boom, as contractors. Her grandfather had made some excellent connections at the school he'd attended, you see. Old school tie, and all that." John winked, knowingly.

Sadly, I recalled only too well how poorly a working-class girl from Wales had been treated by that very same "network" when she'd arrived in London to build a life and career for herself almost thirty years back. It was the first time I'd encountered the titanium mesh that binds together those who've endured the particular brand of cruelty and indoctrination that's the stock-in-trade of the English public school system.

John looked a little puzzled – probably because I was frowning as I remembered any number of slights I'd endured back in those days – then pressed on. "So, you see, Bella grew up in a well-respected, extremely wealthy family with ties to many of the great landowners in London and its environs – so pretty much everyone with a title. In less than a hundred years, the Asimovs became utterly integrated into the upper *echelons* of English society."

"Is that the public version of the family's history, or the private one?" I was curious.

John glanced at the teapot as he replied, "My investigations haven't been able to uncover much else – though Bella's grandfather and father were both rumored to be pretty good at sharp practice, if not men who were ever known to have actually crossed the line to illegality. Bella's father was also a significant supporter of Shakespeare…not exactly a scholar, but he put some money onto getting the Globe Theatre rebuilt, and he set up, and funded, a scheme that takes the Bard's plays into schools – the ones where the children might not otherwise have a chance to see them in a real theater."

Philanthropy is alive and kicking in the twenty-first century, I thought. "How benevolent of him," I replied.

"Bella says the only thing of any real importance the public has no idea about is how utterly toxic her father was as a person. That's why she chose to have so little to do with him; she was afraid he'd poison her life. Before his death – before she even knew he was dying – she said he was so difficult to live with that none of his wives could stand him for long. As I said earlier, I never met the man, so can't comment, but the record might bear out Bella's words. Oleg had four wives: his first died in childbirth, as did the child; his second was the mother of Bella and her sister Sasha, they divorced, and Bella's mother died some years ago – five or six, I believe; the third was the mother of Bella's half-brother, Charles – they also divorced, but she remarried…a chap with even more money that Oleg, Bella tells me, and she's now some sort of countess living in the south of France; the fourth gave Oleg no children, but they divorced nonetheless. You might have heard of her: Felicity Sampson."

"The model?" Even though I'd never followed the society or "what to wear this season" pages – because I firmly believe the fashion police should be lined up against a wall and forced to show us what they all wore when they were teens – even I knew of Felicity Sampson…the fashionista "IT" girl about thirty years ago, usually snapped by the paparazzi while falling out of a taxi at four in the morning, draped over the arm of some young blade with a title and a pot of money.

"So-called model," replied John disdainfully, as he poured my tea. "Reckons she's an 'influencer' nowadays. Though goodness knows who would want to be influenced by her. On the occasions I've met her she's struck me as vacuous and more than a little hedonistic. She might be well-connected, and even high-born, but she's lived most of her life as a C-list celebrity, rather than being a productive member of society. Not that I know a great deal about her, of course, but Bella's known her since she was quite young; Felicity was a friend of the family long before she became the fourth Mrs. Oleg Asimov."

I reached for the plate of shortbread biscuits as I allowed my tea to cool. "But you say Bella had little to do with her father during his life?" I asked a question I hoped would lead to a long answer so I could enjoy my biscuit.

"Bella and Sasha, and Charles of course, were away at school for years," began John. "Cheltenham and Eton, respectively."

Oh, the delights of moving in circles where the assumption is that all children go to boarding school, was what I thought. "Of course," was what I mumbled through crumbs.

"They were spared her father's oversight for most of their young lives – Bella's words – then they each struck out on their own at university and their follow-through careers. Well, Charles didn't take the university route; he's a hairdresser. Some might say *the* hairdresser. More rock star than coiffeur. Heard of Charles A?"

I shook my head. "Not big on hairdressers," I muttered. *If only you knew…I've cut my own hair since my twenties, following a disastrous experiment with high- and low-lights for which I still haven't quite forgiven the entire profession.*

"Well, Charles is a big noise in London society, too. Bella seems to like him alright – says he's mainly harmless – but, I tell you, he's the most aggressively heterosexual hairdresser I've ever encountered. Known for 'dating' any female with a title, a nicely padded bank account, or possibly just a pulse…single, or married. He's annoyingly flamboyant, and women tell me he's irresistibly raffish and good-looking. Personally, I don't understand what they all see in him – I reckon he's overcompensating for something, though I don't know what."

Possibly an unhappy childhood, packed off to board with the well-heeled but not necessarily super-bright? Was what I thought. "Hmm…" was what I said.

"Anyway, Sasha did her thing, and Bella did hers," continued John. "Bella studied jewellery design at university, then got her goldsmithing qualifications. You must have heard of Bella Zoloto. Bella's a brand, as well as a person."

I felt I was letting John down shockingly when I had to shake my head again. By way of explanation, I waggled my hands in the air. "Just the wedding and engagement rings, and a watch. That's it. Oh, and a few pairs of serviceable earrings. You know what I'm like, John; just not the flash jewelry type."

John looked a little hurt.

I tutted inwardly. *Foot in mouth, Cait.* "Sorry. I don't mean to suggest your fiancée panders to a clientele that should favor something more significant than personal adornment. It's just not my thing – hence the lack of knowledge. I'm assuming Bella designs gold jewellery, thus *zoloto*, the Russian word for gold. Playing on her heritage?"

John nodded. "She's got such a good eye. Her designs have won awards, you know." I didn't, but made every effort to look impressed. "She designed this," he added.

John surprised me by opening two buttons of his shirt. I was even more taken aback to see he was sporting a large gold medallion on a heavy chain. I didn't have my handbag with me, nor, therefore, my reading cheats, so I squinted at his chest.

"Is that a centaur?"

John's chin lifted. "She said that's how she sees me – man and beast in perfect harmony." He rebuttoned his shirt.

Too much information! I thought. "Very nice," was what came out of my mouth. "She's obviously a talented designer – it's a beautiful piece."

John rubbed the precious object through his shirt. "She is, and it is. She's known for individual pieces like this – commissioned work is her primary passion. Though the Bella Zoloto brand exists to allow people with a bit less cash to own something she's designed, even if it hasn't been made by her. She has a workshop where those pieces are made by a team she oversees, and her own private facilities at her home."

"Quite the businesswoman," I observed.

"Not really – she's an artist in the true sense of the word, so she mostly sticks to the creative aspects, with a bit of quality control too – it's Sasha who's the brains behind the brand. Got her father's ability with numbers, has Sasha…so says Bella, in any case. Sasha's a big-wig in PR. She and her husband run their own agency. Lobbyists. You were in that line of work yourself, once, weren't you, Cait?"

I nodded. It seemed like another person had lived that life. Anything "BA" feels that way to me: "Before Angus" and my time at Cambridge, my world – and possibly I, myself – had been so different.

I snapped out of it. "Yes, I was, though more on the advertising side, rather than lobbying," I replied. A cog rolled into place. "I worked with a woman named Asimov. Though she was Alex Asimov, not Sasha."

"Really?" John stared at me, open-mouthed, across his cup of tea. "Bella's sister's proper name is Alexandra...though she's always been called Sasha within the family. Nowadays she's Tavistock. Of Tavistock and Tavistock PR. Sasha's professional name is Alex. Alex Tavistock. So, you know Sasha? Gosh. Small world, eh?"

I sipped my scalding tea carefully as I recalled Alex Asimov when she and I had been at The Townsend Agency all those years ago; we were there at the same time, but had never worked on the same client accounts. She'd been pompous, and not as good at her job as she'd thought, despite the fact she was – invariably, and annoyingly – first into, and last out of, the office. Cold eyes, whip-thin, and a tongue as sharp as a scimitar. I wondered if she'd changed, then hoped she had, for John's sake...she might be just about to become his sister-in-law, after all.

"She always put in the hours," I said. It was the most charitable comment I could summon. "Did she marry someone in the business. Oh, hang on...not Piers Tavistock? Is she married to Piers Tavistock?" *Please say no!*

"Don't tell me you know Piers too?" John beamed. "Yes, they run their own agency. Together. How wonderful you know them both. This might help, Cait. There'll be quite a different atmosphere when we get there this evening if you already know Bella's sister and brother-in-law."

John seemed genuinely heartened, and set down his cup onto his saucer like a man who'd just quaffed the elixir of eternal youth.

I forced myself to smile. The last time I'd seen Piers Tavistock had been at the party thrown for me when I'd left the agency. He'd launched himself at me in the ladies' toilets in the pub, and I'd had to fight him off with my handbag. It was at that point – just as I was thwacking him across the head while he drunkenly fumbled with my blouse – that Alex had walked in on us. She'd thrown a glass of red wine in my face, grabbed Piers, and hustled him back into the crowded bar…calling me a slut over her shoulder, loud enough for everyone to hear.

That was the last I'd ever seen of the pair of them and wasn't at all sure how reacquainting myself with them would turn out…but I thought it best to not bring John down from his happy little cloud by mentioning it.

"Probably best I wake Bud," I said, having checked my watch. John nodded and I padded away. Bud would have to get by with just a little less sleep than we'd planned; I needed to bring him up to speed with what the evening might hold for us.

Bud's earlier use of the term "muddy waters" echoed through my thoughts.

"...the memory be green..."

Bud and I had done all we could to achieve "London smart casual" status: I was wearing my multi-purpose black bouncy two-piece with a paisley over-thingy in tones of brown, beige, and gold; Bud looked relatively comfortable in a jacket and slacks, and his blue shirt almost exactly matched the color of his eyes. We presented ourselves at the front door at the appointed hour. Bud was still looking a bit dazed, and I was less than my sparkling self, because I was – frankly – worried about how the evening might turn out.

"Vinnie will have the car ready for us at the back of the house." John looked incredibly dapper in an eye-wateringly expensive jacket, teamed with a shirt that had probably cost more than what both Bud and I had spent on our entire get-ups. "Follow me." He sounded quite like himself as he led us to the top of a staircase which descended below the one I'd climbed to reach the upper floor.

"You have a basement this close to the river?" I was surprised.

"Indeed," replied John nonchalantly. "When they began excavations in the 1960s they discovered the original Georgian houses had basements, so the chap who was developing the site managed to get basement level usage grandfathered into the building permissions – which is why I'm fortunate to have this facility."

We were in a gloomy space that seemed to have only one wall. John flicked a switch, illuminating a large garage, housing a gleaming, red Mini Cooper, with space for another vehicle.

"What, no Aston Martin?" I mugged. Bud didn't even register a smile. *What's wrong with you, Husband?*

"Hardy, ha, ha," replied John. "Parking is – as one might imagine – at something of a premium around here. It's a bit of a faff to come downstairs, then go back up again to the street behind the terrace, but there's no way a car could collect us at the front; bus lane and all that."

Bud nodded, a bit vacantly.

"Come on, this way." John led us up an incline, pushed a button, and the entire wall slid sideways. In front of us was a deserted narrow road, bounded by a high wall.

John looked at his watch. "Vinnie said he had to pop out to get some petrol. Should be here any minute. Let's take advantage of this shelter until I spot him."

John wasn't going to get any argument from me. "Good idea," I replied. Sleet was falling, and it was chilly – not something I'd expected us to encounter in London, where the temperature is usually maintained at a slightly higher-than-elsewhere level, because of the density of its buildings.

"Isn't it wonderful that Cait already knows Bella's sister and brother-in-law, Bud?" John shuffled from foot to foot as we waited; his overcoat was beautifully cut but didn't seem to be keeping out the cold very effectively.

"Sure," replied Bud sounding distracted. I'd described to him the nature of my past working relationships with Alex – who I kept doing my best to refer to as *Sasha* – and Piers, but he hadn't seemed to be firing on all cylinders at the time. "I'm sure Bella will come round," he added, with so little conviction that John began to chew at his lip.

"Yes. Yes, old man, I'm sure you're right." He leaned out into the lane. "Ah, there's Vinnie. You two go ahead; bundle yourselves into the back, and I'll shut up shop."

Bud opened the rear door of the sleek Mercedes and I slithered inside. He followed, with John taking the seat beside the driver. "Thanks, Vinnie. Beulah House, please. This is Bud and Cait, as advertised." John glanced around as he buckled up. "I've told Vinnie and Vaseem all about you both." He flashed a grin, "Well, not *everything* I know, of course – but they're the ones to thank for your room being kitted out. Vaseem decorated it himself."

"With my help; slave labor," added Vinnie. "Nice to meet you both. I hope you have a grand visit."

"Is that an Irish accent?" I asked. I reckoned Dublin.

"To be sure, to be sure." Vinnie laughed throatily. "Thought most of the edges had been knocked off living in this godforsaken place for the past twenty years," he added. "Whenever I go home, they tell me I sound like a real Cockney."

"No danger of that," I replied, "but it's nice to hang onto the accent you started out with, isn't it?"

"It is that, Boyo, it is that." Vinnie pulled out into traffic, and we were off. "John tells me you're from Swansea, originally. I've got two aunties in Wales – one in Llandudno, one in Cardiff. Love it there, so they do, though they both make out their priests were sent to their parishes as some sort of punishment, because of all the godless chapel-goers they're surrounded by. Me? I've been there a few times and think it's green and lovely, unlike London. Will you be going there this trip?"

"The plan is to rent a car and go for the weekend," I replied.

"That'll be grand," said Vinnie.

"Yes, I'm really looking forward to it. It'll be our second wedding anniversary in a few weeks, and we were married there, so it'll be nice to visit a few favorite places again." I could almost taste the Joe's ice cream I knew I'd have as soon as we arrived in Mumbles, and told myself Saturday wasn't too far off…all we had to do was get through this thing with John and Bella, see them married, and everything would be fine.

As we chatted, my eyes greedily drank in the once-familiar sights we were passing. I supposed the development along Queenstown Road was bound to happen – with such wonderful views across the river, then Battersea Park – but the scale of it amazed me. Beyond the park the changes along our route were few and far between; I was glad, because the general architecture was not without Edwardian charm.

"Staying with family in Wales?" Vinnie's almost-inevitable question was innocent.

"Mum and Dad died in a car accident more than ten years ago, and my sister, Siân, lives in Perth, Western Australia. So no, Bud and I will stay in a hotel; they have some nice ones in the area." I tried to make my voice sound as though I wasn't keenly aware that when I told people where we both now lived, it sounded as though Siân and I had made a real effort to live as far away from Wales, and each other, as humanly possible.

"Sorry to hear that. May they rest in peace." Vinnie's tone conveyed genuine regret. "Mine are still kicking. Both of them. Often each other, or one of their many, many, grandchildren. I'm pleased to say my four sisters have more than made up for my lack of procreation. I'm the baby of the brood, so can do no wrong, thank the Lord. Though they still choose to believe Vaseem is my flatmate."

Judging by the back of his neck, and a slight view of the side of his head, I gauged Vinnie was in his late thirties or early forties. From my seat directly behind him I could see he had broad shoulders, and suspected his taut jawline meant he worked out more than a little. I wasn't sure whether the totally bald head was purely a style choice, or a response to a receding hairline.

"Vinnie and Vaseem have been together for ten years," said John wistfully. "I can't say any of my relationships have lasted half as long, though I had hoped…"

"Hey, this one's agreed to marry you, so you're set now, John-boy." Vinnie shoved John with his elbow.

I mused about the relationship between these two men. It obviously wasn't one of an employer and employee – it was far too jocular for that. More a meeting of equals who were both benefitting from what John had described as a "quid pro quo"? But if they were "equals", what did that mean? I wondered if Vinnie's physique might be something he'd developed in the services; was there something militaristic about him? Being Irish, and knowing about John's connection to all sorts of security services around the world, that raised some interesting questions in my mind – none of which I suspected I'd ever ask.

Bud said, "Where are we going, by the way? I mean I know we're going to meet Bella, but where will we be doing that?"

John twisted so he could at least see me, though not Bud, who was directly behind him. "Bella's house. Well, Bella *and* Sasha's house really. Their late mother left it to the both of them. Bella actually lives in the coach house; it's cozy there – everything just the right size for one, and I manage to fit in, at a pinch. The main house is a joy. Big old place. I think of it as a bit of a Frankenstein house – not that it's stuffed full of horrors, or secret laboratories or anything like that, but it's been changed so much over the centuries that it's all a bit of a mishmash. Started out as an early Georgian delight – solid, symmetrical. Then they added bits here and there. Anyway, you'll see for yourselves later on. You might know the area, Cait. Upper Norwood? Highest point in the area – they used it during the Anglo-French survey in the mid 1700s when they were measuring the exact distance between the Royal Greenwich Observatory and the Paris Observatory – it's not far from

Greenwich, as the crow flies. Close to Dulwich; there's a blue plaque commemorating the house where Raymond Chandler lived not far away – you know, when he was at Dulwich College. I bet none of those thrillers of his would have been written if it hadn't been for the classic education he received there as a boy."

"Chandler? Really? I had no idea," said Bud, "I thought he was American."

John turned to face forward again, "Yes, he was, but his Irish mother brought him to London so he could receive a good education, and Dulwich managed to produce him, PG Wodehouse, and CS Forester, so it certainly earned its reputation. It also produced me, too, so there's that."

Bud cracked a smile, which warmed my heart. "Yes, there's that, but you can't expect them to turn out brilliance every time."

"Ha, ha," replied John dryly. "Chandler also spent a little time in your neck of the woods. Vancouver. Quite a chap."

"I didn't know you were such a Chandler fan," I said.

"Not a fan, as such. I find his books readable, but the similes annoy one after a time. I very much enjoy his work for film – more than his books." John's voice sounded hollow. "He certainly knew how to write manipulative female characters. *Double Indemnity* is a case in point. Women have a much greater ability than men to be desperately cruel."

Given that we were on our way to try to talk a woman out of cancelling her planned marriage to him, I thought I'd better try to cheer him up a bit.

"So, come on – tell us how you and Bella met," I said brightly.

"All thanks to this chap here," he said, patting Vinnie on the shoulder.

Vinnie replied happily, "That it is, though I can only claim to have played a part in it. It was because of Vaseem, really. Got a lot to answer for, he has, that boy."

"Oh, that sounds interesting – do tell." I did my best to sound gushingly enthusiastic.

"It's funny how things work out, isn't it?" John began. "Vaseem got to know Sasha through a job he was doing, and he invited me along to a party she was hosting at her house. Bella was there too, and she and I…well, we just hit it off straight away, didn't we, Vinnie?"

Vinnie chuckled throatily. "You could put it that way, yes. Pure lust it was, from the off. Couldn't keep their eyes, or their hands, off each other, truth be told. Then they got to know one another, and it turned out they actually liked each other, too – and now they're set to walk down the aisle. Who'd have guessed it?"

It was clear that John hadn't told Vinnie about Bella calling off the wedding.

"Yes, who'd have guessed it," said John, sounding bleak again. He added, "Clapham Common looks as though it could gobble you up and never spit you out, doesn't it?"

I tried to rally him. "Oh, I don't know. It's wonderful that it's survived. A breath of slightly fresher air with all its greenery."

"It's no more than a giant, rectangular roundabout, I always think," was John's succinct way of shutting me down.

We skirted Clapham and headed along the South Circular; I was pleased our route gave me a chance to be driven past my old flat at the top of Brixton Hill, but my reaction to seeing the place wasn't what I'd expected. As I gazed up at the block, I experienced the jolt of familiarity I'd imagined I'd get; I'd loved the building since the moment I'd laid eyes on it decades earlier – classic 1930's architecture inspired by ocean-going liners, with rounded corners and white concrete trim…just the sort of place Poirot would have lived, I'd always thought. But then I saw someone closing the curtains in what had once been my bedroom, and the sight sent a chill through me. Unreasonably.

That home that was no longer mine. It was just a setting, a place in which I'd once lived part of my life. My old life. But still…someone was in *my* bedroom…and I wondered how they'd redecorated it.

I held Bud's hand, and settled back into my seat to allow more of my history to flash past me: the pubs that had been my locals; the bus stops where I'd stood for what must have amounted to days of my life; the places I'd done my shopping, and more pubs that had been a little further away from home, but inviting enough to warrant a longer walk at the end of the evening. In this part of London, not much had changed – except the names above the doors of the kebab shops and pizzerias…and there seemed to be many more nail salons than I recalled.

We finally began the ascent from Streatham High Road toward our destination. This wasn't territory with which I was as familiar, so was able to see it with fresher eyes, which was good. Before long Vinnie turned off the main road into a narrow and rather bumpy lane, which led nowhere, it seemed. The car slowed to a crawl, then he took a sharp right into what appeared to be a copse, with the word PRIVATE spray-painted on a large piece of hardboard; it didn't look terribly salubrious, and I wondered if he really had the right place.

I shouldn't have worried, because after about twenty yards a driveway opened ahead of us and we were facing a wonderful house, that had once been – as John had said – a symphony of early Georgian symmetry; carriage lights either side of the front door glowed against the yellow London stock brick, and a small, paved area containing a fountain provided the center of a turning circle. To the left was an almost-detached building, which I assumed was the coach house where Bella lived; it certainly had the characteristic massive wooden double-door at one end, but it looked too small to have also provided stabling for the horses. However, what really drew my eye was the roofline of the main house, which glinted in a flash of moonlight peeping through the shredding clouds.

"Is that a giant greenhouse up there?" I was puzzled.

John chuckled. "When the original Crystal Palace was all the rage, just a little way down the hill, the then-owner of this place decided to stick that on top of his house. It uses the same principle – glass in an iron framework. As you can see, it means the house offers an even better vantage point than it once had. They refer to it as the palace room," he cleared his throat, "because that's what it's always been called – not because they claim to be somehow vaguely related to the Russian royal family – which Oleg apparently did. But, you know, the name isn't about that. They're a wealthy family, but not…pompous, in that way."

"It's quite something," said Bud.

I wasn't sure if my husband's tone meant he thought it was a good something, or not; I thought it remarkable, in the true sense of the word.

Vinnie pulled up in front of the porticoed door. "The wine's in the boot," he said, as John unbuckled his seatbelt.

Bud and I also got out, and I gave Vinnie a little wave as I passed his window. He waved back, his face illuminated by the car's interior lighting; well-balanced features, blue eyes that were even paler than Bud's, big smile, great teeth.

John was already at the door to the main house, a bottle in his hand. "We're early, but Bella will have come over by now, in any case," he said. He didn't need to check his watch – he'd done so a thousand times on the journey. "She's always in charge of drinks – and exceptionally good at it. I don't think Sasha would know how much tonic to add to a gin if you paid her; she's far too used to others providing her a service to worry about that sort of detail."

She certainly used to know how to tuck away a fair few G & Ts when I knew her, I thought. "Ah," was what I said.

"Everything's going to be fine," whispered Bud to John, who squared his shoulders, then tugged at the brass bell pull.

I heard jangling inside, then we waited; three nervous people standing in the chill of a winter's evening wondering what the next few hours would hold.

"…more than kin, and less than kind…"

The door opened and I squinted in the brilliance of the scene in front of me: heavy velvet curtains were held back by tassels each side of the front door, which struck me as both practical – to keep out draughts – and theatrical. A glittering chandelier hung above a black-and-white tiled entrance hall; beyond, I could sense, rather than see, a more dimly-lit expanse of house.

Muted chatter wafted toward us, over which the silhouette that had dramatically pulled open the double doors declaimed, "Welcome. See, I told Glen you'd be early. Always plans for the worst traffic, doesn't he, that Vinnie of yours? He's a good boy. Come on in before you get frozen. Does Vinnie need to use the facilities before he goes?"

As she stepped toward us, the illumination of the lamps either side of the front door allowed me to make out the features of the speaker: taller than me by a few inches – so probably around five seven – the woman ushering us into the comforting warmth from the bleakness of the doorstep was older than any of us, somewhere in her mid-sixties. She wore a plain, black, shift dress, which sagged a little across her flat chest, but strained at her broad hips; she smiled at John as though she were welcoming her son home from war.

As she stood back for us to enter, John said, "Thanks, Julie. Vinnie said he'd drop into the pub for the evening; I'll text him when we've got some idea when this little shindig will be finishing." He turned and waved at the car; I saw Vinnie wave back, smiling.

"All out by ten thirty, that's what Mrs. T said she wants." Julie nodded her head toward the body of the building. "Now come on, let me take them coats of yours." It was wonderful to hear her South London accent.

I took off my coat and was delighted to see a magnificent Christmas tree in the corner of the entryway, tucked in beside the front door. It was tastefully decorated in red and gold, and the star on its top glinted, the only part of the tree to be lit.

John introduced us. "This is Julie. She and her husband Glen run the place – between them they can do just about everything that's needed."

Julie's arms were full of coats, so I waggled my hand at her and flashed a smile; I've never quite got the hang of how to deal with folks offering service inside a person's home, as opposed to in a public space – the idea of "staff" or "servants" or "help" is completely alien to me, and not something I think I'll ever get used to. Not that I'm likely to have the chance.

"Come through, I'll announce you. Miss Bella's doing her thing with the drinks trolley, she'll sort you out." Julie smiled, then leaned toward me and stage-whispered, "Go on, ask her for something really complicated – she loves that, she does." She winked, walked briskly into the salon – leaving us trailing behind her – and announced John, then bustled off through one of a number of doors set into the wall on our far left, all of which were decorated to blend in with the panelling of the wall itself, which instantly appealed to me, because I've always had a bit of a thing about hidden doors; I blame Nancy Drew.

To our right, a wide staircase swept up and around the double-height entry hall, leading to a wooden balustrade that ran the width of the house, while ahead of us, the main salon beckoned. John took the lead, clearing his throat as he strode out. Bud and I shuffled behind him, but I managed to spot an almost-familiar face over John's shoulder.

Alex Asimov – *Sasha* – had changed since I'd last seen her; she was more rounded in every way…her body, and even her features, had a surprising softness about them, and it was obvious from the way her face had wrinkled that she was more used to smiling than looking miserable. Her once-reddish-blonde hair, which she'd invariably worn in a tight chignon during our office times, hung in waves over her shoulders; now a less lustrous shade, threaded with gray, it almost exactly matched the color of the velvet, medieval-inspired gown she wore. I felt a tad underdressed, but reasoned I couldn't have foreseen every wardrobe requirement of our trip when I'd packed. I'd always imagined Sasha to be a good deal older than myself, but judged she was probably still only in her mid-fifties. Overall, I was amazed at how happy and glowing she looked. *Maybe she's had a personality transplant?*

I knew I'd put on a good few pounds – well, maybe a few dozen pounds – since she'd last set eyes on me, and I've never colored my hair, so it's not as brown as it once was, but I'd expected some glimmer of recognition when my ex-colleague saw me. However, there wasn't anything in her eyes to suggest we'd even met. That said, she wasn't looking at me at all – she was gazing at John, her eyes dewy. *Odd.*

Sasha moved toward John, and he to her. They flung their arms around each other as she cried, "Oh Johnnie, my darling Johnnie, I've been such a fool. I love you so much. Of course I couldn't possibly live without you. Can you ever forgive me?"

The kiss which followed gave Bud a chance to shuffle his feet and clear his throat, while I felt my mouth fall open.

What's happening?

A couple of seconds later, a booming voice called, "Is that Cait Morgan, I spy? No, surely it can't be." I looked across the room and spotted an enlarged, ruddier version of the Piers Tavistock I remembered; he was lounging in a chair, waistcoat buttons straining, with a look of astonishment on his face. "Good God it is. As I live and breathe, Cait Morgan. Are you one of John's 'friends from Canada'? Is that where you disappeared to?"

I breathed deeply as I mentally edited several potential responses and was about to utter possibly the most wittily pithy riposte of my life, when I heard the distinct nasal tones that had irritated me all those years ago.

"Yes, that's Cait Morgan alright." I spun toward the sound – and there was Alex Asimov looking almost exactly as she had when I'd known her, though it seemed someone had kept whittling away at all her sharp features to bring them to even more prominence. Her gold-gray hair was pulled into a tight chignon above a severely cut gown of a similar color. I stared at her, then turned to look again at the woman who'd now been released by John.

Twins!

"Hello everyone," said John a little too loudly, "my friends Bud Anderson and Cait Morgan. Cait, Bud – please allow me to introduce you to my beloved fiancée, Bella."

The softer version of Sasha moved toward me, her arms stretched wide, coming in for a hug. The kisses on each of my cheeks were delicate and carried with them the strong fragrance of patchouli and sandalwood. As I looked into her warm, amber eyes, I judged Bella's delight at seeing John to mean she'd changed her mind about calling off the wedding. I was relieved and pleased for John; they'd make a handsome couple, and possibly – *hopefully* – a happy one.

"Wonderful to meet you, Cait. I've heard so much about you, and Bud." She turned her attention to my husband who almost managed to contain his discomfort at being kissed by a total stranger.

"You're both welcome, of course, and I'm sure John won't mind if I make the rest of the introductions…though it sounds as though my sister and brother-in-law both recognize you, Cait." A frown creased Bella's brow for a fleeting second. "Do they? How can that be?"

"Alex – sorry, *Sasha* – and I used to work at Alistair Townsend's advertising and PR agency at the same time. Piers joined the company not long before I left to pursue my new career, which eventually took me to Canada." I wanted to be the one to present my life path since I'd left the agency.

Bella's eyes and mouth grew round. "How absolutely wonderful," she said softly. She looked directly at her sister and beamed. "Isn't that wonderful, Sasha – you already know Cait."

"Oh yes, indeed I do," replied Sasha.

I noted how different the siblings sounded; Bella's tones lacked the sharpness of Sasha's. Even as I was wondering if that was because everything Sasha said – *she's Sasha here, not Alex* – usually dripped with disdain, I noticed Piers had struggled up from his seat, and was approaching Bud and me. *Oh no, don't let him want to do the cheek-kissing thing, please.*

With an outstretched hand he made a beeline for Bud, who responded by extending his own.

Piers boomed, "So, are you two married, or just having a bit of a trial run? Making sure she's up to snuff before you sign your life away, eh?" He leered at me and winked at Bud as he spoke; there was twice as much of Piers as when I'd fought off his advances, and all of it was as greasily unpleasant as the slimmer version had been. "Piers Tavistock. Welcome to our home. Did John say your name was Bud? That some sort of nickname?"

I didn't dare look at Bud, and wondered how he'd respond; he's good at weighing people up, and I'd given him a quick primer on Piers back at John's place.

Bud was shaking Piers' hand with much more vigor than was normal for him. "Cait and I have been married for almost two years. And I'm Börje Ulf Dyggve Anderson. Hence Bud. Pleased to meet you, Piers. Is *that* some sort of nickname?"

Piers' brow furrowed. "What? Piers? No, that's my…ah, yes, very amusing." He fake-laughed, then added, "Can I offer you a drink, Bud? A cocktail, maybe – Bella's an excellent mixologist. Or maybe you'd prefer a beer?"

To be fair to Piers, he'd been sharp enough to guess Bud was a man who'd more happily nurse a beer than something requiring a recipe – or maybe he was relying upon his preconceptions about Canadians, which was probably more likely. However, the way he'd spoken made it sound as though the idea of someone requesting a beer under his roof would be quite a novelty.

"I'll take a Negroni, if I may," replied Bud smoothly.

"I'll have the same, thanks," I said, by way of something to cover my shock.

"Oh, Negronis, delish," enthused Bella. "Long, or short?" She looked at Bud, who looked at me. I saw panic in his eyes.

"We'd better pace ourselves," I said brightly, "so make them long, then we can sip. You never know when the jet lag's going to kick in." I laughed. Possibly too loudly.

Sasha's whine set my teeth on edge. "That doesn't sound like the Cait I used to know. You'd knock back three or four at lunchtime, then a lot more in the pub after work, wouldn't you." It wasn't a question. "You were always a G & T girl, as I recall."

I'd been apprehensive when I'd realized I was going to have to spend the evening with Alex/Sasha, but had told myself it would be for just a few hours, and it was for John, after all. Unfortunately, I hadn't been prepared for the effect that seeing – and *hearing* – the woman would have upon my psyche: the past twenty-five years hadn't been a ball, but I'd certainly learned how to stand on my own two feet, even if that had required some painful lessons. However, with those disdainful, accusing amber eyes gleaming in the light from the roaring fire, I felt as though I was that twenty-five-year-old once more, the one who'd discovered she had to turn her back on her dream of becoming an account director at a top London advertising agency because the life she thought she'd wanted had been revealed to her as nothing more than a sham…an illusion. I'd left London disappointed by the entire world of marketing communications, and myself. Now here I was, slithering down a time-traveling wormhole to a psychological funk I hadn't re-visited in half a lifetime, and I didn't like it.

I took a step toward Bud, and he instinctively reached for my hand.

I'm not that Cait any longer. Bud and I have talked about that Cait at length, and I neither can, nor want to, deny the fact she existed; she's the reason I'm the Cait I am now.

I made a decision: I would thrust and parry with Sasha, but as politely as I could, since she was the sister of John's future wife. I would leave in a few hours and never have to see her again. *You can do this, Cait.*

I made sure my voice sounded steady when I replied, "Ah yes, the days when I'd walk into the Coach and Horses on Greek Street and Norman – who, for your information, Bud, was renowned as being the rudest landlord in London – would call out, 'Here's Miss Wales. Gin and slim coming up!' Bless him, he might have been horrible to some, but he was always a complete and utter gent to me." I remembered the time he'd barred Alex/Sasha because she'd tried too hard to get his attention at the bar. I wondered if she would, too. *I hoped she did.*

"A disgusting man, and a dirty little place. I've no idea why everyone idolized him," she sniped.

"Oh, come on, Alex – sorry, Sasha – he was quite the institution; there aren't many landlords who get their autobiography published and have a successful West End play written about their pub. But there, once he barred you, you were spared having to enter the place at all, weren't you?" As the words left my lips, I felt a pang of guilt. *Or was it pleasure?*

"Norman Balon barred you from the Coach and Horses, Sasha?" Piers spluttered. "That's quite a badge of honor. I'm surprised you've never mentioned it."

"Really? Not worth it." The woman I'd always felt uncomfortable sharing air with all those years ago pushed back her shoulders and lifted her chin. "A grubby man, running a grubby pub, with grubby patrons. It was no great loss, believe me."

Bud's grip on my fingers loosened slightly – he could tell I was going to be just fine, and I knew it too. *I'm wearing armour I've crafted through years of adversity, and no barbs about my past can pierce it.*

The jangling of the front doorbell seemed to mark the end of the first round of our match, and I felt, rather than heard, John heave a sigh of relief.

"I hope that's Charles," said Bella as she handed a large, cut-crystal glass to Bud; its weight seemed to surprise him. She passed me my drink, which I took with a smile and a nod, then she moved toward the hall. "Yes, it *is* Charles, how wonderful." It seemed Bella found many things to be full of wonder.

A tall, skinny man in his late-thirties, with tousled, long, dark hair, and a slightly straggly beard and mustache, entered the room, dragging Julie by the waist. "Look at this one," he said, holding her chin in his hand, "she gets younger every time I see her. But that hair? I keep telling you, Julie, you must come to the salon for me to work my magic on it. We cannot have people coming to the house and imagining I'm responsible for that, can we? It'll do wonders for your sex life, too. A new hairdo? Glen won't be able to keep his hands off you." He kissed her cheek. "I know I wouldn't."

I watched Julie as she smiled, and seemed to melt a little in Charles's arms, then she gently removed herself from his embrace. The primness of her dress jarred against his flamboyant, figure-hugging rock-star-chic outfit, which was a cacophony of various shades of purple. I also couldn't help but wonder what the state of his own hair signalled to his clients. *Wash and go is "in" this year?*

Julie giggled like a smitten schoolgirl. "Charles, you'll be the death of me, you will. I'm old enough to be your mother."

Charles Asimov mugged a cute pout. "I refuse to believe that, as you well know, Julie, darling. But if you want to treat me like a child then you go ahead. I mean it, now – all I need is a phone call, and you'll be in one of my chairs with these very hands cutting and styling your hair – yes, me, myself. And you know I don't do much but oversee, direct, and primp these days. Go on –" he bent down to stage whisper into Julie's ear – "call me. You know you want to."

Julie flushed, and said quietly, "I'll just put this overcoat away. And…um…Mrs. T? Sir Simon's car is outside – his driver said he's just finishing a phone call, then he'll be in. Vinnie must have caught a quiet spot in the traffic tonight, because he might have brought Mr. John early, but now everyone else is going to be late. Half an inch of snow and London grinds to a halt. Do you want me to push dinner back by fifteen minutes?" Julie looked toward Sasha as she spoke.

Sasha nodded. "Yes. There's something I want to say to everyone at the table, before we start to eat, too. So make it twenty, for food service."

No please or thank you. Typical of Sasha, I thought. "So, this is your brother, Charles, the famous coiffeur," was what I said to Bella.

Bella didn't have time to respond, before Charles lurched forward and grabbed my wrist, then my arm. He bent his head to kiss my hand, which should have been a gallant gesture, but I felt uncomfortable as he touched me.

He said, "And who do we have here?" Until that moment I'd never considered a voice to be capable of slithering, but Charles's did.

"This is Professor Cait Morgan," said Bud, offering his hand to Charles. "I'm Bud Anderson. Her husband. We're friends of John's. Visiting from Canada. Pleased to meet you."

Charles Asimov's head popped up and his eyes scanned Bud from head to foot. He stood upright, nodded at me, and shook Bud's hand. "Likewise, Bud, likewise," he said quietly.

"The usual, darling?" Bella called to her brother as she waggled a bottle of vodka at him.

"Extra, *extra* large, please, darling." Addressing the room Charles added, "Been a sod of a day at the salon. One of my best cutters is pregnant, if you please, which means she'll have to be replaced, and I don't know what on earth is going on with the girl you've sent to do my PR, Sasha. Does she have a brain, or just good hair? I can make anyone's hair look fabulous, what I need is someone who can string two thoughts together and come up with the odd bright idea. Where on earth did you find her?"

"I'll have a word, Charles, but give her a chance. She's only been with you a fortnight. I was in school with her mother and promised her I'd get Lolli some experience. Let her at least get her feet under the table." Sasha sounded bored. "But let's not talk shop tonight. Tonight's about Father, as you know."

Bella handed a drink to her brother as Bud and I gravitated toward the hearth.

"To the old bastard!" Charles raised his glass toward the massive portrait hanging above the carved marble mantlepiece, then he surprised me by adding, "The most cold-hearted man I ever knew."

Looking up I recognized that the sharpness of Sasha's jaw and nose were a mirror of her father's – who'd been as lean as she – whereas Bella's extra pounds helped her look a great deal less cadaverous, and disdainful. The late Oleg Asimov sneered over us, though I was a little puzzled about why he was dressed so strangely in the portrait.

My face must have given away my confusion, because John said, "Bella's father is represented as King Lear, on the heath."

The ragged cloak and storm-tossed skies should have given it away, but it hadn't occurred to me that anyone would ever want to be shown as such a dreadfully tragic character, unless they'd acted the role at some point; I wondered if amateur dramatics had been a part of the man's life, given that John had mentioned he'd been a great fan of Shakespeare's works.

To avoid the glowering portrait, I tried to focus on the rest of the room's décor, which was tastefully lavish, and the work of a designer with a good eye. Subtly painted paneling, good oak doors and trim – with two sets of paneled double doors in the wall opposite the fireplace. Dotted around the walls were depictions of many pivotal scenes from Shakespeare's plays; I assumed they'd been chosen, and hung, by Bella's father. The only decorative objects connected with Christmas in any way were the tree beside the door, and a few sprigs of holly placed on the mantlepiece. I was glad about that, because the room had a stately energy, which didn't need any sort of additional adornment.

My eyes were drawn to the hypnotic portrait once again. "What on earth possessed you to ask for a Negroni?" I hissed at Bud, trying to distract myself from the late Oleg Asimov's wild and piercing gaze. "Not really your thing, is it?"

Bud sipped. "No, it's not. It's disgusting. But I've seen you have them a few times and they look good, and sound fancy. And I remembered the name. How can you drink this? It's so bitter."

"And sweet, and complex," I added. "Give it some time. It's an acquired taste."

"Like Charles's PR girl, I guess," quipped Bud. *Oh good, you're sounding a little more like yourself, Husband.*

We shared a private smile, then our attention was taken by Julie's call of "Miss Sampson," and the arrival of a whirlwind wrapped in a sheath of bronze. "Darlings – how wonderful to see you all again. It's been an age."

Sasha replied drily, "We saw you at the funeral, Felicity. That wasn't so very long ago."

So, this was the famous Felicity Sampson, in the flesh…of which there was quite a lot on display. The party-girls' party-girl of the It-set decades ago looked good for her age, which I judged to be around the mid-fifties, making her a contemporary of Bella and Sasha. Well, most of her was about that age, though I suspected some body parts were a good bit younger; heavy make-up and overprocessed hair topped a wraith-like figure, and while her jewelry suggested she had shares in a gold mine, her heels told me she'd probably done irreparable damage to her back over the years.

Lots of air-kissing and mock-hugging ensued, and finally Bud and I were introduced, just as a short, bald man announced as "Sir Simon" entered and began his own round of hugging.

Felicity floated off when Bella hoisted a bottle of champagne into the air, and John introduced us to the latest arrival, Sir Simon Pendlebury, about whom I'd read an article just a week or so earlier.

When we were finally alone again for a moment I hissed to Bud, "Pendlebury's is a chain of upmarket department stores…last bastion of those for whom shopping is a thing to be savored. There are a lot fewer stores than there used to be, but he seems to be diversifying quite successfully."

Bud's eyebrows rose. "John's fiancée is tied up with some real high-flyers. Pots of money in this room tonight, I'm guessing."

"Pendlebury owns one of the world's largest super-yachts – known for it, in fact. An honest-to-goodness billionaire. In pounds, not Canadian dollars." I winked.

Bud's brown furrowed. "Doesn't seem the yacht type. Not very outdoorsy-looking, is he?"

"I mean big motor yacht, as in a small cruise ship, not a yacht with sails; swimming pools, helipad…that sort of thing."

"Why on earth would you need a helipad on a yacht?"

"Why not? Easy way to get ashore without getting your feet wet."

Bud's face told me he thought this made little sense to him, just as another person joined what was now feeling like a throng. This person's arrival differed from everyone else's insofar as she entered without announcement, or the apparent need to be hugged or kissed by everyone. Instead, she made her way to stand behind the chair Piers had been using upon our arrival, where she all-but disappeared into the shadows, largely due to her mud-colored trouser-suit, and hair. Sasha handed her a glass of what looked like water, they exchanged a few words – which I read as being less than friendly – then she abandoned her. I found this very odd, and mentioned it to Bud, who looked bemused.

"To be honest, Wife, this is all odd to me; everyone's…oh, I don't know…it's as though they're acting parts, declaiming to each other, all for show. It all feels so…unreal." He sighed. "But, hey, I've decided to take everything in my stride tonight, until the jet lag kicks in, at which point you and John will have to pick me up and carry me out. I feel as though I'm starting to fade already…not sure how I'll make it through dinner." He almost spilled what was left of his Negroni when he was startled by the furious beating of a gong in the entryway.

"Please be ready to take your seats for dinner in fifteen minutes," called a disembodied male voice over the suddenly quietening chatter.

I was surprised by what happened next: as though it were some Pavlovian response, everyone, except Bud and myself, found somewhere to deposit their glass, and they all moved to leave.

Sasha left first, through a set of French doors at the rear of the salon, which I could see led to a covered terrace and the garden beyond; she was followed by the quiet woman in the mud-colored suit.

Bella followed Piers to the stairs who said, "I'll use my own."

Bella replied, "I'll use the yellow."

"I've a call to make," announced Sir Simon; he slid open one of the sets of oak doors which revealed the dining room.

"I'll beat you to the pink," called Felicity playfully toward Charles as she moved swiftly toward the entryway.

"Bags I the blue," called Charles as he followed her.

Bud and I looked at John and shrugged.

"Time to prepare your bladders for a rich meal and a fair old quantity of fluids." He grinned. "Facilities all over the house – take your pick."

"We'll follow you," said Bud, quite sensibly.

"You mean we're not allowed to leave the table once we sit down?" I asked – equally sensibly, I thought.

John chuckled. "Of course you may. It's just that the early announcement, then everyone taking care of what they need to before dinner, is a bit of a family thing here. Sasha's probably gone for a smoke with Renata – who's her PA at the agency –

and everyone else is, well, yes, preparing for the evening. But, you know, if now's not a good moment for you, Cait…"

"I'm fine, thanks, I'll just wait here, and take my chances later," I replied.

"Right-o," replied John. "Come with me, Bud, there are a couple of WCs off the entryway. I'll lead."

With Bud and John gone, I was alone in the salon and couldn't help but notice how cavernous the place looked now that it was no longer filled with people. We'd be ten for dinner, and ten people can make a large room look merely adequate.

I took my chance to examine the prints and paintings which adorned the walls – some of which were very fine indeed, and indicated a preference on the part of their selector for the Great Bard's tragedies, as opposed to his comedies. I admitted to myself as I wandered around that I'd never found any of Shakespeare's comedies to be especially amusing; I find them sharp, sometimes bitter, and even cruel, but rarely with laugh-out-loud moments…except when played by actors whose skills allow the raw, crowd-pleasing one-liners to zing. I checked my watch; surely everyone would be back soon.

I was taking what I hoped would be a final look at the late Oleg's portrait above the mantle when I heard the jangling of the front doorbell, then banging. I wandered toward the door, but wasn't sure what to do – it certainly wasn't my place to open it to whomever was bashing at it.

"All right, all right, I'm coming," shouted Julie as she crossed the entry hall.

When she pulled open the front door, Vinnie all-but fell inside.

"Don't go out there, Julie." He tried to push the woman bodily into the hall even as she was peering around him.

"What is it?" There was a jagged edge to Julie's voice.

I felt the tingle on my arms before I saw anything other than the changes in Julie's body language. She wasn't as tall as Vinnie, and she certainly wasn't as well-built, but she managed to push him aside and get past him, nonetheless.

Then the screaming started.

I dashed toward the front door, where Vinnie was trying to pull Julie back inside the house. Beyond them I saw a ragdoll body, lying crumpled on the driveway, and a crimson stain creeping across the freshly-fallen snow.

"…the gloomy shade of death…"

The next few moments were a frenzy of activity and emotion, and one of those times in my life when I knew I had to observe as much as possible to be able to recall it accurately later on; my eidetic memory can be useful, but only if I've perceived something in the first place. The shock of seeing the body shot adrenaline around my system, so I wanted to make use of my heightened senses as best I could.

Bud emerged from a hidden door in the wall of the hallway, rushed to my side, and took in the scene. His eyes narrowed, and he shouted, "No one touch anything," which seemed a bit over the top considering only Vinnie, Julie, and I were on the spot at the time.

A wiry, gray-haired man I'd never seen, but assumed was Julie's husband, Glen, appeared through the door in the wall I'd seen Julie use earlier and rushed to her side, trying to calm her – but horrified himself – at about the same moment that John emerged from yet another concealed doorway. He, like Bud, took in the scene in an instant, but his reaction was quite different.

He screamed, "Oh my God, Bella!"

As he made to move toward the body in the snow, Bud managed to grab him back. "It's no good, John. She's gone. Her neck…her entire body. The blood."

John wrestled with Bud as Sir Simon rushed from the salon. "What the devil is…oh, dear Lord. Who…? What…?" He grabbed at John.

"Bella!" John was screaming, wailing, and trying to get away from Bud.

"What's wrong?" Bella appeared at the top of the stairs looking pink and panicked. John spun around in Bud's arms, his mouth open.

"Bella – my love!" Bud released his friend, who raced up the stairs, taking them two at a time, while Bella ran down to meet him, sweat beading on her brow.

Piers stood on the top landing. "What the bally-hell is going on?"

John was kissing Bella. "I thought you were dead. Oh, Bella…my Bella."

"What do you mean, dead, silly Johnnie?" Bella stroked John's hair.

John was still sobbing, "There's a body. Outside. On the drive. I thought it was you. But it's not. So…it must be…oh my darling, I'm so sorry. Your sister. She's gone."

Bella slipped from John's arms and ran down the stairs to the front door. John followed, then it was his turn to hold back Bella from the body and to be the one to try to provide comfort, and reason. Bud and I moved toward each other in the hallway, and he held me tight. Beside the suddenly-incongruous Christmas tree.

Piers stomped down the staircase, peered through the door, then stepped back. He clung to the banister. "Sasha?" It wasn't much more than a rough whisper.

"What's all the fuss about? Have you started a party without us?" Charles appeared at the top of the stairs, with Felicity Sampson a step behind him. She looked flushed, her dress was crumpled, and her hair looked…different. They both stopped on the top landing and stared down.

Felicity let out a little giggle, then froze. "What's happened?"

It was at that moment I realized someone was missing – Sasha's PA, the woman I hadn't been introduced to.

"We went outside for her to smoke, but she was chilly, so she came in to get something to put over her shoulders." I swung around. The mousy woman was standing in the entrance to the salon, a look on her face that suggested resignation more than shock. "Has anyone called 999?"

"Don't worry, I've taken care of things," said Vinnie grimly. He added, "John, we need to talk. In private. Now."

John held Bella tight, and pulled her face into his shoulder so she couldn't see her sister's body. His voice trembled just a little as he said, "Could a couple of you get Piers out of here? Bud, old man, would you take charge of Bella, please, and maybe sort out some brandies for everyone? I suggest decamping to the dining room and waiting there for the authorities to arrive. Away from here. From this. Vinnie, let's talk."

We all headed to the dining room, except for Vinnie and John who disappeared through the front door, pulling it closed behind them.

We were an odd, and distraught, group as we took what should have been our seats for dinner. We all stared at what would, I assumed, have been Sasha's seat at the head of the table. It seemed to pulsate with emptiness, a sensation which was only heightened by the fact there was a large portrait hanging on the wall beside it, depicting Oleg Asimov and his three children as they'd all have appeared about thirty-five years earlier.

Julie and Glen presented themselves in the doorway of the dining room. "Everything is already set up on the sideboard for brandies," announced Julie, her voice still thick with tears, "so Glen will serve drinks, while I bring in the soup. You all need something warm inside you – the brandy will be a start, but we could be here for some time."

"Thank you, Julie," replied Piers. "I know you'll do us right." A small, lost boy's voice coming from a suddenly deflated man, curled into a chair that seemed to swamp him.

"Indeed I shall, sir. Mrs. T would have wanted that." Julie left the room, while Glen poured brandy into bowls which Bud offered to pass around. Glen made it clear he wouldn't hear of such a thing, so Bud sat, patting Bella's heaving back, his eyes silently begging me for help.

I was sitting next to the woman John had told me was Sasha's PA. I reached out my hand. "Sorry we're meeting like this. I'm Cait Morgan. This is my husband, Bud Anderson. We're friends of John Silver."

"I know," she replied. A dry voice to match her dry eyes. "I'm Renata Douglas, Mrs. Tavistock's personal assistant."

I answered, "I used to work with Alex – Sasha. It's hard to use the right name for her, isn't it?" Immediately the words left my lips, I felt such a fool.

"The two names helped her keep her business and family lives separate," replied Renata quietly. "Even Mr. Tavistock muddles it up sometimes, but never at business meetings – he always manages to call her Alex then, because she really is quite a different person. Utterly professional. And the hair helps, too, of course."

"The hair?"

"She always pins up her hair for business, lets it down when it's personal. It's quite magical to see her do it, actually. It takes her about four seconds. Quite something to behold. I was surprised to see she had it up tonight – she must have been thinking of this evening as more of a business function. Maybe her father's ghost had that much power over her. I know mine does."

I've met many people in situations where they're struggling with the trauma of losing a loved one, or someone close, and I know – both from my experience and training – that there's no specific way one should expect them to act, or react. But there's a range of responses one might label "normal", and others which are at either end of the bell curve…as was Renata's. It made me wonder about her real feelings toward both Sasha and her late father, Oleg.

John sidled into the dining room and beckoned toward Bud. "A word, in private, old man?"

Bud rose. "Cait will take care of you, Bella, won't you, Cait?"

I smiled as sweetly as I could and placed my arm around Bella's shoulders. "How are you feeling?" I asked, knowing I'd get more quiet sobbing in reply. I rubbed Bella's back as I watched my husband. Bud's shoulders straightened as John whispered to him; Bud nodded, John whispered again; Bud shook his head, looked at his watch, nodded, and slipped out into the salon; he pulled his phone from his pocket as he left.

When John came to the table and took over my Bella-consoling efforts, I looked around the room and considered the nature of the people gathered there: a knight of the realm, and a billionaire to boot; a hairdresser to the stars, and tabloid favorite; a world-famous, blue-blooded, fading "model"; a titan of the public relations world, and well-connected lobbyist; a revered artist; a liaison across the British secret services, as well as those around the world. I had no idea about Julie or Glen's backgrounds, nor did I know much about Vinnie or Renata, but I wondered who'd turn up to investigate the death of a woman who herself had apparently no small reputation, while surrounded by such a significant group. I knew John well enough to realize he was certainly going to try to get the tragedy handled by as carefully selected a team of investigators as possible.

"How did Sasha end up…out there, like that?" Piers sounded like a child too young to truly understand the finality of death.

Quietly, Charles replied, "She must have come off the roof. That's the only way she could have wound up where she did." He was staring into his brandy.

"How on earth could she fall from the roof?" Piers sounded shocked at the idea. "Why would she be on the roof…unless she meant to…"

Charles shook his head. "I say…has anyone been up there, yet?"

John's attention was captured. "No one's going anywhere. We'll leave that to the authorities, when they arrive."

"When will that be?" Piers sounded close to tears – though he'd shed none so far.

John moved to Piers' seat. "They're on their way, Piers. I promise this will be discreet, and swift. No sirens, no press. I'm sure that's what the family wants." He glanced toward Bella. She lifted her eyes to his, and silently thanked him with her gaze.

I sipped my brandy, and encouraged Bella to do the same with hers, despite her protestations that she couldn't stand the stuff. As I did so I noticed that Renata had polished hers off, while Charles was looking around for a refill. Felicity fidgeted, and kept looking at her watch – which seemed terribly unfeeling.

Then a bizarre scene followed, as Julie carried a tray into the dining room, set it on a sideboard, and began to serve soup to each of us. She was still snuffling, and clearly deeply upset. Everyone was in their own little world, focussed on their grief in their own way; no one acknowledged Julie's presence, let alone her thoughtfulness. I felt the anger swell in my tummy, blooming with the warmth of the brandy. When she placed my soup in front of me, I said, "When you've done this, just let us look after ourselves, Julie. We'll manage."

Julie's face suggested I'd offered to dance naked on the table. "You can't do that," she snapped. "I can organize everything that won't be eaten this evening so it doesn't go to waste; Glen and I are more than capable of fulfilling our duties."

"I didn't mean to suggest…" *Foot in mouth again, Cait.*

"What were we supposed to be having?" Charles was eyeing his soup with some disappointment. "I've only had a couple of apples and a banana today – I was saving myself for tonight. I'm starving."

I was shocked by his seemingly heartless statement, but a quick glance around my tablemates told me he wasn't alone in hoping for a larger meal.

"After the cauliflower and stilton soup, there was to be salmon with purple sprouting broccoli, then roast beef with all the trimmings, fruit, and cheese, of course," replied Julie.

"Any reason we can't have the lot?" Charles adopted what I assumed he thought was a cute smile.

Julie paused beside me, took one big sniff, and replied warmly, "No reason at all, Mr. Charles. I can finish the preparation and serve the entire meal as planned. If that's what you'd like. Would that be alright with you, Mr. Tavistock?" She looked at Piers, who was staring into his soup. I doubted he was seeing it at all.

"As you please," he replied.

I got hotter. "Hang on a minute – I know I'm merely a guest of a guest here, but if people are hungry, isn't there some way we could all just get a plate of whatever we fancy and let Julie and Glen have a bit of alone time. They're people too, you know."

Bella wiped her eyes, and said, "Cait's right. Julie, why not just open up the kitchen, put everything on the counter, and let us help ourselves? This is no time to stand on ceremony. And who knows how long we'll be here, anyway. I dare say we'll all have to be interviewed…give statements, and what-not. If we treat this as a buffet, we can keep picking away at bits and pieces as we choose." She stood, and addressed the room. "Look, this is terrible, just terrible, and I feel responsible, in part. I was Sasha's sister. I could have done…more. She didn't have to end her life that horrible way. But we all need to eat – so let's at least do that, while we wait." She stepped away from the table and stood in front of the sideboard, blocking my view of the large slate clock; for a moment it seemed as though she herself were ticking. Then she turned, holding a fresh drink, and retook her seat. She gulped down the entire contents of the brandy bowl; she appeared to have developed a taste for the stuff, after all.

Julie shifted her weight. "I could do that, I suppose. The Yorkshire puds haven't even gone in yet, so I could forget about them. Everything else works well hot or cold. I'll do as you ask, Miss Bella."

I'd been the last person to receive soup, so Julie left through the swing doors with her empty tray, then reappeared as she pulled back sliding, paneled doors which comprised one entire wall of the dining room. I was surprised to see they opened onto a large, well-appointed kitchen, then realized how cleverly the ground floor was designed: two sets of double doors led from the kitchen, one to the salon, one to the dining room; if both sets were opened, as well as the set dividing the dining room from the salon, the entire floor was more or less one large, open area. Whenever needed, the kitchen could be shut away from prying eyes and the dining room given a more formal, private air – as it had been for this evening. Neatly done.

Now that we could see Julie and Glen scurrying around the kitchen, laying serving platters and trays on the counter, most people raced through their soup. I gave in to the wonderful texture and flavor, knowing I could opt for cheese alone thereafter; the brandy had gone to my head, and I feared jet lag might come knocking at any time, so I decided it would be best to load up on fatty proteins.

Oliver Twist-like, we each took our empty soup plates to Julie at the large island counter-top, and she handed out dinner plates, upon which we each piled whatever it was we fancied from the wide range of foodstuffs presented before us. Bella took something for Piers, the rest of us fended for ourselves. I hoped Bud would return soon, so he didn't miss the chance of hot food. I popped a few bits of cheese into my mouth, then put my plate on the table, and slipped out into the salon to try to find him.

The front door was wide open, cold air wafting in. Bud, John, Vinnie, and two people in overcoats were all standing around the Christmas tree, looking almost festive. Arms were being waved at the windows above the door within the atrium, and making the shape of what I assumed must be the edifice on the roof.

I was desperate to know what was being said, so headed for the group. "Julie's opened up the kitchen, and everyone's grazing from what would have been dinner. If any of you need some food, now would be the time to claim a plateful, because I fear it'll be well picked-over quite quickly."

Bud's expression softened as he looked toward me. "Thanks, Cait, but I don't think we'll be stopping for food."

As I got closer, I could tell that one of the figures in what were almost-matching, and exquisitely cut, inky overcoats was a woman, the other a man. The man had a head that seemed just a little too big for his body, even allowing for the bulky outerwear; it looked as though someone had slapped several Brillo pads onto it, while his skin told a tale of terrible teenage acne, and his teeth – on full display as he smiled broadly at me – were equally loquacious on the topic of British dentistry…if teeth function perfectly well, don't bother with fripperies like realignment. He spoke first, with an air of authority that marked him as having a rank superior to the woman, whose fluttering hands poked from her sleeves like a skeleton's…her skin was so pale it was almost blue, and her lank brown hair seemed determined to escape from the loose bun at her thin neck.

"That her?" The man's voice boomed as he looked directly at me; I didn't imagine there were ever many people in a room who'd tell him to speak more quietly. Bud and John nodded. The man shoved out his chin and rolled a little on his toes.

John nodded. "Absolutely solid."

Bud added, "And, as you know, fully cleared."

I felt goosepimples prickle my arms, and told myself it must be because of the chill of the night air, though I feared it wasn't.

The man extended his hand in my direction. "I'm Worthington. This is Enderby. You're Professor Morgan." I shook Worthington's hand and nodded at Enderby…whose thumbs were occupied with her phone. "I hear you're an asset worth utilizing, and your track record is impressive – both professionally, and in less formal situations."

It seemed someone had been digging into my academic reputation, as well as building an insight into the sort of challenges Bud and I had faced in our personal lives.

"I've checked your clearances in Canada. They suggest you're trustworthy and discreet, and we're down a few members at the moment due to…let's just say an 'incident' at an address sometimes used by a certain front-bench spokesperson. So, all hands to the pumps. We're part of a select group specializing in cases where discretion is critical. That's all you need to know. Except for one more thing – I am in control, and that's that. My word is final, do you understand?"

Not really, but I'm sure that's your intention, was what I thought. "Absolutely, officer," was what I said.

"Worthington will do. Mister. Enderby is a Miss. Ranks are immaterial, and only serve to cloud matters."

"Yes, Mr. Worthington," I said, feeling like a schoolgirl meeting her new headmaster.

He continued speaking quickly, which I suspected was normal for him. "Our scene of crime specialist tells us the position of the body, and the injuries sustained, suggest Mrs. Tavistock fell straight down. As you've surmised, Silver, Anderson –" he nodded at both men – "she couldn't have landed where she did by falling from a window – all the upper windows at the front of the house, directly above the locus, are inaccessible, being set into the walls of this entry hall. Thus, the point from which she fell must have been the roof. Our SOCO has gloves and protective bootees for all of us. I suggest we follow her to the structure on the roof."

"It's called the palace room by the family," offered John, as Worthington strode toward the stairs, "because of the Crystal Palace."

Worthington shrugged. "Off to the palace we go, then."

I wanted to beam at Bud, because there are few things I hate more than missing out on something, and it was obvious that, between them, he and John had managed to get me an "in". But even I knew that grinning like an idiot was inappropriate, so I followed meekly at the rear of the procession up the staircase, holding my paper shoe-covers and latex gloves, silently fizzing with excitement.

"*...the stars above us...*"

John gave directions to the SOCO, to whom no one had bothered to introduce me. She led, John at her shoulder, with Worthington, Enderby, Bud, and me following. At the top of the stairs, we all plodded along the balustraded landing off which led a few doors. I saw two bedrooms – one pink, one blue – and a separate bathroom, then we found ourselves at the foot of a spiral staircase; it was of gothic design and crafted from wrought iron. My heart sank; I hate spiral stairs...I'm not built for them, and can never seem to make my feet work properly on the tiny steps, even though my feet are small enough to theoretically fit. We all pulled on our bootees and gloves. Quite how the SOCO woman managed to get up so fast I couldn't fathom, until I began my own ascent; unlike most spiral staircases this one was wide, with deep, shallow treads. I surmised it had been built to accommodate Victorian ladies' garments, bustles and all...which is handy when you have your own built-in bustle.

Once I reached the top, I paused to take in the room we had entered. It was extraordinary: the entire thing was made of curved glass, bounded by meticulously forged cast iron which was painted matte black; above the glass canopy was the night sky, and on the horizon – below, and all around us – the entirety of London and its suburbs, in all their glittering glory. I felt as though I were on top of the world, and did my best to blot images of Jimmy Cagney from my mind. The staircase emerged about one third of the way across the room, which was massive, because it was as large as the entire footprint of the house beneath it. The skill of the engineering used to achieve such large spans with glass and metal alone wasn't lost on me, and I gave myself up to the grudging acknowledgement that – for all their hypocritical puritanism, desperate colonialism, and utter disregard for those for whom an unfortunate birth inevitably meant an unfortunate life – the Victorians really had taken leaps and bounds in terms of the technology of the day. This addition was no carbuncle on the top of an elegant Georgian pile, it was an opulent celebration of engineering, and I was fascinated to see what the Asimov family had chosen to make of the opportunity it afforded them.

The palace room looked like a set for a Jules Verne film – not quite steam-punk, but not far off. Originally-expensive carpets were strewn across the expanse of the floor, but all were well-worn, their colors subdued by possibly hundreds of years of wear; the furnishings were plentiful, also well-worn, with lashings of Victorian over-zealous decoration about them. I realized everything I was looking at must have been brought to the room up the spiral stairs, so it wasn't a surprise that the scale of the furniture was small. Then I saw the desk. It was so huge I suspected the only way it could have got there was either to have been brought up in pieces and constructed inside the room, or hoisted onto the roof before the edifice had been glazed; given it was high art deco in design, I suspected the former method had been employed. Standard lamps provided pools of illumination as the SOCO switched them on; she moved carefully across the room and finally turned to face us.

"There," she pointed.

I'd noticed the room was chilly, and had put that down to there being no obvious source of heating, however, now I could see there was an opening in one of the walls. As the light from the SOCO's torch played around the doorway, then around the room, it was clear that each of the four sides of the glass canopy had a metal-framed door set into it; one of them was open – the one which, if my bearings were correct, would give a view over the center of the front of the house – just where Sasha's body had fallen.

"Follow my path," instructed the SOCO, and she reminded us with the beam of her torch where she'd walked. We did as instructed, then stopped when she raised her hand. She bobbed and weaved, pointing the light this way and that, before directing the beam from her torch out onto the roof beyond the glass walls.

There was a walkway, about a foot or so wide, with a metal railing – another gothic delight – that came up to mid-thigh height. Even to my inexperienced eyes it was the sort of railing that would send any modern building-code enforcer reeling, as it only served the purpose of appearing to offer safety, rather than actually promising to be of any use if one leaned or fell against it. It wouldn't have taken much to step over it, or to be pushed over.

And that was the question, of course, that had been in all our minds since our grisly discovery: what had caused Sasha's demise? An accident? An intentional deadly deed? Or had she chosen to end her life in a way designed to cause shock and horror, as well as grief, for those who loved her?

"Indistinct marks in the slush, directly above the landing site," said the SOCO. "Not much doubt she went over from here." Her camera flashed, then she filmed the scene. "Nothing visible on the rail."

"Anything else?" Worthington's voice cracked as he spoke.

The SOCO bobbed, peered, stepped outside, stood, flashed away again, then returned. "A soaked and disintegrating cigarette butt. There had been slush, which has held some evidence of foot traffic, but the fresh fall on top of that layer hasn't helped. I've taken photos, and have recorded with live footage. I'll bag the butt." She peered upward at the arc of glass. "Not much chance of securing a protective covering here. I'd prefer to do my detailed examination now, before the snow gets any thicker."

Worthington replied, "Agreed. Remember, personal safety first. It's slippery out there, take care. We'll observe in here, and summon you if anything pertinent is spotted."

"Sir." The SOCO nodded, as did we all when Worthington scanned our faces.

"Obviously, touch nothing." Worthington sounded grim. "Let's take north, south, east, and west quadrants." He waved us away, and we did as we were told; he chose to join me.

I took the north quadrant, which offered the best view toward Greenwich, Canary Wharf beyond it, and the City of London itself. The skyline rose like a jagged, dazzling tiara against the velvet of the now-clear night sky; north of the Thames, it looked as though the snow had blown through at last. The fairly sizeable brass telescope affixed to a tripod which would have allowed me a much better view of the distant horizon was off limits, because I'd have had to raise it from its position – with its lens pointing toward the floor – to be able to take in the sights. Instead, I noted the two occasional chairs upholstered in rather tatty leather, and a rug that had once been, possibly, red and blue. A small side table – octagonal and topped with intricately-patterned brass – provided a resting place for a cigarette box, a burlwood veneered humidor, and a marble-based table-lighter. It was a pretty standard range of items to find on a smoker's table, which was what this clearly was.

"I have something," called John, capturing everyone's attention. He'd taken the eastern quadrant, which overlooked the front of the house, and was where the large desk was situated. We all turned. He added, "It's a handwritten note. Signed by Sasha. Can't say if it's her handwriting or not, because I'm not aware I've ever seen her handwriting before."

"SOCO, now," called Worthington.

We all waited while the position of the note was recorded, and it was placed in a protective plastic bag.

Worthington beckoned to his bunny-suited minion, and took the bag. Extending his arm, he read aloud. "'He'd have been eighty today. His shadow will never leave me. It's too late for me to try to be whatever I could have been, had he not been my father. I thought it would end with his death. But now it seems that was a foolish hope on my part. It will never end, until I end it. So I shall. No procrastination. No more...anything. Sasha.' That's it."

A clock tocked in the silence.

"Looks to be intentional." Worthington's tone suggested he'd expected a suicide note, and was relieved to find one.

John shifted his weight. "As I say, I can't be certain it's her handwriting."

Bud and I caught each other's eye; Bud's spine became more rigid. "I'm sure Mr. Worthington will be seeking assurance it's written in Sasha's hand."

Worthington looked across the room. All I could see was the back of his head, but I could feel his eyes boring into Bud. "Of course, Mr. Anderson. We'll take every measure necessary to ascertain the origin of this note. Silver, you knew the woman, even if you didn't know her writing. Sound like her?"

John chewed his lip. "She wasn't someone who chose to show me her emotions and, to be honest, we haven't spent a great deal of time in each others' company. When we did mix, I always found her to be a little sharp...businesslike. Most of what I know about Sasha is what Bella has told me about her, though Bella tells me she and her sister didn't share an overly close relationship beyond their teen years. You see, Sasha was older than Bella by ten minutes, and their father favored her as his firstborn. Sadly for Bella, this meant she felt she never met her father's expectations of her, though Sasha could do little wrong in his eyes. Of course, Bella and Sasha were at school together, but they moved in different sets; Bella was always quieter, more artistic, whereas Sasha was outgoing, sporty, and…well, Bella mentioned that Sasha was rather more keen on boys than she was – you know the way it is with teens, I dare say. Anyway, when they weren't in school, or abroad on trips, they spent their holidays here, together. This was the family home, you see, when their father was married to their mother; he moved out when they divorced. Bella and Sasha continued to live here, with their mother, until they each left to attend university. As you've seen, it's a large house, and Bella tells me they didn't need to, and rarely chose to, spend a great deal of time together. Bella moved into the coach house after her mother's death; shortly thereafter Sasha and Piers sold their home and took up residence in the main house. But, even then, Bella said their relationship revolved around their professional connections, rather than them being personally close. Sasha just couldn't come to grips with Bella's artistic flair, you see."

Worthington looked a little bemused. "I see. So are you saying your fiancée's late sister might have written this note?"

"Certainly Sasha wrote notes. Not emails, notes. On paper. Though she's never shown me any of them – as they are all private, I understand – Bella says Sasha's very keen on writing notes for many people, herself included. Sasha seemed to think a person needed to see something written down before they'd take it seriously. At least, that's what Bella told me. On balance, I would say the tone of this note matches what I myself know of Sasha's personality, and it would be in line with what her sister has told me about her. It's a very…businesslike note. Though some elements are puzzling."

Worthington swung around to face me. "Professor Morgan?"

I took a deep breath, "The note doesn't contain an apology. That's unusual, for most people. The woman I knew twenty-five years ago would also not have apologized; she was entirely focused on herself – her own needs and desires – back then, and nothing I saw this evening made me believe she'd changed in that respect." I paused, then added, "But I was in her company for only half an hour or so tonight, and wasn't studying her with…this sort of analysis in mind."

Worthing nodded thoughtfully. "Thank you, both. Has anyone seen anything else they feel we should take note of, that they haven't yet mentioned?"

I raised my hand. Worthington nodded. "I have a question for the SOCO," I said. "Which of these lamps were illuminated when you first entered this room?"

"Only the lamp beside the telescope," she replied.

I thanked her. "And I have one more question: how did Sasha even get here? I saw her leave through the doors leading to the garden, and I remained in the salon. She didn't return to the house that way."

"I might be able to help there," said John. "Sasha and Piers' bedroom is at the rear of the house, overlooking the garden. It has a little terrace, which is, in fact, the roof of the bowed window of the salon beneath it. There's a staircase at the side of the house leading to that terrace. Renata said Sasha felt cold outside and wanted a shawl or something – she might have used those steps to go to her room via the terrace. That, in turn, would have allowed her to come here from the upper hallway."

"Enderby and I shall, of course, be establishing if anyone saw Mrs. Tavistock in the moments before her death," replied Worthington. "Anything else, anyone?"

"Nothing here, sir," said Enderby. Her voice was surprisingly deep for such a slight woman. "No signs of a struggle. Nothing disturbed, it seems."

Worthington cleared his throat. "Once the SOCO has completed her work, get the husband up here, so he can tell you if anything's not where it should be – you know the drill, Enderby."

I suspected we were about to be ushered out of the space, so took one last look around the entire vista offered by the room, drinking it all in. "I wonder if anyone in any of the homes this place overlooks saw Sasha…fall," I said. Glowing windows – thousands of them, in every direction – seemed to offer innumerable opportunities for witnesses, all with an unrestricted view.

"Impossible to ask everyone," said Worthington quietly, "even if we were the types to go knocking on doors. I dare say if anyone saw anything amiss, they'd phone it in."

I didn't share the man's belief that people would rush to report seeing something that might, possibly, have been unusual.

Before we were politely invited to leave, I took one final glance upward; all I could see were the icy stars in the clearing sky. A wave of sorrow washed over me: how dreadful to be unable to see a possibility of continuing to live, when so much of life was literally displayed at one's feet, and above one's head was the beauty of nature. Sasha's brief note didn't give any real explanation of why she'd done what she'd done – it was vague, to say the least, though of course I wondered what she'd meant by the reference to her dashed hopes, and what it was that wouldn't end until she, herself, no longer existed.

It also didn't sit well with me that she'd apparently chosen to kill herself in such a dramatic, and horrifying way – a method of suicide that was bound to cause as much trauma as possible for everyone in the house. I wondered if I should share my concerns with Worthington, but decided to keep them to myself until I'd at least had a chance to talk things through with Bud, and – maybe – even John.

I found it much more of a challenge to get down the spiral staircase than I had to get up; Bud waited to see that I reached the upper hallway safely, and we shared a hug before we joined the others, in the master bedroom.

"The terrace I told you about is here," said John, indicating a glass door discreetly tucked to one side of the large double sash windows which gave a view over the inky garden at the rear of the house. The fresh covering of snow was rapidly melting on the terrace, allowing black patches to appear here and there in random places. "Look, footprints," he added, pointing to a defined track in the slushy covering of what was clearly the roof of the room below us.

Worthington nodded. "Let's not disturb anything out there until the SOCO's taken some photographs and so forth. You take some shots for now, Enderby, in case all that snow melts and everything disappears. Where's her backup, by the way?"

"Still at the other locus, sir," came Enderby's businesslike reply.

Worthington rocked on his toes. "Hmm, no idea when that'll all be dealt with. Better warn ours she's in for quite a night of it here. I want all this lot recorded –" he waved toward the terrace – "and I dare say there'll be a bit for her to do downstairs, and more outside too. You can point me in the direction of the way by which the victim could have come up from the garden when we get downstairs, Silver."

"The body's been removed. Plain vehicle, no fuss," said Enderby, reading from her phone. "Want uniform to hang about, sir?"

Worthington scratched his neck. "I want the entire area where she landed searched in daylight, so it needs to remain undisturbed. One uniform until that daylight examination is completed. The others can go. And I want a victim support officer here pronto. Let them know."

"I don't think that'll be necessary, sir," said John.

Worthington almost smiled. "I dare say, but it's something we need to be seen to have done, Silver. Make sure the family knows the offer was made. You catch my drift?"

John nodded. "I'll be staying at the coach house with Bella tonight; I'll be around tomorrow as needed, to liaise."

"Always good to play to one's strengths," responded Worthington. *Was there a hint of sarcasm in his tone?*

John spoke to Bud, "You two won't mind going back to my place alone tonight, will you?" He sounded concerned. "I dare say Vinnie will be able to drive you."

"We'll be fine," replied Bud.

The four of us were arranged in a semi-circle around Worthington's back, all of us still staring out at the terrace. Worthington turned, the light from the bedside lamp casting deep shadows beneath his eyes. "It'll be quite some time before anyone's leaving here," he said. "And until then, none of you will share a scintilla of information about any of our discoveries, or beliefs. I shall choose who gets to know what, and when. Silver, you can begin your liaising by gathering everyone in one room, downstairs. I need to talk to all those present at the time of Mrs. Tavistock's demise. Enderby will be taking formal statements later on; I shall allow my initial conversations to go wherever I need."

John stepped forward. "I know just the place. There's an office-cum-meeting room beyond the dining room, in what were the servants' quarters. Sasha and Bella use it when they have business meetings themselves, or when clients visit the house. I'll talk to Julie and Glen about sorting that out for us, and maybe they'll organize some coffee. I think it would be better suited to your needs than the main salon, or even the dining room."

"Indeed," replied Worthington, "gravitas is important, thank you." The ominous shadows on Worthington's face shifted as he turned toward me; his teeth gleamed like uneven tombstones in the lamplight when he smiled. "And I happen to have my very own victim-profiling expert on the spot." It sounded like an accusation. The seconds of silence that followed were counted by an invisible clock. "Let's get to it." We all breathed out. He strode between Bud and me, out to the hallway.

We trooped along behind him, and Bud squeezed my hand. "Don't let him intimidate you, Cait. He's pretty high up the food chain in these parts, it seems."

"Intimidate me?" I was surprised. "How could he do that? I mean, what have I got to lose? Besides, he's not my boss, and I don't plan on undermining his authority at all. It's just that I want to..."

"...*know*," said Bud. He smiled, warmly. "I understand, Wife. Go get 'em, girl."

I tutted. "At fifty years of age I'm hardly a 'girl', but thanks anyway. Come on, let's catch up – I don't want to miss a thing. And by the way, I expect you to shadow Enderby, so between us we get the full picture. Right?"

"Sure thing." Bud mugged a salute, and off we went.

"…I come to bury Caesar…"

If you hadn't known that our hostess had just been carted away in a body bag, you'd never have guessed it from the scene that met our eyes when we all returned to the dining room; I wondered exactly how much brandy, and other alcohol, Glen had served. Felicity and Charles were giggling like schoolchildren, their heads bobbing up and down, close together; Piers was waving his arms expansively as he illustrated some critical point to Sir Simon, who was looking shocked, yet entertained; Bella and Renata were holding hands, smiling at each other, and toasting the family portrait on the wall; Julie and Glen were a blur of activity in the kitchen, as pots were being washed and food rearranged on the countertop. Vinnie was the only person who seemed to be a little adrift; he was standing beside the kitchen island, nibbling at something, and looking for all the world as though he were the only person in the room who was aware someone had died.

Worthington announced our arrival with a melodramatic clearing of his throat. The seeming-conviviality stopped instantly; everyone turned toward him and froze. DaVinci would have loved the scene. I took the opportunity to examine each face, every expression, knowing I'd want to revisit it in my mind's eye later on. The moment passed when Vinnie let something clatter onto his plate; the tableau shifted, though Worthington retained everyone's attention.

"My name's Worthington. This is Enderby. We need to take statements from everyone. I have no doubt you expected as much." There was a general, tentative, nodding.

John spoke quietly to Glen, who made a beeline out of the kitchen, after whispering something hurriedly to his wife. She swooped into action, pulling trays, mugs, pots, and plates from a variety of cupboards. I perked up when I realized this activity was a precursor to there being coffee available in the meeting room, because I knew I was beginning to tire; I hoped jet lag wouldn't hit me until Bud and I were able to get back to John's house, which I assumed wouldn't be for hours. I also hoped Bud would manage to push on through, then realized he was actually looking a good deal more chipper than he had on the drive from the airport. *The thrill of the chase, no doubt.*

John announced, "Julie and Glen are just setting up the meeting room to accommodate us all. I'm sure Mr. Worthington will want to start as soon as possible. Maybe if folks could begin to make their way through, then we can get going."

"Good, I have an early flight to Jersey in the morning." Sir Simon Pendlebury threw down his snowy linen napkin and began to push back his seat.

Felicity Sampson said, "You're not the only one who wants to get away from this place as fast as possible, is he, Charles?"

She turned to seek assurance from Bella's brother who replied, "I thought I might stay over. That'll be alright with you, won't it, Piers? I'll use the yellow room. Close enough if you need anything during the night. Can't abandon my dear brother-in-law in his hour of need."

"I'll be here if Piers needs anything," said Bella. Her voice cracked as she spoke; her amber eyes looked darker than they had upon our arrival that evening.

"But you'll be in your own little hidey-hole, with John-boy," replied Charles. "Too far away to be of much practical use. No, I'll stay. I insist. The room's all made up, isn't it, Julie?" His tone was forced. *Odd.*

"It always is when you come for dinner, Mr. Charles," replied Julie from the kitchen.

Charles blew her a kiss. "How well you know my love of the wine cellar in this house."

"Follow me, please, ladies, gentlemen," said Glen, emerging from yet another door all-but hidden within the paneling of the dining-room's wall. I was right behind him.

We crossed a dimly-lit hallway, which appeared to run from the front to the very back of the house, then entered a large, mauve, damask-papered room. An ornately carved partners' desk sat beside a window which would doubtless offer both users a fine view of the garden in daylight, but most of the room was filled by a stunning, walnut-veneered oval table, surrounded by a dozen matched chairs. Wall sconces flattered the room's décor and gave it a clubby feeling, despite the delicacy of the *object d'arts* dotted on the surfaces of several serviceable sideboards and chests of drawers around the perimeter of the room. The art on the walls seemed to be a variety of depictions of Beulah House through its various incarnations, and the local area when it had been a good deal more bucolic than it now was.

"This will do nicely," said Worthington, who removed his overcoat for the first time since his arrival.

Glen took it from him. "We'll bring coffee, and some biscuits, as soon as possible," he said, turning to leave.

"And I'd like both you and Julie to join us too, Glen, thank you," called Worthington, as he skirted the table and took a seat at the center of the long side of the oval, facing the door. He gestured that we should all take seats, as we arrived; I was first in, with Enderby at my shoulder.

Felicity Sampson entered the room as I was beginning to believe she'd entered every room throughout her entire life – with an air of expecting all heads to turn to look at her. I was already staring at the door, so all I had to do was not smile at her

– something I was certain she'd notice; Worthington's complete indifference to her arrival was even more satisfying. She upped the ante by sighing tragically as she sank onto a chair opposite him. Worthington still didn't look up from his phone; he went up in my estimation by at least two notches.

Piers was accompanied by John and Bella; Sir Simon straggled along behind with Charles, and Renata brought up the rear of the group, with Vinnie beside her. Eventually, Bud rushed in; the only people missing were Glen and Julie, who followed momentarily, each carrying a tray.

"Thank you," said Worthington. "I'll begin, while coffee is served." He nodded at Julie and Glen who set about delivering mugs of coffee to everyone around the table. He continued, "We're all here, now, which means I can ask Mr. Tavistock a question." Piers looked up from the bowl of brandy he'd brought with him. "Enderby, the note, if you please. Can you tell me, Mr. Tavistock, if this is written in your wife's hand?"

Piers took the plastic bag from Enderby and frowned. "What's this?"

"Please, sir, if you'd just examine it, as Mr. Worthington asked." Enderby's voice wasn't just low, it reverberated in the now-silent room.

Piers pulled a pair of pince-nez from his waistcoat pocket. I wouldn't have been surprised if he'd produced a monocle, but the pince-nez were adequate for the caricature the man had become since I'd first known him. He peered at the note. His lips moved as he read silently.

"Good God! Where did you find this? When? This is…oh my poor Sasha." He shoved the note toward Enderby, who only just managed to catch it before it fell to the ground. Piers grabbed the glass he'd placed on the table beside him and took a swig.

"Did your wife write that note?" Worthington's voice rumbled.

Piers nodded. "It's her handwriting alright. Her signature, too. But...but what does it mean? That she took her own life because...because of what?" Piers pushed himself out of his chair and reached to take the note from Enderby's hand. "Give it to me. What did it say?" He scanned the note again, his eyes darting, sweat beading on his brow. "Why?" He waggled the note.

Worthington replied, "I had hoped you might be able to tell us, Mr. Tavistock."

Piers all but threw the note at Enderby, "Well I can't. Sasha must have...she must have been disturbed about something. Not in her right mind. I mean, of course she wasn't in her right mind if she killed herself, which this note tells us she did. But why? She could have...she could have talked to me about it...whatever it was."

Worthington reacted coolly. "Now that we have confirmation it was written by the deceased, this note makes Mrs. Tavistock's intentions quite clear. We're so terribly sorry for your tragic loss, and I very much appreciate your patience this evening. In due course you'll be contacted by the coroner's office to allow arrangements to be made, and, of course, we'll make sure all our personnel and paraphernalia are removed from your home as soon as possible. But, in the spirit of completing my task with due diligence, I would like to ask everyone here just a few questions. I need to give a full report to my...superiors...about the events leading up to Mrs. Tavistock's tragic death. I'm sure you all understand why."

I could tell from the faces around the table that was not the case.

As John and Bud avoided each other's gaze, Bella stood, her eyes glittering. "May I see the note, please? I'm her...*was* her sister." She sucked her lips. "You know what I mean. May I see it, please?"

Worthington nodded at Enderby, who passed the note to Bella. She cradled the precious object for what must have been two, long minutes. It was as though Bella was trying to absorb every word with her eyes. Eventually she looked up. Tears rolled down her pale cheeks. "It's...it's definitely her handwriting, yes. But...oh, poor Sasha." She sat down on her seat again, hard. The note fell from her fingers. This time Enderby had to retrieve it from the floor. She slapped it into a folder, which she snapped shut.

Felicity wriggled on her chair, fussed with tendrils of hair at her neck, and cleared her throat as though she had black lung. Finally, Worthington gave her his attention. His broad smile made me think of a shark about to attack, but Felicity didn't seem to pick up on the threat, and simply mirrored it with a coy one of her own.

"I'll be direct," said Worthington, "and I trust you'll all be the same. Did anyone notice anything amiss this evening, prior to Mrs. Tavistock's unfortunate demise?"

Felicity tilted her head, dropped her chin, and smiled coyly at the big man. "Not a thing."

"When did you last see Mrs. Tavistock, prior to her death, Miss Sampson?"

Felicity lifted her chin. "The gong rang, and we all headed for the loo. That's what we do here. An old habit of Oleg's. My ex-husband. He didn't like meals to be disturbed, not even long dinner parties, so he let it be known that one should avail oneself of the facilities prior to sitting down to eat. Sasha kept the old system going." She giggled. "It's strange, I suppose, but then this house is so strange, anyway."

"How so?"

Bella sat forward in her chair, her eyes wide with…what? *Anticipation?*

Felicity waved her arm. "I never lived here, of course." Her tone suggested she was relieved by that fact. "Oleg did, as did the girls and their mother –" she indicated Bella – "but I've often stayed over. There's a ghost here. I've heard her, but haven't seen her. Sasha told me they say it's a woman who walks the hallway upstairs looking for her dead babies. Crying. It's quite a dreadful sound when one hears it. Pitiful. Chilling. I should have thought a good number of women had lost a good number of babies in this house over the centuries; I've no idea what sets this particular woman apart, nor why she sees fit to scare the wits out of unsuspecting house guests, but there you are. Maybe the ghost of that poor woman shoved Sasha off the roof; they can manifest in many ways, I believe. Possibly Sasha finally saw the phantom, and fell off the roof with shock. Oh…but…the note. Ah." She stopped talking and twirled her coffee mug.

"Setting aside the possibility of ghostly intervention for a moment, can you tell me exactly what you did when you left the salon, Miss Sampson?" Worthington took a mug from Glen, and settled himself.

"I used the bathroom, then heard a terrible commotion downstairs. That was when I found out what had happened." Felicity's tone suggested Worthington was extremely stupid for having asked a question to which the answer was glaringly obvious.

"In detail, please," pressed the man, whose tone betrayed not a hint of impatience.

Felicity looked at her coffee, but didn't touch it. "Each of the bedrooms has its own attached bathroom, and there's another guest bathroom available upstairs, too. There are also a couple of guest washrooms off the hallway. I prefer to have a bathroom to myself, when I need one." She took in the assembled group, her neck flushed a little, and added, "I don't think those little cupboard things you've got downstairs are adequately…you know, not terribly private. Anyway, when I stay here, I always sleep in the pink bedroom. It's got a lovely view toward London. That's why I prefer to use that bathroom; I know it. I think I fiddled about with my hair a little – it just wasn't behaving as it should when I left home this evening – then, as I said, I heard screaming. I made my way to the top of the stairs, and since then I haven't been alone for a moment. Is that what you wanted to know?"

"So, you were alone, in the bathroom attached to the pink bedroom, for how long, would you say?"

Felicity rolled her eyes. "I don't know. However long it takes to do the necessary and wash one's hands. Five minutes?" Her tone was testy.

Worthington looked at me. "How long were you in the salon alone?"

"Approximately thirteen and half minutes."

Felicity laughed. "That's ridiculously precise. How do you know that? Did you time it?"

I looked at Worthington as I answered. "In fact, I did. The gong rang when the clock on the mantle in the salon read twenty-nine minutes past seven; I checked my watch, because I'd had to re-set it to the local time when Bud and I arrived at Heathrow, and I wanted to make sure it was correct – at least, correct according to the clock on the mantlepiece. I was a few minutes off, so I put my watch right. I spent some time looking at the art in the salon, but happened to be looking at my watch again when Vinnie started hammering at the door. That was, in total, thirteen and a half minutes later. Miss Sampson appeared at the top of the stars approximately a minute and half after that. Alongside Charles."

Worthing looked at Felicity, whose mouth was open. "You and Mr. Asimov arrived at the top of the stairs at the same moment?" His tone was polite.

Felicity shut her mouth and swallowed. "I dare say we might have done. He'd have been in the bathroom attached to the blue bedroom, which is next to the pink bedroom. He'd have heard the noises downstairs as I did."

"So you arrived at the top of the stairs separately, but at the same time?"

Charles interjected, "Yes. Felicity and I arrived separately, but at the same time. I was using the blue bathroom, as she said, and – frankly – for much the same reasons. Why does that matter so much?" He scratched at his beard.

Worthington rumbled, "I wondered if you might be able to provide each other with an alibi."

Felicity leaned forward and flung out her little hands. "Why on earth would we need an alibi? For what? Sasha threw herself off the roof, didn't she? The *note*! Though, God knows Charles would have good reason to have shoved her. She never left you alone for a moment – constantly pushing and pushing you to diversify into this, or stop doing that. Why on earth she couldn't just let you be a hairdresser and be done with it I don't know. That's your forte – and you're a wizard at it. But she never let up. However, as for Charles throwing her off the roof? Don't be absurd. He doesn't need an alibi. Neither of us does."

Worthington didn't respond.

Sir Simon Pendlebury jumped in. "I really do need to make a move, so let's get on with this, shall we?" He stared at his ruinously expensive wristwatch before returning his gaze to Worthington.

"Your reason for being here this evening would be a good place to begin," said Worthington.

Sir Simon's eyebrows shot up. "It's no secret: prior to his death, Oleg Asimov appointed me chairman of the board of the Asimov group of companies. I'd known the man for years, through various business connections, and he wanted a safe pair of hands to run his business empire after he'd gone. None of the children are interested in the businesses, as such."

"Construction companies, aren't they?"

I judged that Worthington knew full-well the nature of the Asimov companies.

"Yes, traditionally they were, though they also moved into demolition back in the 1960s, and the past couple of decades has seen a shift of the business focus into waste disposal. Hence the group name of Asimov CD&D: construction, demolition, and disposal. I was here tonight with some papers that needed to be signed by all three of his children – to whom Oleg bequeathed equal shares in the group. They're large contracts for one of the businesses." He paused and looked sympathetically toward Bella and Charles, then added, "It shows a great deal of foresight on your late-father's part that, when they banned the use of asbestos in construction, he knew there'd come a time when there'd be a need for companies who could get it out of buildings ahead of demolition, or refurbishment. You see, Worthington, the Asimov companies carried out so many government construction projects before, during, and after the war, he knew he stood a good chance of picking up the asbestos removal contracts too; the Asimovs had all the original plans, put the stuff in there, then got paid again to take it all out. Brilliant. And necessary, too. Surveying, removal, transportation, then disposal – I'm not going to say it's the group's biggest earner, but it's the steadiest, and those are the contracts up for renewal."

Worthington sucked the end of the pen with which he wasn't taking any notes. "They can't destroy that stuff, can they? Too dangerous."

Sir Simon leaned forward, totally engaged, "Ah, now that's where Oleg was ahead of the game too, you see. He'd already invested in a couple of research companies looking into chemical ways to destroy asbestos. It'll happen, one day, and I intend to ensure the Asimov group is leading the way. It's taken decades to build their reputation as the go-to people when you've got something to pull down, or remediate, or dispose of, and playing a leading role in technological developments will be critical."

Worthington said, "So, you were here to enjoy dinner, remember the late Oleg Asimov, and get his children to sign some papers – that about it?" Sir Simon nodded. "And did you notice anything unusual about Mrs. Tavistock this evening?"

Sir Simon didn't even think. "No, I didn't. She was her usual self in every regard. However, given the way you never quite knew where you were with her in any case, I dare say that's not saying much. Sorry Piers, but I must be honest, and open." Piers didn't look up from his brandy. "Tonight? Tonight we got to share the company of the slightly hyper hostess, but that's hardly surprising given the reason for the gathering. I've seen Sasha several times since her father's death, and she's not taken his loss well. Of his three children, she was the one with whom Oleg spent most time, so – again – I would think that's to be expected. Her state of slightly elevated anxiety this evening was, therefore, normal for her, and the situation." Sir Simon sat back in his chair, his fingers tracing the edge of the table. He was obviously a man at ease, or at least doing an excellent job of portraying one.

"And could you please share with me your exact movements between the sounding of the gong and the discovery of the body?" Worthington used an almost warm tone.

Pendlebury puffed out his cheeks. "I had an important phone call to make, so I came into this very room to make it. More privacy. I was alone, and while I'm sure you could get all sorts of warrants to allow some twelve-year-old to tell you exactly who I was phoning, I would much prefer you didn't. It was to be a conversation of the most delicate nature and the person I was calling has a role within the government which propels him, and therefore our communication, into a...sensitive...realm."

"Would you be prepared to share that person's name with me in private?"

Pendlebury sat a little more upright. "I shall not, unless legally compelled to do so. It's not your business. Besides, what would be the purpose of wanting such information?"

"It would give you an alibi."

I watched Pendlebury's brow furrow, in stages, as he thought through the implications of what Worthington had said. His fist clenched. "I have to agree with Fliss on this point, Mr. Worthington – why on earth should I, or anyone else, need an alibi? Poor Sasha killed herself. That note you found states her case. Grief, I'd say. Yes, grief at her father's death. No one needs an alibi."

"And yet..." Worthington didn't finish the thought.

I leaned forward and raised a finger, looking at Worthington. He nodded. I said, "What were you and Piers talking about when we all joined you, while you were eating?"

Sir Simon Pendlebury stared at me as though I were a talking dog. "Pardon?"

"When we all joined you, in the dining room, you and Piers were talking about something that involved him showing you how big something was, if I'm not mistaken."

Pendlebury stared at Worthington, who tilted his head, then he looked at Piers, who was oblivious. Sir Simon's expression changed, and a smile creased his face. "Ah...Piers was reminding me of a time, back when we were at school, that he and some other boys erected a large tent inside the gymnasium, in the dead of night. No one ever found out who had done it, of course, and we were all given the task of making good the damage to the property. It might have been that." He shrugged.

"You and Piers were at school together?" I was interested. Piers wasn't.

"Indeed. Eton, of course. Same year. But I was elected to Pop, and he wasn't. After school we didn't see much of each other until he and Sasha developed their PR and lobbying business. Then, of course, the connection was forged anew."

I could feel Bud tense beside me, and realized he probably had no idea what Sir Simon was talking about when he'd said he'd been elected to Pop at Eton; I made a mental note to tell him all about the way boys are elected to join the elitist group, within the elitist school, at my first opportunity...then smiled as I imagined what his response was likely to be.

I suspected Worthington had noticed the change in my expression, because he glared at me as he asked Sir Simon, "Are you certain no one saw you when you were in this room, during that critical quarter of an hour?" Worthington seemed to be pleading.

"I could hear noises in the kitchen when I passed by, so one assumes Julie and Glen were in there doing...whatever they were doing."

Glen and Julie looked at each other, and both nodded in Worthington's direction.

Julie said, "We was both in the kitchen, wasn't we, Glen love? But we didn't come in here at all. Didn't think anyone would need to use this place tonight." Glen nodded his agreement with his wife's statement.

Worthington signalled his thanks.

Sir Simon continued, "I didn't imagine anyone would mind if I came in here. I was sitting at the partners' desk over there – in the dark, if you must know – totally focused on trying to get through to the person I needed to speak to. It was very frustrating."

Worthington pounced. "Are you saying, now, Sir Simon, that you didn't actually connect with the person you were trying to reach?" His voice had a sharper edge to it.

His altered tone seemed to rattle Pendlebury. "Ah, yes, well that's the thing, you see. No, I couldn't. I hesitated to leave a message. Then called again when I realized I had to say something. The answerphone gave me the opportunity to rerecord my message, which I did, because I needed to think about what I wanted to say. It took a little time, but I would be surprised if it had taken a quarter of an hour."

"And you remained in this room the entire time?"

"Indeed. Until I heard a commotion at the front door."

Worthington leaned forward, but said nothing.

Pendlebury looked at his watch. "If that's all…" He shifted in his chair. "As I said, no alibi needed. Sasha must have been grieving and…well, you know. Terrible for old Piers, of course. And a loss to the world of public relations in toto. She'll be missed by her family, of course, and she had a great talent. Highly driven woman. Laser focus. Extremely effective."

"Does Tavistock and Tavistock act on your behalf?" Worthington sat back. I noticed a large tear roll down Piers' cheek, but he still wasn't interacting with anyone in the room – it was as though none of us existed.

Pendlebury stared at Piers, and sighed. Heavily. "Yes. Have done for about…oh, I'd say maybe ten years."

"And the nature of the business they conduct for you would be…"

"General public relations planning and execution, reputation management, crisis planning, some internal communications stuff – conferences, that sort of thing. And lobbying, of course.

That's what they're known for. Representing my business to politicians on an ongoing basis."

"Any politicians in particular?"

Pendlebury ran his tongue along the edge of his top teeth. "A wide range, across the spectrum. I have business interests in many countries around the globe. You probably know of my department stores, but you might not be aware that – having started out needing to fill those shops with appealing goods – I now run one of the biggest import-export groups in the nation, supporting thousands of jobs here, and overseas. My customers are also global. My businesses are impacted by almost every political decision made in this country, and different aspects of my businesses touch almost every MP's constituency. It's a symbiotic relationship, and Sasha and Piers help those in political power to better understand that symbiosis."

I wondered if he really believed a word of what he was saying.

"An interesting endeavor," said Worthington blandly. "When do you return from Jersey?"

Pendlebury was already out of his seat. "Morning meetings, I shall lunch there, then return. Pre-Christmas drinks at the House of Commons tomorrow evening, and I shan't miss that. I just hope the weather doesn't muck up my flights."

Worthington nodded. "Me too. We might need to talk again. Please make sure you confirm your statement before you leave. Enderby will see to it. And give her a number where you can be reached, should I need to contact you." Worthington's tone seemed to take the wind out of Pendlebury's sails; he simply nodded and all-but scurried out of the room, followed by Enderby.

"When may the rest of us leave?" Felicity was an inch away from whining.

Worthington ignored her, and said, "Mrs. Quiller, did you notice anything in your sister's behavior this evening that might have indicated she was planning to take her life?"

Bella grasped John's hand on the tabletop, gave him a look that spoke of desperation and replied, "I wish I had. I might have been able to stop her from…you know. And please, call me Bella. I haven't been Mrs. Quiller for many years."

"Indeed," replied Worthington. "She didn't say, or do, anything that would not have been her usual habit, or manner?"

"Not at all. As Sir Simon said, Sasha was a little overwrought about this evening's dinner, but it was to be a gathering to mark what would have been my father's eightieth birthday, had he but lived to reach it. Somber, yes, but we all wanted to recognize his birthday out of respect. He's gone, but not forgotten."

"And when the gong rang, you also used the facilities?"

"Yes. The yellow bedroom. It used to be my mother's room, when we were children; Sasha and Piers have what used to be Daddy's room as their bedroom, now. I followed Piers upstairs; he went into his room – well, his and Sasha's room, of course – and I went into the yellow room. Both are at the rear of the house. I, like Felicity and Charles, only came to the top of the stairs when I heard the commotion. Piers was just behind me, as I recall." She bent her head and spoke more softly, saying, "I'm telling you about Piers because it really doesn't look as though he's up to any of this…I hope that's alright?" Worthington nodded. Bella finished with, "And that's it, really. You know what happened after that."

Worthington turned his attention to Renata. "So, Miss Douglas, it seems you were the last person to be in the company of Mrs. Tavistock by some moments. You say she asked you to accompany her to the terrace beyond the salon, where she wished to smoke before dinner? Was that usual for her?"

Renata's hands were laid flat on the table in front of her, one either side of her empty coffee mug. "She did smoke before dinner, sometimes, but only at private dinners, like this. Never before a client function. Here, she never smoked inside the house, except for up in the palace room. We stepped outside, then she realized how chilly it was, and headed off around the side of the house to go up the steps to her bedroom, to fetch something to put over her shoulders, she said. That was the last I saw of her, until she was dead."

"Do you have any idea why she used the outside stairs instead of coming back into the house?"

Renata gave her answer a few seconds' thought. "We were at the back of the house, her room is at the back of the house. It was quicker."

"And what did you do after she left you?"

"I waited for her."

"Outside? In the cold? Why not return to the salon?" I was glad Worthington had asked such a direct question – because that had been worrying me, too.

Renata squared her shoulders. "I started out in life as the daughter of a hard-working lorry driver from Solihull, and have now been the personal assistant to one of the most influential lobbyists in the country for a good many years. I am proud of my achievements, and have only retained my position by being utterly reliable. Let me ask you this, Mr. Worthington: if you were to tell Miss Enderby to wait for you, and you returned to find she'd wandered off to a place where you'd had to hunt her down, how long would she continue to work for you?"

Touché!

"Renata's the most reliable assistant I've ever known," said Piers, surprisingly. His speech was slurred, his eyes staring at something far away. "We used to share you, didn't we, Renata? In the early days. Then it all grew so fast...so many hours of work, and meetings, and events, and dinners, and it all got bigger, and bigger." He finally focused on our inquisitor's face. "She's only here tonight because she puts duty to the company above all else, right, Renata? Sasha, of course, had to invite Sir Simon, so we had one man too many. Good God – this poor woman has sat through countless dinners making up numbers, listening to clients drone on and on about their businesses and Lord only knows what else, all so we've been able to have a balance of genders sup together. She's a good woman. Made a huge difference to Sasha when Oleg was dying. Knows what it's like to watch a father face his mortality, you see, and how that can affect a family. I'll hear nothing said against her." He raised his brandy bowl toward Renata, realized it was empty and added, "Glen – bring more of this, now. Fetch the bottle."

Glen glanced at Worthington, who almost imperceptibly shook his head, saying, "Maybe Mr. Tavistock would prefer a coffee, Glen."

Piers stood, grabbed the table to stop himself swaying, and barked, "I'm in my own house, and my wife has just seen fit to go and kill herself. I'll bathe in brandy if I choose, man. Glen. More. The best in the house. Now." He sat down again. Hard.

Felicity shifted in her seat, and Charles stared at Piers as though he were an alien, which I thought was a bit rich, considering he looked as though he'd tucked away a fair amount of booze at the dinner table.

"And you?" Worthington looked directly at John, who seemed shocked to be addressed.

John spluttered, "I showed Bud where the WCs were in the entry way, and we each used a cubicle. We almost ran into each other when we heard Julie screaming in the entry way. Cait was already there."

"And I'd remained in the salon, as you know," I said. I was going to add a few of my own observations – but Worthington reacted to his phone, which began to vibrate on the tabletop.

We all sat in silence as he gave his attention to the instrument, reading, and typing.

"Thank you all, for now. I need to make an important call. If I might have the room, please. See Enderby about your statements." I looked around to realize the woman had slipped into the room again, unnoticed by anyone; she and Renata seemed to share the ability to melt into their surroundings, becoming almost invisible by dint of their not projecting any personality at all, and favoring bland costume.

We were dismissed, and all got up, ready to move to the more comfortable areas of the house, which everyone did as Worthington dialled, and Enderby ushered.

"*...unloose this tied-up justice...*"

I hung around for a few moments, wanting to create an opportunity to ask Worthington a few questions in private. However, he made it quite clear he had no intention of giving me any of his time, so I left the meeting room, walked across the rather bleak hallway and entered the dining room. It was empty, but the doors to the salon were open, and I could see everyone there. Everyone except Sir Simon, in any case; I guessed he'd decamped as soon as possible.

I headed straight to the entry hall where I located one of the hidden doors to a guest washroom. I reckoned if Bud and John had used those facilities it would be fine if I did the same. Refreshed, I headed to the salon, and could see Enderby deep in conversation with Piers, with Bud by their side. I managed to catch Bud's attention, and beckoned him over to me. He sidled away, then headed in my direction.

"Come with me," he whispered, and pulled me through the French doors, shut them behind us, then hustled me along the chilly terrace. Finally he pulled me close to him.

"I'm going to cuddle you to keep you warm, but it's also going to give me a chance to talk to you in a way that no one can hear what I'm saying, right?"

"It's always lovely when you cuddle me, Husband, but why all the cloak-and-dagger stuff?"

"Later. For now you need to know this; something's wrong. I don't know what, but it's something that might bring this investigation to a halt. I suspect it will stink to high heaven, and I don't want you kicking up a fuss."

I pulled back to be able to see Bud's face. "What on earth...?"

He pulled me close again. "Just listen. Now's not the time for anything but this – keep quiet, don't say anything to anyone about anything. Just take orders from Worthington. Got it?"

I wriggled away. "Bud...I'm not..."

The French doors leading from the salon opened, and Enderby's head poked out. "Ah, there you are. I wondered where you'd...ah..." Enderby coughed as Bud kissed me. Hard. "I'll be inside. Mr. Worthington wants a word with everyone – including you two. When you have a mo." Bud kept kissing me for about five seconds after we heard the doors closing, then released me.

"You're so strong, and powerful," I mugged. Then I pecked him on the cheek and added, "That was nice. Unexpected, but nice."

Bud winked. "Good cover, eh? Okay, let's get this over with. Please, Cait, bite your tongue. We'll talk later, I promise."

Upon entering the salon, it was clear Worthington had been waiting for us; I didn't have to fake the heat that rushed to my cheeks. I steeled myself for what was coming – I judged I knew what Worthington was about to say, and do.

"As you know, I have had the opportunity to establish that the note we discovered in the palace room was written by Mrs. Tavistock. It is clear that Mrs. Tavistock didn't make her intentions known to anyone here tonight. It appears there is no more investigating to be done; this is a terrible tragedy, of course, but it seems the coroner will have sufficient grounds to rule that a suicide took place here this evening. You have our sincere condolences. Enderby and I shall now take our leave of you. I'm sure you'll all be glad to have some privacy. Thank you for your time. And, once again, our commiserations for your loss." Worthington ushered Enderby toward the front door, where Julie magically appeared with two overcoats, and they were gone.

I was almost cross-eyed with the effort it had taken for me to not say anything, but my absolute trust in Bud had helped me to keep quiet. I finally made eye contact with him, and his face creased into what I recognized as a smile of gratitude. John placed his arm around Bella's shoulders as she wept. Piers retreated to the fireside seat, and Glen rushed to his side.

"How about a nightcap, Mr. Tavistock?" Piers nodded. Glen looked around the room. "Anyone else?"

I was torn between wanting to leave – so I could be alone with Bud to find out what on earth was going on, and wanting to stay – to see how whatever was going on played out. If Sasha really had thrown herself off the roof, in the middle of a dinner party, having dashed off a suicide note during a loo break, I wanted someone to at least talk openly about why she might have done that. Did Bud know? Did someone else in the room know?

A moment later my decision was made for me by John. "Vinnie, if you're ready, I'd be grateful if you'd get Cait and Bud back to my place, please. I'll be staying with Bella, and I know Charles will be here – as will Julie and Glen, of course – if Piers needs anything during the night. Renata – do you have some way to get home?"

Everyone looked at Renata, who had more or less disappeared into the most dimly lit corner of the room. "I was planning to use the company car service." Matter-of-fact tone. She looked at her wristwatch. "I'm not much later than I would have been had the evening gone according to plan."

Others also checked their watches; I felt as though I'd fallen into some sort of looking-glass world, where a tragedy hadn't taken place a few hours earlier. I glanced at the clock; it wasn't quite eleven, so I supposed at least Renata's assessment was accurate, if pragmatic to the point of cold-heartedness.

"Whereabouts do you want to be getting to?" Vinnie sounded almost jovial.

Renata looked horrified. "Oh no, I couldn't possibly impose. The car service is exceptionally reliable. But thank you for offering."

"Only too happy to help, then you wouldn't have to be waiting about here, you know, with the family." I wasn't certain if Vinnie had meant his comment to be so pointed.

Renata's body language told me it had hit home, as she gushed, "Oh, yes, I see what you mean." Red patches crept up her throat as she scanned the room. "I'm not far from Vauxhall tube station."

"We're going your way," said Vinnie, beaming; he moved from his perch beside the drinks trolley. "We can drop you off, no problem at all. Come on, let's get out of the way of these poor people now."

"Thanks, Vinnie," said John. "Talk in the morning, Bud, Cait." He returned his attention to Bella, and I caught Bud's eyes steering me to the door.

"See you out front, at the car, in a tick or two," said Vinnie, and headed off.

I had no idea what to say to the host of a dinner party that hadn't happened because of his wife's death. The fact the person in question was Piers Tavistock didn't help at all.

Bud came to my rescue by walking toward me, putting his arm around my waist and saying, "This has been a dreadful experience for you all. We're terribly sorry. We'll leave you to your grief." Then he pressed my side, and I followed him meekly to the front hall, where – yet again – Julie appeared with her arms full of coats.

I thanked her and patted her on the shoulder, which I realized as I was doing it was an odd, and possibly quite patronising, thing to do, so I stopped, grinned idiotically, and left. I got into the back seat of the car, offering the front seat to Renata; even if Bud and I couldn't talk, we could at least be close to each other for the journey back to John's place.

As it turned out, the entire trip was silent, until we began to get close to Renata's neck of the woods, when she told Vinnie exactly where she lived. We deposited her outside a squat Victorian block of flats that enjoyed a position on the corner of a busy main thoroughfare and a small park.

"Thank you. Goodnight," was all we got when she left us.

"Chatty type, isn't she though?" said Vinnie as he pulled away and headed for Vauxhall Bridge.

Bud squeezed my hand and I whispered, "Not long now – we're very close."

He whispered back, "Good. I'm done. Think I might have nodded off back there for a while." *He had.*

Vinnie drove in through the garage entrance, then turned and handed over a bunch of keys John had given him for us. "I'll be seeing you tomorrow, I dare say. Himself likes me to drop in to do a fry-up for him on occasion. Any interest? I do a fine full Irish."

Not having eaten much for what seemed like days I was tempted to ask Vinnie to cook the lavish spread right there and then, but thought it best to ask, "Would I be right in guessing there's food in the fridge we can raid, and breakfast supplies in John's place?"

"Thanks to Vaseem, you'd be right on both counts. Just give me a bell on my mobile if you need anything. Hold out your hand, I'll write it down for you."

"Just tell me what it is, I'm good with numbers," I replied lightly. He did, and I made a mental note.

Finally in our room, I collapsed onto the bed, kicked off my shoes and said, "Okay, spill your guts, Bud. What just happened tonight?"

Bud flopped onto the chair in the corner of the room. "You've no idea."

I sat upright. "Yes, you're right, I don't, so please tell me – directly, and fully, or I might blow a gasket."

Bud smiled. It was a tired, loving smile. "I was so proud of you tonight, Wife. Worthington checked you out before he let you into our little cabal, and he was obviously impressed. It was a great feeling."

I stood, getting hotter by the minute. "Thank you. Spousal pride. Lovely. Now tell me what's going on, or I might have to strangle you."

"I don't know much more than you do about who, exactly, Worthington and Enderby work for, nor report to. John reckons they might be part of a special unit of the Metropolitan Police who tackle politically sensitive cases. I know there's one law for everyone, but I also know the realities of life; it's not so very different anywhere in the world – politics add a dimension to crime that has to be taken into consideration, even if the courts and the law act the same way regardless of position."

"You mean Lady Justice is blind, but not every crime is put before her for judgement, because they don't get that far?" I could feel my heckles start to rise alongside the heat rushing up my neck. *Not a hot flash...not now, please.*

Bud sighed. "As I said, reality."

"And?"

"When he found the body, Vinnie made a call. As I believe you might have already guessed, he and John go way back; John met him when he was liaising under some pretty challenging circumstances. They had each other's backs then, still do. So Vinnie knows...people. Phoned one of them, realizing immediately he saw the body that there'd be an issue, due to the nature of the folks who were on the spot. You know how it goes, Cait. Wheels were set in motion. Once John saw what had happened, he also made a couple of calls, then he asked me to make a couple too. 'Covering all bases,' he said. That's when you and I were kind of vetted, I guess you could say. Worthington didn't know if he was walking into a situation that might blow up in his face; he was short-handed, so accepted the national and international help offered to him by...various agencies. Then, just before he made his abrupt exit, both John and I got texts from our respective contacts. No detail, just saying that suicide was most likely, due to the note. Family to be left to get on with...whatever they're getting on with as we speak."

"And that's that, is it?" I contemplated shoving my wrists under cool running water to try to get my body's thermostat under control. "Worthington was pursuing lines of enquiry that suggested he suspected foul play, long after we'd found that note. Is he not as high up the food chain as you'd initially led me to believe? Did he simply get shut down by someone he reports to?"

Bud stood and stretched. "To be honest, I can only say I guess so. Everyone's got a boss, or even multiple layers of bosses, Cait. I don't know who his masters are, or even what type of people they are. Home Office? Maybe MI5? Or the Met? I don't know. And, to be honest, at this moment, I am too, too tired to care. I've been running on fumes for hours. Please can we save everything else for the morning? If I don't get some sleep soon, I might just collapse."

My husband's usually twinkling blue eyes had no lustre, and there were deep bags sagging beneath them. Even as he said the words, I knew he wasn't the only one who needed sleep, so I agreed, and hit the bathroom. Within ten minutes I joined him in bed, where he was already snoring. I hoped the wall between our room and Vinnie and Vaseem's home next door was a thick one, because I feared I might make it a two-part harmony when I finally managed to shut away the images of Sasha's body in the snow, and the sound of Bella's keening wails.

TUESDAY

"...all is mortal in nature..."

I pulled open the curtains to discover that the sky was robin's-egg blue, and all the slush had disappeared, which bode well for the day I hoped lay ahead of us. I couldn't believe we'd slept for as long as we had, given the amount of traffic on the road just beyond our window. I still didn't feel completely rested; I'd hoped to bound out of bed ready to face the world around seven, but it was gone nine before I eventually woke Bud to tell him I'd prepared tea and toast for us.

Given the number of buttons and dials on every piece of kitchen gadgetry John had hidden away in cupboards about the place, I congratulated myself that I'd found what I'd needed and made it work as I bit into thick toast, oozing with butter and blackcurrant jam.

Bud joined me looking his usual bright-eyed self. He'd showered and shaved, had selected a shirt from the two I'd hung in the wardrobe, and seemed intent upon making me feel as special as possible, which was lovely.

He also slathered his toast with jam, and ate almost half a piece with one mouthful. After a couple of swigs of what I'd made certain was strong, properly brewed, tea, he said, "So what's today? National Gallery, or Piccadilly Circus?" He winked, telling me how proud he was of himself for having remembered two of the long list of places I'd been enthusiastic to visit on our trip.

"It looks as though it might be a dry day, so Piccadilly Circus, and then along Piccadilly itself, to Hatchards and Fortnum and Mason, then on to Green Park, via the Ritz, would make sense…but I really don't want to miss visiting old friends at the National Gallery, so maybe we could start there?" I checked my watch. "It's going to be a late start…so how about I phone the Ritz and see if they have any spaces for tea? I mean, given the time of year, and the short notice, I doubt it very much, but we won't know if we don't ask. Failing that, I'll try the same at Fortnum's. And failing that – well, maybe the Criterion Restaurant for an early dinner…though we'd run into the theatre crowd then and—"

Bud held up his hand. "Hang on a minute, I thought we were going to take it easy this trip. Just wander where we please, when we want. This is beginning to sound like a military operation. Can't we just show up for tea somewhere? If you're intent upon having tea, that is."

I shrugged. "I wish we could, but it's prime Christmas shopping time, and people will have booked tea weeks, or even months, in advance. I can't imagine they have a lot of cancellations – but that's why I thought it might be at least worth trying to—"

"Why don't we let fate decide, and just show up where and when we want tea?"

"Because there are set times for tea, it's not some sort of casual, rolling affair…there are several sittings at the Ritz, and only so many tables, or you book a table at a set time at Fortnum's, and so forth. Oh, that's an idea – the Ritz might be able to take us later this morning. You'd have to wear a tie of course…"

Bud shook his head. "Hang on a minute. A tie? I never wear a tie, you know that. I'm not even certain I own any, and I certainly didn't pack one."

"You're okay, I did. I knew we might get called upon to show up in any number of carefully-calibrated dress codes at various places, so I covered all our bases."

Bud chomped into a second piece of toast. "It doesn't sound very appealing. All a bit too marshalled and stuffy for my liking." He sighed. "But if you want to make a few calls, who am I to stop you? Have at it, Wife. Be your most charming self – if charm is likely to play any role at all. I want you to be able to experience all the things you've been missing since you moved to Canada. You spend your life studying those who have been touched by crime – by those who seek to do harm, and act in a societally deviant way. You deserve the chance to revel in normality. By the way – was taking tea at all these swanky places something you did often? And, if so, why is it I'm only finding out about this now?"

I began to head to our room to get my phone. "Agency days, Bud. If you wanted to try to sway a potential client to use your services, or thank an existing one for doing so, you might have got a big fat 'No' when you invited them to even an excellent restaurant for lunch. But make it breakfast at the Savoy, or tea at the Ritz, and they'd bite your hand off. Claridge's was just about the only luncheon place most folks would agree to meet – so, yes, I did eat at places like that, for years. And, to be honest, I thought I'd had my fill of them because it was always all about schmoozing whomever your guest was. I'd like the chance to indulge for the sake of it, for the fun of it…and with my husband."

I'd reached the top of the stairs as I heard Bud call, "Good luck."

I couldn't tell if he really meant it.

Twenty minutes later I joined my husband again, feeling rather subdued. It had been as I'd feared – no bookings were to be had, at all, anywhere I wanted to go. I got a hug and a fresh cuppa to try to buck me up, but it didn't work.

"National Gallery it is then," said Bud, trying to jolly me along.

I agreed, and began to shove my dishes into the dishwasher – which I'd managed to locate behind a devilishly clever touch-to-open lower cupboard door.

As we cleared away Bud mused, "Last night feels as though it all happened in a dream. It did happen, right? Sasha Tavistock really did kill herself, and we were there when it happened; I didn't dream it all, did I?"

I chuckled, wryly. "Yes, Husband, it all really did happen. But I know what you mean – it feels as though we fell into some sort of weird story that wasn't our own, and now we're here, in unfamiliar surroundings, without the anchor we thought John would be for us on this trip. I hope this doesn't scupper his wedding plans – though the way Bella was last night I can quite understand she might not want to go through with it. If she does call it off – again – how do you think John will cope?"

Bud stood, a jammy plate in one hand, an empty mug in the other. "Devastated, I guess. I mean, he'd understand – who wouldn't? But he'd be real upset. Poor John."

"Is there anything we can do?"

Bud handed me his dirty dishes. "Not a thing. He's on his own for this, Cait, though we'll be here for moral support."

"And what about the case?"

Bud tutted. "There's no 'case', Cait. I told you I'd been warned off, in no uncertain terms, if the suicide note was authenticated. It was. Nothing for us to do – other than support a friend who's soon-to-be sister-in-law took her own life."

I nodded, and closed the dishwasher. There was no point running it for so few dishes – besides, I wouldn't have had a clue how to, since there were no obvious buttons. "Right then, let's get going so we can make the most of the weather, while it lasts. Don't bother with a tie; let's go out dressed as exactly what we are – tourists here to see as much as we can in a short time. I'm looking forward to introducing you to Jean de Dinteville and Georges de Selve before we grab something for lunch."

Bud chuckled as I headed to the stairs again. "You love it, don't you?"

"What?" I called playfully.

"You know very well 'what', Wife." *And I did.*

It was almost eleven by the time we reached the National Gallery. When I'd lived in London, Trafalgar Square had still been surrounded by traffic, so I found it a delight to not have to dodge buses and taxis, but to be able to take the time to enjoy the square itself, and the new approach to the wonderful façade of the gallery. The pigeons weren't as numerous as they were in my memory, and the square was quite peaceful as we stared up at the towering Christmas tree.

"It's big," observed Bud, rather unnecessarily. "Does it have to come far? Moving that thing around these streets must be a nightmare."

"It comes from Norway, so it's had a few adventures before it winds its way to this spot. The Norwegians gift a tree like this to Britain every year, in thanks for the British support from 1940 to 1945."

"Nice," said Bud. He can be a master of understatement when he wants.

A gaggle of folks all wearing matching black overcoats and jolly crimson scarves suggested carol singing was about to break out; we decided not to wait, but to head off so I could make my introductions to Bud.

There's something magical about walking into the National Gallery; yes, I know it's a world-class gallery, but – for me – it had been a place of refuge during my agency days. My office had been in Soho, not very far from Trafalgar Square, and I'd found I needed to decompress sometimes, in a way other than throwing gin and tonics down my throat at the Coach and Horses. This had been my sanctuary; a place where most people automatically spoke in hushed tones, where each room offered a new insight into the way artists had used their talents in different countries at different times, and where I'd been just another person perching on a bench gazing at awesome paintings.

On this occasion I all-but dragged Bud to the room I had to visit even if I missed everything else: the one where the paintings by Hans Holbein the Younger were displayed. I knew it would be busy there – it always had been, in my experience, and probably always will be – but I didn't care. I introduced Bud to *The Ambassadors*, otherwise known as Jean de Dinteville and Georges de Selve, which had been painted in 1533 by the artist whose talent and skill never, ever cease to amaze me. Bud was incredibly patient as I – possibly over-enthusiastically – shared my knowledge about, and love for, the piece with him.

He nodded and smiled in all the right places, even when I went on – and on – about the way that Henry VIII decided to upend the stability of the Western World, bound together at that time by the common religion of Roman Catholicism, by breaking from Rome…all so he could marry the woman he lusted for.

"So these two blokes are in England, dispatched with the task of pointing out to a man who wants nothing more than to bed Anne Boleyn, that he's messing with the entire power structure of the known world and everything is out of whack because of it. See the ways the artist shows us how things are not right…all through the device of objects that are broken…" I could hear myself, but couldn't shut myself up.

When I'd almost finished – and stopped to draw breath – Bud said, "That globe thing of the stars is amazing, and the satin of his sleeve looks…well, real. Which I mean as a compliment."

I was thrilled. "But this is my favorite bit," I said. I pulled him to the right-hand edge of the piece. "Now look at that blurry thing side on – the thing that seems to be a shapeless disc when you view it from the front."

Bud shrugged. "Yeah, I wondered about that…" He bobbed his head about, squinted, then said, "That's amazing. It's a skull. A perfectly painted skull – but it's all at an angle from the front. How on earth did he do that in, what, 1533, you said? I mean, how would a person even do that now, without using computer graphics, and all that sort of stuff?"

I was bouncing. "I know, it's fantastic, isn't it?"

Bud stared again. "Indeed it is." He looked surprisingly grim. "Bit of a hint for the two guys in their fancy clothes to never forget we all face the same end, I guess."

I nodded. "Maybe for Henry VIII, too. And, of course, Sasha; even though I remember her as a bit of a blight on my life, all she really was, was a woman, who's now dead." I looked at the painting. "Alas, poor Sasha…I didn't know her well, though I didn't want to."

"Holbein the Younger, *and* Hamlet?" Bud mugged a shocked look. "Yes, even *I've* heard about Yorik. Trying to make me less of a Philistine this morning, are you?"

"I wonder why her hair was hanging loose," I said – aloud, as it turned out.

"Whose hair?"

"Sasha's. Look at the ermine on the coat he's wearing, there. You can see every hair in it. Like the broken string on the lute – such incredibly fine detail. It made me think of Sasha's hair, fallen across her face as she lay in the snow. Her hair was pinned up when we were having drinks, and a chignon needs a lot of grips to stay that way. But when she was on the ground it was hanging loose. I wonder why. And I wonder when, and how, it came down."

Bud turned from the painting, the skin around his eyes creasing into a smile. "Can't leave it alone, can you?" I must have set my jaw, because he added, "And don't look at me like that. There is no investigation. She jumped. There was the note."

"Yes, the note…"

Bud shook his head. "Listen, the poor woman decided to kill herself and she dashed off a note. The fact it doesn't make sense to you or me is neither here nor there."

"It didn't seem to make any sense to her husband or her sister either," I replied. "And the way she chose to do it – flinging herself off the roof like that. It was bound to be a scene everyone there would see. I know I told you Sasha was completely self-involved, and pretty cut-throat when it came to business. But to do that to her family? She must have hated them. Her body was so terribly mangled…"

A woman with a gray bob and a small child in tow approached and hissed, "Excuse me, please think about what you're discussing. So loudly, too. There are children here."

Bud and I realized we'd become the center of attention; I apologized, we clamped our mouths shut and wandered toward Holbein's portrait of a woman with a squirrel, which is another of my favorites…though Bud preferred the one of Erasmus – not at all due to his dislike of squirrels, he assured me, in no more than a whisper.

Having made a real effort to focus on the art, and not mention the previous night's incident, we completed our tour of the room, and I suggested we headed to see the Caravaggio around just a couple of corners, but Bud claimed to need a loo; we were quite close, so made our way swiftly past the Canalettos, Guardis, and Tiepolos, and reached the toilets in record time.

Refreshed when we emerged, Bud surprised me when he said, "I need some air, Cait. Do you mind?"

My tummy clenched. "Are you feeling alright?"

"I'll be better outside. Come on." He whisked me out.

Standing at the top of the stone steps, looking down into Trafalgar Square and along Whitehall, where Big Ben stood proudly above the Houses of Parliament, I felt a surge of nostalgia for London that I hadn't been expecting. The power surrounding me was palpable; the heart of London, and all its attendant government buildings, was designed to inspire awe, and it does. I grabbed Bud's hand.

He spoke quietly. "We've been asked to…requested to…"

I looked at my husband sideways; he was being unusually dithery. "What?"

"That's Canada House, just there." He nodded to a building to our right.

"I know. I mean I knew anyway, but the maple leaf flags are a bit of a giveaway, too, don't you think?"

"Ha, ha." He didn't smile. "I…well, we…need to meet someone, just for a few moments probably, and they're in there. Now. Just texted, asking me to drop in."

I didn't like the feeling creeping up my spine. I glanced around. "How did they know we're this close?" I noted the numerous CCTV cameras in the area.

Bud managed a smile. "Oh, I don't think they did. It was just a request. Drop by, as and when."

I nibbled my top lip as I worked out what I should say. "I trust you, and I love you. Of course we'll go. Right now. Do you need to text back?"

"I did."

"…thou art wedded to calamity…"

I led the way. I wasn't angry, I didn't even feel terribly put out; I was more puzzled than anything, and a little anxious, because this wasn't the sort of request I imagined was normal. Then I reasoned that Bud's relationship with various law enforcement and intelligence gathering agencies around the world also wasn't normal, so – despite the fact he could never tell me *everything* that was going on, or had happened – that had to be factored into the situation too, on top of what had happened to Sasha the night before.

When we presented ourselves to an underwhelming security guard, we were directed along a marbled corridor to a desk where Bud explained who we were. A phone call led to a small woman in flats and a trouser suit leading us away from the fancy areas into a disappointingly plain room that didn't have a single window, nor any adornments on the walls. We sat at the table which almost filled the space. I was working hard at being quiet, but had so many questions I wanted to ask…starting with who exactly was Ralph MacDonald – the man Bud had told the woman at the desk we'd come to see.

A moment or two later three gray-haired men in gray suits entered silently. One shook Bud's hand. "Thanks for coming, Bud. This must be your wife. Professor Morgan, a great pleasure. I've heard a lot about you."

Ordinarily those words wouldn't have filled me with dread, but they took on a complex hue, under the circumstances. I replied, "Mr. MacDonald, I presume?"

The man's face creased into what appeared to be a genuine smile. "Indeed. We won't take much of your time. We don't want to spoil too much of your visit."

We were pointedly not introduced to the two other men, who sat on a couple of seats set against the wall, rather than at the table.

"We can all speak freely in this room, so please do so," opened MacDonald. "Last night's incident is most tragic and regrettable, and, of course, Mrs. Tavistock's loss will be felt deeply by those closest to her. I understand John Silver was – or possibly still is – due to become married to her sister." Bud nodded. I wondered how MacDonald knew that; had Bud told him?

"Furthermore, I'm aware of the various ways in which you and Mr. Silver have worked toward goals our two nations have had in common at certain points in the past." MacDonald might have said we could speak freely, but it was clear to me he wasn't planning to do anything of the sort.

Bud nodded again. I played quiet little wifey with as much aplomb as I could muster.

"I understand it was happenstance that you were on the spot when Mrs. Tavistock died, and I have in my possession the findings of the team sent to ascertain the true nature of the incident, as well as a list of those present at the time, along with some briefing materials about them. Professor Morgan, you understand that here in the UK the Coroner's Office will be the final arbiter of cause of death?" I nodded, silently. *Duh!* "It is believed at this time that the finding will be one of suicide, largely due to the discovery of a note stating intent, as well as a lack of any evidence to suggest anything other than suicide. As I mentioned, you may speak freely in this room, at this time. Is there anything you think I should be made aware of that might suggest suicide was not, in fact, the cause of Mrs. Tavistock's demise?"

I found it strange to hear a Canadian speaking in such a formal way. Bud must have been more used to it than me, because he didn't bat an eyelid, he just shook his head and replied, "Nothing concrete."

One of the men sitting beside the wall shifted in his seat.

"Meaning?" MacDonald leaned forward.

Bud looked at me, and tilted his head.

I ran through my still somewhat scattered thoughts about Sasha's hair being down when she died…about the way the lamp on the table where the note had been found wasn't illuminated when we arrived in the palace room…about what possible reason there could be for the big brass telescope being found pointing at the floor…but…I didn't feel able to speak about any of those factors coherently. It was frustrating, but even I am capable of erring on the side of caution – especially if I'm in a windowless room with a bunch of men in gray suits.

I replied, "I knew Sasha a little, many years ago, and have to say I don't believe it would have been within her character to take her own life. She was too utterly selfish, and driven. So, since we're speaking openly here, I don't believe she would have jumped, but I think she was the sort of person who might have said or done something to someone that might have made them to want to push her. But, no, I have nothing concrete to support my…suspicion."

MacDonald looked at Bud, whose grave expression cheered me no end. "Cait's good, very good. You know that, because you'll have checked. I've never known her to be wrong."

MacDonald sucked at his bottom lip as he looked at me, then he returned his attention to Bud. "I understand you were both privy to the interviews conducted last evening. Anything you'd like to tell me?"

Bud replied dryly, "Worthington appears to be under the thumb of his masters, whomever they might be. He was less than transparent on that point. His evidence gathering oversight was sound. His questioning thorough – to the extent it was allowed to be."

"Is there anything you'd like to share with us about your observations last evening, that might not be apparent from the official record, Professor Morgan?" MacDonald's polite tone seemed almost genuine. Almost.

I pushed aside my desire to scream, and replied, "The man who introduced himself to us as Mr. Worthington allowed everyone to believe he suspected them of some sort of involvement with Sasha's death. This was despite the fact he'd already read the note you mentioned, and had been told it had been written by the deceased. I found this approach to be odd at the time, and I then found the way the entire investigation was shut down, abruptly, to be quite worrying."

"So, was your immediate response to suspect foul play of some sort?" MacDonald's tone had shifted.

I weighed my response. "In thinking more deeply about last evening's events, and considering my knowledge of the dead woman, I've said all I feel comfortable saying. Though I would welcome the opportunity to remain involved in any further investigation." I tried to make sure my voice sounded calm.

"Hmm. Well, I'm afraid that's where we have…well, let's not call it a problem, eh?"

At last, a tangible bit of Canadiana within MacDonald's vocabulary, I thought. I said nothing.

He continued, "What I thought it might be useful for you to know is that we've received certain representations about the presence of two Canadian citizens at Beulah House last night; the only two persons present who were not normally to be found within the dead woman's social circle. One of these persons used to work with said woman some time ago. That same person threatened, publicly, to sue a national daily newspaper represented by the dead woman, and the same person was present when the ex-employer of the dead woman – a man with whom the dead woman had enjoyed an intimate relationship – was himself murdered."

I was amazed my jaw didn't actually hit the table. Bud tensed beside me, and clamped his hand onto my thigh. "Now just a minute, Ralph…" he began.

Ralph MacDonald held up his hands and smiled, coldly. "I'm not saying these points are damning – they are factually correct, yes, and might lead one to travel a certain path if they were all connected together in a way our friends sitting in offices not half a mile from here have chosen to do. But we know better, don't we, Professor Morgan?"

I was almost speechless. Almost. "Are you telling me that Sasha Tavistock was a PR advisor to the rag that kept sending photographers to hunt me down, even when the inquest had made it clear that my ex had died from internal injuries sustained in a fight I was miles away from?" I struggled to stop my voice quivering.

"Indeed she was," replied MacDonald.

I sat back in my chair, and let it all sink in. "All I can do is be honest and tell you I had no idea. When I let my ex-boyfriend, Angus, into my flat in Cambridge I had no idea I'd wake up to find him dead on the floor. I understood why the local police arrested me on suspicion of murder – there was no one else in the place, and the way he'd treated me during our relationship gave me a pretty good motive for wanting him dead and gone. However, they discovered incontrovertible evidence proving I had nothing to do with Angus's death, and released me. But the newspapers? *They* wouldn't let it go, would they? One particular tabloid was ruining my life; everywhere I went there was a photographer leaping out at me, or taking shots with long-range lenses. It became impossible for me to continue with my teaching, or even with my research. My solicitor advised me to threaten to sue, and also advised I should do so publicly, rather than in a private letter, which she said they'd probably just ignore…or add to the piles they received on an almost daily basis. Eventually, things got so bad for me that – as you know – I left the country. But I honestly didn't know Sasha was connected with them in any way."

The two men in suits shifted on their chairs.

I continued, "And you're also telling me Sasha had a relationship with Alistair Townsend, who owned the agency we both once worked for?"

MacDonald nodded.

"Well, that might explain why she was always first into, and last out of, the office, I suppose. But, again, I had no idea. When was that, exactly?" I hadn't noticed anything at the time, but had no doubt these people would know.

MacDonald looked across the room. The thinner of the two suited men replied, "While you were at Cambridge, gaining your masters degree. Their relationship lasted about a year."

I reacted more angrily than I should have done. "So, hang on a minute…that means that when Alistair Townsend bumped into me in Nice, and invited me to attend the birthday party he was throwing for his wife – the party during which he died – he knew very well his agency had represented the newspaper that had made my life hell? No wonder he remembered me when he saw me in the Cours Saleya that day." I let the realization settle. "I wonder if he ever felt guilty about it?"

"Cait…" Bud squeezed my hand. "Don't torture yourself."

My mind was scurrying through Sasha's every look, gesture, and comment the previous night, interpreting them in the light of all this new information. "And you're saying that someone, somewhere, suspects I might have done Sasha harm last night?" I couldn't believe I even needed to ask, it was all so preposterous.

"I wouldn't go that far," replied MacDonald.

I tried to sigh my anger away. "Look, first of all, Bud and I came to London at John Silver's invitation to meet his new fiancée, whose name he told us was Bella Quiller. Which it is. But that didn't lead me to imagine she would be related to a woman I'd known donkey's years ago as Alex Asimov. Until we got here, we didn't know we'd be meeting Sasha, let alone that I'd have the chance to kill her – had I wanted to. The note which both Sasha's husband and sister say was written by her is not something I could have conjured out of thin air…I didn't have the opportunity to produce a forged suicide note. And I've never been to Beulah House before, so how on earth would I know how to navigate it, or get Sasha up to the roof to throw her off it? It's all totally ludicrous." I could hear my voice getting higher, and my Welsh accent thickening with every sentence, but I couldn't stop it; I was livid.

"Yes, Professor Morgan." MacDonald leaned toward me as he spoke. "I agree with everything you've said. All I'm doing is laying before you the fact that there are certain conversations taking place."

Bud was raking his hand through his hair – his way of trying to manage tension. He looked at MacDonald, then at me. "Cait, Ralph is doing us a favor by telling us this. It's really way beyond his remit. We…we might consider returning home sooner than we'd planned."

I couldn't take it anymore. "Are you nuts? There's a bunch of old-school-tie chums, and tabloid darlings, who think they can cast these aspersions upon my character? No way. I allowed myself to be run out this country once before. Never again. I'm staying, and we're going to enjoy our time in London, then we're driving to Wales where we shall equally enjoy recalling our wedding."

"That would be the wedding when a chorister was murdered, and the local authorities had to rescue you from a marooned castle?" The gray man with more girth had a falsetto voice. Which didn't help.

"Death and chaos do seem to stalk you, Professor Morgan," observed MacDonald, sagely.

"He wasn't a chorister, he was a choir master," I snapped...then I sighed. "Yes, I see what you mean."

MacDonald cleared his throat and stood. "Bud, I'm so sorry I didn't have time to meet with you today. Maybe next time?" He extended his hand.

"It would have been wonderful if we'd had the chance to say hello and reminisce a bit, Ralph, but I guess you're a busy guy. Too busy to see me, anyhow. Totally understandable," replied Bud.

I stood too. "Yes, um...pleased to have not met you," I added. The three men left, silently.

"I'm sorry, Bud." *This is all so...confusing....annoying.*

Bud hugged me. "Nothing to be sorry for. Ralph's a great guy. Met him a while back. I bet if ever I'd needed to call him at any time – maybe if you and I were in a bit of a tight spot – he'd have helped, no question."

"In that case," I replied heavily, "let's make sure you apologize that I was snappish to him next time you don't text him?"

"Agreed."

We left the building, waved off by a different underwhelming security guard.

"...he that filches from me my good name..."

"Which way?" Bud and I stood on the edge of Trafalgar Square, just two individuals among the bustle of humanity swirling around us.

I looked toward the corridors of power that Whitehall represented, then turned and said, "Let's hit Soho – there's bound to be somewhere we can grab something to eat there. I know it'll have changed since I worked there – all the grime and grit has probably been replaced by millennials sipping overpriced coffee on the pavements, but there'll be somewhere that's still serving hearty food at affordable prices. Failing that, we'll get something from Maison Bertaux, which must still be there. No, hang on, I know – let's go to Chinatown. I could kill for Peking duck."

"Maybe not the sort of language to use, given our recent non-conversation, and our surroundings, Wife," replied Bud, steering me through a gaggle of schoolchildren all peering up at Nelson's Column.

We didn't talk much as we trudged through the throngs; to say the pavements were busy would be an understatement, and there certainly wasn't an opportunity for the heart to heart I wanted. I'd known when we'd planned our trip that I'd be facing up to my past – but I'd expected to only be challenged by memories of my life in London. What I hadn't foreseen was that so many other periods of my personal history would be being viewed through a distorted lens by people I didn't even know existed...but who, apparently, knew me at the granular level. They knew where I'd been, what I'd done, and when. I hate it when I feel I've been blindsided by something – and this? This was just too much.

We found a restaurant on Gerrard Street with dozens of ducks hanging in the window, so at least I knew I'd be able to indulge in what my tastebuds were craving – for whatever reason – and the bustling lunch-crowd atmosphere was just what I needed to allow me to talk freely, if quietly, with Bud. We ordered, and the immediately-presented jasmine tea warmed me, though I hadn't realized I was feeling chilly, while the Cantonese chatter, the aroma of spices promising flavors to come, and the simple décor helped ground me again.

Bud began with, "I know we're not leaving London earlier than we'd planned, but maybe we should give John a bit of a wide berth, given what MacDonald said."

"Sure you don't want to refer to him as just 'M'?" I managed a smile, as did Bud.

"It's good we know." Bud sipped his tea.

I sighed. "I know it's good we know…but it's bad that it's happening at all. Look, I thought it was clear that Worthington had been stood down on the basis of suicide being decided…by the powers that be, if not yet the coroner. So why would someone – anyone – be raising my track record in any case? I mean, what's the point? Suicide doesn't require a whispering campaign to be mounted against me, does it?"

Bud poured more tea. "My thoughts exactly," he said. "It's…odd."

"You could say that."

"I just did." Bud winked. "Come on, it'll be fine."

I poured more tea for myself. "I know you're saying that to try to cheer me up, but we both know it's not true. It won't be fine for Sasha's family for a start – she's dead. It might not be fine for John either – Bella's more than likely going to want to at least postpone their wedding, even if she'd realized she'd made a mistake by saying she wanted to call it off. And as for us? Well, if someone wants to put two and two from my background together and come up with five hundred and forty-seven, I have to ask…is someone acting with malice toward me? Because I cannot imagine it was Worthington pushing that bizarre linking of myself and Sasha back through the years; he struck me as an intelligent man, and that's not at all an intelligent connection of dots. So who? And why?"

"Who would have anything to gain by undermining your reputation?" Bud caught the eye of our server and asked for another pot of tea.

"If this were a murder inquiry, then I'd say the answer to that question would be, 'The guilty party,' because that's who would want me off the case."

Bud tried to hide a grin. "Not full of yourself at all, are you?"

I realized what I'd done. "No, not really – but you know what I mean."

"I do."

I continued, "But this isn't one of our situations where we're trying to work out who killed someone – at least, I'm still forcing myself to believe that Sasha did, indeed, jump. But – to play devil's advocate for a moment…"

"A role you were made for…" Bud poured fresh tea.

"Thank you, sir. So, what if Sasha *didn't* jump? What if someone pushed her?"

Bud shook his head. "Oh, that's hot!" He nodded at the tea, then added, "But the note."

I gave the note some thought. "It wasn't addressed to anyone. It wasn't in an envelope. And – let's be honest – it didn't make it clear that she was planning to end her life."

Bud put down his tea. "Go on then – remind me exactly what it said. You know you're dying to."

I was. "It said: 'He'd have been eighty today. His shadow will never leave me. It's too late for me to try to be whatever I could have been, had he not been my father. I thought it would all end with his death. But now it seems that was a foolish hope on my part. It will never end, until I end it. So I shall. No procrastination. No more…anything. Sasha.' Which isn't a clear statement of intention to kill oneself, is it?"

Bud sat back as our server almost covered our table with plates, most of which had food on them. She smiled, and left us to it, so I dug in and pulled the meat from the bones of the glossy bird in front of us. Bud started preparing wraps, and we both allowed ourselves to focus on putting together that first, magical rolled pancake that bursts with what seem to be a million flavors from the meat, the sauce, and even the vegetables. I bit in, and my tastebuds were in heaven; the delight of not just eating, but licking my fingers too, wasn't lost on me for a moment. Even so, my mind was galloping.

"I reckon the only person with enough clout to get the investigation shuttered like that would be Sir Simon Pendlebury. He was out of there last night quickly enough to have had a few key quiet words on the phone and get Worthington stood down. And that old-school-tie network can act fast, when one of their own calls upon them."

Bud was also licking his fingers, with glee. "But why would he want to do that?"

"Well, maybe he saw something, or suspected someone of playing a role in Sasha's death." I was thinking and speaking at the same time, which isn't unusual for me, when I'm just with Bud. "What if he wanted to protect someone?"

"What if he pushed her off the roof himself?" I could tell Bud had thrown out the idea as being ridiculous.

I sighed. "No, I've discounted him as a suspect from the outset." Bud chuckled as he chewed. I glared at him, and pressed on. "I don't think he could have got upstairs without either me seeing him come from the meeting room through the salon, or – if she was where she said she was – Renata would have seen him on the terrace beyond the French doors. In fact, if we believe Renata, Sir Simon's about the only person who couldn't possibly have got up to the palace room unseen. Sitting in the meeting room, in the dark, he had a view to the back garden. But...what could he possibly have seen out there?"

Bud reached for more sauce. "Glad you've managed to talk yourself out of that theory pretty quickly."

I paused, a forkful of duck mid-air. "Come on, Bud – let's be honest with ourselves and each other; it's most likely Sir Simon shut down the investigation and has – for some reason – started Whitehall tongues wagging about my reputation. There must be a reason for that. And if he's protecting someone, that person would have to be closely connected with the success or failure of the Asimov group. Which includes Bella and Charles, because they are Asimovs...Piers, because he's married to one – or was – you know what I mean..."

"Don't forget Felicity was an Asimov, once upon a time." Bud's voice was muffled as he chewed. "Renata works for an Asimov, and works on Sir Simon's business at the Tavistock and Tavistock agency."

"And John is about to marry an Asimov," I added, a little sheepishly.

Bud glared at me. "Do you reckon Sir Simon would bother to protect Julie, Glen, or Vinnie? Or is the servant class beneath him?" He winked, though I had to admit he made a good point.

"Piers was the first to suggest suicide, and extremely quick to accept that note as proof, wasn't he? Bella too. Though, as I've said, I think it's far from conclusive. Piers could have been with Sasha in the palace room. They could have argued. Fought. It could have been an accident that...well, that he sought to pass off as a suicide to protect himself from blame. His reaction to his wife's death wasn't what one might call normal, was it?"

Bud tilted his head, and gave me his full attention. "As I have said before – and shall repeat – none of these people seem 'normal' to me, in any way, Cait. The worlds of artistic or esthetic endeavor, politics, and public relations seem to demand folks present themselves as larger than life. But I know what you mean in Piers' case…he seemed almost jolly when we rejoined everyone in the dining room. Though he sank into his brandy a fair bit after that – which I guess is to be expected."

"Odd behavior all-round, then, and the possibility that Sir Simon knows something he wants to keep secret, to protect someone within, or close to, the family business. We could talk to Worthington about that…"

Bud said, "Not happening, Cait. Heed the warnings. Now – what about these last three pancakes? Why on earth did they give two people an uneven number? So unfair, for one of us." I knew he knew which one of us that would be.

We each raced to create another filling for our next pancake, and it was such a wonderful feeling to be doing something so normal together…then Bud's expression changed. He put down his wrap, wiped his hands, and pulled out his phone. "It's John," he said. "Mind if I answer?" I shrugged, and he did – while I happily stuffed my face, gloating.

I'm pretty good at reading Bud, and didn't like what I was seeing. I made up the final rolled pancake, and got that inside me too, because I had a feeling we wouldn't be dawdling over lunch. Bud put his phone away, and poked at the food on his plate.

"Go on, tell me," I said. "Just rip off the Band Aid…get it over with."

Bud scratched his head. "It's not good, Cait. It's been a busy morning at Beulah House, and now it's become a tragic one. It seems Julie Powell – that's Julie's name, by the way – disappeared around ten this morning. Very unlike her, apparently, and, given the circumstances, everyone – including her husband – was at a loss as to where she might have gone."

"And…?"

"Apparently, she turned up at Felicity Sampson's flat and attacked her with a knife when she opened her front door. A struggle ensued, and Julie…well, she sustained critical injuries. She's been rushed to hospital, and Felicity's being interviewed by your friend and mine, Mr. Worthington. He sent a car to Beulah House to drive Glen to be at Julie's bedside – hence John knowing, and calling me."

"Julie attacked Felicity Sampson?" I asked. Bud nodded. "Good grief. That's…unexpected. But…why?"

Bud shrugged. "John has no idea. No one does. But he says it's pretty chaotic at Beulah House, as I can imagine. Piers is now under the care of a doctor – which John says means he's drugged to the eyeballs; Bella and Felicity had a fight this morning, and she's really upset—"

I interrupted, "Maybe Piers is wracked with guilt for killing Sasha? Or…hang on – what do you mean Bella and Felicity had a fight this morning?"

"John says Felicity phoned Bella early this morning, and they had what he called 'a right old ding dong', by which I guess he means a shouting match." I nodded. "So, as I was saying, Piers is out for the count, Bella is distraught, and John tells me Charles had irritated Julie beyond reason at the breakfast table, so everyone thought she'd gone off in a huff…until Glen realized she was nowhere to be found. Then word came in about the attack."

I stood. "I'm going to find the loo, and you can get the bill. Let's go to Beulah House."

"Cait, I really don't think that's a good idea."

I leaned over to kiss Bud's head. "John needs his chums at a time like this, right? He's in the midst of a tempest, and we can be his rock. Besides, you know what? Julie didn't strike me as the sort of woman to go off on some sort of homicidal rampage. She appeared to be level-headed, and devoted to the family. So, if she went after Felicity Sampson, she must have believed she had a good reason to do it. And I want to find out what that was."

I looked around for signs indicating washrooms.

"But going to Beulah House isn't going to help; she's not there, and her husband's not there. No one there knows why she did what she did."

I knew Bud was right, but I also had my answer ready. "Maybe not – but I can guess what everyone who's there is going to be talking about, and I want to be in on those conversations. And I want a chance to talk to Piers, too. If he was involved with his wife's death, he might let something slip."

I spotted the universal symbol for male and female facilities, and headed off, with a full, happy tummy, and knowing there was more to find out about what on earth was going on among those present at the previous night's dinner party.

When I got back to our table, Bud had paid, and he'd called John Silver. "Vinnie's going to collect us outside the fire station opposite the Palace Theatre. He seemed to think you'd know where that was," announced Bud, looking a bit panicked. "He'll be there in ten minutes – said he was in Seven Dials. Have I got all that right? Can we get there in time?"

I chuckled. "Yes, you have, and yes we can. Handy he was in the area, eh? It's almost as though we have a guardian angel watching over us."

As we left, I realized it was really to our advantage to have Vinnie to drive us – at least we could talk. And there was a lot to talk about…

A cut and dried suicide? Maybe not.

An unprovoked attack? Unlikely.

Me sticking my nose in where I'd already been told it wasn't wanted, and where I ran the risk of having it cut off? Most definitely.

Sometimes Lady Justice needs to peep out from her blindfold, just to make sure she's getting everything dumped onto her scales that should be there.

"...the map of honour, truth, and loyalty..."

Vinnie was as good as his word, though Bud and I had to hurl ourselves into the back seat of the car pretty sharpish, because it was almost impossible for him to stop. As it was, he drew the ire of several motorists and the horns were still blaring as we zipped off toward Piccadilly Circus, avoiding cyclists, and pedestrians more interested in their phones than the traffic.

"Any requests for our route?" Vinnie sounded chipper.

"Parliament Square, then Lambeth Bridge, if that's okay?" I replied. "Then if we could go through Brixton instead of Clapham this time, I could have a squint at my old stamping ground."

"No problem," was Vinnie's cheery reply. "I bet John'll be glad when you two turn up. Sounds like he's at the end of his tether, poor fella. I told him to just keep pouring cups of tea into everyone, but it seems he's running out of both tea and sympathy. You two will be just what the doctor ordered."

I still wasn't sure about Vinnie: if he and John went way back, as Bud had told me they did, then I hoped I'd be able to talk openly in the car. I decided to test the waters, to help form my own opinion.

"Bud tells me you've known John for some time," I opened.

"I have that."

"And John said you each have the other's back."

"We do that."

"How so?"

Bud's mouth fell open.

Vinnie replied, "We met under extreme circumstances, Cait. Formed a bond of trust. Never looked back. He's a grand man, John. Though I must say, Bella's got him by the heart. They say there's no cure for love but marriage, so I hope this business with her sister doesn't delay the nuptials too long. The poor fella will lose it, for sure, if she does." Vinnie was a patient driver, as he demonstrated while we idled behind several buses, with no room to pass; it seems bus lanes don't always work out too well for the rest of the traffic on the road.

"Will he move in with her – or she with him?" I asked.

Vinnie sounded a bit grim. "Now that's what I don't know. Might be they'll want a new place, together."

"Will that mean that you and Vaseem will have to move too?" Bud jumped into the conversation at just the right moment, and with just the right question.

Vinnie sighed. "We haven't had that talk with John yet. Vaseem thinks we should start looking for somewhere now, but I reckon John'll give us plenty of time to get ourselves sorted. We might even consider buying the place we're in now – if John were prepared to sell it."

I was wondering how Vinnie and Vaseem earned their livings, so it amazed me that Bud asked, "What is it you guys do for jobs? If you don't mind me asking."

Vinnie curled a bicep. "Personal trainer, me. Can't tell you who me clients are, of course, or then I'd have to kill you. But let's just say they're prepared to pay for the best. Do the lot, I do, you see; nutrition, exercise, body sculpting, and self-defense. The full package."

Why am I not surprised, I thought. "Oh, interesting," I said. "And how do you manage at times like this? Have you no clients today?"

"Ah now, that's where I rely upon my secret weapon – the surprise long-distance run. All I do is tell them they have to get out and do a five-mile run, and they think I'm a hero for not putting them through their paces indoors."

I shuddered. "Good grief, what do you make them do when you're with them, if they'd prefer to be out running on a day like today?" Vinnie chuckled wickedly. "And how do you know they do it anyway?" I immediately thought of several ways to get out of such a challenge.

"Ah, now that's where modern technology comes into play," he replied triumphantly. "They all have to wear those watches that let me know exactly what they've been up to, all the time. I track them on my laptop, when I need to – or even just using my phone."

I commended him upon his resourcefulness.

Bud added, "And is Vaseem in the same line?"

Vinnie chuckled. "Nah – too soft for all that sort of stuff, he is. The sight of a barbell makes him go all weak at the knees, so it does. But see this?" He rubbed his head. "He makes wigs. Makes us both laugh, sure it does. Sometimes I model them for him, if my giant noggin won't stretch them. He says it's handy having a baldy about the house."

Bud's tone was genuine. "That's a full-time thing? Making wigs?"

Vinnie turned as we sat at a red light on Whitehall. He was smiling. "He doesn't do many for regular people, though he fits in what he can for the cancer patients, now and again. Does a lot for telly, films, and the stage. Postiche, as well as wigs. That's all the other stuff they wear – you know, moustaches, sideburns, that type of thing. I model those too, sometimes. He's mobile – goes to the sets for fittings and so on. Loves it, so he does. I've been taken along on occasion – seen some big names up close and personal. It's amazing what a difference it makes to them. The actors, I mean. When Vaseem's done with them you'd not recognize half of 'em in the street. Big part of it all, he is. Won awards, too. It's how he met Sasha – through the Shakespeare for schools scheme her father set up. She gets…sorry, got…all the sponsors, that sort of thing. Vaseem did a load of wigs for them, and they seemed to get on. He was upset when I phoned him last night to tell him what had happened to her. Couldn't believe it. He'll be fine with it, eventually, he said. He took it badly, sure enough. But, there…he's so busy at the moment, he won't have time to dwell on it." Vinnie's pride in his partner's achievements was obvious, then he returned his attention to the traffic as we approached the Houses of Parliament.

Big Ben struck the half hour just after we'd passed by. "Should be there by about half two," said Vinnie, "if the traffic's not too bad up Brixton Hill. Like I said, John will be glad to have you there. I'll hang about too, see if he needs me. Vaseem's at a big old house in Sussex, working on some Victorian TV series this week – you won't be seeing much of him, I'm sorry to say. Me neither. He's staying locally. Got a lot of upkeep to see to through the shooting, he said. He uses out-workers for some of the jobs he gets – these TV types won't wait months for him to get everything made, you see, so he had all the fittings to do, then there's always fix-ups to be seen to when they all take their bits off after a day's shooting, and he has to make sure they're right again for the next day."

I felt I didn't need to know any more about the wig-making business. "When you spoke to John, did he say anything about Felicity and Julie?" I wanted to know if we'd missed anything, so far.

"Sounds like a right old mess, if you ask me," he replied. "Though I cannot fathom what Julie was thinking. I mean, she's a bit of a tartar if you step out of line, but a kind and welcoming soul, under normal circumstances. But this isn't normal, is it?"

"Have Julie and Glen been working at Beulah House for long?" Bud was being delightfully Bud-like.

"About five years, I believe. I've had many a cuppa with them in their own little kitchen over the past several months. John's been spending more and more time there, so I have been too. They live in a little flat above the meeting room we used last night. All part of the servants' quarters block built after they put that big glass thing up on the roof. Old servants' quarters used to be up in the attic, see, then they kicked 'em out and built a new bit for them. Nice place, they've got. What is it the estate agents call it, now? 'Compact, and bijou.' Kitchen, sitting room, bedroom, and bathroom – all they need, they said. Their own space. Like me and Vaseem, though, in our case, it's a bit of a different arrangement, because they're employees, and we're John's mates."

I tried, "Do you know anything about them – as people?"

Vinnie's tone was thoughtful. "Glen got into a bit of trouble some years back. Big bit, to be fair. Did fourteen years for armed robbery. Since then, straight and narrow is his road. Julie took him under her wing, and there he's stayed. Julie knew Sasha's mother. Not sure Julie ever told me how, exactly. In any case, the connection was made, and Sasha has employed the Powells since not long after she and Piers moved into Beulah House."

"Sasha and Piers had their own place, but chose to move back into Sasha's old family home, after her mother died, I understand," said Bud.

"So they did. As Julie tells it, it was one of those fancy houses in a square with its own private garden in the middle, in what people are pleased to call Fitzrovia. Must have been worth a pretty penny, I'd have thought. They sold up, and moved out to Beulah House. Plenty of room for them, because Bella never lived in the main house. Said she preferred the coach house. Though I wonder if she's ever regretted that decision."

"How so?" I was interested.

"It's nothing she says, outright. More a look here, or a gesture there. I think she feels her sister casts a long shadow…though she's always quick to point out her focus is her art, and the creation of beautiful objects. But, sometimes, when she looks at her sister, she has that air about her that a woman does when she's at someone else's wedding – you know?"

"The 'I wish that were me' look?" I offered.

"There you go then," replied Vinnie. "I knew you were the type to understand."

"Is fourteen years a long time for armed robbery, here?" Bud leaned forward a little.

"Don't know that it is, don't know that it isn't. I know you can get life for it, but I think it all depends upon the nature of the armament, the way used, and if any harm was done, as opposed to being merely threatened. Probably it depends on what was robbed, too. Possibly more than if any harm was done, truth be told. He was in Brixton prison – leastways, he was just before he came out. Met Julie when she was a barmaid at a local pub. The rest, as they say, is history."

"Which pub?" I asked.

Vinnie chuckled. "The big one at the top of Brixton Hill. Was that your local?"

"You don't get much more local than living diagonally opposite a place," I replied. I mused aloud, "I wonder when they met? Julie didn't look familiar to me, so likely not during my time there."

"No, you'd have been off in Cambridge by then," replied Vinnie.

I wanted to ask how on earth he knew when I'd been in Cambridge, but assumed maybe John had told him. I was getting the impression more people knew a great deal about my life than I'd ever imagined. And I didn't like that feeling.

Vinnie said, "Here we are now, coming into your old neck of the woods. Quite the going concern now it is, Brixton. Not that it was ever a backwater."

I looked around the world that was no longer mine: the arches beneath the railway line were buzzing with shoppers, the tube station was bustling, and Marks and Spencer's was still there – and busy. The market stalls on Electric Avenue were rather quiet, I thought, but there were queues at all the bus stops, and two 159 buses were approaching. The Ritzy looked cleaner than I remembered it, but Lambeth Town Hall was still the dominant presence in the area – in its swaggering red Victorian brick, with wedding-cake-style Portland stone corners, and the clock tower looming over the somewhat bleak expanse of concrete that had replaced the old Tate Gardens.

"What's that?" Bud pointed at the open area.

"Windrush Square," I replied, "in honor of the Windrush generation, who came to London from the Caribbean Islands after the second world war, answering the call for willing members of the workforce, and the promise of a better life for their children than they could expect on their home islands."

"Ah," replied Bud.

Vinnie's tone was bleak. "Poor beggars didn't find the warm welcome they'd been led to expect, though, did they? There were infamous notices in boarding house windows: 'No Blacks, No Dogs, No Irish'. See how we managed to even come last in that list? And that right through to the 1960s."

"Are things better now?" Bud spoke cautiously.

"There'll always be eejits who think one human life is worth more or less than another, but I'm luckier than many – folks don't know where I'm from until I open me mouth. Vaseem, now, that's a different matter. But there, two gay men, one Irish, one brown, have to decide they're going to be resilient, right? We're both masters at pretending we're ducks, letting all those sideways looks and half-whispered comments roll right off us, let alone ignoring the outright slurs we get if we so much as hold hands in some places. Too many people are annoyed by us just being around them for us to have a truly normal life. All we want is to be taken for who we are, not what we represent in someone's befuddled little brain."

I commiserated with Vinnie. He shrugged. I decided to change the subject. "John told Bud that Piers had been seen by a doctor this morning; do you know him and Sasha well enough to judge how he'll be coping with her death?"

Vinnie shook his head. "Not my type, that man. What do they say? Full of sound and fury…"

"…signifying nothing." I completed the quote. "So, he's not changed much over the years, then."

"You and him have crossed paths before, I gather." Vinnie glanced at me in the rear-view mirror.

"Yes. He joined the Townsend Agency just a little while before I left it. As far as I know that's where he and Sasha – or Alex, as I knew her – met and began to work together."

"Though it's not him who told me," said Vinnie, "I happen to know they took a slice of business away from that place when they left it. Poached a lot of key clients. The owner sold up, after that. Retired to France, so the story goes."

"He did, where he tried to teach the French how to farm snails," I said.

Vinnie threw a curious glance toward me via his reflection. "Is that so? Sounds like he was a special type of person himself, so it does. Maybe he and Piers had more in common than they thought – because I also happen to know that when he and Sasha moved to Beulah House, he tried to tell the local historical society how they should do better research into the area, and 'his' house, in particular."

"How so?" I was all ears.

"Something to do with that ghost Felicity was on about last night. Piers thought they should have done a more thorough job of investigating the claims over the years – but they told him they had nothing on record at all, which got his goat, it seems. Now don't go getting me wrong, I'm a firm believer in there being things we don't understand – but I don't hold with ghosts, so I don't. If a soul is unquiet, it might hang around for a bit, but to go wailing about the place for hundreds of years? No. All hogwash, that's what that is. I reckon it was Piers just wanting to make the house more notorious, so it would be worth more. You could ask Julie, she'll tell you...oh no, of course, you can't be doing that, can you? Not unless she recovers...and what John told me about what happened didn't make that sound too likely. Poor woman. And poor Glen, too. I should think he'll not cope well with losing her. That much I can tell you. Even if I can't say the same for Piers. Which is not to say he'll be dancing on his wife's grave – just that I have no intel about him...other than what John passes on to me." Vinnie added, "Almost there – your old flat that is, Cait. Want me to pull over so you can take some photos or something?"

We turned off Brixton Hill onto the South Circular Road and I answered, "No thanks, I'm good. Let's not keep John waiting any longer than we must." Having seen a figure at the window the last time we'd passed, I was now keenly aware someone else lived in the flat I'd once called my own, which meant I felt less of an attachment to it than I once had. *I'm happy to put that part of my life behind me.*

"On we go then," Vinnie replied, and we spent the next couple of miles all sitting in silence.

Eventually I asked, "You've got no guesses why Julie might have taken off and attacked Felicity Sampson, have you, Vinnie?"

"I've wracked my brain, sure enough, but can't come up with anything sensible. So unlike Julie. The only time I've ever seen her really lose her temper was when a cake she'd ordered for Sasha's birthday arrived and it wasn't right. Julie was – *is* – a good cook, but admitted she wasn't the best of bakers, so she'd given in to getting a professional to make a cake. When it turned up, they'd spelled the name wrong – they'd piped SACHA on top of it. It stuck in my head, because it seemed a small thing for her to get so upset about. The woman lost it – out of her mind with rage, she was. Ranting and raving about how someone had let her precious Sasha down. Thing is, it was a cake for both Bella and Sasha, of course, them being twins, and they'd got the Bella bit right. Julie went on and on about it, and ended up doing her best to change the C to an S herself. I don't think Sasha even noticed. I told her to stick a candle in that bit of the cake to cover up the problem, but she said Sasha deserved to have her name done right, because Miss Bella was the one who always got everything she wanted, and Sasha never asked for anything she hadn't worked for."

I gave what Vinnie had said some thought. It seemed Julie had quite a different impression of the relationship between Bella and Sasha than I'd had a chance to witness – and absolutely at odds with that which John had described, when quizzed by Worthington in the palace room. "Is that a dynamic you've seen for yourself, Vinnie? Bella being the sister who always gets what she wants, rather than Sasha?"

We weren't far from our destination when Vinnie replied, "To be honest, I thought that strange at the time, because it's poor Bella who seems to always get the pointy end of the lollipop. John's often talked about how brave she's been when she's been let down by a supplier, or a client – and he does his best to help her out, or at least put her in touch with someone who can, if he's able. In the end she pushes through it all, so she does."

"How do you mean?" I pressed.

Vinnie paused for a moment, then said, "Well, it seems like Bella's had lots of practice at having to face difficult situations. It's funny how that happens in a family. See my Auntie Brid, she'd be the one in Cardiff. Her poor old husband attracts bad luck like you wouldn't believe. I swear if he dropped a pound he'd bend down and pick up a bit of old chewing gum instead, so he would. Can't hold a job for long enough that everyone can learn to like him – nor for them to find out he's good at anything he turns his hand to, says Auntie Brid. And John says it's always been a bit like that for poor Bella. Sasha casts a long shadow. But as for Bella always getting what she wants? Well, I dare say she ends up with it, but only when folks have noticed she was suffering for lack of it in the first place."

"And Sasha?" I wondered what Vinnie would say; if it was as fascinating as his insight into Bella's personality, it would be worth hearing.

Vinnie gave his reply almost no thought at all. "Ah now, there you have a woman who never left you in any doubt at all about what she expected, and you knew right off she'd do whatever it might take to get it, or make it happen. A force of nature, that woman. Quite different are – *were* – Bella and Sasha, for twins, like. Maybe as a psychologist you might know why that would be?" His reflection winked at me as we swung into the driveway of Beulah House which – without the benefit of carriage lamps and a smattering of snow glinting in their light – looked smaller, and less impressive by daylight. That said, the palace room looked, if anything, even bigger, possibly because of the way it was reflecting the still-blue sky, and scudding clouds.

"Here we are then. I'll drop you at the front then take the car around the side," said Vinnie.

"Where exactly do you take it?" I asked.

"Along the far side of the coach house there's a track that leads to what were once the stables. Beyond that is the old farriers' place, though it's Bella's workshop now. The stables are a sort of summer house in the garden, but they use the track for cars they don't want littering up this entry circle. I'll cut through at the back of the house once I've popped it there. Catch up with you inside, so I will."

Bud and I got out, thanked Vinnie and, once again, stood on the doorstep of Beulah House uncertain of what would greet us. This time, of course, at least I knew it wouldn't be Julie who would open the door. I wondered if the next twenty-four hours would be as deadly as the last, and grabbed Bud's hand as I hoped not.

"...this tiger-footed rage..."

Charles Asimov opened the door, his face sweating, his hair wild, his eyes blazing. When he recognized us, he deflated a little. "I thought you were that Worthington man. He's on his way. What are you two doing here?" To say his tone suggested he wasn't pleased to see us would be an understatement.

Bud took a step toward him and held out his hand. "Terrible times, Charles. All such a shock. And after last night's tragedy too. John gave us a call – thought you guys could do with a bit of support. Cait and I know our way around a kitchen, and we're here to lend a hand – keep things ticking over while everyone – well, you know...grief's a terrible thing."

Charles hooked his long, matted hair behind his ears, and shuffled backward a little. With the wind well and truly taken out of his sails, his features settled into lines and furrows I'd not seen the night before. "Yes, very kind of John to think of it, and of you to offer. It's hellish, you know. Just hellish. What on earth made Julie snap like that I cannot imagine. Felicity's lucky she wasn't killed. Once I told her Glen had left the house, she said she'd come here with Worthington. He said he wants to examine our kitchen knives. Isn't that awful? One of *our* kitchen knives...Julie."

He continued shuffling backwards until he stood in the middle of the entry hall, and we assumed we'd been invited in, so crossed the threshold and shut the door. We kept our jackets on, largely because there was no one to take them from us, and no obvious place to hang them up.

Charles muttered, "Piers is in bed, of course, and John and Bella are in the kitchen – steering clear of any sharp objects, as per Worthington's request, and I'm just…well, seemingly superfluous to requirements. But I can't go to work. I know I should be here, for Piers, but, honestly, I don't know what to do with myself. I got the doc out to see to Piers in the early hours – he gave him something to calm him down a bit. Renata's been and gone, with some papers it was apparently critical that Piers signed – but even she couldn't bring him out of his funk. I mean, it's to be expected to a certain extent, I suppose, but I didn't think he'd fall into a complete state of physical collapse like this. He seemed to be a bit quieter, but sort of rallying until…well, until Renata left, then he just toppled over the edge, so to speak." He paused, and his face fell even further. "Sorry, poor choice of words."

"What can I be doing to help out?" Vinnie appeared through the door I'd seen Julie and Glen use the previous evening.

"You too?" Charles shuffled toward the bottom of the stairs. "Alright – I'm going to shower. Can't be looking like this when the house is full of…you know, not family. Best you find your friend John. Bella will be with him – she can be in charge until Piers is up and about. You can all deal with that man when he arrives. Tell Felicity I'm upstairs. She can find me there. Only bit of privacy I'm going to find…" He was talking to himself as much as to us as he climbed the staircase.

We filled Vinnie in, and all trooped into the salon, where the doors were open to the kitchen – but there was no sign of either John, nor Bella.

"They might be at the coach house," said Bud, "even though Charles thought they were here."

"No, they won't be there," replied Vinnie, "the coach house is all locked up with no one home – you can tell that from the outside because of the giant latch thing being down, and there's no lights on…it's not got a lot of natural light in there, so Bella always has the lights on when she's at home."

I looked toward the garden which – now that I could see it in daylight – was much larger than I'd imagined; it seemed to go on forever, and was wide, as well as long. Over to the left was what had obviously once been a stable block, but now the doors stood open, and I could see a variety of furniture inside, offering a tempting place to sit to enjoy the delights of what would – were it not frozen solid – be a bubbling rill which ran the full length of the garden bounded by formally-cut flagstones, as well as the variety of wonderful planting, which was putting on a colorful show despite the season. But both the garden and the summer house seemed deserted.

We were all peering through the window when John's voice called to us. "Hello folks. Thanks for coming." We spun around, and there were John and Bella looking just a little pink in the face, and happier than I'd imagined either of them would be, given the circumstances. "We were just…um…checking that everything was as it should be, up in the palace room, you know?"

Bella smiled coyly. Too coyly for a woman in her early fifties. "It's such a pretty day but chilly – and that place is, well, magical seems to be the wrong word, but I'm sure you know what I mean. We heard you arriving. We're so pleased you came. Now, can I offer everyone tea? I don't often have the chance to host here, but I'm sure Piers won't mind. I mean, I know it's my house, now that Sasha's gone, but it's his home. I'll just play hostess while he's…incapacitated."

"I'll help," I said, keen to have a chance to get some time alone with Bella.

She beamed. "Oh thanks, Cait. We can hunt out what we need together. I don't like to tread on Julie and Glen's toes, usually. My little kitchen over at the coach house is quite adequate to my needs, and – if I ever want to entertain anyone – Sasha's always been most accommodating about my being able to use this kitchen and dining room."

I wondered what it was like to be the co-owner of a home, but an outsider at the same time – uncomfortable, on occasion, was the impression Bella was giving me.

We left the men in the salon, where I could hear Bud saying, "Nice set-up with those old stables out there. Big garden too…" Then they wandered out of the French doors where they were going to explore for themselves, I supposed.

In the kitchen, Bella stood looking around as though she'd never seen the place before. I judged her seeming lack of focus to stem – quite naturally – from her grief at her sister's death, so I was the one who pulled open doors, hunting for tea and biscuits…both of which I managed to locate before the kettle was even fizzing, let alone boiling; Bella at least passed mugs down from a cupboard.

"Those are high cupboards, for a short person like me," I said.

Bella's eyebrows shot up. "I didn't realize they were unusually high. Mum was tall, and so are Sasha and I, I suppose. Julie too. So no one's ever really commented." She peered down at my five-four from her five-nine.

I felt myself shrinking, then rallied. "A tall family, eh?"

Bella paused, a mug in her hand. "I suppose so. Daddy was tall, too. Over six feet. Just like John." She glowed. "There was a time when Sasha and I were by far the tallest girls in our class at school; we had a spurt during the hols, once, and Mummy had to keep getting us new clothes while we were away. Luckily, we were in Italy at the time, so at least they were nice new clothes, though Sasha got to pick everything, and I just had the same. Mum said taking me shopping was too time-consuming. I find it difficult to make decisions, sometimes." Bella seemed to be addressing the mug in her hand when she added, "That was our last holiday together, the three of us. The next year Mummy took only Sasha. To Wales. You know, where you're from." She made it sound as though this was somehow my fault; I even felt a bit guilty. "They went alone. I stayed here. I had to cram that year. Sasha…" She finally looked up. "Sasha had other things to deal with, but I had to focus on my studies. I always had to work harder than Sasha. Think about things for longer. You know?"

Nope, sorry Bella, I don't, thanks to my sometimes-wonderful eidetic memory.

Her eyes had clouded over, and I realized she was talking about two dead parents and a dead sister – not the cheeriest of topics. I tried to change tack. "It's fortunate we're all different – and your strengths lie in the creative field, where considered decisions are critical, I'd have thought."

Bella focused on me, and a tired smile turned up the corners of her lips. "I suppose you're right. Sasha was so…dynamic. Always made snap decisions, and followed through. All go, she was. All the time. Didn't understand my process at all, really. You're quite right, Cait; thinking for a while before you do something is terribly important when one is creating something that will exist for a long time…maybe forever."

"It must be marvellous to see your work adored and enjoyed by those you've made it for," I replied, hoping that focusing on her own achievements would help rally Bella.

She sighed. "Oh, I don't know. All they see is the finished product – not the hours of planning, sketching, redrawing, then crafting a piece…making my vision a perfect reality. Though it's always lovely when people say nice things, of course." She forced a broader smile.

Not being a particularly creative person, I fell back on the only possible parallel I could speak about. "Back in Canada, we have a large garden. Planning and planting, then crossing your fingers that it all ends up looking as good as you'd hoped, is about as close as Bud and I get to creating anything, but we're not exactly in control. Are you much of a gardener? You have a beautiful garden behind the house. The color for this time of year is amazing. Ours was just brown and dead-looking when we left. I reckon there's an artist's eye at work out there. Yours?"

Bella looked across the kitchen and out of the dining room's bow window, the mirror of the one in the salon. I looked too, and could see the men strolling about pointing at things outside in the remainder of the sunshine, which was fading fast. Bella was becoming a little agitated, bobbing her head about.

She sounded distracted as she replied, "Yes, Sasha was happy for me to oversee the garden. She didn't really have time for it – other than as a place where she could host drinks parties in the summer, of course. Glen does all the work, though, because he says I don't have a green thumb. But it's lovely, as you say, to see something in your head, then watch as it becomes manifest, through the seasons. I wonder what will happen...now. Oh, no, they're not going into my workshop, are they? They mustn't do that. I don't like my things disturbed."

I looked out, and saw the men still ambling around, chatting, not seeming intent upon making a beeline for anywhere in particular. A crash snapped my attention away from the window.

Bella had dropped the mug she'd been holding. She looked at the shards of crockery on the tiled floor with surprise. "Oh dear. Did I do that? I'm so clumsy..."

She was paying more attention to the men in the garden – who were all bending over, looking at something – than to the mess she'd made. I put my arm across her midsection, as though she were sitting, unbelted, in the front of a braking car. "You stand back, I'll clear it up," I said, suddenly aware of the fact she was barefoot beneath her heavily embroidered kaftan. "Go on, you go into the salon. I'll find a dustpan and brush for this lot. Or something."

Bella hooked her long, gold-gray hair behind her ears and wandered off. "There's a cupboard in the outer hall for that sort of thing," she said.

I beetled off to find what I needed, which meant I had to venture along the hallway between the dining room and meeting room. I found a light switch, which helped; the only natural light came from the half-glass door at the rear of the house, so I was pleased that long fluorescent strips ran the length of the hall, only one of which had been used the night before. Now at least I could see what I was doing. Needless to say, I felt the desire to explore and get the lay of the land. John had been correct when he'd described Beulah House as something like Frankenstein's creation; I seemed to be in what – from the outside – was visible as an addition, a way to link the main house to what Vinnie had told us were the servants' quarters. It smelled a little damp, and had a generally unwelcoming air. I found it odd that nothing had been done to smarten it up, given that anyone using the meeting room had to cross it; it wouldn't make a great impression upon any clients Sasha might invite over.

At one end was the door leading out to the garden, about halfway along on the right was the door I knew gave entry to the meeting room. Opposite it was another door which turned out to be the one I'd seen Julie and Glen using the previous night. Beyond that, half the width of the hall was blocked by…well, I wasn't sure what it was. It was certainly a structure – then it dawned on me…they were the guest washrooms off the main entry hall; they'd been built into the back hallway at some point. There was still a space wide enough to walk through behind them, and each WC had a door, allowing access for those who needed to clean them, I presumed. I tried the door of one, and it opened. Inside was the functional space I'd used the previous evening – though I'd spotted no door to the hallway in my haste to get in, get done, and get out. I shut myself into the cubicle and was amazed at how cleverly the doorway had been set into the panelled wall – no wonder I hadn't noticed it. Upon closer inspection I noted a hooked device, to secure the rear door from the interior. *Good idea.*

I returned to the hallway, and tried the other loo door, but it wouldn't open; locked from the inside, I presumed, then continued along the hallway, which was now full-width again, where I found another half-glass door; this one gave a view to the long, windowless side of the coach house, and a double-width track leading to the front, and back, of the property. I assumed this was the track to the old stable block Vinnie had spoken of. The door was locked, but it occurred to me that the warren-like nature of the buildings on the property allowed for any number of people to secrete themselves about the place…and it suddenly dawned on me that Sir Simon could have used the hall to gain access to the front as well as the back of the house. Then I realized he'd still have had to enter the house by the front door to have been able to get upstairs to the palace room, and I'd have seen him from the salon, so, no, he was still a non-starter for being a possible killer.

Disappointed, I rattled the knob on the door. It was locked, which I thought eminently sensible. Then I walked along the hall again opening the doors to cupboards in the wall which abutted the meeting room until I found one housing a vacuum cleaner, some mops and brushes, and I found a dustpan and brush too. I made my way to the kitchen again, poured boiling water into the teapot, and swept up all the bits of china I could see. I opened the doors beneath the sink – the most likely place to find a dustbin, to my way of thinking – and found a pedal bin, but it seemed silly to put my foot inside the cupboard to operate it, so

I simply lifted the lid with my free hand, ready to tip in the shards of broken mug.

As I bent down, something in the bin caught the light, and my eye. It looked metallic. Substantial. I put down the dustpan, pulled a piece of kitchen paper off the roll on the counter and reached into the bin. I was surprised to find I was holding John's gold medallion – the one with the centaur he'd so proudly shown me just the day before. My tummy clenched. Did that mean the wedding was off again? But no, it couldn't; John and Bella had looked so incredibly happy when we'd arrived. So why was John's medallion in the bin? I stood there for what must have been a whole minute, trying to decide what to do. I flipped the medallion in my fingers. On the back was a large letter C. John hadn't shown me the back of his medallion; if this were his, why would Bella have marked the back with a C, not a J? In the end I popped the medallion, still wrapped in kitchen paper, into my jacket pocket – only then realizing I still had the blessed thing on.

When I entered the salon I asked, "Is there somewhere I can dump my jacket, please?"

Bella looked up from the hearth, which was filled with only glowing embers, despite the fact there was a stack of logs beside it. "Pardon? Oh, yes. In the back hall. There's a wardrobe there." She waved vaguely and I realized I wasn't going to get much more out of her.

"How about I pop some more logs on the fire? Warm things up a bit?" I said.

"That would be so kind of you," said Bella, smiling wanly. "I'm no good with the fire. Daddy always said so. I'd probably set the house alight." She stood out of the way, then flopped into a chair.

I shoved some logs onto the embers; they were good and dry, and I had no doubt they'd catch of their own accord, so said,

"Right, I'll dump my jacket, and by then the tea should have steeped."

"You're so very kind," she replied, weakly.

I told myself she was in mourning, and that I shouldn't get annoyed by her apathy, then headed to the back hall the way I'd left it, via the kitchen. I pulled open more doors, and finally found the wardrobe, but – as I dragged my cross-body purse over my head, before taking off my jacket – I decided to pull the gold medallion out of my pocket, to keep it safe in my handbag. I wondered why I was bothering, but I've learned over the years that I should trust my instincts, so I did.

Back in the kitchen I could see the men wandering toward the house, and it was just as I was waving at them, and pointing at the teapot, that I heard the noise upstairs. Crashing, banging, footsteps thumping about, then a bellowing that sounded as though a wild animal was coming down the stairs. I abandoned the teapot and rushed into the salon, to discover Piers, in a flapping robe and underpants, running toward me screaming. Spittle flew from his mouth, his eyes were ablaze.

"Stop her! Stop her!" Thunderous screams. Arms flailing, he grabbed me as I stood, aghast, in the middle of the room.

Bella rose from her seat, and hid behind it; Bud, John, and Vinnie came in through the French doors from the garden; the front doorbell began to jangle.

"I'll get it," called Charles as he trotted down the staircase. "What was all that commotion?"

Charles's hand was already on the front door when Piers abandoned me and bolted.

"Get away. Get away. Let me get her." Piers was screaming, flailing.

Charles had already unlocked the door, and a second or two later Felicity Sampson walked in, with Worthington at her shoulder.

Piers roared and grabbed the woman by the throat before anyone could stop him. Luckily, Worthington was on the spot, and he leaped into action; Bud, John, and Vinnie took just seconds to get there, but, by then Worthington had wrenched Piers' hands off Felicity's neck, she'd collapsed onto the floor, almost taking the Christmas tree with her, and Piers had fallen onto the stairs. Bud and John grabbed Piers, while Vinnie and Charles helped Felicity. Worthington stood in the doorway taking in the sight about him, and we locked eyes.

Something deep in my dark little soul wanted him to say, "'Allo, 'allo, 'allo, what's all this 'ere then?" and flex his knees. I suspect I might have smirked a bit when the totally inappropriate thought flashed through my head, because Worthington's expression changed, an eyebrow rose, and he shook his head, ever so slowly...almost as though he knew what I was thinking.

"...the lady doth protest too much, methinks..."

The attack on Felicity – the second she'd suffered within a few short hours – had shocked us all...her more than anyone, of course. She was shaken, and shaking, when I helped her to a seat in the salon.

"You sit there, and I'll bring you a nice strong cuppa with three sugars," I said.

Felicity managed to gather her faculties sufficiently to reply, "I don't take sugar."

"You will today," I answered and turned to head to the kitchen, but Bella caught my eye.

"Me, too, please. And I'll also have three sugars. For the shock." Bella fluttered her hands, sank onto a sofa, and John made a beeline for her, having relinquished his Piers-wrangling duties to Vinnie.

"Oh my darling..." I heard, as I prepared a mug of tea for each of the women.

Bud and Vinnie guided Piers to another sofa, where he collapsed in a heap. I made a mug of tea for everyone I could from the first pot, and stirred in three sugars each, whether folks wanted it or not. I immediately filled the kettle to make a second pot, and Bud joined me in the kitchen.

He leaned close and whispered, "Never a dull moment around this lot, is there?" I managed a smile, which was good, because I felt I was going to burst – an odd response to a tense situation for me.

"I can't wrap my head around what just happened," I responded under my breath. "Did Piers say anything to you about why he flew at Felicity like he did? Do you think he's suddenly developed some sort of desire to attack women for no reason – the first being his wife, maybe?"

As we waited for the kettle to boil, Bud tutted, and shook his head. "He was pretty incoherent, then was crying like a baby. John told me when we were out in the garden that Piers' doctor gave him something to make him sleep earlier on this morning – Piers was up and about, stomping around the place for most of the night. And no, he didn't start ranting on about being sorry for having killed his wife, so you can take that look off your face right away." He winked. "Charles called John and Bella over to help him calm the man, but they weren't able to get him to stop, so Charles phoned his doctor. Came here from his home, apparently. I guess that's what it's like for the rich – you'll get seen to when you need it, and in your own house at that."

I checked the kettle. Not ready. "If it wasn't a guilty conscience, maybe it was a reaction to whatever the doctor gave him? A nightmare he couldn't wake from, and he was acting within that mindset? It could happen. But…"

"He might have killed Felicity, had Worthington not been right there." I like it when Bud finishes my sentences. "She's a slight woman. It wouldn't have taken much longer to do some real damage."

I glanced over at Felicity, who was being consoled by Bella, and John; the victim of Piers' attack was still trembling. Worthington was towering over Piers' slumped figure, texting. Vinnie and Charles were standing in the entry to the salon, each with a mug in hand, and a look of bafflement on their faces. They made a strange-looking pair…but then the entire tableau was like something out of a stage play…and a pretty melodramatic one at that.

Piers eventually sat a little more upright, and seemed to become aware of his surroundings. He tried to stand up.

Worthington stopped texting, and put his hand on Piers' shoulder. "Just stay there for a little while, sir. I'm sure you'll feel better that way."

Piers looked confused. "What's going on? Why are all these people in my house? Why are you here? What have you found out about Sasha? Have you discovered something about her death? Felicity? Why are you here? What's going on?"

He was still pink in the face, sweating, and seemed to only realize his state of undress at that moment. Despite my suspicions about the man – and my deep-seated dislike for him in any case – I felt rather sorry for him as he tried to hide his underwear, and his embarrassment, by wrapping his robe around his midsection while he fished about for its tie-cord. There was none.

He continued, "Let me go, man, I must go to my room to dress. I can't have people seeing me like this." Worthington stepped back and Piers managed to get to his feet, though he was wobbly.

"Shall I come to give you a hand, old chap?" Charles's offer was waved off.

"I can manage perfectly well on my own. I am not a child." Piers seemed to have regained his faculties, but his speech was a little slurred, and he still wasn't terribly steady on his feet.

We all watched as Piers stomped up the stairs, grasping the handrail.

"He doesn't seem to have any idea of what he's just done," said Bella, as I poured boiling water into the pot for a second time.

"Well, you all saw him do it," replied Felicity. Her voice was hoarse.

"The doc did give him something pretty strong earlier today," explained Charles. "Maybe he really didn't know what he was doing?"

"Tell that to my throat," whispered Felicity. She sipped her hot tea, and rubbed her neck, which looked terribly long, thin, and vulnerable above her deep V-necked, powder-blue sweater. "First Julie attacked me, now this. What on earth is going on? Have I got a big target painted on me, or something? I've never done anything to anyone to warrant being treated this way – not by Julie Powell, nor Piers." She glared up at Worthington. "And don't you go telling me there's nothing you can do. I know Julie's lying in a hospital bed, and I absolutely understand that I gravely injured her. How do you think that makes me feel? I told you all about it – I had to defend myself…she was slashing at me with that knife, on my own doorstep, for no good reason. Not that there could be one. And Piers? What on earth was that all about? I've been a part of this family for decades – first as a friend, then as Oleg's wife, and now – I hope – as a valued member of a small group of people who know what it's like to be an Asimov. I don't deserve this, and I'm not going to hang about here until he feels like attacking me again. Charles, organize a car for me, there's a darling. I can't go back to my flat, so I'll stay at a hotel for a while, until this lot allow me back into my own home." She glared at Worthington again – in case he'd missed her first set of daggers, I assumed. "I don't even know why I came here. I was concerned about how you were all coping with the loss of dear Sasha…and now this."

Bella jumped in. "You poor, poor thing, Felicity, you must feel just dreadful. I can't imagine what it's like to know you've taken someone's life." She leaned forward in her chair, and reached out to touch Felicity's knee with her long, slim fingers.

"I haven't killed anyone." Felicity's tone was razor sharp. "Julie's not dead. She might pull through. And, anyway, defending oneself against an attack is absolutely not the same as taking a life intentionally. I would never dream of such a thing. This man's investigation will prove everything was above board, won't it?" This time her gaze toward Worthington was a direct challenge…which he ignored, as he continued texting. I wanted to cheer.

Bella patted Felicity's knee. "Of course she'll pull through, Felicity. I mean, I know Julie's injuries are life-threatening, but they can do some marvellous things these days. And you're right, her life shouldn't weigh on your conscience at all. You weren't responsible, in the true sense of the word, because she initiated the attack. Her blood isn't on your hands." She paused, sighed, and added, "Well, yes, I know they said you were, in fact, covered in her blood, but killing her wasn't in your heart. And she's not even dead. Yet." She sat back in her seat, smiling sympathetically. "Poor Felicity. And, of course, poor Julie…and Glen."

Felicity stared into her mug, then at Bella. "Yes," was all she said.

Worthington finally gave his attention to Felicity. "You said you have no idea why Mrs. Powell attacked you at your home this morning, and now you say you have no idea why Mr. Tavistock attacked you moments ago."

Felicity shook her head. She gazed absently into the now-crackling fire as she replied, "Not a clue. He must have been over-medicated, as Charles suggested." She looked up. "Charles, don't bother with a car – I'll stay a little while. I do care about how you're all coping after Sasha's death. The two of you have lost a sister. We're family, of a sort. We must stick together, right?"

Charles and Bella stared at each other, then at Felicity.

"Of course we must, darling," said Charles, and he moved to take Felicity's empty mug from her. He walked to the kitchen and handed it to me, which threw me a bit, but I took it as graciously as I could, and put it on the kitchen counter.

Worthington joined Bud and me. "I trust word reached you that I'm interested in examining any knives in this kitchen."

I nodded. "It did. I haven't touched anything with a blade. At all. There's a knife block over there, with one missing. I've looked, and it's nowhere to be found."

Worthington flicked through what I imagined to be crime scene photos on his phone, pulled on a latex glove, removed the largest knife remaining in the block and held it next to his phone. He nodded. "To my eye, that's a match. The knife used in the attack appears to have come from here."

"Which means Julie took it with her," I observed.

"Precisely," he replied. "But why she wanted to do that is still unclear."

"She didn't say anything?" I was desperate to know.

"Unconscious. Significant loss of blood." Both his eyebrows rose, then settled again.

I leaned in. "What are her chances?"

He looked grave, and shook his head. "As good as gone. We did what we could to get Glen to her quickly."

"Two tragedies in such a short time. And now Piers going on a rampage," I said. "It's all a bit...much, isn't it?"

Worthington's eyes glinted. "And here you are, on the spot again, Professor Morgan. What brought you and your husband back to Beulah House, I wonder?"

"John was having a challenging time coping with Piers, Charles, and Bella, so Cait and I offered to help out," said Bud. "John mentioned things were spiraling a bit, especially with both Julie and Glen not here to do all the things they usually do. Bella's not exactly a whiz in the kitchen, it turns out, and John's not up to catering for more people than himself."

"Unlike me," said Vinnie, entering the kitchen. "Hello again, Mr. Worthington."

"Mr. Ryan, we meet again, and so soon. You're at home in a kitchen, then?"

Vinnie beamed. "In my element," he replied. "Ask John Silver – he'll tell you. If ever he has folks over, I'm the one who preps it all…leaving him to serve it up, and take all the glory, of course. If there's to be a full house this evening, I'm your man – if everyone wants feeding, that is. I'm thinking Julie keeps the place well stocked, so once you're done with your collection of evidence here, I'll start to work out how to feed the five thousand with whatever I can find in the fridge and cupboards. Will you be staying yourself, sir?"

Worthington rocked on his toes as he dumped the knife into a plastic bag. "I think not, Ryan."

"So, no interrogation for Piers, about what might have motivated his attack on Felicity?" I was surprised.

Worthington's eyes narrowed. "I don't believe it'll prove to be a highly productive conversation, but I shall be having it, nonetheless, before I leave. In the privacy of Mr. Tavistock's room."

I smiled my prettiest smile. "But of course. You wouldn't want someone with a questionable track record like mine to have a chance to listen to you questioning a suspect in a dangerous, and unprovoked attack, would you? After all, I've been arrested on suspicion of murder, was on the spot when one of Sasha's past lovers was killed, and have even threatened to sue one of her clients – so heaven forbid I should hear what you're going to ask Piers. By the way, maybe I should tell you he once made an incredibly aggressive pass at me, which forced me to fight him off. Sasha witnessed the aftermath of the pass, and her treatment of me last evening suggested she'd neither forgotten it nor forgiven me for it…despite the fact she and Piers weren't an item at the time."

A hint of a smile played at the edges of Worthington's lips, and made definite crinkles at the corners of his eyes. "I appreciate your frankness, Professor Morgan. I was aware of most of those facts prior to meeting you last night. Though your final insights are news to me. Thank you."

Vinnie leaned toward me. "Piers made a pass at you? Naughty boy."

I shrugged. "It was half a lifetime ago and I dare say I was more pass-worthy back then...though there are passes, and passes, and what he did was absolutely inappropriate. He was lucky Sasha showed up when she did, or I might have done some real damage with my handbag. Filofaxes weighed about the same as a brick, and I was never without mine during my agency days." I conjured my trusty, battered, old, leather-bound tome in my mind's eye; I'd never really needed a way to record names, addresses, and telephone numbers, because I can always recall them, but clients had expected note-taking at meetings, so I'd schlepped the thing around for the sake of looking as though I was the same as everyone else, like a prop. It didn't make the cut when I migrated.

A thought occurred to me. "How did Julie carry the knife to Felicity's flat? And did she drive? I don't even know if she had access to a car, or if she could drive."

Worthington's eyes grew steely, then softened. "She drove her own car – at least, the one she and her husband own jointly. We believe she carried the knife in her handbag. It was already in her hand when Miss Sampson opened her front door."

"But Felicity opened it anyway?" Bud's surprise was perfectly reasonable, I thought.

"The knife was not being held aloft at the time," replied Worthington coolly.

Vinnie made stabbing motions accompanied by squealing noises, a smirk on his face. By way of explanation he said, "You know, *Psycho*?" Worthington tutted aloud. "Sorry. Of course. Poor Julie. Too soon." Vinnie added.

"I'll take the chance to speak to Mr. Tavistock, alone, now," said Worthington, walking away with the bagged knife sitting, uncomfortably, in his hand. I wondered why Enderby wasn't with him – possibly overseeing the crime scene at Felicity's place?

As Worthington crossed the salon, Bella called out, "If you're planning on quizzing Piers, please be gentle with him, and please be brief. He's very confused. Probably jabbering nonsense by now, I'd have thought. The poor man needs his rest."

Worthington didn't turn, or respond, though his back became even more rigid, if that were possible.

"You two have a cuppa, I can tell you're dying for one," said Vinnie, nodding at the pot, "and I'll have a quick scan of this place. John tells me Bella's good at spag bol, but that's about it. I reckon I can do better – and it won't be long before everyone realizes they're hungry enough to eat."

As Bud and I arrived in the salon, and I started to wonder where we'd sit, Felicity rose from her chair. "Charles, be a darling – come and see what you can do with this hair for me? I feel wrecked." She headed for the stairs, and Charles followed like a lamb.

"I'm just popping over to the coach house, John," said Bella, also standing. "I'm feeling a little chilly, so I'm going to put on something warmer." She'd been sitting right next to the fire, and looked pink in the face, but who was I to mention that?

"Shall I come with you?" John was at her shoulder.

Smiling, Bella kissed her fiancé's cheek. "No. I'll be just fine, darling, thank you. Look – we've been in each other's company almost every minute since…all this began…and I really do appreciate your loving support, Johnnie. But I *can* manage to change my clothes on my own, when that's absolutely necessary." She winked wickedly. "And I won't be a mo." She left – still barefoot, which I thought foolhardy, to say the least.

Once again, only we visitors remained in the salon – all the family members had gone. It felt odd – as though we'd been abandoned. When the doorbell jangled, we all jumped. Vinnie called from the kitchen, "If they've got a weapon, don't let them in."

John said, "I'll go." Bud and I followed him to the entryway, and all three of us were surprised to see Renata standing on the doorstep, a sleek black car pulling away. She was carrying a backpack, and two obviously-heavy briefcases, which John and Bud rushed to take from her.

Once relieved of the briefcases, she took off the backpack. "Piers is expecting me," she said calmly. "Could someone tell him I've arrived, please?"

I replied, "He's up in his room, with Mr. Worthington. They might be some time."

Renata blinked – which I was beginning to think was a strong reaction for her. "Oh, I see." She blinked again. "No, I don't see, actually. Why is Mr. Worthington here again? Is it something more to do with Sasha being dead?" Her tone had an almost-childlike quality; no emotion, just curiosity.

"I understand you came to see Piers earlier today?" I replied, ushering her toward the salon; Bud and John followed with her bags.

"Yes. I had to clear Sasha's diary, of course, and he didn't want me telling anyone why. I cleared his too, because his PA is off with a terrible cold at the moment. But there were papers that had to be signed. Client contracts, some artwork to be approved by a director, and so forth. I knew Sasha would have wanted them sorted, Piers too, so I brought them here." Renata took the seat I offered, beside the fire. "He did what he had to do – but he wasn't really *compos mentis*. He asked me to come back later – now – with some other paperwork as a matter of urgency. So here I am. Such a lot of what the agency does is only committed to paper, you see. Confidentiality issues." She stared at Bud and John. "Those bags mustn't leave my sight."

The men placed the bags beside Renata. "Can I offer you a cup of tea?" I asked.

Renata opened her mouth, then stood. "I shall take tea, thank you. No milk, or sugar. And I shall trust you with my bags while I…use the facilities. It's a good drive from the office. I'm sure you're all to be trusted." Her look suggested she wasn't one hundred percent certain.

"I'll keep an eye on your bags," said John, and beamed his most trustworthy smile.

Renata didn't look convinced, but said, "I'll be upstairs. I don't like those tiny little ones out there."

She left, Bud and John stood like bookends at either side of the fireplace, and I joined Vinnie in the kitchen, where I just about managed to eke out another cup from the pot. "I'd better put the kettle on again," I said.

"Already done," replied Vinnie. "Where's the chatty one gone?"

"To use the upstairs guest facilities, I gather. It's one long round of tea-drinking and relieving oneself, in this place, it seems."

Worthington appeared in the salon, just as I entered with Renata's mug. "All done?" I asked.

"For now," was his quiet reply. "I heard the front door bell. Who was it?"

"Renata, with some papers for Piers. Apparently, he asked her to bring them to him, when he saw her this morning," said Bud.

"Ah," replied Worthington, nodding. "Maybe that's what he was talking about, though why he'd need papers concerning

Renata's father I don't know. He's still a little incoherent. Confused. I think another call should be made to his doctor. I'm no expert, but I don't think he's reacting to whatever it was he was given in the healthiest manner."

John said, "I'll get Charles to make the call, when he and Felicity rejoin us. I'm afraid I don't have the number."

Worthington didn't reply, but took a moment to look intently at each of us: Bud and John at the fireplace returned his gaze quizzically; Vinnie stood in the doorway to the kitchen, with a tea towel in his hand, wiping a knife; I hovered with Renata's mug in my hand.

"Quite the quartet of helping hands, aren't you?" Worthington's tone was grave. "A family facing this much trouble could do worse, I suppose. All of you security cleared to the heavens, all with special training behind you – as appropriate to your roles. I dare say I couldn't have pulled together a better team if I'd tried. Especially if I were facing a situation where an investigation I felt was far from over was quietly closed. And if a post-mortem had found an injury on a person's body, that could not – necessarily – be explained by said person falling to their death. Indeed, an interesting group. But there – what am I talking about? Nothing at all. Now I have a victim of two attacks just fine and dandy, while one of her attackers lies at death's door unable to explain her actions, and the other is a jabbering mess, with his actions likely to be attributed to some sort of misdirected medical decision to prescribe him inappropriate pharmaceuticals…so I'm unlikely to be proceeding with further investigations in those directions, either. If only all my tasks were this easily, and neatly, dealt with. I tell you what, how about you all do the best you can to make sure no one else within this circle is attacked, or dies, while you're around? That would make my life a lot simpler still. And it would certainly please their highly influential friends. I have been told there's nothing more for me

to do here, so I have to take my leave. Goodbye. Again."
Worthington left.

At Worthington's mention of an unexplained injury, I felt a jolt of excitement; another clue that maybe an altercation had led to Sasha's demise?

Vinnie slung the tea towel over his shoulder, and returned to the mound of vegetables he'd piled on the kitchen counter. It was only then I noticed he was spinning and twirling the knife with his fingers...completely at ease, and not even paying attention to what he was doing. I wondered where, and how, he'd acquired such significant knife-skills...as part of his training as a nutritionist, or were they something he'd picked up while developing his expertise in self-defense?

"...richer in your thoughts than on his tomb..."

Once Worthington had left, I caught Bud's eye and said, "He's telling us Sasha's death wasn't a suicide, but that he can do nothing about it, right?"

John and Bud exchanged a glance. They both nodded.

"Don't mind me out here," called Vinnie, "I'm just the kitchen skivvy I know, I know...but don't go making any plans without your boy here being brought in on the case."

Bud moved to my side and hugged me. "We need to..." We drew apart as Renata presented herself.

I said, "I think your tea's cold, by now, Renata. Sorry. I poured it, not realizing you'd be away so long."

She cleared her throat. "A call came through while I was in the bathroom. Private. Confidential. I took it there. Cold tea will be acceptable." She spotted the mug I'd perched on a side table, and took the seat beside it.

Charles and Felicity were chattering as they made their way down the stairs; I was amazed the two of them always managed to find something to giggle about.

"Ah, Renata, were we expecting you?" Charles's greeting wasn't as pointed as the one he'd given Bud and me earlier on, but it was hardly hearty.

"Piers needs some paperwork," replied Renata, and she picked up her mug.

"And what Piers wants, Piers shall get," said Felicity. "But why are you here, not his girl?"

"She's poorly. Head cold," replied Renata.

"Lucky thing," remarked Felicity. "She's well out of all this mess. I bet you don't mind though, do you, dear? What will you do now Sasha's gone? You've been with her a long time, haven't you?"

"She took me to Tavistock and Tavistock from Townsends. I've been Sasha's PA since before she and Piers were even a couple, let alone business partners. They shared me after the start-up, then I was hers alone again." Matter of fact. No anger. No sense of loss. *Odd.*

Spotting a point of connection I said, "As I mentioned last evening, I used to work at Townsends, too. When exactly did you join?" I had no recollection of Renata at all.

"After you'd left. Sasha spoke of you sometimes." Renata looked up at me, over her mug of cold tea. "She wasn't very pleased when you threatened to sue one of her clients. She thought it was personal – they were difficult clients at the best of times, but were incandescent when they discovered you used to work for Alistair Townsend. They fired the agency not long after that. Which turned out to be a good thing for Sasha, because that was when she realized she had a real chance to pick up some of his clients for herself. So, for her, that was the chance for a new beginning."

I wanted to say so much – but realized I, too, had found a new start because of the actions of that newspaper; no migration to Canada would have meant no Bud and me. So there was that…*which is everything.* I looked at Bud, and bit my tongue.

"It's uncanny how small the world seems, don't you think?" Felicity was twirling a curl at her throat; Charles had done a good job with her hair, as she looked as lustrous and radiant as she had the night before. I wondered how many hairdressing tools and products he kept at Beulah House.

"Hello everyone, have I missed anything…oh, Renata, you're back." Bella entered the front door and shook an umbrella all over the floor. "It's snowing again – wet stuff. Oh dear, look what I've done…how silly of me…"

John moved to her side, took the umbrella and said, "Don't worry, I'll sort out mopping up the floor. You go on in and join everyone. Do you feel a little warmer now, my love? You look…wonderful."

Bella beamed and smoothed her emerald velvet skirt, which she'd topped with an amber sweater. She kissed John's cheek, then came to claim her seat beside the fire while John disappeared toward where I now knew there was a wardrobe, and cleaning supplies.

"Yes, I agree with you that it's quite surprising how incredibly small the world is, Felicity," said Renata, calmly, "but that's a wonderful thing, you know." *Odd.*

Vinnie gained everyone's attention by calling from the kitchen, "Who's for veggie soup and sandwiches? I've found everything I need. I can have it ready in an hour. Good enough?"

Charles grinned. "Fine by me, I'm starving."

The rest of us nodded.

"Might there be a salad?" Felicity was pushing it, I thought.

"I'll be long gone by then, of course," said Renata. "Do you think I could go up to see Piers now? He impressed upon me that only he was to be given these papers." She stared vacantly at the briefcases and backpack.

Charles shrugged, Bella flapped her hands, Felicity said, "Why not?" Her tone dripped with disdain, which didn't surprise me, given Piers' actions toward her earlier on.

Renata stood. "I wonder if someone could give me a hand?" She looked helplessly toward John who was returning from his cleaning duties; he immediately bent to pick up the briefcases. "Thanks," she said, sounding anything but thankful.

The two of them headed upstairs, and I realized I was stuck with a room full of people I wished would disappear, because I desperately wanted to talk to Bud about what Worthington had said before he'd left. But I couldn't think of an excuse to be alone with him, nor where that might happen.

"Fancy a turn around the garden, Cait? Before the snow really comes in. I saw something in the summer house I think you'd like – you know, for our garden back home. It's a great idea…" Bud walked toward me, grabbed my arm, and steered me toward the French doors. "See you all in a bit," he said.

I was so pleased he'd thought of a way for us to have a quiet chat and was congratulating him when we heard John's shout.

We turned, to see him run into the salon, his phone to his ear. "Bud, Vinnie, Charles, come with me…yes, that's the correct address…chaps, Piers is unresponsive, on the floor in his room…yes, Beulah House, that's right, as I said." John held up his hand, to stop everyone who wanted to, asking a question. He spoke into his phone. "Yes, unresponsive. Blue lips. Ragged. Irregular. Diazepam. No idea, sorry. About eighteen stone. Around sixty. Not that I know of. Yes, I'm getting someone to help me do that right now. Good. Thank you." He shoved his phone into his pocket. "Bud, Vinnie, with me. Charles you too. We need to get Piers upright, to the extent that we can, and keep him that way until the ambulance gets here. If we can get a response, we have to try to keep him alert. Come on, it'll take all of us…he's no lightweight."

Bella was on her feet, wailing. "Oh Piers, not Piers too! This cannot be happening to me. What's become of my family?"

John was clearly torn. "Darling…we'll do all we can for him, I promise. Cait? Cait, could you…?" He gestured toward Bella, then joined the other men running upstairs.

I stepped up and tried to calm Bella. "Come on now – he's in good hands." I felt as useless as she obviously did.

"This place is a madhouse," said Felicity. She looked at her watch. "I don't think I'll stay for dinner – if dinner there will be."

How can you think like that, at a time like this? Was what I wanted to ask the woman. "How long will it take for an ambulance to get here, do you think?" was what I said.

Bella wailed, "What if they can't find the house? Lots of people can't find the house – it's so well hidden. Do you think I should go out onto the road to wave at them when they come?"

"Only your dozy friends can't find it, Bella," snapped Felicity. "Everyone else can because they use GPS, you know? Your lot are all out of the ark – too involved with ancient ways of refining gold in your hovel out there, or hammering bowls and chalices and so forth to know what day of the week it is, let alone how to use a GPS system. This house has been here for hundreds of years – it's on every map ever drawn of the area since the year dot. Of course an ambulance driver will be able to find it. Besides, they've only got to come from Forest Hill or Croydon – hardly the far side of the moon."

Renata came downstairs, looking flushed and sucking her bottom lip. I took this to be a sign of great distress on her part.

"How is Piers?" I asked.

Renata looked blank. "I don't know," she replied. "They didn't seem to think he was breathing. Vinnie was giving him the kiss of life, John was making some more phone calls – I don't know who he's phoning though."

"This is all so terribly shocking," said Bella. "Cait – brandy. We all need brandy, don't you think?"

You lot must go through gallons of the stuff if you fall back on it every time there's an emergency, I thought. "I'll sort it, now," I said.

It was clear that – before she'd headed off to attack Felicity that morning – Julie had cleared away the trolley of drinks that had been set up in the salon the previous night. I looked around, but couldn't see anything that looked like a drinks' cupboard.

I asked, "Any hints as to where I might find some?"

Bella did an impersonation of a fish, as Felicity stood. "Over here…I'll show you. They hide it all in a seventeenth-century cabinet, thereby making it seem more glamorous when it emerges. That said, they do usually keep a very good brandy here. I'd better have a drop myself – it's been a trying day."

With nothing to do but sip our drinks, we four women sat huddled beside the fire, all straining to hear the sound of an approaching siren. At least, I was – and I had to imagine the others were, too, because it would have been utterly heartless to not be. Finally, I thought I heard something, and ran to open the front door. Sure enough I could hear the ambulance approaching, and it finally made its way into the drive. The paramedics ran up the stairs two at a time, then I returned to my brandy, since there was nothing to do but wait. Again.

Bud was the first down the stairs. I didn't need to ask him how Piers was doing – his grim expression told me everything. He approached, and stood beside Bella. "I'm sorry, it was too late. They couldn't save your brother-in-law's life. Vinnie did his best to try to revive him, but he was past help, I'm afraid."

Bella let out a little squeal, and clapped her hand over her mouth. "My father, my sister, and now Piers. Why? Why?" She put both hands over her face and shuddered.

Bud spoke softly to Bella. "John will be down soon." He put his arm around my shoulder, and kissed my cheek. "John's called Worthington. He's on his way," he whispered.

"Now there's only John left to look after me," said Bella quietly. She seemed to have forgotten she still had a brother – even if he was only a half-brother.

"And he will," said Bud, sounding his most reassuring self. "He just has to answer a few questions the paramedics have for him. They might want to speak to you, too, Renata."

"Why me?" Renata sounded genuinely puzzled.

"Because you and John were together when you found Piers," replied Bud. "It's just a formality."

Renata sipped at her brandy. "I'd better make a phone call. In private," she said, then drained her glass, stood, and took herself off to the garden, closing the French doors behind her.

"I wonder who she's calling," I whispered to Bud.

He shook his head.

"Was Piers already dead when you got there?" I asked, quietly enough that Bella couldn't hear.

Bud nodded. "Looks like an overdose, though I'm no expert. Paramedics seemed to think so. Could have been something wrong with him none of us knew about, I guess."

"But his doctor saw him this morning, Bud. He's the one who gave him the medication. Did John mention diazepam?"

Bud nodded.

"Tricky stuff. Did you have a chance to see if he'd taken too many? Might this be Piers' way out, having killed Sasha?"

Bud hugged me. "Back to that idea again? Look, time enough to find out," he said, and kissed my cheek. "I hope John comes down soon; Bella looks as though she needs some attention."

Indeed, Bella was staring into the fire as though it held the answer to every question in the universe. Her head snapped up at the sound of John's voice.

"Darling," he said, and rushed to her side.

Her expression put me in mind of John William Waterhouse's painting of the Lady of Shallot as she faces her fate – vulnerable, wistful, and tragic...which reminded me that Bud and I had planned to visit the Tate the next day...and that in turn reminded me of Millais' depiction of Ophelia, singing her way to madness and death as she floats downriver. I wondered how much more Bella could take – she seemed close to the edge, psychologically speaking. I hoped John's warmth and love would be able to comfort her.

As if to answer my unasked question, Bella rose, and wrapped her long arms around John. He responded, and the couple held each other in front of the crackling fire for several moments. Felicity shifted in her seat, looking away from them, taking her turn to study the flames. It took Renata's arrival to break the sombre mood.

"Sir Simon Pendlebury will be here in an hour or so. Piers had told me only he himself, or Sir Simon, were allowed to take possession of the papers he asked me to bring here. Sir Simon's private jet just landed at Farnborough. He'll stop off here to take the papers from me on his way back to Central London." Renata spoke quietly, drawing no reaction from Bella other than a nod.

"Thick as thieves, Piers and Simon, since school. It'll have been a shock for him to hear the news. How did he take it, Renata?" Felicity's tone suggested a certain amount of unpalatable interest.

"He was a little upset, I'd say." If Bud was sometimes the master of understatement, I judged Renata to be its queen.

"I dare say Sir Simon will be glad to have a chance to pay his respects," observed John, largely to Bella. He turned. "Bud, old man, we all might have to stick around a little longer than any of us had planned. Of course I'll stay here another night, but I have a feeling Worthington will want a chat with us all. He won't be long; he hadn't even made it back to his office, it seems."

Bella actually stamped her foot. "Why have you asked that man back again? He's quite horrid." She spoke with the vehemence of a six-year-old.

John's expression told me he was surprised by Bella's reaction. "He's a sound man, Bella, and his involvement with…well, with everything that's happened to this household over the past twenty-four hours means he's bound to want to take a look at how Piers died."

Bella pulled her hand away from John's, to wipe away a tear. "He must have taken too many of those silly pills Dr. Swain gave him. I warned him they were nasty things, but he said he needed to sleep. Unfortunately, Piers always thought he knew better about everything than anyone – he probably took more whenever he felt like it, and they accumulated in his system. That would be Piers all over. It was his nature to believe that too much of something was never a bad thing. Always wanted more gravy, more wine, more everything. It looks as though that's what's finally finished him off."

Felicity looked taken aback, "We don't even know that's how he died, yet. Though…maybe he felt badly about what he'd done to me. Flying at me that way. For no good reason."

"Mr. Tavistock was a hard-working, thoughtful person. He'll be missed terribly by everyone who knew him." Renata almost whispered. "He was so kind to me when my father needed my attention, toward the end. I'll never forget that."

"We all know you'll miss him a great deal." Felicity stood, smoothed down her blue leather skirt and added, "I dare say it's alright if I pop upstairs to powder my nose?" She was addressing Bud.

He shrugged, "I don't see why not, though you might find it's a bit busy up there still. And I'd allow the paramedics to do whatever they need to be doing."

Felicity's eyes swept Bud from head to foot. "Why on earth would I want to get in their way? I only want to use a decent bathroom. And to get away from all this…" She waved her arm, indicating our assembled number, then flounced off, taking her over-large handbag with her.

"We're cursed, John. This family is cursed, I told you before you shouldn't marry me. Now I know that's true," said Bella melodramatically. We all gave her our attention.

John held her shoulders, and bobbed his head about, trying to get her to lift her eyes to his. "Come along, darling, I know you're upset. We all are. But this is not the time to be making snap decisions. We talked about this for hours last night. I'm sure that Sasha, and even Piers, would have wanted our wedding to go ahead as planned. What's to be gained by postponing it?"

Tears ran down Bella's cheeks. She looked up, her eyelids puffy. "But I'm not a strong woman, John...I don't know that I can go through with it. My heart is broken..."

John's expression as he glanced toward me and Bud was a silent cry for help, which Bud gave. "John's right, Bella. I have some understanding of grief. You might not know this, but my wife died about three and a half years back. That might sound like a long time to some, but I can tell you this...there's not a day goes by that I don't think of her. But there is more life, after death...look at me and Cait. We're happy. Truly happy. We're just coming up to our second wedding anniversary, and we're both so glad we did what we did, when we did it. The start of your marriage to John might be tinged with tragedy, but it's a tragedy that will still be there whether you marry him or not...so why not do it? Make the commitment to each other you know you want to right now, when things are tough. Because that's what marriage is about – telling each other, and telling the world, that two people have agreed they'll be there for each other whatever happens."

I couldn't have been more proud of Bud, and I could see the light in Bella's eyes change as he spoke. He was getting through to her.

"If you lost a wife, you know how I feel," she said...which I thought an odd response, given she'd lost a sister and brother-in-law, rather than a spouse. "There's always going to be a void in my heart where they each had their place, but I suppose you make a good point."

John rallied. "Yes, listen to Bud, Bella. He knows what he's talking about. We can have what he and Cait have. Sasha and Piers aren't…well, I hate to say it, but they weren't ever going to be central to our lives, were they? We were planning on finding our own place, moving away, and moving on. We could still do that…"

Bella looked around the vastness of the salon, kitchen, dining room, and entry hall. "It was always too much for just me. But, maybe, you and I could move into this house, John? It's the sort of house that consumes a person if they're alone in it."

As she spoke, her eyes grew round, and I noticed the fire was dying to embers. The whole place seemed to get a little darker, despite the fact all the lamps were lit.

The now-familiar jangling of the bell caught us all off-guard again, and there was a communal shudder at its sound.

"I'll go," said Bud.

As he marched toward the door I wondered what it would open to this time – and if the house would be pleased to greet this new arrival.

"...we have seen better days..."

No one had turned on the lights at the front of the house, so Worthington stood in darkness when Bud opened the door to him. He brushed the snow off his shoulders and entered. His face was a mask; grim, etched with lines, shadows beneath his eyes. His tombstone teeth were a memory – I didn't expect he'd smile any time soon.

Bud and he talked for a moment; their despondent body language spoke of the tragedy we were all experiencing, despite the gleam of hope of the twinkling star atop the Christmas tree, beside which they stood. Worthington glanced up the stairs, nodded toward those of us in the salon, then ascended. Bud returned to our group and whispered to John.

John said, "Bella, darling, Bud and I are needed. I'll be as quick as I can, alright?"

Bella nodded, still crying, and John and Bud took off.

I settled Bella in her seat again, then Charles thudded his way downstairs.

"Scotch," he said, as he plonked himself in the seat Felicity had vacated.

I guessed he was asking "someone" to get him a drink, so I said, "Do you mean you'd like me to pour a whisky for you?" He nodded, without looking up. "And how do you take it? Neat?"

"Yes."

I sucked up my annoyance, once again telling myself that I was dealing with people *in extremis*, but cursed inwardly that this family was blessed with very few manners, and a boatload of entitlement. I get it that the rich lead different lives, but the entire Asimov clan seemed to assume everyone owed them something – even if nothing more than service. True, Charles had been the one to whom Bud had presented us as being people who could take up the slack when it came to domestic duties, it was just that the reality of that "cover" was wearing a little thin, for me. The amount of soothing I was having to do was weighing on me – it's not my forte.

I handed a crystal tumbler with a substantial amount of scotch in it to Charles. He looked up, his eyes rimmed with crimson, and actually thanked me. I felt my multi-purpose eyebrow shoot up – and hoped he didn't know it meant I was thinking, "*About time, too.*"

As I watched Charles nurse his drink for a moment, then gulp it down, I couldn't help but wonder about Piers' death. Had he intentionally overdosed, wracked by guilt at having killed Sasha, then having also attacked Felicity? But, even if that was the case, why *had* he attacked Felicity? And what about Julie Powell – what could possibly make sense of her attacking Felicity, too? Might Julie have seen something that would have implicated Felicity in Sasha's death? Could Piers have seen Felicity do something…or had she seen him do something? My mind was whirring…in circles…so I was delighted to see Bud, John, and Vinnie coming down the stairs; they all descended in step, which was weirdly distracting.

"Listen up, folks," John began.

"Wait for me," called Felicity as she bounced down the staircase. "I don't want to miss anything."

Does she look like a woman who's possibly caused three people's deaths?

John waited until Felicity was seated on a small sofa, beside Renata; neither woman looked comfortable with the situation, and they both shuffled to cling to their respective arm, rather than touch in the center.

John forced a smile. "Right, then…Worthington says he needs to know everything that happened to all of us today – and he means *everything*. So, we'll all have to put on our thinking caps. He's got that Enderby woman joining him as soon as she can get here, but – in the meantime – he's asked if everyone can please write down what they were doing, as well as where, and when, today, so he can get as full a picture as possible. It doesn't matter if you were here, or elsewhere – he wants to know the ins and outs of everyone's day. I'm going to round up some supplies from…somewhere, and I thought we could each find a spot where we can think, and write notes. Meanwhile, Vinnie's kindly offered to push ahead with making a meal for everyone. So how about we take that time to get our notes sorted out, then we can all eat? Bud's volunteered to help set up the dining room, and we can all pitch in, right, Bella?"

Bella stood. "I'm sure you'll find everything you need for us in the meeting room, darling. And, actually, I'd rather oversee setting up for dinner, myself. If we're going to dine, even if it's just on soup and sandwiches, we should do so comfortably. I know where to find the table settings I want to use. My notes would be exactly the same as yours, John, so they won't take long to write up, because I can just copy them out. So I'll get the place set up for dinner. How many will we be?"

Bella's tone was different; for the first time since I'd met her, she sounded like someone with a purpose, and I struggled to wrap my head around this Bella being the same person who had, earlier in the day, seemingly not known where I could find a dustpan and brush. Now she knew where everything was?

"We'll be eight, plus the Worthington man, plus whomever else decides to drop in to examine us all." Felicity sounded angry.

John demurred to Bella, then headed off toward the meeting room, returning moments later with a stack of lined pads, and a

box of pens, all of which were printed with the Tavistock &
Tavistock corporate logo. He distributed the supplies.

Renata twirled her pen sadly. "What's to become of me, I
wonder? Sasha and Piers looked after me so well."

Until that moment, the realization that there was now a
public relations firm that had lost the two people who'd set it up
hadn't occurred to me; I know from experience that it's the
people at the top who are the draw for the clients of a business
of that nature...there was little likelihood the company would
survive the deaths of both its founding directors. The clients
would find new suppliers, of course; I suspected there might be
a few account directors at the place who'd be able to cobble
together enough of the accounts to strike out on their own.
However, I feared Renata would soon be without a job. As the
PA to a woman who no longer needed one – and having worked
for only Sasha for so many years – she might have a hard time
finding a new post, once she'd stayed on long enough to wind
things up, as necessary.

"Don't worry about it, Renata. I'll find something for you to
do at Bella Zoloto. I know Sasha and Piers trusted you
completely – there's no way I'd ever...abandon you. Indeed,
there's no way I'd ever let anyone down who had my family's
interests at heart. I would always find a way to look after them.
You must know that, surely."

A smile managed to creep across Renata's face. "Thank you."
She sounded...*triumphant?*

Worthington's arrival was a surprise; he'd come downstairs
and entered the salon without my noticing – I'd been absorbed
by watching the jarring interaction between Bella and Renata.
Thus, his blustering, "Good, I see you're all getting ready to
write up those notes I need," took us all aback. Heads turned in
his direction, and everyone slapped a smile on their face – as
though a teacher had just entered a room full of unruly pupils.

"I managed to find supplies, and everyone's going to find a quiet spot so they can focus," said John in a very prefect-like tone.

"Good job, Silver," said Worthington.

Worth a gold star? I wondered, *Or maybe house points?*

He continued, "I'll let you all get on with that. The paramedics are leaving, and my lot will be along shortly. They're moments away. We'll try to not cause too much disruption. That said, I'd like everyone to think of the upstairs as out of bounds, until I say so. I'm sure you all understand why."

Renata held up her hand. "I don't," she said.

Worthington rocked on his toes. "We need to establish how Mr. Tavistock died. That question is likely to be answered, ultimately, by a post-mortem, but there's a good deal of information we need to gather at the scene of his death."

"Bella thinks it was an accidental overdose, born of Piers' belief he knew better than any doctor how much medication was good for him." Felicity's voice dripped with disdain.

Worthington gazed at Felicity, and said, "We don't yet know his cause of death, so maybe that idea's somewhat premature. We'll see what we see."

Before he disappeared upstairs again, I knew I had to take my chance. "I wondered if I could have a quiet word, please, Mr. Worthington?"

Worthington seemed to be performing a total body scan on me, then Bud, then John. His shoulders dropped a little. He nodded. "Meeting room. Just you."

I glanced toward Bud, threw him a smile, and followed Worthington's lead. We sat in the two seats at the table where we'd sat the night before. He rested his hands on the table. "Yes?"

"May I speak freely?"

"No one's stopping you."

"You know what I mean."

"If you mean can you say anything to me without fear of reproach or reprisal, yes, you may. I am a functionary, not an ogre." He almost smiled.

"Be that as it may...I have some questions. Relating to the comments you made just before you left Beulah House earlier today."

"I made no comments, other than to politely take my leave."

I was starting to get annoyed. I counted my top teeth with the tip of my tongue – it's a technique I've recently adopted to help me take time to think before I speak; I've been surprised by how often I've used it. Eventually I said, "I'm getting sick of 'not having' conversations or meetings with people, and of 'not hearing' comments people have made. It's like it's a game. But it's not. People are dying."

"I had noticed."

I sighed. "May I ask you a question?"

"I can't stop you asking."

I felt like screaming! "Did Sasha Tavistock have a headwound that couldn't be definitely categorized as having arisen from her fall?"

"It was a considerable fall. The coroner's office is still determining the possible nature of all her wounds."

"If there were to be such an injury, might I suggest an examination of the large brass telescope that's in the palace room?"

"You may. Thank you."

"And was any paper matching that which was used for her suicide note found in the palace room?"

Worthington's eyes glinted and his brow furrowed. "Not in that room. No writing supplies of any sort were found there. However, we did find matching paper in a small study used by the decedent, located adjacent to the main bedroom she shared with her husband."

I said nothing.

Worthington said nothing.

I had a suspicion we could have gone on the same way for some time, so said, "I believe Sasha Tavistock did not commit suicide. However, I have an open mind about whether she died as the result of an accident, or if she was intentionally killed. And I had a suspect in mind, though he's now dead."

Worthington's eyebrows slowly concertinaed his forehead. "Her husband?"

I replied, "We both know it's usually the spouse who's to blame in most murders. Or a close friend, or family member. So, if not Piers, maybe Felicity?"

"Or any one of the other family members and close friends who were here last evening?" His tone was dismissive. "But I'm pleased you're keeping an open mind about whether Mrs. Tavistock was murdered or not, at least. May *I* speak openly?"

I couldn't help but smile. "If you mean without fear of reproach or reprisal, fire away."

"I mean may I speak to you in complete confidence? Are you prepared to agree you will not tell anyone what I am about to say? And I mean *anyone*."

I didn't hesitate. "In that case, the answer is no. I don't keep secrets from my husband."

Worthington's gaze seemed to pierce me to my core. "But he keeps secrets from you. He has sworn to do so."

I stood. "He has to. It's his duty. And he does. I've accepted that fact. But I have taken no such oath. What you tell me, I reserve the right to tell him. Take it or leave it."

Worthington also stood. "In that case, I'll leave it, for now. Thank you, Professor Morgan. We'll take a look at the telescope, purely for the sake of being thorough. While you understand there is no ongoing investigation into Mrs. Tavistock's demise, there is one just beginning that concerns her husband's death. It might be that he was up in the palace room earlier today – so we should make sure everything is as it should be up there. I suggest you and your husband leave here as soon as possible – Mr. Silver will be wanting to attend to his fiancée's needs, I'm sure."

I was dismissed. But I knew I'd given the right answer to his question. For me, and for Bud and me.

I returned to the salon. Bud wrapped his arms around me and we gravitated toward a dim corner. I whispered, "Look at them all, Bud. This is an unhealthy place. I know we're seeing people on what must be their worst day, but Charles is drinking his face off and trying to engage Felicity in what? Some sort of pointless banter? She's glowing – which is so far beyond normal given the fact she's been attacked twice today, and has all-but killed a woman, that I have no words to categorize her body language. She's not carrying an ounce of guilt, that's for sure. Which has given me pause for thought…which I want to discuss with you. Renata's sitting there taking everything in as though she's a woman who knows she's holding the winning ticket to the lottery, but hasn't told anyone yet. Vinnie is…well, I can't tell if he's the most callous man I've ever met, or if he just has a weird sense of humor that's blacker than coal. And John? I thought he fawned over Lottie in Jamaica – but the way he is with Bella is…well, it's a little disturbing, to be honest. Look at him now – following her around the dining room doing what she tells him to with the glassware…that's not John. When Vinnie said she'd taken him by the heart, he wasn't kidding. John's more than besotted, he seems to have been absorbed by Bella – he's become nothing more than a doting lapdog. I feel as though we're the only normal people here, Bud."

My husband held me tight. "You're right, this is a real bad day for these folks, and I don't think I'm getting any really useful insights into them. But we've both met enough people on their worst day – professionally speaking – to also know that these are the circumstances where you get to see the inner person, with all the dressing stripped away. I honestly don't feel comfortable talking about these folks, right here, right now. But I do think we should get away from here as soon as we can – and spend some time alone."

I agreed.

"You can all come and serve yourselves from the platters Vinnie has prepared, and take your soup etcetera into the dining room," announced Bella. She was smiling so broadly that I could see her perfect teeth gleaming, which filled me with dread for some reason…and forced into my mind's eye the sight of Sasha's teeth, which I'd noticed upon meeting her again had been surprisingly far from perfect; in PR, image counts for a great deal, and I was amazed Sasha hadn't either taken better care of them, or had them attended to by a professional.

John grabbed Bella by the waist, kissed her cheek and said, "Marvellous job, darling, under the circumstances."

Bella was glowing, and smiled coyly. "You helped so much."

"I followed sound instructions." John kissed her again.

Pass me a sick bag! "Great teamwork," I said. "Come on Bud, you know we agreed to head off as soon as the food was out. I hope you all understand – there's nothing we can do to help, here, and we thought we'd grab a bite somewhere…somewhere tourists go."

Vinnie began to usher us toward the kitchen, "Aw come on now, come on…I've slaved away over a hot chopping board buttering enough bread for an army, sure I have. You've got to at least try one of my blue cheese and walnut ones, or maybe even a cheeky little smoked salmon with dill and chilli-speckled cream cheese. Bella's opened some fine wine, and the soup's a good 'un, too – me Ma's famous veggie mix. It'll fill yer up, and put hairs on yer chest, so it will. Unless you don't fancy a hairy chest, that is, Cait."

He was irrepressible, alright. Bud and I exchanged a glance that told each of us we'd surrender, and I smiled at Vinnie. "No hairy chest, thanks, but the sandwiches sound impressive."

Vinnie leaned in, "I also rustled up a nice Greek salad for Lady Muck, over there, and I made enough to go around…but I'll not answer for the olives, because they're Italian, not Greek. And I'm guessing the feta's not been flown in from the Cyclades, though, knowing the Asimov clan, I wouldn't put it past them. Come on, dig in – and I'll drop you off at a nice place I know where you can have a romantic dessert later on."

This time at least Bud and I got to sit down together, and we both got to enjoy some food – but to say the conversation at the table was weird would be an understatement of Bud-like proportions. Bella kept swooning at John, and when she wasn't doing that she was patting Renata's hand as though it were the paw of a favorite dog; Charles and Felicity sat beside each other, and knocked back more wine between them than I've seen two people do in a long time; Renata ate her food in silence, sipping at her wine; Vinnie sat beside Bud and kept both of us entertained with tales about Vaseem's encounters with famous actors in unflattering circumstances…and through it all not one word was spoken about Sasha, Piers, or Julie, nor the fact there was a pretty constant procession of people coming and going up and down the stairs.

Absolutely weird.

"…leave not a rack behind…"

After being assured by Bella that she and John could manage to clear up alone, Vinnie drove us back toward Central London. Renata had declined the offer of a lift, because Sir Simon Pendlebury had failed to arrive by the time he'd said he'd be there, and she assured us it was imperative she handed over the bags of papers she'd brought to the house to him, personally. Our journey was largely silent – because Bud and I had stomachs full of carbs, and it had been a long and stressful day…which meant we both nodded off.

The first thing I was aware of was Vinnie's booming, "So the restaurant I was telling you about isn't so far from John's place. You'll be able to get a cab back no problem."

A tell-tale dry mouth and damp chin suggested I'd been snoring and dribbling, and Bud's dazed look told me I hadn't been the only one enjoying the effects of jet lag. "Lovely," I answered, rather half-heartedly. The desire for a chatty soirée with Bud had evaporated, and all I really fancied doing was getting a proper sleep.

Bud rubbed his face with both hands, then said, "Thanks, Vinnie. We'll rally. Where are you taking us?"

"Just delivering…don't panic. I've some laundry to take care of, and I'm putting together a few bits of fresh clothing, and so forth, for John that I'll drive over to him first thing. I'll drop you off, and let you have some alone time. Nice place. A brasserie on Brompton Road. Been there for…well, a good, long time, anyways. First all-day brasserie in London, so they say. Good menu, excellent service, and a dessert trolley to die for. Quite literally…it's always covered with the best ways to con your body into overdosing on sugar and fat, so it is."

"I know the one you mean," I said, sitting upright, and orientating myself. We didn't take much longer to reach our destination – which was a place I'd wanted to share with Bud in any case. We waved Vinnie off, and I pulled at Bud until we were teetering on the edge of the pavement. I pointed at a window above our heads. "I had a boyfriend who lived up there. We used the restaurant a great deal. We broke up, he left for the shires…so I got 'custody' of this place. Came here often, throughout the time I lived in London. I had planned for us to come here to eat anyway – so now's as good a time as any."

Bud hugged me as we walked into the restaurant, which looked as though it had been plucked from a Parisienne street and dropped not much more than a stone's throw from the Victoria and Albert Museum, relatively speaking.

When we walked in, I remembered the *maitre d'* we were greeted by from the time when his hair had been brown and there'd been more of it…but his slight overbite and general pallor hadn't changed. I said, "You were once a waiter here, I recall. It's Yves, isn't it?"

The man looked amazed, then a little sheepish. "I've been here since I was in my twenties. You used to come here regularly?"

"I did. For some time." I suspected I'd blended into the many thousands of faces Yves must have seen over the years, but, now that I'd established my credentials, and explained we only wanted desserts, he led us to the end of a red-upholstered banquette which ran the length of a mirrored wall, facing the splendid – and well-stocked – bar.

Yves bent to us and spoke quietly. "The party requiring these seats will arrive in an hour. They are delayed. Bon appétit." He pulled the dessert trolley to our side, then returned to his post.

"Do you come here often?" asked Bud, with a wicked grin, as he surveyed the scrumptiousness laid before us.

I returned his smile. "It's pretty much where I learned to eat. I was a girl who came to London from what was, as you know, a relatively poor family in Wales. I'd never been introduced to anything more exotic than the Welsh interpretation of curry before I began to come to this very restaurant. It's where I learned to read a French menu, order the right wine to match every dish, where I first grappled with tongs for escargots, and was shown – in the hallowed kitchen – how to make a perfect omelette. It's also where I was able to discover the difference between champagnes. I learned a lot here. It'll always be an incredibly special place for me."

"And the guy who lived upstairs?" Bud tilted his head. His eyes weren't playful.

"I've mentioned him to you. He was the one who spent his work-weeks in London, and weekends in the country…with his family, as it turned out."

Bud nodded, "Ah yes, the one who wasn't quite as 'separated' as you'd thought."

I nodded. "That's him." I reached out and touched my husband's hand. "It hurt, back then. But now? It's all so far in the past…that distant land I choose to visit only infrequently."

"But more often at the moment, I guess," replied Bud, squeezing my fingers, then drawing back as a young, long-faced, aproned man approached, with a hopeful air.

Bud licked his lips as he surveyed the splendors before us, and whispered, "Everything looks so good. Bad, but good. Do I just point?" I nodded. He did, and we ended up with five desserts between us, and two glasses of champagne – because we were on holiday, after all.

We began by sharing the *pot au chocolat*, a light, silky mousse, with a little brandy poured into the top. As we oh'ed and ah'ed at the flavor and texture, Bud asked about my time alone with Worthington, which I recounted in every detail, though we were both careful to use no names, because the party beside us could overhear every word.

His look of concern about Worthington's offer to share confidences with me abated when he savored the first mouthful of *crème caramel*. "Thanks for telling him we're a team, Wife," he said, eventually. "J and I have chatted about the man you speak of, and we've agreed he's a decent enough chap."

I chuckled. "Picking up the local lingo, I hear. Oh – oh, let's try the *tarte au citron* next; I hope it's well-balanced between sharp and sweet." Bud carefully sliced the little pastry in two – with me watching him like a hawk.

As I bit into my perfectly-judged half of the crumbly delight, I wished everything about Beulah House would vanish into thin air, so we could float on a cloud of happiness, but I knew it wouldn't, so was just about to pick up our conversation when the foursome beside us paid and departed, for which I was grateful. We enjoyed the distraction of the balletic flurry of activity that followed, to clear and reset the table.

"How did Worthington react when you told him about the telescope?" Bud wiped a crumb from his chin, and licked his fingers. "That was good," he said, smiling.

"Said he'd check it out. And I think he will have done. I'm glad he found paper that matched the suicide note somewhere other than the palace room," I added. "That could explain a great deal."

"So where was it he found it, exactly?"

"When we were in the master bedroom, it was clear it only used half the upstairs space. Remember? It was above the bowed window of the salon below – so there had to be another space above the bowed window of the dining room. It sounds as though Sasha had a place next door to her bedroom where she had a bit of an office set-up, or maybe just a small study, or something like that."

"But would she really sit there to write a suicide note, then take it up to the palace room with her?"

"Come on, Bud, Worthington told us something was off about Sasha's injuries; I believe there was some sort of altercation up in the palace room, and that – somehow – Sasha fell or was thrown or pushed to her death because of it. Her hair being down suggests to me she was meeting someone who put her into her non-business mode of thinking; Renata told me she usually had her hair down, then wrapped it into a chignon for business. The telescope's position suggests she could have been hit by that – it wouldn't have been pointing at the floor of the room for any other good reason. The SOCO told us the lamp wasn't lit at the desk where the note was found. I mean, who writes a suicide note then does that? If they've written it, they want someone to find it, right?"

"I guess."

"Of course they do." Bud shrugged, and I continued, "So the question is – who could have been up in the palace room with Sasha?"

"And the answer is…?"

"I still think Piers is a good option, despite the fact he's dead. If he's found to have overdosed, that could be his remorse enacted. But – to think beyond that for a moment, if it wasn't Piers, then who? Renata went out of the French doors with Sasha, who she said left her, and went up the outdoor staircase to get a wrap, or something, because she was cold. Do we believe what Renata said about Sasha?"

Bud didn't answer; he was sipping his champagne and eyeing the *tarte tatin*. "Oh, sorry. Umm…I don't see why not. There were footsteps in the slush on the roof terrace leading to the master bedroom, so there's some physical evidence to support

Renata's story that Sasha went up there, and she must have done, because how else would she have got to the palace room without you seeing her, right?"

"Right. Renata says she remained on the lower terrace, however, she *could* have followed Sasha up the outer stairs, and then into the palace room. She joined us all in the entry hall by entering the salon through the French doors, but she could have retraced her steps to do that. Agreed?"

"Agreed. Shall I cut the *tarte tatin* now? Into two perfectly equal halves, of course."

I grinned. "Yes please."

He did, and I allowed myself to luxuriate in the texture of the wafer-thin apple slices and their caramelly goodness for a moment or two.

I finally returned to our reality, and said, "Next, Charles and Felicity. They said they were using the pink and blue bathrooms – which we now know means the *en suite* bathrooms attached to each of those bedrooms. Felicity said they weren't together, but they each seem to have taken an awfully long time to simply powder their noses…unless that is, in fact, what they were doing."

"I'm not with you," said Bud as we both sat back, wiped our sticky lips with our napkins, and reached for our drinks.

I said, "I reckon they might both be using cocaine: they seem to have mood upswings at the same time as each other, and always after they've been alone somewhere. It could be that they have that in common, too."

Bud sighed, "I can't say I noticed, to be honest. I'm usually pretty good at that – though, to be fair, there was so much nervous tension in the place that what might have stood out under normal circumstances looked pretty average." He paused, looking a little sad. "There's only the *crème brulée* left – shall we dig in with our spoons at the same time?"

I nodded, but let my spoon hover for a moment. "What I can tell you with certainty is that Felicity was lying when she said she'd been alone in the pink bathroom the whole time. Her body language was screaming that she'd filled those moments with something she doesn't want us to know about. When she presented herself alongside Charles at the top of the stairs, her hair was arranged differently than it had been earlier in the evening. She was a little flushed, and her dress was crumpled. My most charitable thought at the time was that a woman with uncooperative hair had sought and received aid from experienced hairdresser."

"And your less charitable interpretation of what you saw?"

I weighed my response as I allowed the silky, crunchy, sweetness in my mouth to linger for as long as possible. "Felicity and Charles aren't that far apart in age. She's probably not even twenty years his senior. Such an age difference, were the genders reversed, wouldn't be seen as unusual. In this instance, if there is a relationship – beyond a sniffing one – I believe both parties would prefer it to be kept secret due to the fact she was once married to Charles's father, so was – technically, at least – Charles's stepmother. Maybe not even their set would accept that? That inconvenience aside, they are two people who both understand only too well the opportunities and challenges associated with being a darling of the tabloids, so their shared world view might make for a relationship built on some common ground."

Bud grinned. "The inside of your head must be a fascinating place."

I reached across the table and playfully tapped his hand with the back of my spoon. "Setting all that aside for a moment," I continued, "if they were together, they could alibi each other. If they were not together – which is what they both said – then either of them could have followed Sasha up to the palace room."

"Oh dear, I see where this is going."

"And, of the two of them, I think Felicity could have been the one who had a spat with Sasha that got out of hand, and who threw her off the roof – well, okay then, pushed her, because I don't believe Felicity would have been capable of throwing someone even of Sasha's weight off the roof."

"What about Piers? He's now a suicide because of grief, not guilt? And Felicity meant to gravely injure Julie all along?"

"See – my mind's not much more of a cesspit than yours, when you try," I said.

Bud sighed. "I can't see Felicity doing all that. In any case – why would she?"

I shrugged. "That's what I don't know – so, moving on…Julie and Glen were clattering about in the kitchen, they said; I know at least one of them was, because I could hear noises, and singing – though I couldn't tell if I was hearing a male tenor, or a female contralto. The other one could have been anywhere – and I can tell you right now that I wouldn't be surprised if Beulah House had a way by which they could have gained access to the upstairs without my having seen them do so from my vantage point in the salon."

"Yes, they could have done." Bud sounded triumphant. "There's a servants' staircase – John mentioned it. It was built to allow the servants to get up and down without having to use the…you know, the real stairs. I'm a bit fuzzy about its exact location, because John just waved his arm. But I guess that puts at least one of the Powells in the frame as possibly able to get to the scene of the crime – if that's what we're now calling the palace room."

"Good – well, not good, but, you know what I mean. Oh now, that's something…if there's a staircase I didn't know about, I wonder if Sir Simon could have used it to get to the palace room without me or Renata seeing him? That puts him back onto my list of suspects – and it might explain his actions in trying to shut things down – he wasn't trying to protect someone else, he did it himself."

"So now you're saying it wasn't Piers, or Felicity, but Sir Simon?"

I took what was, sadly, the last sip of my champagne, and Bud did the same with his. "Come on, we're talking through every possibility, here. So, moving on…Bella said she used the yellow bathroom upstairs, and she said Piers used his own. Either of them could have gone up to the palace room. You and John were in the two downstairs WCs – which I discovered have doors which would have allowed either of you to nip out of the back without being seen…"

Bud said, "Now hang on…it just so happens that what Felicity said about those little cubicles is bang on the money – they have almost no insulation, and John and I…well, we carried on a bit of a conversation while we were each in our own. He was keen to know what I thought of Bella, as you might guess. So I can tell you that both of us were there, that whole time. Probably why it took us so long – he asked a lot of questions. And I couldn't get the soap out of that little dispenser thing they had in there."

I squeezed his arm. "Good to know – that means you and John can alibi each other, so that leaves me, and I'll admit that while I know I remained in the salon the whole time, I could also have gone upstairs without anyone seeing me do it. Finally, there's Vinnie who was…well, why was Vinnie even there? I thought he'd left, and Worthington didn't get around to asking him last night."

"Now that's where I can help again." Bud beamed. "Vinnie had planned to spend a few hours at a local pub – was going to get something to eat there, and so forth, then give us all a ride back to John's place. But when he got there, they were hosting the grand final of some local area pub quiz – which I gather is a big deal. He couldn't park, and didn't think he'd be able to eat – so he came back to the house to use the facilities…not knowing everyone else would be doing the same at that time, I guess. And that's when he found Sasha."

"So there's not one single person who couldn't have done it, if they'd wanted to."

"Everyone could have done it? If by 'it' you mean gain access to the palace room to push Sasha off the roof – sounds about right."

"Not helpful, is it?"

We both surveyed our empty plates and glasses, and agreed it was time to leave, so Bud caught our server's attention to ask for the bill.

Yves brought it himself, about thirty seconds later. He leaned toward me and said, "We shall be closing our doors for good, in just a few weeks. Geri has been our head barman for many years; he and I have spoken about you, and I can see now who you once were. I am pleased you have a happy life. I believe you used to know Gaston, the owner?" I nodded. "I am sorry to say he has decided to sell. To retire to a family farm in France, in the south, not far from Biot. This might be the last time you are able to dine with us. As such –" he tore our bill into pieces – "everything is on us tonight. I wish you both a happy future. I shall retire when we close – it's a good time to do so."

I was suddenly aware that – while a few of the ghosts from my previous life were reaching out to touch me – some aspects of my previous life were dissolving, or at least losing their meaning for me. I looked around; I'd never imagined this place would cease to exist.

Bud and I thanked Yves, wished him and the team the best for the future, and I waved to Geri behind the bar, where the customers were standing two-deep. As we were leaving, a group of six took over the corner where we'd been huddled; their red-and-green hats, with giant elf ears attached, suggested they were thoroughly enjoying the Christmas spirit.

When we left the joyful din and warmth behind us, the traffic suggested there was no such thing as a Central London surcharge on cars, and we waited patiently, trying to spot a taxi we could flag down. We could have been any couple out to enjoy a spot of dinner and the Christmas atmosphere, but we weren't.

The cab ride back to John's didn't take long, and I was glad it took us through Sloane Square, where the skeletal trees were decked out with sprays of snowflake-inspired lights, the buses were Santa-red, and Peter Jones's department store was a glittering presence dominating the entire place. The sight lifted my spirits…but not enough, apparently, to allow me a good night's sleep when we finally hit the sack: my dreams turned out to be full of faceless people running up and down endless flights of stairs, entering and leaving a countless number of bathrooms…like some irritating Brian Rix farce, but without any funny one-liners. I blamed the *crème brulée*.

WEDNESDAY

"...nothing either good or bad, but thinking makes it so..."

As is often the way with jet lag, I found myself irritatingly wide awake at five the next morning. Bud was still sleeping soundly, so I did my best to not disturb him as I abluted, then crept upstairs, where I made breakfast for myself – an omelette prepared the way I'd been shown all those years ago in the kitchen of a brasserie that was about to no longer exist. At least the lesson had endured, and the omelette was, indeed, pillowy, moist, and flavorful.

I cleared away the mess I'd made, then sat in John's lounge, looking out at the Thames rushing along in the darkness, thinking about times past, people past, and places past. That old saying is right – you can never step in the same river twice, which made me immensely grateful for my eidetic memory.

I happened to be holding my phone when it began to warble, so answered it quickly.

"Is that you, Cait? Glad to know you're up and about. I saw the lights shining onto the back garden from my kitchen, and hoped it would be you. I know it was a fifty-fifty thing, between you and Bud, but I reckoned you'd be more likely to be up before sparrow peep." Vinnie's voice was unmistakable.

"Yes. Couldn't sleep." I looked at my watch. "You're up early. Everything alright?"

"Not so's you'd notice. Our man John phoned me just now. It's all gone off over at Beulah House again. They were stuffed to the rafters last night, it seems. Sir Simon eventually showed up, and had to stay over because he was as sick as a dog. Not pleasant, I understand. Must have picked up something nasty in Jersey, John said. Felicity stayed, too – though why, John didn't say. Maybe because she wasn't allowed to go back to her flat? Anyways, about four this morning there's a big hoo-ha, because Charles is running amok about the place, telling everyone the ghost's the one who's done for Piers, and now she's after him, too. John was called over to the main house by Felicity, and he's been onto the doc who came to see to Piers, who's on his way there now, none too pleased about it, from what John-boy said."

"What a family," was the first thing out of my mouth, quickly followed by, "can we do anything to help?"

"I was due to take some clean clothes over there for John this morning, so I'll do that now. But I don't reckon you can help at all."

"So what's all this about the ghost? Is that the one Felicity mentioned? Some woman who goes about the place crying because she's lost her children?" Even as I spoke I wondered why I was talking about a ghost as though it were a real thing.

"As I've said, I don't hold with them myself, but the notion of it has quite turned Charles's head, it seems. John's not got much idea about what's going on with the man. Seems like there's a madness running through those who stay the night there, one at a time. Must be something in the water."

I ruefully agreed with him. "Well, if there's nothing we can do to help, maybe Bud and I will go ahead with visits to some places I had been hoping to make today. But you know how to reach us if we're needed."

"I do sure enough. Have a wonderful day, you two lovebirds, you. And don't give another thought to that lot over at Beulah

House. John'll be right enough. Off you go now and have a good time," and he was gone.

Bud and I managed to get out of John's place without much ado, and decided to walk to Tate Britain; I didn't like the idea of being cooped up on a bus. We talked as we walked, but kept hitting snags when discussing who might have killed Sasha – if, indeed, she had been killed.

"If we can't get any further with that, what about a reason for Julie attacking Felicity? Any theories on that topic?" Bud sounded a bit exasperated.

"She must have had a reason to do it," I replied. "There's always a reason for a person doing something; it's not always a good reason, nor even a logical one, but they always *believe* that reason – which is why they do what they do. Humans are, at their essence, *reasonable* creatures. She took a knife from Beulah House with her – why would she do that if she didn't intend to at least threaten Felicity? What's really confusing is…why did she attack Felicity as soon as she opened the door?"

"We only have Felicity's word for that," noted Bud, sagely.

I pounced. "True. Oh rats, that's what I meant to do – I meant to ask what it was that Felicity and Bella argued about on the phone yesterday morning. Remember, John told you when you spoke to him that they'd had a bit of a ding dong? I didn't ask him more about that, and I meant to. Maybe Julie overheard something? Maybe it set her off?"

"Team Bud to the rescue on that aspect. I asked John about it when we were out in the garden yesterday. Bella told him that Felicity had phoned her, accusing Bella of having something to do with Sasha deciding to kill herself. Bella said it was typical – that Felicity had always hated her, so she'd decided to forgive and forget, which John says is very much in-character for Bella. But you're right…there's no reason why Julie couldn't have overheard at least Bella's side of the conversation. John mentioned that the call came through on the landline to the house, rather than on Bella's own phone, so I guess Julie could have even listened in to both women talking. But what on earth could Felicity have said that would make an otherwise perfectly normal woman – which Julie seemed to me to be – go and do something like that? I've interviewed enough perpetrators over the years to know there really is a huge chasm between someone who lashes out in the heat of the moment, and one who takes a weapon with them to confront another person. The law differentiates between manslaughter and murder with malice aforethought for good reason, and it looks as though something gave Julie a 'reason', in your words, to plan the latter."

I gave my response some thought. "As you said, we only have Felicity's side of the story. What if Julie went there on some perfectly innocent errand, didn't attack Felicity at all, but Felicity invented the story of Julie's actions as a way to cover up all-but murdering the poor woman? Maybe Julie saw or knew something that implicates Felicity in Sasha's killing?"

Bud turned to face me, and smiled. "Now Felicity killed Sasha, and initiated the attack on Julie? And I guess the knife just walked to her place from the kitchen at Beulah House all by itself?"

To save my blushes, I paid attention to the traffic as we scurried across Vauxhall Bridge Road. "Not far now," I said, then added wickedly, "Oh look, I wonder what all your secret-squirrel chums are up to this snowy morning?" I pointed toward the 1990s toytown-style MI6 headquarters, across the river. "Ugly thing, isn't it? I'm surprised they really didn't blow it up in that James Bond film – then they could have started again."

Bud chuckled. "One: not 'my chums' at all. Two: it's not that ugly, and it's possibly highly practical – fit for purpose, you know? And three: Judy Dench's face when it exploded was one of those great moments in movie history you never forget. I wish

Vinnie's Vaseem had some stories about her – I bet she's quite the character."

I agreed, and we strolled in silence until we walked up the steps to enter Tate Britain. I was almost salivating at the prospect of seeing so many more old friends; during my London days, if I'd had enough of the National Gallery I'd headed off to the Tate when I'd needed to escape.

Once we were inside, I dragged Bud to a room where I wanted him to look at a painting with which I'd had a long, and troubled, relationship. "There – tell me what you see," I said, after sticking him in front of the portrait in question.

Bud leaned forward and read aloud, "'Thomas, 2nd Baron Mansel of Margam with his Blackwood Half-Brothers and Sister, by Allan Ramsay, painted in 1742, when the artist was…wow…not even thirty. A Scot, I see, and this is…ah, very funny. A Welshman? Is Margam near where you're from, Wife?"

"Come on Bud – look at the name…Baron Mansel. I'm from Manselton, Swansea. He's a forebear of the family who owned the land where my neighborhood was built. But let's not dwell on that. Other than a bloke with his two half-brothers and half-sister, what do you see?"

Bud stared. He bobbed about; I suspected he was looking for some sort of visual trick of the type I'd pointed out to him in the portrait at the National Gallery, though I knew there wasn't one. He stood back, leaned forward. Finally, he read the label again, then mused, "Hmm…portrait probably commemorates the children's mother. That's sad. Thomas Mansel. Half-brother Shovel and sister Mary, who was partially sighted. That must have been tough, in those days…though it looks like she was okay for money, which I guess would have made a difference. She's got her hand on a dead bird, and this reddish-brown mark is apparently part of the partridge's natural plumage. Okay – I love it that some poor kid was called 'Shovel', which I never imagined was a name, but nope, I give up. I see exactly what it says is there. Nothing more, nothing less. Though I think that rather good-looking dog should have got a mention. What am I missing?"

"I used to come here and get a bit nauseated by some of the art they have on display – a lot of the Victorian era stuff's a bit too chocolate-boxy for me. But then I started looking at things in a different way. Forgetting for a moment that this is an incredibly skillful piece, what used to intrigue and amuse me would be things like that little note. Would you agree with me that the main subject, Thomas, is clearly holding a gun?"

Bud nodded. "Looks like it to me – long, tubular, gunmetal color. I'd say so."

"And there speaks a man with decades of experience of firearms. Now take a look at that so-called natural part of the bird's plumage. To me that's always been obviously a shot to the heart of the bird."

Bud peered. "Yep, I'll give you that – though I have to admit I can't claim any expertise when it comes to the natural plumage of a partridge; I've only really seen them on Christmas cards…you know, when there's one stuck up a pear tree."

He mugged a smile and I replied, "Lovely Christmas-themed joke there, Husband. Good job. Now look at Thomas's face. I know it's 'just a painting' but isn't there something a little too 'knowing' about the way he's got that crooked smile, as he looks down at his step-sister. And if she's got a visual impairment, do you think she knows she's placed her hand on the bloody hole through the heart of a bird he's shot? I think he's a young man looking at a very young girl in an overtly sexual manner, and she's been 'hit in the heart', though she might not know it yet. It's always given me the creeps, that portrait."

Bud stood back. "Well, now you've explained it that way I can see what you mean. But, if that's what the artist intended, why doesn't the note about it say so?"

"Because art is subjective."

"As is your interpretation of it."

"Agreed. But my entire career in criminal psychology has been about interpreting what's overt, to give insight into the covert. And that's why I wanted you to see this. Because I disagree with the experts' interpretation of the painting, in the same way I disagree with the experts' interpretation of what's happening at Beulah House. There's a great big cover up going on, and I point the finger at Sir Simon for that. I've been mulling over my observations, trying really hard to not jump to conclusions, and believe that if only I could find out the answers to some key questions, I could make sense of it all."

"Questions like what, for example?"

"Well, one question that got answered was about the paper upon which Sasha's so-called suicide note was written. I honestly think it's just half of – or the last portion of – a letter she'd written for some entirely different purpose, and that fits with her having written it using paper found in her personal study, as opposed to paper found in the room from which she fell, jumped, or was pushed. You see, if I'm right about that, it points to a certain sort of mind at work here…"

Bud's phone rang, and quite a few heads turned. He answered it quickly, and we scuttled away so we didn't disturb people's silent enjoyment of the magnificent Hogarths in the room.

Bud mainly listened, his expression giving away very little. Eventually he said, "Whenever you want," at what was apparently the end of the call.

He whispered, "We've been summoned to Beulah House. Worthington wants us."

Outside, the snow was easing. As we stood on the kerb, each of us watching in a different direction for a cab with its light on, I asked, "Why are we needed? Did Worthington say?"

"No idea. It was Enderby. She said a lot, but communicated almost nothing. However, I sensed urgency in her tone, so there's that."

"…a stage, where every man must play a part…"

With a cabbie delighted to take us to our destination – because he wanted to get home to Croydon, south of London – Bud and I sat in comparative silence as we took our now almost-familiar route to Beulah House.

"Never been there myself, before today," the jolly cabbie told us as we got close. "Passed the Knowledge in three years, me, but there's still some places even I don't know."

Bud hissed, "What's he on about?"

"The exam all black cab drivers in London have to pass to be able to get a licence to drive one of these taxis," I replied. "It's rigorous – they have to know thousands of places, routes, junctions, streets – all to be able to navigate London, and get a fare to their destination by the shortest possible route."

"Why don't they just use GPS?"

"Not allowed. The Knowledge exams set these black cab drivers apart from mini-cab drivers. This type of cab is still properly called a Hackney Carriage, because a lot of the horses used to pull the original carriages were from Hackney. They were first licensed in 1654. The Knowledge was introduced back in 1865."

"You'd probably pass an exam like that in a couple of weeks, with your special memory," observed Bud, with a wink.

"Oh, I don't know, it could take months to drive all the routes you need to know and see it firsthand, once, to even be able to memorize the information you'd need. But, funnily enough, I did contemplate doing it when I was thinking about leaving the Townsend agency…but decided I'd be too nosey to be a decent driver, so reckoned I'd do better with a career in criminal psychology."

"I'm glad you did what you did," said Bud, as we swung into the drive, which was – surprisingly – deserted.

"Nice house," said our cabbie. "I'll add it to my list of secret places," he said, and waved as he left us.

"Have you any idea how much that trip just cost us, given the exchange rate?" Bud sounded horrified.

"A necessary expense," I said, as I rang the bell. "Wonder what's the other side of this door today."

Bud pulled me back from the top step. "I'll find out first," he replied.

To our amazement, Glen opened the door. "Hello. Come in." He sounded half asleep. I couldn't imagine what he was even doing there – nor why he'd be performing any housekeeping duties.

We hadn't received an update about his wife's condition, so I said, "We were sorry to hear about Julie. Is she…how's she doing?"

"Passed in the early hours. To be expected, they said. She never woke up, but at least I was with her at the end, thanks to Mr. Worthington." His eyes focused – they were bloodshot. "It's been the right thing for me to come here. To be near her things. But I can't deny it's difficult having to face Miss Felicity. I can't believe what she said about Julie, see? That's not my Julie she's talking about. Why would Miss Felicity want to hurt my Julie like that? Kill her. That's what I don't understand. And…and why's she here…in there, with that lot, instead of being locked up? I don't get it."

We'd stepped into the entry hall, and the salon was empty – indeed the house felt as though it were as deserted as the courtyard outside. The tiled floor echoed with our steps.

"Where is everyone, Glen?" Bud used his calming voice.

"After they took Mr. Charles away, they all went into the dining room and shut themselves in there. Without me. Asked me to wait here for you, and fetch you to them when you arrived. I'm surprised Miss Enderby hasn't come already – she must have heard the bell."

"Who took Charles away? To where? And why?" I asked.

"That black van from the coroner's office, that took Mrs. Tavistock." Glen seemed surprised by my question, then added, "Didn't they tell you? Isn't that why you're here?"

Bud and I shook our heads.

"Mr. Charles is dead, and Miss Bella says she's terrified she's going to be next. But they'll tell you all about it, I dare say. I'm going over to our flat, now. They've asked if I can get some clothes ready, for Julie, for when she goes to the undertakers, you know?"

I really didn't have the words to be able to speak to a man grieving for his wife, who'd apparently died after unleashing an unprovoked attack, killed by a woman sitting just a few yards away – so I rubbed his arm, and thanked him for greeting us. Glen led us to the dining room, knocked, and opened the door.

Worthington was seated at the head of the dining table, and he beckoned us inside. "Thanks, Glen. Let me know when you need a lift, okay? I'll sort it." Glen nodded and left. Felicity shuffled in her seat and cleared her throat.

At the opposite end of the table sat Sir Simon Pendlebury – but he was far from the dapper figure we'd met less than forty-eight hours earlier; his skin was papery and gray, he looked as though he'd lost ten pounds, his hair was matted in clumps, and his shirt looked as though he'd slept in it – which he might have done, for all I knew. John was at least better turned-out, in what was clearly a fresh set of clothes, though he looked drawn, with dark circles beneath his eyes. Felicity looked as though she'd been dragged through a hedge, backwards; smeared make-up spoke of tears, her hair was doing a good job of escaping from a topknot, and her clothes were looking less than fresh. Vinnie looked his usual perky self, and Bella looked…well, not like a woman in fear for her life. She was composed, well coiffed, and gazing serenely at John with something in her eyes that wasn't passion. *Proprietorial pride? Odd.*

Enderby was hovering behind Sir Simon; she moved to pull out a chair for me. She did the same for Bud, beside me. We took the offered seats. There was a notable absence of refreshments; this get-together was all business.

"Thanks for coming," said Worthington with an almost genuine, closed-mouth smile. "In case you haven't heard, Mr. Charles Asimov died this morning. In his bath."

Bud and I exchanged a glance.

"They've all gone, now," said Bella quietly. "Charles was convinced that something in this house meant him harm. And it seems he was right." She reached for John's hand. "I'm afraid I'm next." There was that Lady of Shallot look again.

John straightened his sagging torso. "Come on now, darling. You've nothing to worry about. I'll take care of you. And look, we've got Vinnie and Bud here too. No one's out to get you. This is your home. You're safe here."

Felicity snapped, "Sasha, Piers, and Charles weren't safe here. Why do you think any of us are? Charles was right – there's an aura in this place…an aura of death. It's everywhere. I nearly died here myself. Something's after our blood. Even Simon had a bad night of it here, you can't say he didn't." She was panting, wild-eyed, appearing to be truly terrified.

Sir Simon's voice had lost its blustering edge when he croaked, "On come on, Fliss. I picked up some sort of bug on my little jaunt yesterday. You're paranoid. There are no such things as ghosts, and this place hasn't got an aura. It's just a house." He turned his attention to Worthington. "I keep telling you chaps there's nothing to investigate here. It's just a terrible run of bad luck for the family. Sasha killing herself led to Piers needing to be medicated, and Charles probably dropped off in his bath; he was always either bouncing off the walls or half asleep. All this talk of ghosts is what got him so worked up that he just passed out with exhaustion, Fliss. Best you calm down and get yourself home. Which is what I plan to do as soon as my man is here with my car." He looked at his watch. "Which will be within the hour."

Worthington stood. "With all due respect, Sir Simon, there have been three deaths resulting from what any reasonable person would label 'unusual circumstances' at this property within the past two days, as well as a death resulting from injuries sustained during an attack at another location, involving two persons intimately linked with this house and family. There comes a point when even the most innocent-minded among us can no longer miss, or choose to ignore, the connections. This is not a litany of misfortune. Coincidence cannot be the underlying reason for all that's happened here."

His tone when addressing Sir Simon was respectful enough that I knew my belief that Sir Simon had shut down Worthington's initial investigation was correct. And I was even more convinced it had also been Sir Simon who'd caused questions to be raised about my reputation, too. With Piers dead, he'd shot to the top of my list of suspects alongside Felicity. But…what about Piers' death? Had Sir Simon been responsible for that, too? And what about Julie attacking Felicity? Or Charles's death? I sighed inwardly. I was going around in circles. Again.

As a means of calming my inner turmoil, I focused on assessing the body language of both Worthington and Pendlebury. I took account of the latter's compromised state of wellbeing, but could still tell I was watching a knight of the realm who was determined to have things happen the way he saw fit. His fists were clenched, his jaw set, the tiny muscles around his eyes twitching. He didn't like being told that the world was operating in a way contrary to his wishes, and that can be a tremendous motivation for…well, what was turning out to be quite the killing spree – if one person were responsible.

"But…" he began.

Worthington stepped away from his chair and spoke firmly, "There are no 'buts' on this occasion, Sir Simon. My superiors have assessed this is an investigation that must run its course, and it will be one that seeks to explain all the events of the past forty-eight hours."

Pendlebury folded his arms and sat back from the table…like a small boy determined to not eat his vegetables.

A feeble knock at the door led Miss Enderby to open it. Renata was standing outside, with Glen at her shoulder.

"Thank you for coming, Miss Douglas," said Worthington. "Please join us."

Renata moved with economy, and sat beside Bud, doing her best to disappear into the chair, an illusion aided by the fact her trouser suit more or less matched the mahogany. She hooked her bob behind one ear, and folded her hands on the table in front of her. She hadn't made eye contact with a soul, not even Worthington.

"Now that we have our full complement, I can tell you why you're all here," began Worthington. "I have been tasked with investigating the deaths of Sasha and Piers Tavistock, Charles Asimov, and Julie Powell." Felicity jerked in her seat, then settled herself, as best she could. I could see her knee bobbing up and down beneath the table. "You were all kind enough to furnish me with information about your activities for yesterday morning, but I now need to talk to you all, individually, to clarify some further details."

Sir Simon leaned forward and seemed to be about to speak, but clearly thought better of it, slumping back into his seat.

Worthington continued, "I shall use the meeting room to conduct my interviews, which will be recorded by Miss Enderby. I shall require everyone to remain here, and I ask you to be patient while this investigation runs its course." He took a moment to glance down at his phone, then returned his attention to our group. "Thank you all. The sooner I begin, the sooner I shall be finished."

He stood, and headed toward the meeting room, with Enderby in tow. He opened the door to take his leave, but turned and added, "I want no one discussing the events of the past couple of days with anyone here, before I have questioned them, or even afterwards. I hope that's absolutely clear. To everyone." He made a particular point to look at me when he spoke.

"I'll come and fetch people in turn," said Enderby before she closed the door behind them.

No one spoke. No one moved. It was as though we were all frozen, awaiting our fate.

Vinnie popped up out his seat. "Who's for a spot of lunch? If we all muck in, we could whip something up before you know it."

Felicity seemed to not have heard him, because she said, "If we're not allowed to talk about what's happened to us, what on earth else is there to talk about? I can't even think about anything other than this nightmare. I just want it all to stop so I can go home and…well, alright then, go to a hotel and put it all behind me."

"I'm sure you'd like nothing better," said Bella. "But how do you think I feel? In less than a month I've lost my father, my sister, my half-brother, my brother-in-law…and my housekeeper. My entire family is dead."

"We're all at the end of our tethers, darling," said John. "I'm sure Felicity can't fathom what you're going through." He glared at Felicity. "Look at poor Bella – she's numb with grief. Don't you understand?"

"I could whip up some sandwiches again," suggested Vinnie. He sounded a little too perky for the situation.

"Thank you, but I couldn't possibly face anything," said Sir Simon, looking nauseous at even the thought of food. "But maybe a pot of tea?"

"All over it, like cat hairs on a spinster," said Vinnie, and he took himself off to the kitchen.

I was livid; there was an investigation taking place in which I had no role to play, and I'd been told – in clear terms – to not ask anything of anyone that could help me lift the veil that was clouding my understanding of what was really going on at the house. I ran through ways I could glean information from the people around the table without appearing to do so, then had an idea.

I stood. "Just off to…you know," I said. Bud looked at me with a little concern; he always tells me I'm a terrible liar, and it appeared my inability to mislead him had failed, again.

"I won't be long," I added as I left.

I wasn't sure how to get to my destination, but headed out into the entry hall, used the door Julie and Glen always used to get into the outer hallway, then stopped: there was only one door I hadn't tried so far, so judged that must be the one I needed, because there had to be a way to get to Glen and Julie's flat that involved stairs, and John had told Bud there was a servants' staircase.

I crept along the hall, past the meeting room – hoping Enderby wouldn't pop out all of a sudden – and reached the back door. I turned the knob of the door beside it, which opened easily, and silently. I did my best to be as quiet as possible as I climbed the carpeted stairs to what I hoped would be the Powells' living quarters. I could hear a doleful air being sung, by a voice cracked with grief. I knocked, quietly, on the door at the top of the stairs, and waited, peering along the corridor which led away to the main house – yes, I'd found the servants' stairs alright.

When Glen appeared, it was clear he'd been crying. It was understandable, of course, but he graciously invited me in in any case. I was relieved.

He waved me into a long, narrow space; at one end was a small sitting room, at the other a small kitchen. The esthetic was surprising – minimalist almost explained it, but purist would have been closer to the mark. Each piece of furniture had a purpose, and its form was high mid-century modern. The walls were sparkling white, there were few adornments in the space, and the kitchen was a stark arrangement of utility. I was surprised, because I'd expected something more...homey.

"Thanks Glen. You have a lovely flat."

"All Julie, this. Loved this sort of thing, she did. Knew her stuff, too. That sideboard is by some Danish bloke. Or was he from Finland?"

"Finn Juhl, from Denmark. He more or less sent everyone else who was designing modern furniture at the time in the direction of using teak."

Glen's face lit up, "That's right. That's him. Funny you should have heard of him. He was one of Julie's favorites."

I was thrilled I'd found a connection, but knew I didn't have time for idle chatter. "Look, I hate to bother you, Glen, but I wondered if I could just ask you a couple of things about Julie..."

Glen didn't seem to hear me. "Since you're here – and I know you didn't really know her, but you're a woman – would you mind taking a look at a few things I've pulled out of the wardrobe for her? Give me your opinion…for…you know."

Glen had already opened the door to a small bedroom, which housed a bed, wardrobe, and dressing table that, between them, would, I estimated, have cost the better part of forty thousand Canadian dollars. I was amazed. Maybe Julie had been a whiz at spotting bargains at junk shops and jumble sales? The bed was covered with clothes.

Glen picked up a suit with a lavender jacket and toning floral skirt. "Had this made for her niece's wedding, she did. Cost an arm and a leg. Found it difficult to get clothes that would fit top and bottom, see, so had them made by a woman she knew in Streatham. She only wore this the once, though; didn't think the color flattered her. So maybe not?"

He sounded as though he really needed help, so I threw myself into the role. "If she didn't like it too much, maybe not. What was the thing Julie wore most often?"

Glen chuckled. "That's easy, that is. 'My old frock'." He picked up a red shift dress, almost the same shape as the black one she'd been wearing when I'd first arrived at Beulah House. "That's what she always called it, see? 'My old frock'. She'd wear it if we went out for dinner, or even down the pub. She'd be in here putting things on, and taking them off again, then she'd come out wearing this and say, 'Nothing for it, Glen, but for me to wear my old frock again.' And she'd laugh, and I would too."

I smiled. "I think maybe that would be what she'd choose then, don't you? It sounds as though she really liked it – and it also sounds as though it was with her on lots of special occasions. How about that one?"

Glen caressed the dress as he said, "She had a lipstick that matched it perfect, and she always wore a bit of scent, too. No scent allowed in the house, at work, of course, but she liked to dab it on her wrists before we went out anywhere. Would they put scent on her, do you think? At the undertakers. If I asked."

"I'm sure they would, Glen."

His face creased into a broad grin. "Good, she'd like that. Now you ask whatever you want while I find her bits and bobs."

He sat at the dressing table and started fiddling about, so I took my chance.

"I wondered if you had any idea why Julie—"

He didn't turn, but addressed my reflection in the mirror. "No, I bloody well don't. And I don't even believe she did what they say she done. There's no way she'd attack anyone, even if she didn't like Miss Felicity. She's no better than she should be, that woman. Spent her whole life flaunting herself in the papers, she has, and made Mr. Asimov's life a right misery when they were married, by all accounts. Dragging him around the place to go to parties with her silly friends. He needed to be working, but all she wanted was to spend his money. Mrs. T was the one who took it all in the neck, of course. There she was running her business, and her father always coming here and ranting about how Miss Felicity wouldn't leave him alone even though they was divorced. He used to sit in that dining room and the stories he would tell. He gave her money all the time – Julie and I knew that, because we'd hear Mr. and Mrs. T talking about it. Thousands, whenever she asked for it. Mr. Oleg must have had more money than sense. There was that time he bought her a car, and then another time she wanted to do up her flat, and he just put his hand in his pocket and paid out for it. Mrs. T told him he shouldn't keep doing it, but Julie said he'd told Mrs. T off because she didn't understand. Miss Bella had no real idea about it all. Never came into the big house when her father was here – talk about oil and water...those two never were in the same room as each other, as far as we knew, anyway. And then when he died, Miss Bella went potty about him, she did."

He stopped sniffing the lipstick in his hand and drew breath. I took my chance. "Any idea why?"

He tutted. Loudly. "Look, it was Mrs. T what took us in, and it's her who pays our wages. Not Miss Bella. Has as little to do with us as possible, she does, until she needs something. Then Mrs. T would ask us to help out, see? No idea why, because Lord knows they might be twins, but those two women were so unlike each other in every way it's hard to believe they're even from the same family, sometimes. Never a kind word for anyone, Miss Bella, not unless they're standing right in front of her, then she's all sweet as honey, ain't she? Now there's a woman who had no truck with Miss Felicity – not only did Miss Bella never have a good word to say about her, she had quite a few choice ones, on occasion. Like I say, I don't think she knew her father was paying Miss Felicity's way as much as he was, but I know for a fact Mrs. T talked to her about it in general terms. Julie heard them shouting and going on about it…things like 'paying up', and that 'a woman should pay her own way'. Poor Mrs. T – she was a martyr to her nerves, she was. Always having a bad stomach, and Julie having to clear up after her. Worst before she had big client things to do, I think. And Miss Bella being so wrapped up in her gold and stuff, out in that workshop all hours, she was. I have no idea how she could spend so much time out there. It's a terrible place – cold, and damp, even though she's got that fire thing going out there half the time. What's it called now? Oh, never mind. Anyway, gives off a lot of heat, that thing, but otherwise the place is like a fridge."

I leaped in with, "I understand Bella and Felicity had a row on the phone the other morning."

Glen nodded. "Oh, you heard about that did you? Not surprised. Miss Bella could have woken the dead. Julie was…where was she now? Oh, I don't know – doing the beds, I should think, at that time of day. Anyway, Mr. T was a bit quieter because the doctor had just gone, and Mr. Charles was back in his bedroom – so maybe she wasn't doing the beds, after all…but she wasn't in the kitchen, in any case, because that's where I was. And I hear Miss Bella screaming down the phone, 'Not blinkin' likely, Felicity, you won't leech off me, I'm not my blinkin' father.' Only she didn't say 'blinkin', you know? And then she was off about how she could get everyone to be talking about some woman called Jocasta – was it? – if she wanted to, because of what she'd seen, and then about how she knew Felicity was just out to become what she called 'The Empress of Asimov', and how she knew she'd…um…sleep her way to it eventually, only she didn't say 'sleep'. You know. She was very angry, and said she wasn't going to play any part in it, so Felicity could forget about her getting the center after all. She didn't say the center of what. I told Julie about it all later on – but I don't think she was listening to me proper 'cos she was pulling the kitchen apart looking for her best knife that had gone missing…her favorite one for when she was making stew, and that's what she had planned for dinner later on. And then she was called in to see Miss Bella for a while. Goodness knows what they were talking about. She didn't tell me, but I guessed they had to have a chat about the plans for the housekeeping and so forth, because of Mrs. T being dead, you know. Then…then Julie weren't here no more. I wish…I wish I could remember what it was I said to her last. I can't recall it at all. One minute she was there, then she wasn't. They say she went over to Miss Felicity's and had a go at her, and then Miss Felicity done for her. And here we are, now. See? I don't understand it."

"The knife was missing? Which knife? The one they say Julie used to attack Felicity?"

"They haven't told me nothing about what knife it was Miss Felicity used on my girl…but it can't have been Julie's knife, because it weren't there."

A knife that wasn't there? What was so familiar about that concept? What else hadn't been...where? I knew it was significant that there hadn't been any writing paper at all in the palace room...so what else...was I trying to recall? That was it!

I had a vision of the smokers' table in the palace room...when I'd seen it I'd known something was wrong with it, but it was only when Glen mentioned the missing knife that it dawned on me. "Like the ashtray," I said.

Glen's brow furrowed. "What ashtray?"

"The one in the palace room. There's a smokers' table up there, with everything a smoker might need, except for an ashtray."

Glen's entire face screwed up. "There's definitely an ashtray up there, for Mr. T's cigars. Big cut-crystal thing it is. Weighs a ton. Mrs. T used it when she smoked up there too, but it was Mr. T's to start with. Had it as a presentation gift he did from...somewhere, I forget, now. Something to do with some client or other. Waterford crystal, it is. You say it's gone?"

I nodded.

"Oh dear." Glen sighed. "Well, I don't suppose it matters now, does it? Both Mr. and Mrs. T have gone too, and Miss Bella won't be using it. Very much against smoking, she is. Though she makes enough of a stink down in her workshop. Probably does herself just as much harm down there, if the truth be known."

Glen pushed a bottle of perfume into the carrier bag he had balanced on his knees.

"Make sure you bring that back with you, Glen," I said. "You'll find a quick spray of that will help you remember Julie, whenever you want. Smell is one of our most powerful senses when it comes to trying to recollect something, or someone. Even the smell of her lipstick reminds you of her, doesn't it?"

Glen's brow furrowed. "What makes you think I'll need this scent to remember her? She was my life. My whole life. I'll never forget her. If I close my eyes I can see every line of her face, every curl of her hair, and I can hear her voice as clear now as if she was standing in the doorway, telling me to get a move on. None of that will fade. It can't."

He spoke with conviction, and I realized it wasn't my place to disabuse him of his certainty.

He stood. "Look it's been a real help, chatting like this. And I'm ever so grateful for the advice about the frock, but I should be going, now. I said I'd be back there this afternoon. So, if there's nothing else…"

I also stood, so he'd know I was about to leave. "There is just one more thing…is there any reason you can think of for Felicity wanting to hurt your wife? You see, if we accept that Julie didn't attack her – why might Felicity have wanted to do her harm?"

Glen stared into the carrier bag, then snapped his gaze to meet mine. "That's easy. Miss Felicity didn't forgive Julie for telling Mr. Asimov about the affair she was having behind his back."

"I thought you and Julie hadn't been working here when Oleg and Felicity were married…and, anyway, they didn't live here as a couple, did they?"

Glen looked surprised. "No, we weren't, and no, they didn't, but Julie knew Mrs. T's mother, you see, years ago, so had come to meet Mr. Oleg too, through her. So, when Miss Felicity started knocking around with that rugby player who drank at the pub where Julie worked, well…Julie saw them, and felt she should tell poor Mr. Oleg. Which she did. Then he divorced Miss Felicity, and I think Miss Felicity found out all about it quite recently. See, the last time she was here – right after Mr. Oleg's funeral, that is – she was horrible to Julie, and poor Julie hadn't done anything to deserve it, so we guessed she must have found out about what Julie did. Miss Felicity went to see Mr. Oleg in the hospice just before he died, so maybe he told her then. They say folks do some strange things when they know they're going to die. I'm not sure what good that does. Maybe they want to meet their maker with a clear conscience." A sigh rattled his entire body. "Oh my poor Julie. She was a good woman. She'll not have any trouble at the Pearly Gates, she won't. They'll be glad to let her in."

All I could muster was, "I'm sure they will, Glen. Thanks, for your time. I'm sorry to have kept you. Will you...will you be alright?" As I asked the question, I knew how stupid it was.

"You've been very kind, but I'll be honest and tell you that, no, I'll never be alright again. Julie was my everything. She saved me. That's not too much to say. And now...I can't see a way forward. I can't imagine Miss Bella will have any use for me here. With all her lot gone this'll be her place now, and I dare say your friend, Mr. John, will come to live here with her. Which will be good, because the old place needs people in it to stay alive. Julie and I rented a little flat in Streatham Hill before we moved in here, so I suppose I'll have to try to find somewhere just for myself, now. But there, Miss Bella's always wanted this house to be hers, so now at least she's got her wish. Funny how everything always turns out alright for her in the end."

"But I was told Bella chose to live in the coach house after her mother's death, rather than the main house, even before Sasha and Piers moved in."

Glen shook his head. "No, I know for a fact she lived in the big house after her mother died. Then she moved out so they could move in. It weren't no secret." He leaned toward me. "I'm not speaking ill of the dead when I tell you this – and I wouldn't speak ill of Mrs. T in any case, because if Julie saved me, then Mrs. T saved the pair of us – but they had no choice but to sell the place they was living in before. Needed the money quick sharpish, they did. Must have been for the company, Julie always said, but I didn't know about that. They lived well all the time they was here, but not in a flashy way. Worked hard, too, they did – but never seemed to have a lot to spare, if you know what I mean. Not like some who go spending loads of money on all sorts of rubbish. Don't know where it all went, to be honest with you, because Mrs. T was always all over Julie to keep the housekeeping costs down. But there…"

Glen had been gradually shuffling toward the bedroom door, herding me toward it, and it was clear he was telling me it was time to go, so I left, creeping past the meeting room, where I was sorely tempted to stop and listen.

"...what's past is prologue..."

"Good grief, where've you been? We were starting to worry you'd flushed yourself down the loo," said Felicity when I entered the salon. She looked me up and down and muttered under her breath, "Not that you'd fit."

Vinnie's voice floated from the kitchen, "Scrambled eggs on toast for you, Cait?"

I debated the wisdom of having scrambled eggs for a late lunch having already eaten an omelette for breakfast, so wandered in to find Bud standing at the kitchen island, with Vinnie clattering pots about the place. "There isn't anything else on the go, is there?" I asked, flashing my cute smile.

Vinnie grinned. "Baked beans on toast? Sausage sandwich? Bacon butty? It seems Julie Powell shopped for fresh food often – so there's not a lot on offer, because...well, she's not been shopping, has she? I'm guessing from what's here that she cooked a full breakfast now and again, and it looks like there's half the world's cheese supply in the fridge too – maybe there was a cheese and wine do on the cards? No idea. But I could rustle up a—"

"If that's proper British back bacon, I'd love a bacon butty," I said. "It's not easy to get that cut at home."

"Brown or red sauce?"

"Tut, tut, Vinnie, brown, of course."

Vinnie pulled at a non-existent forelock, and headed to the fridge.

"And where have you been, exactly?" Bud whispered.

"Talking to Glen," I replied.

"About?"

"Guess."

"Despite Worthington's formal warning?"

"Glen wasn't there when he warned us, so wasn't included." I didn't even blush as I answered.

"What can we do with you, Cait?"

I hugged my husband. "Just love me," I replied. "Right, I'm going to join the others."

"Be…careful," said Bud.

I mugged a salute, and wandered to the hearth, from where I could see everyone. Sir Simon had commandeered an entire sofa and was on the phone; he seemed to have a little more color about him. Felicity had tidied up her make-up and was examining her manicure as she relaxed in a fireside seat. Renata sat upright on a straight-backed chair, rather like a small girl would in church, her hands on her knees; she was looking out of the window to the garden, where I could see the snow had settled. Bella was pink-faced, and perched on the edge of the chair nearest the fire, which was roaring. John was nowhere to be seen; I assumed it was his turn to be grilled by Worthington.

"He looks like a man who knew what he wanted," I said to Bella, directing her attention to the portrait of her late father above the mantle. She wasn't the only one who looked up. "Sometimes men who know what they want from life can be difficult to live with," I added.

"I'm the one who knew how difficult he was to live with, not her. Those two were hardly ever under the same roof, were you?" Felicity's voice was sharp.

Bella smiled. "Oh, I don't know. He wasn't at home very much when I was small, of course, and then I was at school. But there were always the hols, growing up."

"Which you spent with your mother, not your father. Except for that one she took with just Sasha — I heard that was to somewhere in the wilds of Wales." Felicity rolled her eyes in my direction. "Did Mummy leave you alone and give all her attention to your big sister one time?" Felicity was sounding shrew-like.

Bella looked at me sadly as she said, "Daddy was a man who had a great deal to put up with during his life." Only then did she return her gaze to Felicity.

"I know he had a deep fascination with, and love for, Shakespeare's plays, so is he the one who accumulated all the artwork around the house?" I asked because I was curious about why it had all remained, even though he'd left.

Bella smiled wistfully as she cast her gaze around the salon. "Yes, Daddy was highly...acquisitive. He created this collection for this house, which is why we still have it. I have to say I find much of it to be far too theatrical to live with happily. I'll try to find a museum, or some sort of organization connected to Shakespeare in some way, so they can have it."

Renata's head snapped up. "There's a great deal of money tied up in it all. You should have a proper valuation carried out before you gift it to anyone, or choose to sell it. After all, you might be glad of the income."

I thought this an incredibly odd thing for Renata to say, but Bella didn't seem to be at all fazed. Her, "I dare say you're right," was spoken in an accepting tone, with no hint of surprise.

"Renata might well be correct," I said. "I can see that's a print of the Edwin Austin Abbey portrayal of Lear banishing Cordelia, over there –" I waved my arm in the direction of the print in question – "but I think there are a couple of originals here by him too. Do you happen to know how your father managed to acquire them?"

Bella stood, and stretched out her back. "Oh, you mean the one of Hamlet, and the other one of Lady Macbeth? Yes, they're originals. Daddy's pride and joy. There's also a magnificent piece in the main bedroom. He didn't say who he bought them from but, of course, he was attracted by the subject matter, and it's rumored the artist stayed at this house, on occasion, when he lived in England. Abbey spent a lot of time with Millais and Sargent, you know? Oh, and we have some illustrations he did, upstairs, too. Daddy kept the best stuff out of the public spaces."

As Bella was speaking I became aware that, other than the palace room, and the main bedroom – which had been pretty dark at the time – I hadn't seen the rest of the upstairs. However, I decided to keep going on the track I was following, rather than miss this chance.

"Other than his love of Shakespeare, and his support for taking his plays into schools, did you get to see lots of productions, when you were growing up, Bella?" I asked.

Again that wistful smile. "Of course. We were fortunate. Lots of trips with Daddy to Stratford-upon-Avon –" she glanced at Felicity, whose attention was now focused on rubbing some sort of lotion onto her hands from a small bottle she'd produced from her giant handbag – "and Sasha, Daddy, Mummy, and I would sit just here, beside the fire, and read the plays aloud, all playing different parts, you know?" I nodded. She looked up at the portrait of her father. "Daddy was Lear, of course, Sasha would read Goneril – because she was ten minutes older than me – and I would read Regan. Mummy was always Cordelia." She paused, then added, "Which wasn't at all fair, because I was the youngest and I always loved him the most."

I hesitated for no more than a few seconds before I said, "But he didn't banish you, did he? And he certainly didn't lose his mind and go running around the blasted heath."

Felicity's laugh was explosive, and cruel. "Oh yes he did – when Bella and Sasha were in their late teens, Oleg began to stray, and he met Charles's mother, which led to a desperately bitter divorce – which Bella's mother would have claimed to be ample evidence of him losing his mind. And he convinced her to pack Bella off to university. I know Bella 'said' she couldn't wait to leave home to be able to begin her studies in those interviews she gave to the Sunday supplements when her Zoloto brand was being launched, but I'm equally aware that Sasha's the one who wrote those pieces, not Bella. Of course they'd have been designed to make Bella look as good as possible, because that's what PR people do for their clients, isn't it? But at least Bella was able to come back to her darling Beulah House, weren't you? To her precious smithy in the garden." Felicity took a final look at her hands, which glistened red in the firelight, then stared directly at Bella. "This is where she's been ever since, and now, of course, she'll never have to leave…even when she gets her man."

A thought struck me. "Do you fire gold here on the property? I'm guessing it needs to be brought to extremely high temperatures. Is that safe?"

Bella beamed. "I create artisanal pieces, so, yes, I work on every aspect of the piece right here. I get my gold from people who belong to international networks supported by those who help them earn a living through mining without damaging themselves, or the planet. Then I do some final refining work on it when I get it, so I can create pieces to my exact requirements. It's wonderful to be absolutely in control." He eyes shone as she spoke.

"But isn't it dangerous to have to heat gold so you can work it?" I pressed.

"Not at all. I've done it for years, so I'm quite used to it by now. Of course, one must employ all the appropriate safety measures, but a good crucible and a trustworthy source of heat is all one really needs. And it's worth the extra step, to ensure that what one creates is exactly what one wants." As Bella spoke, her eyes lifted, so it looked as though she were speaking to her dead father.

"How long's that man going to keep us here?" Sir Simon had finished his telephone call. He peered into the kitchen, spotted Bud and Vinnie, and hoisted himself out of his seat to join them. He rubbed his belly as he moved. "Almost nothing of me left," he said – his observation being almost ridiculously inaccurate.

With us women in the salon, and the men in the kitchen, it felt as though some weird dinner party was playing out; the fact there was another of our number currently being questioned by an investigator of dubious origin wasn't lost on me, but it seemed to be on my companions, all of whom looked…well, bored was what I saw – but that seemed so inappropriate, under the circumstances.

Since I wasn't allowed to ask about the events of the past couple of days, I decided to try to find out more about the Asimov family, so said, "Was running your father's group of companies not something that ever interested you or your siblings, Bella?"

Bella leaned forward in her seat. "I admit to a passing interest in architecture, but I think that stemmed from my artistic tendencies. Sasha certainly would have had the head for it, but I don't think she fancied all the grubbiness that would have accompanied such a profession. As for Charles, well he wouldn't have wanted to do anything that would have taken him away from the ladies, and you don't find too many of them on your average building or demolition site, or at the local dump."

"Did that upset your father? That the family business might not continue, after him."

Bella looked surprised. "No danger of that. We were all summoned, individually, to his death bed and told how things would be, after he'd gone. I hadn't seen him in…some time, so was surprised to be included. He'd put a succession plan in place;

as Sir Simon explained the other evening, he's the new chairman of the board of directors, and he'll oversee everything. Sasha was to have been an executive director, as were Charles, and I – the family shares were split three ways, between us. It will continue to be a going concern. Though I don't know what Sir Simon's plans are for it, I dare say I'll agree with them."

"Typical of you, Bella," sniped Felicity. "It's all about John and the house for you now. And the gold, of course. Always the gold."

For a woman who was dripping with the stuff, I thought Felicity was being incredibly off-hand about Bella's realm of endeavor, and achievement.

"You've been glad enough to wear and gift pieces I've created for you, Felicity," replied Bella coolly.

"John showed me the medallion you gave him," I said. "It's beautiful." I wondered how she'd react: did she know the piece was no longer adorning her mate's chest, but in my handbag?

Bella looked coy. "I didn't know he'd shown anyone, but it's nice to know he's proud enough of it to do so. I was just saying when I was looking at it this morning that it needs a good cleaning – gold stands up to everything, forever, but it doesn't like some of the perfumed products he uses."

I was puzzled: if John had been wearing his medallion that morning, whose was it I had found in the bin in the kitchen the day before?

"He told me it's a one-off," I added.

Another coy look accompanied her reply. "He's the only person who really deserves it." She shot a puzzlingly venomous glance toward Felicity.

Sir Simon wandered in to join us. "Did I hear my name mentioned a moment ago? Not being taken in vain, I hope."

"I was just talking about your new role overseeing Daddy's businesses," replied Bella.

Felicity yawned, dramatically, while Renata sat very still, grasping her knees.

"Ah yes, I'm looking forward to it. Not that I would have wished that end on anyone, least of all old Oleg, but he was right to talk to me about taking the reins when he did; we had the chance for some meaty discussions about his plans for the future. Speaking of which, we'll need to talk, at some point, Bella, but not until…well, you know…all this is behind us. Though we can't wait too long – those contracts need to be signed very soon…" He paused and drew breath, rubbing his chest as he did so. "Sorry. I know now's not the time." Sir Simon sagged, visibly, then clutched his stomach. "I think I'm going to be sick again!" He ran in the direction of the WCs in the entry hall.

"Has he been seen by a doctor?" I asked.

Felicity replied quietly, "The doctor who came to…to see about Charles took a look at him. He said Simon had probably managed to get himself poisoned by something he ate. Of course, he couldn't tell the doctor everything he'd eaten and drunk, because goodness knows the man shoves anything into his face without paying any attention. It's why he's so…" Felicity paused and turned, as we all did, when we heard a crash.

Bud and Vinnie flew out of the kitchen.

"Hallway WC," I called, and they headed off, with me right behind them.

Sir Simon was lying on the tiled floor in the entryway, his face puce, his groans loud, and his body writhing.

"I'm calling an ambulance," said Vinnie, pulling out his phone. "Bud, go and tell Worthington what's happened – just in case he's got some way to get one here quicker than I can."

Bud shot off toward the meeting room.

"Can someone bring a pillow over here," I called, as I tried to support Sir Simon's head; he kept banging himself on the tiles.

Renata arrived with a cushion, which I put to good use.

"He was fine just a moment ago," said Felicity, sounding panicked, as she joined our throng.

Bella stood beside the fireplace, as though she were attached to it. "I'm sure he'll be okay," she called.

Worthington, John, Enderby, and Bud all arrived together.

Worthington was on the phone. "I'm taking advice from a paramedic now," he announced. "Keep his airway clear, loosen any tight clothing, keep him warm, try to stop him hitting his head, check for any pharmaceuticals he's ingested and have them here when the ambulance arrives. Got it." He hung up, but made it clear he was in control. "They're on their way. Who knows how to get in touch with the doctor who saw him this morning?" He looked around and spotted Bella raising her hand. "Good, get hold of him – I want to speak to him, pronto." Bella nodded and pulled a phone from her pocket. Worthington continued to speak loudly enough for everyone to hear him. "Where did this man spend the night?"

John replied, "In the blue bedroom, upstairs."

Worthington nodded, and looked at Enderby. "Go there, gather anything that belongs to Sir Simon, and check the bedroom and bathroom thoroughly for anything he might have ingested." She ran up the stairs.

"What's he eaten here, today?" Worthington barked.

Vinnie replied, "Nothing, that I know of. He said he wasn't up to it, couldn't face so much as a bite. He had a cup of tea in the kitchen a while back. Had it out of the same pot as Bud and me." He looked at Bud. "You feeling alright?" Bud nodded. "Me too."

"You suspect poison?" I was pretty sure I knew the answer.

"We can't rule anything out," snapped Worthington.

Sir Simon stopped groaning and thrashing. It wasn't a good sign. Worthington felt for a pulse. "Damn it! Right, everyone stand back." We all did, as he began to perform live-saving measures. He kept going until the ambulance arrived, but it was no use.

Sir Simon Pendlebury was pronounced dead a few moments later. Worthington stepped aside, his expression grim. "Everyone into the salon, please. I'll deal with this."

To say the mood was one of disbelief would be an understatement.

John went to sit with Bella, Vinnie paced around the perimeter of the room, Renata retook the seat she'd been in before, and Felicity flopped onto a sofa. Bud grabbed my hand and pulled me toward the French doors. "Just getting some air," he announced.

Once we were outside he hugged me close, and spoke quietly. "Every time we get together in that salon, there's fewer of us," hissed Bud.

"No need to tell me that," I hissed back, "it's terrifying. If Sir Simon was poisoned, as Worthington suspects – where did the poison come from?"

Bud shrugged. "No idea – but I'm not going to have so much as a glass of water here from now on, and nor should you." I nodded my agreement. "Good," he said, with finality.

"Worthington's keeping his cool incredibly well," I observed. "He's now overseeing five deaths, either here or connected to this family, with only Enderby's help. Surely he needs backup? Why don't they send more people? Whoever 'they' might be."

Bud sighed. "No idea. Not certain what's going on, who's calling the shots. But if people keep dropping like flies around here, there'll be some serious repercussions, you can be sure of that. Especially if it was – as we suspect – Sir Simon who was doing all the string-pulling to get the investigation into Sasha's death shut down."

"But why?" I said.

"Why what?"

"Why any of it? There can't be any one person who benefits from all these deaths. I admit I had Piers marked as the most likely to have killed Sasha, and could see his death as a guilt-ridden suicide. But is there any way he could have killed Sir Simon – from beyond the grave? I don't think so. And that suicide note…that was always a bit too clever for him."

"Piers didn't leave a note," said Bud.

I sighed. "I know. Which is not exactly unusual – we both know that not all those who choose to end their own life leave an explanation. I mean the note that he identified as having been written by his wife."

Bud's brow wrinkled. "It was too clever? I don't understand."

"Sasha's death? For an attacker to make her murder look like a suicide, they'd have to be clever, or at least cunning, to come up with the idea of using part of a letter written for another purpose as a suicide note."

Bud nodded. "That's true. And Piers wasn't the brightest light bulb in the box, was he? Sir Simon, on the other hand, was pretty sharp."

"And yet they're both dead – which isn't the best way of remaining at the top of a list of murder suspects."

"You've not found out anything else that might be useful, then?" Bud was almost pleading.

I sighed away my frustration. "No, not really."

Bud raked his hand through his hair. "There's something we're not seeing, Cait," he said.

"I'll grant you I haven't done terribly well, so far, in lining up suspects, and I believe we have to consider the only viable candidates are those who…well, aren't dead. There's not 'something' we're not seeing, there's a heck of a lot we're not seeing," I replied. "And I know who might be able to help – if only he would choose to do so. I'm going to take another run at Worthington."

"Not without me, you're not," replied Bud.

"You're right – we're better as a team. Though I wonder if, this time, and even as a team, we stand any chance of working this all out? We're not infallible, and we're not omnipotent – this could be the time we fall flat on our faces, or worse."

"Go Team?" Bud mugged a smile, and feebly punched the air.

"...*to be, or not to be...*"

I suspected the blokes who drove the unmarked van that took away Sir Simon's body must have been placing bets on when they'd be back at Beulah House to pick up their next "passenger". However, once they'd left, the house seemed to settle into the evening almost as though nothing had happened. Maybe, given its age, the loss of life it had witnessed was just a blip in its history, that might end up being referred to only briefly in any future account of its existence.

The humans rattling around inside Beulah House were another matter; there's no way people can experience as many losses as we all had and not be impacted by it. The person most directly affected was, of course, Bella, though she was the one who seemed to be coping best. She was calm, almost regal, with John her doting servant, whereas Felicity was more than a little eager to be allowed to leave, and Renata kept pointing out that Tavistock and Tavistock needed to put out a news release that dealt with the sudden absence of its two managing partners. Vinnie was pacing in the kitchen – having run out of things to cook, or clear away.

I spotted Worthington sending Enderby scurrying out to the meeting room, and decided to take my chance.

Sidling up to him in the entry way I said quietly, "I'd like to have a word, in private, please."

I was dismissed with a sharp, "Not now. Calls to make," and he followed Enderby.

"Anybody fancy a cuppa?" Vinnie sounded more cheerful than I could have imagined possible.

"You're kidding. Nothing passes my lips until I'm out of this place," replied Felicity, "even if that means I starve to death." She looked horrified when she realized what she'd said.

"It's perfectly safe here," retorted Bella, more sharply than I'd expected.

"Of course it is," added Renata.

"How about when this is all over, we three girls meet up again and have a giggle about it all over a cocktail, somewhere – eh? Not likely." Felicity folded her arms and stared into the dying fire.

"I'd like a cuppa, please, Vinnie," replied Bella. "And I'm sure John would, too."

"Absolutely," replied John, who was actually sitting at her feet. "Want a hand?"

"I think I can manage, thanks," replied Vinnie, who already had the kettle under the tap.

Felicity left her seat and wandered aimlessly, ending up at the French doors. She flicked a switch, and lights illuminated part of the garden. "Everything's frozen out there tonight – look, even the rill has backed up."

John said, "The rill's been frozen since Tuesday morning. The temperature must have dropped overnight on Monday. It's been solid ever since. But that must have happened before – the rill won't be damaged forever, will it, Bella?"

Bella seemed to be a million miles away, then stiffened. "The rill? What about the rill?"

"It's frozen solid. Is the pump underground?" John peered at Bella, concern creasing his brow...more due to her seeming lack of focus than any real concern for an electrical pump, I judged.

"I have no idea about pumps," she replied. "The rill hardly ever freezes, as I recall. It's so bitterly cold this year. But please,

Felicity, don't fuss over things that are none of your business." Bella's voice was brittle.

"I wasn't making a fuss. I just noticed it and mentioned it." Felicity pouted. "Seems I can't say anything without getting my head bitten off. Typical." She turned off the outside lights, and flounced toward the kitchen, where she opened the fridge door and peered inside. "Did Simon eat nothing at all today?"

Vinnie replied, "Not a sausage. Nor anything else, neither." He mugged a grin, but Felicity just shut the fridge door and walked toward the bow window in the dining room.

"I shall miss Charles and Simon terribly," she said. It was the first time I'd heard an expression of grief or loss pass her lips.

"Sasha and Piers too," said Renata.

"And Julie," added Vinnie.

Felicity stared daggers at him.

"Professor Morgan, if you please." Enderby had summoned me.

Felicity stamped her foot. "I'm never leaving this damned place, am I?" She spun to glare out of the dining-room window into the blackness of the invisible garden beyond.

Bud called, "Good luck," as I marched toward the meeting room; I was determined to make this chance count, to make Worthington take me seriously.

At least he didn't ignore me when I entered the meeting room. He stood, in a gentlemanly manner, until I took a seat, then retook his. "Thank you for coming," he said.

I couldn't help but laugh. "You're joking, right? First of all, what choice do I have? Secondly, I want to help as much as I can. And, thirdly – you know very well I have questions to which I'm sure you have the answers, and I truly believe I could help you even more than you might imagine, if only you would choose to be open with me."

Worthington said nothing.

Neither did I.

"Same terms as before?" His voice was low.

"Bud and I are as one," I replied. "I'm happy to take things forward without him being present, but I reserve the right to tell my husband anything you tell me. But only him. I agree to that."

Worthington stood and began to pace along his side of the table. "To start with, I shall be open and honest about this. I have read your files. I understand the work you've done in Canada for the police service there. I have been told by those who should know that you are a valuable asset. But I just don't know if it's best for me to involve you in this."

"What do you mean? I'm already involved."

Worthington threw the glance I now recognized as characteristic of the man – direct, and challenging. "It's understandable you'd think that, but there's a great deal you don't know. If I allow you insights into my investigations – well, that's where we're on tricky ground. Politically speaking."

"Was Sir Simon the one who went over your head to shut down your investigation into Sasha's death?"

"If I answer that question, with anything but this response, I would already have made the decision to give you information you currently don't possess."

"I'll take that as a yes," I replied.

Worthington's eyes flashed. "No, you may not take that as a 'yes', Professor Morgan. Nor may you take it as a 'no'. It was a very specific non-answer to your question."

I sat back in my chair and waited.

He continued to pace. His micro-expressions told me he was having a heated internal debate. He stopped pacing when he pulled his phone out of his pocket and took a call. He nodded toward me, then stepped out into the hallway.

I sat there, counting my fingers, annoyed that he wouldn't tell me what I wanted to know. I was discovering how dreadfully frustrating it feels to be shut out of an investigation.

Returning to the meeting room, Worthington looked even more grim than when he'd left, if that were possible.

"Change of plans," he said. "Enderby and I must leave. Immediately. We'll return in the morning. Please join me as I inform the rest of the…party."

I couldn't resist saying, "Sure we'll all be safe in our beds?"

Worthington turned and replied, "Sadly, no, I'm not. But it's a risk I must take. I have people to brief. In person, apparently." He strode into the salon, and called for everyone's attention. "Enderby and I are leaving. Now. We'll return here at eight, sharp, in the morning. You may all spend the night wherever you choose – but I insist you all present yourselves here at that hour, when I shall be able to proceed with my questioning. Thank you, and goodnight."

Felicity stood as he turned. "Could you please drive me to a hotel?"

Worthington responded, "We aren't providing a taxi service, Miss Sampson. Goodnight."

Felicity whined, "I need to get as far away from here as possible." Her eyes were wild.

Renata stood and pulled out her phone. "I can organize that, Miss Sampson," she said. "Leave it with me. I'll call for a car, and book a room for you. Any particular hotel?"

"I trust you," replied Felicity. "Somewhere nice, of course. Do you think Tavistock and Tavistock might be able to get me a suite? I don't usually pay, of course, because I post photos online, and always talk to a couple of journo friends of mine to tell them how wonderful the place is, and how super the staff have been. Is that something you could manage to arrange, do you think?"

"I believe it's within my realm of capabilities," replied Renata coolly. "Would you also want me to arrange for a personal shopper to sort out some fresh clothes, etcetera, for you?"

Felicity glowed. "Would you? Yes, please. Harvey Nicks. They've got all my info there. Usually do an excellent job – they know what works for my body type, and personality." She looked at her watch. "You'll just catch them."

"I have the number," replied Renata, and she moved to the far side of the dining room to make the calls.

"You'll be glad to have me out of your hair," said Felicity to Bella with surprising tenderness.

"Thanks," was Bella's terse reply.

"Vinnie can get you two back to my place," said John. "I'll stay. Of course." He smiled at his fiancée, who smiled back.

"It'll be just us two here, tonight," he whispered. "You alright with that, darling?"

"Perfectly," replied Bella, and her expression told me she wasn't lying.

THURSDAY

"...now is the winter of our discontent..."

I woke early, having spent a fitful night; my sleep pattern was off, my eating pattern was off – I felt generally dreadful. I couldn't put my finger on anything that was specifically wrong with me, but I did feel as though I was running a bit hot and cold.

When I told Bud, he replied in a very Bud-like manner. "You know what it's like on airplanes – you've probably picked up a bug. Now it's coming out. Hopefully no more than a head cold. Let's make sure you get lots of rest, and fluids."

I sat up in bed and laughed. "Rest and fluids? Will that be before, during, or after we've been grilled by Worthington?"

Bud looked at the bedside clock, and groaned. "It's only half five. Why are we both even awake?"

"I couldn't sleep, and you kept snoring, so I gave you a bit of a shove. A loving one, of course. But maybe it was a bit too hard, because...well, you're awake now."

Bud snuggled under the duvet. "Not for long, I hope. I need an extra hour. You do too. Come on – head down, eyes closed. You'll drop off."

"Thanks, Mum." I remained in my sitting position until he was snoring again – which took about five seconds – then I applied my mind to our situation.

I knew we were in for another big day – one that didn't hold the promise of a single gallery or museum, sadly, but which needed to be used as wisely as possible. As such, I wanted to have everything clear in my head, so I could ask Worthington the minimum number of questions to elicit the maximum amount of illumination and insight. I decided I'd make a list; I like lists – they help me organize the mass of stuff that usually rolls around in my fevered little brain…which made me wonder if I had a high temperature, which made me wish I'd packed a thermometer.

I told myself it was probably just another form of a hot flash, and padded up the stairs to the lounge, where I peered out of the windows, toward the river. It looked bitterly cold outside; the road itself was dark and wet, and the trees along the embankment glistened icily in the street lights. I shivered, then settled myself on the sofa, pulled a throw over my feet, and started to make a list in my head of everything I wanted to know.

It was a long list, because I didn't know much at all. I'd learned a fair bit about Oleg Asimov, had picked up a few conflicting insights into the dynamics between Sasha and Bella, but hadn't learned much about Charles. It occurred to me that no one had really mourned Charles's loss at all, except maybe Felicity, then reasoned that maybe everyone was completely numb, following so many deaths. I'd made up my mind about many aspects of Felicity's personality, and yet couldn't come to grips with Renata's at all; she was incredibly…guarded. *Sly* was the word that slid into my mind when I thought of her – but why? Vinnie was the greatest puzzle; I imagined him sleeping, just yards away, beyond the wall I was staring at. How on earth did he play into this tragic mess?

I made coffee to distract myself from my thinking – which helps a great deal, sometimes. However, not on this occasion. I perched at the counter on a stool, my coffee in hand, trying to work out who had killed Sasha.

I sipped my coffee and once again pictured the scene as everyone had left the main salon that fateful evening – was there a look, a glance, that I'd not recalled? Did anyone say anything when the body was discovered that might suggest they weren't shocked? As I ran through it all in my head, the only reaction that stood out – as it had done on the night – was the way Renata had been so incredibly cool. She'd remained untouched by the death of the woman with whom she'd worked closely for many years. I examined everything I'd observed about Renata, and realized she was…sly – there was that word again! – and guarded…but she was also…fake, in some way. What was it about her that was bugging me?

I put down my coffee, closed my eyes to the stage where everything goes blurry, and began to hum – it all helps me when I need to put my eidetic memory to work, though I really don't know why. I called to mind every encounter I'd had with Renata, since I'd first met her. And that was where I began…

She's entering the salon for drinks, though Julie isn't with her…Julie walks in with everyone else, their coat on her arm, and announces their arrival. Not Renata. She doesn't make eye contact with anyone except Sasha – that's to be expected, I suppose. She moves to stand in a dim corner. Okay – she works for Sasha…she's there to make up numbers at the dinner table, to even out the male/female ratio. Maybe she feels a little awkward? Is it even normal that she's been invited? Maybe. Now Sasha walks toward her. I can see she's holding a crystal tumbler. No ice. Where did that come from? From Bella, who's at the drinks' trolley? I re-run that part…no, not Bella, Sasha poured it herself – I saw her do it. And it's not water, it's vodka. Sasha pulled a bottle out of an ice bucket and poured neat vodka. A lot of it. Okay, did Renata drink it? Yes, I see her take a mouthful – not a sip, a mouthful. That's quite something. Did I see if she'd emptied her glass before she left for the terrace with Sasha? I'm alone in the salon, waiting for everyone to do what they're doing, standing where she had stood, looking at an antique cast list for a performance of Othello…and I see Renata's tumbler, empty, sitting on a ledge, abandoned. Yes, she drank it all. Fast.

I opened my eyes. That was useful – only someone who's used to drinking a great deal could have done what Renata did and remain upright. I asked myself if I'd seen any other signs that might suggest Renata was an alcoholic, or at least an unusually heavy drinker. She didn't drive anywhere – probably a good thing – and she was given to remaining still…maybe trying to manage cravings? The only form of addiction I truly understand is my own to nicotine; when I'm desperate for a cigarette, I try to keep myself busy, and fall back on chewing nicotine gum as though my life depends upon it. I'm down to just a couple a day at the moment…which I'm quite proud of, though Bud thinks I should be past that stage by now. I wondered how Renata managed to function in what was surely a highly pressured work situation if she drank, and told myself to talk to Bud about it. During his career he's worked with several officers who've had to step down and take a leave of absence to get treatment for alcoholism – he'd know more about telltale signs in the workplace than me.

I sipped my coffee, thinking about Renata again, and realized I knew nothing about her background, other than that she'd joined the Townsend agency after I'd left. Could her family background be important? Piers had mentioned that Renata's support of Sasha when Oleg was dying had been born of her own experience. Had his addled brain replayed that motif when he'd been talking to Worthington? Were the papers Piers had mentioned at that time concerning Renata's father something that needed to be queried – or should I take them to be the outcome of his having taken too many drugs? Yes, I decided it was worth asking Worthington about that subject.

Then I considered that, with Sasha, Piers, and Charles all being dead, if it weren't for the political overtones, I knew I'd be looking at this as a case of internal family strife taking a deadly turn...so should I discount the political angle? Was this a situation like the one portrayed in the portrait of *The Ambassadors* at the National Gallery, after all? Were political shenanigans clouding something that had, at its heart, a much more personal, domestic situation? Had the arrival of Worthington thrown me off? I understood why a person like Worthington had been called in: Vinnie had contacted someone who didn't answer a simple 999 call; John had been anxious to avoid any hint of scandal on behalf of his fiancée and her family; Bud had phoned one of his connections – at John's request – which had given a domestic situation an international angle. Yes, it made sense that someone of Worthington's stamp would show up.

But then the shutdown had come...from "on high". Why? Why shut everything down like that? I was utterly convinced that Sir Simon had pushed for it, despite Worthington's "non-answer" to my direct question – so why would he do that? And I came back to my original reasons...to protect himself, or to protect the reputation of the Asimov family, and – by extension – the Asimov business empire. Or was it the other way around?

And there I was again, facing that concept – safeguarding reputation. Not spoiling the legacy. Keeping the Asimov family name free from stain. Oleg was dead, his legacy – his businesses – should have lived on through his three children owning them. Oleg had put plans in place to allow for the professional input and oversight of an experienced pair of hands, in the shape of Sir Simon Pendlebury...who was more than equal to the task, and an old school-friend of Piers, to boot. I stopped – but had they really been friends in school? Or had they merely attended the same school at the same time? There's a huge difference. The conversation between Piers and Sir Simon about "jolly old japes" seemed, to me, to have been Piers' over-zealous attempt to remind the knight of the realm of what they had in common. It had jarred at the time, because it had been an incredibly odd way for a man to be acting when grieving for his wife...unless...yes, unless Piers felt he needed Sir Simon to think of him as an equal. Someone who might deserve to be involved in running the Asimov companies in his own right? I made a mental note to find out who inherited Sasha's shares in the company. I assumed Piers would know the terms of his own wife's will, and possibly what was due to happen to the shares; unfortunately he, too, was dead, so I couldn't ask him...but I could ask Worthington.

I stood and rolled my shoulders to unhunch them; without knowing definitive causes of death for Piers, Charles, and Sir Simon, I couldn't get anywhere. All I knew was that Piers had been ranting, then died in bed. That Julie been ranting when she'd attacked Felicity. That Charles had been ranting, then drowned in his bath. There was a link...a commonality. So maybe Felicity hadn't been lying after all? But...why *was* everyone acting in such an extreme manner? I drew a blank – I needed information before any amount of additional thinking could get me anywhere. I checked my watch. If we had to be ready to leave with Vinnie by seven, so he could drive us to Beulah House by eight, I had to hit the bathroom, then wake Bud.

I padded down the stairs, though, since I was about to wake Bud in any case I wondered, even as I was doing it, why I was bothering to be so stealthy. However, it was worth it to be able to watch him sleep for just a moment. To see him look so peaceful, his hands clasped like otter paws on his chest, his face hardly lined at all. I could see why Othello had acted as he had before he'd murdered Desdemona...though I had no intention of killing my spouse as he slept. However, I knew that waking him would kill his dreams which – whatever they were – appeared to be making him happy. It was a great pity, but it had to be done, so I did it as gently as I could, with a kiss. And it was as I kissed him that I thought of the handkerchief, embroidered with strawberries...

"…all that glisters…"

We were a little later leaving than we'd planned, because Vinnie had slept in. He was apologetic, and explained he'd been up until three in the morning talking things through on a video call with Vaseem.

"He's said I'm not to go back there today," he announced as we waited, with annoyance, at yet another set of red traffic lights, "but I told him I had to. I've brought my own food. And water. You?"

Bud sounded surprised, and concerned, when he said, "That didn't occur to me…"

"It did to me," I replied. "Until someone tells us how everyone died, we'll only consume what we've taken to Beulah House ourselves. I packed appropriately." I pointed at the large tote at my feet.

Bud shifted uncomfortably in his seat, and we both kept quiet so Vinnie could concentrate on the driving.

When we finally arrived at Beulah House, Vinnie dropped us at the front, and drove the car around to the back. The house looked bleak and unwelcoming in the pre-sunrise twilight. We rang the bell and waited…and waited. We'd made surprisingly good time, and it was only ten to eight – but both Bud and I were puzzled that no one answered the door.

"Should we try the coach house?" Bud waved in the building's general direction. "I know the latch thing is down, and there are no lights on, but John and Bella could be there. Maybe they slept in?"

We walked across and knocked on the heavy wooden door. There was no response. Bud knocked again – harder this time, still nothing. He tried the latch, which lifted easily, then pushed open the door. It creaked, loudly.

"Hello? John? Bella?" Bud shouted before setting a foot inside. Silence. He stuck his head in, clicked a light switch, and I leaned in too. The coach house was – essentially – a large open space with a kitchen at one end, a lounge at the other and a bedroom up on a platform, with a balustrade surrounding it. The bed itself was clearly visible, and it was empty. The position of the kitchen, in relation to one of the outer walls, suggested to me the bathroom was hidden behind it – allowing for all the plumbing to be in one general area, I supposed.

The entire place was…well, to say it was a riot of decorative objects would be putting it mildly. Bella's artistic bent had been given full rein, and there wasn't an inch of wall, or surface of any sort, that wasn't bedecked with patterned fabric, a piece of decorative pottery, or a wall hanging or painting of some sort. It was utterly overwhelming, and – given the fact there were only a couple of small windows – terribly claustrophobic. The place stank of sandalwood and patchouli; there were incense sticks, pots of oil, and perfumed lotions, dotted on many surfaces.

Bud made a face that implied he felt the same way as I did about the décor and odor, then we both shouted John and Bella's names again. There was no way they couldn't have heard us, if they were there.

"Hello." We spun around to see Vinnie standing in the open doorway. "Are they not there, then? That's odd. The back door of the main house was open."

We turned off the lights, shut the latch and walked across the courtyard again. "No sign of them there," said Bud. "Are they in the house?"

Vinnie shrugged. "I didn't see them, and got no answer when I called out, but then I didn't go looking for them, either."

We reached the door of the main house and entered. Bud shouted again, and the three of us strained to hear anything at all. The silence was deafening. Bud's body stiffened. He, Vinnie, and I became fully alert; the number of deaths in the house so far was making us all worry about John and Bella's wellbeing.

"The last time we arrived and couldn't find them they'd been up in the palace room," I said.

Bud spoke rapidly. "Vinnie – palace room, Cait – ground floor, I'll take the floor with the bedrooms. Go." We went.

Five minutes later, we all agreed John and Bella weren't in the house, just as a car arrived with Worthington and Enderby inside, and another car pulled up, carrying Felicity and Renata. Bud went outside to talk to Worthington, and I said to Vinnie, "I'm going to check the stables and Bella's workshop, in the back garden."

"Just wait a minute now, Cait, Bud'll be back in a…" But I was gone, before he'd finished speaking.

I rushed through the French doors and checked every open area of the summer house using the flashlight on my phone as I strode past. It was deserted. I noticed the rill was still frozen, but put that out of my mind – other than to remind myself it was still slippery underfoot. I could just about discern the ivy-covered outline of Bella's workshop beneath the lightening sky. I reached it, found the door and pulled it open. Inside, the brazier in the center of the room was giving off a surprising amount of heat, and a reddish glow. I shone my flashlight around the stone walls, rough-hewn workbenches, and dusty floor, until it illuminated a couple of naked figures curled together in one corner, snuggling on a mattress beneath a rather inadequate couple of quilts.

"John? Bella?" I shouted.

John sat bolt upright, grabbed a quilt, and hid his eyes from the glare of the flashlight. "What? Cait, is that you? What time is it?"

"What on earth are you both doing here?" I asked – perfectly reasonably, I thought.

"What do you think?" Bella sounded half asleep.

"Here? In the middle of winter? When it's freezing outside?"

Bud arrived, panting, just as I stepped into the workshop. "What's going...oh...you're here. Are you both okay?"

"We were," replied Bella grumpily. She tugged at the quilt John was clenching beneath his chin, but he wouldn't let go. His face told a tale of confusion, and embarrassment.

Bud touched my sleeve. "Tell you what, why don't we let you guys get your act together, then you can come up to the house. Worthington's arrived – well, everyone's here, in fact. I suggest you don't hang about."

As Bud and I stepped out, John called, "Could someone put the kettle on, please?"

"I'll sort it," I replied, and pushed the door shut.

"Don't say it, Cait," said Bud. "Not necessary. Whatever made them spend the night in there I don't know...but I guess they'll have a reason. Even if it's a dumb one. We'd better get Worthington to stand down; he was extremely concerned that we couldn't locate them."

We walked toward the house, waving, and giving thumbs-up signs to Vinnie through the window. I said to Bud, "Did you manage to take in what that place was like?"

Bud sighed. "Not really. All I saw was a man acting like an idiotic teen for some reason or other."

"It was full of chemicals," I continued. "And one in particular that might be of concern – mercury. Even at room temperature it gives off a toxic vapor that works on the nervous system – one that can cause many of the symptoms displayed by

Piers, Charles, and Sir Simon. Funnily enough, I was thinking about thermometers, and mercury, only this morning…now there it is in Bella's workshop."

Bud was distracted. "Not now, Cait. Besides, we don't know that anyone's been poisoned with mercury or anything else. Can we just get inside, see what Worthington wants, and start to get this all behind us?"

I stopped walking, and pulled on his hand to stop Bud too. "What's wrong, Husband?"

Just one look told me Bud was worried. "John's not…I mean, he's acting…this isn't normal behavior for him, Cait. He's a sound man when it comes to appointments and rules. I don't know of him ever having missed one, or broken one – and to be lolling about, out there like that, when he knew Worthington was due? It's as though…it's like he's gone feral. It's…not right. Not John."

His deep concern was audible, and my heart broke just a little for him; to suspect that someone you've always been able to rely upon might no longer be the rock you'd always believed them to be is an incredibly difficult emotion to manage. It's like grief, in a way. I weighed whether I should help him rationalize, offering excuses for John – like, maybe he'd forgotten to set an alarm call after one too many last night? – but I knew Bud well enough to realize that wasn't what he needed from me at that moment; he was more than capable of working through that thought process all by himself.

All I could do was hug him and say, "When you want to talk, we'll talk. But, meanwhile, know I'm here for you, in any way you need."

Bud kissed my forehead. "Thanks." We walked on, to be greeted by Vinnie at the French doors.

"He's good at being polite when he's livid, is that one," he said, nodding toward Worthington.

"I bet," replied Bud, somberly.

"Dining room, five minutes," called Worthington, leaving the salon.

Felicity had chosen to present herself as though attending a funeral where deepest mourning was the order of the day, while Renata was sporting yet another trouser suit in an unflattering shade of brown. Seeing just the two of them sitting in the salon made the tremendous loss of life over the past few days feel even more real; it was a dreadful toll, and it steeled me to screw up my determination to find out what on earth was going on.

The arrival of John and Bella would have been comical under any other circumstances; but no one even smiled. "Just going to grab some clean clothes," said John, as he and Bella scampered through the salon clutching their quilts. They ran out of the front door – heading for the coach house, I assumed. Bud looked disappointed and embarrassed; my heart went out to him. I felt useless.

"Time to face the music," said Renata as she stood, and headed for the dining room which had been returned to its closed state.

We all shuffled in, without an ounce of enthusiasm, and took our seats. Everyone – without exception – put a bottle of water on the table in front of them that they produced from a bag or pocket. I passed one to Bud, who took it, opened it, and drank half of it right away.

Worthington glared at his watch. Enderby sat quietly. Felicity bounced her knees. Renata placed both her palms on the table. Vinnie kept smiling and nodding at everyone, but was ignored. Bud stared into space, and I counted my teeth with my tongue to stop myself from asking Worthington all the questions I wanted answered right there and then.

John and Bella slid into the room and sat down silently.

"Glen won't be joining us," opened Worthington. "It would be too painful for him to be here, now, and I have spoken with him privately. Thank you all for being here." He made a point of not looking at John and Bella. "This is a trying, and tragic time, for you all, I am sure. For me, it's my job to deal with death on a regular basis – for some of you here I know it's a blessed rarity, but it's the reality we all have to face together at this time. I have good reason to believe that none of the deaths that have taken place here at Beulah House have arisen from entirely natural causes. As such, it behoves me to now speak to each of you in private, with a view to establishing the truth behind these occurrences. No one person is suspect at this time, but I'm telling you all that if you believe you require legal representation, or consultation, prior to my interviewing you, then now would be the time to contact whomever you wish to advise you." His tone was serious, his face set grim. The expressions around the table told me no one was about to rush off to phone a solicitor.

He sighed. "Once again, I shall be using the meeting room for interviews, due to the fact it offers privacy. I would ask everyone to continue to not discuss the deaths of your friends and family members with anyone. Thank you." He stood. "Professor Morgan, I'd like to interview you first, if you please."

My tummy clenched – with excitement. Was he going to let me ask my questions now? And would he be able to give me the answers I needed?

"...of bloody deeds and death..."

Worthington looked as though he were running out of steam. As I took my seat in the meeting room, I could only imagine the stress he must be under, and the pressure he would be feeling from his superiors. I hoped that at least that same pressure was also being brought to bear upon those who might be able to illuminate the deaths through the application of scientific methods.

This encounter involved no preamble, for which I was grateful. He simply said, "You have questions, to which I may or may not have answers. If I have them, I shall share them. If I do not, we can discuss why I should seek them out. I am assuming this is music to your ears, but let's just get on with this, then I can talk to those I need to quiz."

I replied equally directly. "Thank you. Yes, I have some questions, starting with – do you now know the cause of death of each of the victims?"

Worthington nodded. "Mrs. Tavistock died as a result of injuries sustained by falling from the roof. We are certain that's where she fell from, we are certain that's how she died. She had one contusion on her head that was not necessarily consistent with her fall. It would not have been fatal, but could have caused her to become disorientated enough to have fallen, or to have been more easily pushed."

"Was the contusion to which you refer consistent with having been made by the brass telescope in the palace room?"

"No, and no traces of blood or skin were found on the telescope."

"What about a cut-crystal ashtray?"

"I beg your pardon?" Worthington looked genuinely shocked, and I noticed Enderby's head snap up from her tablet, where she was typing notes.

I replied, "There was – I have been told by Glen – a heavy, cut-crystal ashtray that usually sat upon the small table near the telescope in the palace room. When we entered the room, just after Sasha's body was found, there was no ashtray."

"Enderby?"

Enderby's finger swiped her screen several times. "No ashtray in the palace room, sir."

Worthington said, "And Glen told you this? Why did he even bring it up?"

"He didn't, I asked him about it. You see, I thought it odd that a cigarette box, humidor, and lighter wouldn't be accompanied by an ashtray on the smokers' table in the palace room. He confirmed a presentation piece that – as he described it – weighed a ton, was usually present. I think its absence is significant, and I wonder if that might have caused the contusion of which you speak."

"I'll check with those who know better than I, but – having seen the wound in question, which was above the hairline – I can at least tell you that the sort of mark a piece of cut crystal might make could well be consistent with the injury I saw. I don't suppose you've seen the ashtray to which you refer?"

I shook my head. "I haven't searched for it, you understand. And the snow might make it difficult to spot, had it been thrown from the palace room – possibly into the shrubbery and copse to the side of the house."

"We can get bodies searching for that. Thank you." Worthington added, "Enderby, get that sorted." Enderby nodded, and typed. "Next…Mr. Piers Tavistock."

"Just a moment," I said, "has there been a toxicology report carried out for Sasha?"

Worthington nodded. "Yes. My apologies." He referred to his tablet. "A small amount of alcohol, but she wasn't drunk. That was it."

I weighed my next words carefully. "Did the toxicology panel include things like sedatives, prescription pharmaceuticals, heavy metals? I wondered if – under the circumstances – a more thorough-than-normal investigation had been carried out."

Worthington smiled. "You're right. It was. Given the circumstances. But nothing was found."

"Any foreign DNA found on her person – maybe under her fingernails, for example?"

Worthington shook his head. "Nothing under the fingernails but her own DNA." He looked up. "People have been known to scratch an itch, on occasion."

"Were there any surprising findings at all?"

Worthington shrugged. "It would appear that Mrs. Tavistock was bulimic. There was scarring consistent with frequent regurgitation. It appears it was a long-standing condition."

"Yes, I did wonder. Thank you. That explains a few things. Talk about Sasha being sick prior to major presentations, and large events, didn't ring true to me, not for someone with her psychological profile, in any case. And Bella's teeth are perfect, whereas Sasha's weren't – a telltale sign of the condition, due to the effects of stomach acid on the dental enamel during the expulsion of the stomach contents. Good. Well…not good, but, you know? Now – Piers. Cause of death? Other than his heart failing, of course."

Worthington almost hid a smirk. "Yes, apart from that. He was found to have heart disease, liver disease, lung disease – and was, essentially, an incredibly unhealthy man. Had much higher than recommended amounts of diazepam in his system, and enough alcohol in his blood to make that combination dangerous. The pathologist said her best guess was that it was the combination of his generally poor health, the prescribed drugs – taken in too high a dosage – and the alcohol that led to his death."

I let that sink in. "And Charles?"

"Ah, now Mr. Asimov was a different kettle of fish – and by 'kettle of fish' I mean he was stuffed full of drugs, and not just the over-the-counter, or prescribed varieties. Sustained cocaine use over many years was evidenced by damage to his nasal membrane; he – like his brother-in-law – also suffered from liver disease; there was evidence of historic use of injected recreational drugs – between his toes, which were, let me tell you, a right mess." I felt my multipurpose right eyebrow lift at the uncharacteristically blunt observation by Worthington, who immediately added, "My apologies – given all I've seen over the years you'd think I'd be fine with most things, but feet are my nemesis; for some reason, I can't abide feet."

The psychologist in me wanted to say so much, but I remained silent on the matter of feet, instead asking, "Did you also find evidence of any other drugs?"

"Indeed – fentanyl, a small amount. Though only a small amount is needed for the dose to be fatal, this was not the cause of death. There was also a wide range of both illegal and unregulated synthetic cannabinoids found in him, which suggest he had ingested—"

"Spice. Yes, nasty stuff. He'd drunk it, rather than smoked it, right?"

Worthington nodded. "That's what they said. Given the story the man's body told of his habits, and these toxicology findings, the conclusion was that he'd entered a state of drug-induced unconsciousness, slipped beneath the water in his bath, and drowned. Drowning was his actual cause of death."

"And Sir Simon Pendlebury?"

Worthington sat back in his chair. "Toxicology's not done, yet. His symptoms could be accounted for by a number of causes. He didn't have the underlying heart or liver conditions of his contemporary, Piers Tavistock, nor the habitual drug use in his background of Charles Asimov. His symptoms didn't begin until he'd been in Beulah House for a little time, but were lengthier than might be expected if a drug overdose were the culprit, I am told. All of that being said, the man did have a peptic ulcer. The medics are still trying to determine the extent to which the acute vomiting he suffered over many hours might have weakened his heart, which is what his cause of death was finally concluded to be – his heart simply couldn't cope any longer."

"But the cause of the systemic overload that might have led to that is yet to be determined?"

"Yes."

"I have a feeling spice might play a role again. Did the post-mortem on Julie Powell find anything like that?" I asked.

Worthington consulted his tablet. "I can't see that an extended toxicology investigation was performed. The cause of death, in her case, was obvious, you see."

"But the reason for her attacking Felicity is not," I replied.

Worthington nibbled his bottom lip. "Spice again? It would be difficult to drive under the influence of that particular drug," he said, "and we know she drove herself from here to Miss Sampson's – not a route she usually took, and a good distance away, in heavy traffic. I don't think it's likely she'd have made it, without incident. Spice is known as the zombie drug for a reason – though aggression, paranoia, and violence can be its outcome, as well as absolute inanimation. We can have it checked, but I don't believe it likely."

I nodded. "I still think that checking her for a wide range of drugs would be a good idea; if not spice, then maybe cocaine, or some sort of speed. She wouldn't have been used to it, and the 'symptoms' she displayed, including her rage-fuelled attack on Felicity, could be explained by that."

Worthington sat back from the table. "What I'm hearing from you, Professor Morgan, is that you seem to believe all the deaths we're looking into have somehow had the misuse of drugs play a role in leading to a – thereafter – range of actual causes of death. Am I to assume you're suggesting that one person is responsible for all these deaths, insofar as they administered said drugs in the first place, and then…let nature take its course, shall we say?"

Enderby sat forward on her chair.

I nodded. "Except for Sasha – I think there was a violent altercation which resulted in her death. But I have more questions…"

"Please, ask away."

"The bags full of papers Renata brought initially for Piers' attention, but which were then to be handed only to Sir Simon – what's happened to them?"

Worthington glanced toward Enderby, who replied, "Due to be back at HQ by this time, sir, but…well, I happen to know they're sitting in a car outside, waiting to be driven there, as soon as you give the word."

I responded, "Thanks. Good. I'm pleased to know they're accounted for, and in a safe place. I'm even more pleased to know that – with your permission – I can access them. Any chance I might be able to take a cursory look at them?"

Worthington's brow wrinkled. "And you'd want to do that because?"

"I have a feeling they might be pertinent to the case."

"They're copious."

"Just a quick look? I wouldn't take time to read them in their entirety."

Worthington nodded toward Enderby. "Get someone to lug them in here." She typed a text.

I replied, "Thanks. Next, you had everyone write down their activities on the day after Sasha's death. Might I read those accounts, please?"

"Yes, you may read those accounts. Enderby will see to it."

"Thanks. And I'm sure you've researched all our backgrounds, quite thoroughly, so might I be told what you know about Renata Douglas?"

"Miss Douglas, but not Miss Sampson?" Worthington sounded intrigued.

I shrugged. "Felicity's more of an open book. Renata not so much. I'm especially interested in her family and personal life. To be honest, I'd love to read the files you have on all of us – those still living, as well as those who have died. I don't suppose there's a chance of that, is there?"

"I'm trying to be helpful, not lose my job, Professor Morgan," replied Worthington. "Just Miss Douglas."

"Just Miss Douglas," I agreed, with relief. "And there's a bit more, please…do you know what happens to the shares in the Asimov group that would have gone to Sasha and Charles?"

Worthington chuckled. "Ah yes, follow the money. I do know: Oleg Asimov's will made it clear he wanted the business owned by the family, while they survived. So, if his children die without issue, their shares are then to be divided among the living children. It was an arrangement which weighed heavily in Charles Asimov's favor, as he was the only sibling likely to be able to bear an heir; it appears Oleg Asimov saw a future for his empire being continued along the male line, and the male line alone."

"And what happens if all Oleg's children are dead?"

Worthington sat back. "I sincerely hope we manage to hang on to the one survivor we have at the moment, but, when Bella does die, she'll be the one to bequeath them, as the sole survivor."

"Thanks. That's almost it, for now...though I have a question about hair grips. Were any found in the palace room?"

"Hair grips?" He looked surprised. I nodded. "Enderby, any hair grips found?"

"Half a dozen, in Sasha Tavistock's pocket, sir."

"Good. Thank you. That tells me a great deal," I said.

"Fancy sharing what that might be?" Worthington's eyes gleamed.

"Sasha chose to take her hair down. Now maybe you can help me understand just one more thing...was it Sir Simon who managed to get the initial investigation shut down?"

Worthington's mouth set itself into a hard line. Something close to a smile suggesting resignation. "It might surprise you to know that I'm not always given a reason for the orders I have to obey. But I'm luckier than many insofar as I have at least one master who trusts me sufficiently to allow for the odd, off-the-record, chat. If we'd had the opportunity for such a chat, he might have mentioned that Sir Simon had used his not inconsiderable influence to shut down the investigation into Sasha Tavistock's death. Though more than that even he wouldn't have said."

"Another conversation that didn't happen," I snapped.

Worthington looked a little annoyed, but continued, "So what do you have for me?" He leaned forward.

I sighed, and let him have it. "There's a killer sitting in the salon, and I just need to think things through to be able to put this all together. Your information about the toxicological results have helped my process enormously. Thank you. It's what I was missing. The hair grips, and the shares, too. What I don't yet know is how this all fits together, nor even how it was all possible. So what I'd like to do is to be able to read all the files we've agreed I may access, then go away somewhere quiet, and think. But I'd also like your permission for Bud and me to be able to have a good look around this house, from top to bottom. Is that okay? We'll wear gloves, if you like."

"Feel free, with gloves. But please come to me the moment you have anything; your reputation is intriguing, but – as they say in the theatre – you're only as good as your last performance, and I'd like this to be one that deserves a standing ovation. I'm going to try to get more insights from the people out there – but I believe we're trying to pin down someone who's been horribly clever so far, and I'm not sure what I can do about that."

"There's a difference between clever and cunning, and, psychologically speaking, a person who's got away with so much so far might easily be tripped up by their sense of infallibility. I hope to come back to you with something soon."

At that moment there was a knock at the door, and Worthington invited in the young man carrying Renata's bags, full of papers, which he set down on the table beside me.

"Loo break?" I suggested.

Worthington nodded, and they all left the room – so I had Enderby's tablet all to myself…then I opened up the bags on the tabletop and started reading through the mass of papers. It was fascinating…and incredibly revealing. It seemed Renata Douglas had hidden depths, and I wasn't surprised the word "sly" had kept sliding into my head when I'd been trying to assess her character earlier on.

"...one sin I know another doth provoke..."

When I emerged into the salon, every face turned to look at me. I said, "He's a pussy cat, you'll all be fine. Excuse us. Bud, could you come with me, please?" I added, "Enderby will be out to tell you who Worthington wants to see next. Just all wait here. Thanks."

Bud and I had the run of the house, and I wanted us to make the most of our opportunity.

As we mounted the stairs, Bud asked, "So, what's the plan? I'm assuming you have one."

"Indeed I do, Husband. This is our chance to wrap our heads around a few things, and I want to start at the top – literally."

I was delighted to be able to see the palace room in daylight for the first time. "Okay, let's get the lay of the land, so to speak," I said. We walked around the perimeter of the structure – inside, because I didn't like the look of the slippery, dangerous walkway one little bit. Bud peered out, over the edge, while I paced around the area beside what I was now mentally referring to as "the smokers' table", beside the telescope, and – now that I knew it was okay for me to fiddle with the instrument – I pushed and shoved it in various directions. It moved easily on its pivot, and was obviously well-maintained.

"Hey, be careful with that," said Bud. "It's old, but it's got one heck of a swing." He was right, it did.

I positioned it so I could see the horizon where London's iconic skyline rose to meet the leaden skies, and felt a pang of disappointment that I was stuck in one dwelling in south

London when there was so much out there I wanted to be seeing and doing. I allowed the telescope to stay in that position, then stepped away and said, "Right, have at it, Husband. See if you can smack it so it ends up resting in the position it was on the night Sasha had died."

Bud did his best, and the action that made it fall that way was a side-swipe, with a downward motion. We examined the telescope carefully, and Bud found a small, sharp indentation at one point, which cemented my suspicions.

"Okay," I said, "door next." I moved to the doorway that had been open when Sasha had died and played around with it; it was another piece of metalwork that swung easily, and it didn't make a sound. The cold air rushed in as I leaned forward and peered out. I saw the spot where the SOCO had found a cigarette stub, but didn't dare look over the edge – I'm not good with heights, and was operating at the limit of my realm of comfort in any case. I wobbled back inside, where Bud grabbed me.

"Cait, just ask me to be your eyes when we're up this high," he said.

"You're right, I should, and shall. I'm feeling quite woozy. I'll have a little sit down, if you can have a quick look around and describe what's below each of the four sides of the house, please?"

He took a few minutes and talked as he walked. "Okay, the door nearest the smokers' table overlooks the side of the house where there are a lot of trees and shrubbery; the one at the back of the house overlooks the protruding terraces behind the master bedroom and yellow bedroom; the third looks onto the roof of the back hallway which connects the coach house to the Victorian servants' quarters. So, the only door that opens onto 'the best place to jump from if you really want to die' would be the door which overlooks the front of the house. Is that what you wanted to know?"

I nodded. "Yes. So it had to be that door. Thanks. Next – how's this place heated? I can tell it is – but how? Can you find any vents in the floor?"

Bud looked puzzled. "Yes, there are vents here…and here. Hadn't noticed them before, they kind of blend into the floorboards."

"Excellent – that's just what I was hoping for. I've researched the use of forced air heating in the UK; I know it's what we have at home in Canada, but it was something I'd never encountered before my migration, so was surprised to discover it went through a flush of popularity in Europe at one time, though it's never overtaken the use of steam or water-heated radiators in terms of popularity. Given that Beulah House seems to have been the sort of place where various homeowners have been open to 'improvements' over the years, the discovery of those vents allows me to explain another few oddities about the case."

"Oh good," said Bud. He didn't sound impressed.

"Let's have a quick look for the ashtray now," I said, rising from my seat.

"What ashtray?" Bud sounded a bit testy. "You haven't told me anything about any ashtray."

I realized I hadn't. "It's big, and made of cut crystal. Trust me, you'll know it if you see it. Enderby said they didn't find one up here, but we both know that human error is a real thing – and we also know what we're looking for."

Bud grumbled, "We do? Okay, ashtray hunt."

We gave the palace room a thorough going over, but there was no sign of it. Finally, we searched the massive desk. Every drawer was empty, many were locked, some were just fakes in any case – designed to give the desk its balance and symmetry. Eventually I was finished with the place where Sasha had, I believed, been attacked, and we headed down to the study where the paper upon which the "suicide note" had been written was found.

It was a narrow room, located between the master bedroom and the yellow bedroom, containing a *chaise longue*, a desk dotted with a few framed photographs, a chair, and a couple of bookshelves. There was no paper in the blotter on the desk – removed by the SOCO, no doubt – then I opened the desk drawers, where I found a plentiful supply of the rich, cream vellum that had been used for the note we'd all seen. There was also a supply of matching envelopes, and several pens bearing the Tavistock and Tavistock logo.

I sat at the desk, pulled out some paper and a pen, and wrote a note – a duplicate of the one Sasha had written – then took a few more pieces of blank paper, popped them all inside a matching envelope, sealed it, ripped it open again, then put it in my pocket.

"What on earth are you doing?" Bud sounded as puzzled as he looked.

"You never know when you might need a decoy," I replied. "Now let's give these framed photos the attention they deserve. They're the only truly personal items in the room, so they must have been significant to Sasha."

"Good idea," replied Bud. He held one up. "This is of Sasha and Bella with their parents; the girls look to be aged about four or five, and I think they're dressed as nymphs of some sort. Oleg and his wife make a handsome couple in their Elizabethan costumes."

I looked, agreed, and picked up another frame which showed Sasha with her father in more recent times – maybe a decade or so ago. Neither of them had attempted to smile for the camera. Finally, we focused on the third.

I said, "This one's of Bella and her mother standing on the seafront at Aberystwyth. See those buildings? Unmistakable." I paused. "But Sasha was the one her mother took to Wales, leaving Bella at home to cram." I peered at the photo more closely, as did Bud. The girl in the picture was in her late teens, and her long, lustrous hair was blowing in a stiff breeze. She looked desperately sad – her shoulders drooping, chin down, her hands clasped in front of her tummy. Only her eyes were looking at the camera. She was partially turned away from her mother, who was clenching the girl's arm. The girl had Bella's curves, but the Welsh setting convinced me I was looking at Sasha. *Odd.*

"If that's Sasha, not Bella," said Bud, "what happened to her figure? I mean, she's got one there. Puppy fat?"

"Hmm…could mean a lot of things," I replied. But one significant reason had occurred to me.

I wondered if Sasha had chosen to keep any other similarly personal items in the bedroom she shared with her husband, but when we entered that room, it was a mess. The place had been completely devastated by the combined impact of paramedics and the SOCO team; the floor was littered with remnants of supplies used in the fruitless life-saving efforts expended upon Piers, as well as the telltale signs of fingerprint dust on every surface.

"Nice picture," said Bud, nodding toward the piece of art that hung above the bed.

"That's a portrayal of Othello kissing Desdemona just before killing her," I replied, "which seems an incredibly strange, and even tasteless, choice of artwork to have hanging above a marital bed."

"Oh, we didn't do that one at school. Yes, bit of an odd choice, as you say."

A relatively quick scan told us the room had hardly any personal items within it, and even the adjoining bathroom wasn't filled with anything other than the usual range of accoutrements. This suite wasn't somewhere Sasha had taken the opportunity to express her personality, and I began to wonder if there even was such a place. Maybe not. Maybe she'd found an outlet for her psyche through other channels, unlike her sister, whose impact upon her living environment – at the coach house – was not only obvious, but all-encompassing.

We visited the yellow bedroom next, and it, too, was a wreck, as a result of Charles having died in the bath there. This time there was the addition of some water damage.

"It's strange to see these rooms so completely abandoned and ignored," observed Bud, "but I guess setting them right hasn't been top of Bella's list of things to do in the past few days, with good cause."

I agreed.

The yellow room was impersonal, held several more gems of Shakespearean ephemera, but told me nothing. Peering out onto the terrace I noted it shared access with the master bedroom to the steps at the side of the house, which was interesting.

Next, we found that the bathroom attached to the blue bedroom was in need of a good cleaning – as Sir Simon's night of evacuation had left a less than pleasant odor. The best we could do was to open a window, and shut the door to the hall.

Felicity had used the pink bedroom the night she'd stayed – the mess in the bathroom told us that. I remarked, "Look, she dumped all the towels – a couple smeared with make-up – in the bath. I wonder who she imagined would be collecting them to be laundered, given she'd stabbed Julie to death."

"The cleaning fairy?" mugged Bud.

"Ha, ha," I replied. "If you track her down, give her our address."

We then headed downstairs and took the back hallway to the garden, where we bypassed the stable block and headed straight for Bella's workshop…which was where I'd been dying to have a good poke about since I'd so rudely awoken our two lovebirds a few hours earlier.

The stone building was still surprisingly warm, though the brazier was no longer glowing. I was keen to get a closer look at the chemicals Bella had on hand.

I made a beeline for them, and Bud followed. "Look, Bud, some of these are in ancient packaging, some brand new. Good grief – some of this stuff is really dangerous if it were to be used improperly."

Bud peered at a few containers. "Some are just plain lethal," he said. "A poisoner's treasure trove?" It was an odd mixture, and I counted at least ten different chemicals that could be used to maim or kill, either quickly, or over a prolonged period, including mercury.

"Could you snap a few photos of those, so we have a record for Worthington, please. Though I dare say he's had people out here snooping around already."

"Sure." Bud pulled out his phone and got to work, while I hunted through the detritus on Bella's workbench. I ignored the containers of gold and precious gems which were scattered among pieces of equipment that looked as though they'd be at home in a torturer's toolkit, as well as some fancy laser-shooting machines I assumed she needed for fine soldering and cutting. The materials and machinery looked as though they must have all cost a pretty penny; maybe Bella's business was even more successful than her lifestyle suggested. Eventually, I found a battered old book, which I opened; it was an order book. Items were listed, with names, dates, and reference numbers, and sketches were dotted throughout the pages. It looked a bit haphazard, but it told me two critically important things, one of which was that Bella's handwriting and that of her sister were almost identical – which I'd guessed it might be, given they were twins, and had probably been taught their penmanship by the same teacher at the same school, at the same time. Now, at least, I had evidence of that fact. *Good.*

Bud poked at the bedding where John and Bella had spent the night with his foot, and an empty bottle of champagne rolled out. "That could explain a great deal," he observed, and I sensed a little relief in his tone.

"A night alone, taking the chance for an adventure, sleeping in this ancient hut...celebrating the fact the wedding's still on?" I ventured.

"I hope so," replied Bud. "Despite the aisle being littered with corpses."

"Ours wasn't much different," I reminded him.

We shared a grim smile.

We headed back to the house, and Bud pointed out that the rill was finally starting to melt just a little – the day was becoming considerably milder than the previous few had been. As I watched the tiny trickle of water piercing the ice and snow, I was reminded again of how Bella had dropped her mug when she'd seen the men approach her workshop...and wondered what she'd been concerned about – there hadn't seemed to be anything out of the ordinary in there...at least, not out of the ordinary for a profession that required a person to have any number of lethal chemicals close at hand.

"...such stuff as dreams are made on..."

Once we'd crept along the back hallway again, I explained to Bud that I needed a little "alone time". He always understands, and said he'd rejoin the group while I returned to my private eyrie in the palace room, which was the only place I felt I could achieve a sense of peace. It was a good excuse to enjoy a vantage point I was unlikely to ever have the chance to use again...so I sat in one of the small, leather-upholstered chairs positioned to take in the view toward London, and drank it all in.

I needed to rerun the statements everyone had written about their movements on the day Piers and Julie had died, and recalled them as I allowed my body to relax.

Finally, I had the series of events prior to Bud, Vinnie, and me arriving straight at last. Also, having had the chance to mentally review the file Worthington had prepared about the Renata, I'd gained a much better insight into why the common ground between her father's loss – of mesothelioma, I had discovered – and Sasha's loss of Oleg might have borne some poisonous fruit...and knew there was a very good reason for Renata wishing ill to the entire Asimov clan – whatever she might claim to think and feel about Sasha and Piers.

With that information, the centaur medallion in my handbag, the envelope of notepaper in my pocket, and the toxicology reports, I felt I had everything I needed to be able to allow my mind to wander – allowing all the pieces of the puzzle to fit together.

The palace room was warm, and quiet, and I was comfortable enough where I was sitting to undertake my wakeful dreaming technique, where I aim to wipe all my preconceptions of a situation from my mind, and let it float free, to do as it will. And I was sharply aware that – in this instance, possibly more than any other I'd ever faced – there were a good number of preconceptions I had to put aside in order to really understand what had taken place, and how, and why.

I allowed my body to relax, closed my eyes, and drifted into my trance-like state.

Bud's standing in the middle of the palace room looking just like Henry VIII, wearing a silken robe, bedecked with many gold medallions, and an ermine shawl, which Sasha runs and grabs from him, then she flies through the shattering glass roof into the pale blue sky and heads for the sun, which morphs into the seafront in Aberystwyth, where she gradually transforms into a bird with a bleeding breast, crying pitifully that she's lost her children. Bella is beside Bud, wailing for her sister, as Piers scrambles up the twisting staircase into the palace room where he gets stuck, and starts to scream like a little boy.

The floor dissolves, and we're in the kitchen of Beulah House, which is simultaneously Bella's stone-built workshop, decorated just the way her coach house is…and Vinnie is in chef's whites, a machete in each hand, chopping swathes of herbs into tiny pieces which grow into a forest on the countertop. Julie is there too, dressed in a gown made of sheer red chiffon, embroidered with strawberries, her hair long and luxurious, and she's dallying provocatively with Glen and Charles at the table, which is covered with plates of sandwiches and pots and pots of tea, like the Mad Hatter's tea party…even to the extent that Bella is wearing a hat with a price tag stuck in its band, laughing manically, stirring a cup of tea with a thermometer.

Felicity is a miniature version of herself – not a child, just a small version of the adult I have met, and she's sitting on Sir Simon's lap being told a story by him, as though she is an infant…but the pages of the book he is reading from are made of pound notes, which she rips from the spine as he turns them.

I am aware of a cloud above me and I look up to see Oleg Asimov filling the sky with his ragged cape. He's carrying a scythe and is swooping toward each of his children in turn, trying to cut them down. Sasha is still a bird with a bleeding breast; now she flies high and tries to loosen her father's grip on his weapon by battering his face with her wings. Bella is sliding along the frozen rill, as though she's on skates which leave smoke trails, and she's scattering china mugs as she goes, which shatter into a thousand pieces when they land on the hard ground. Charles is lolling on the frozen grass, throwing snowballs into the air, where they burst and sparkle, making him laugh.

Renata appears, like a magician appearing through a puff of smoke, and she's surrounded by a cloud of glittering dust when she emerges, dressed in blazing white, with an illuminated star gleaming on her head. She's lugging a golden backpack, which she takes in her hands, and beats Oleg until he begins to tumble from the sky. His three children cheer his downfall.

I hear fluttering, and think a flock of birds is approaching, but it's pieces of paper…all of them printed with depictions of Shakespeare's great tragic heroes, and they're being scattered from Oleg's disintegrating cloak. As they land in the snow, they each become reddened with blood…

I sat forward in the chair, and believed I had it. Now all I had to do was convince Worthington to get Glen to join us all, and I could bring this sorry tale to its conclusion…though I still needed the help of the authorities in more than one way to do that.

But what about Bud? My heart told me I needed to explain my conclusions to him first – so he and Worthington would be able to prepare to cope with what would follow my revelations.

I returned to the salon; once again, every face turned as I approached. Bella wasn't there, so I assumed she was with Worthington and Enderby. The atmosphere was bleak, despite the logs roaring in the hearth.

Felicity was closest to the fire, nursing an almost-full bottle of water, while Renata's was already empty. Given the glassiness of her gaze I wondered if hers had ever really contained water – then further wondered if she'd brought any more with her. I hoped not, because I needed her to be able to answer some challenging questions later in the day.

It was the sight of John's face that I dwelled on, however; he looked at me with a mixture of hope and fear in his eyes. I approached and said, "I need to steal Bud away from you all for a few moments again. I hope you can manage without him." I winked and smiled. A feeble attempt to raise John's spirits.

"I'm right here, you know," said Vinnie. "Being on the spot, and multi-talented at that, means I can deal with any danger, real or perceived. You take your man away with you now, but be sure to return him to us undamaged." He blew me a kiss, and even John managed a smile.

Once we were alone in the entry hall I whispered to Bud, "It's time for me to share. But we need Worthington, too."

Bud smiled. "So you're not going to gather everyone in the salon and explain the entire thing to us all?"

"Eventually, I hope to be able to do so. But…this case is different, Bud. And there's a good reason for me needing to involve Worthington, and you, before we go much further. I just hope he's not tied up for too long, so we can get everything done that needs to be done."

"I could hang around outside the meeting room until he's free, then bring him to join you in…what, the palace room?"

"Yes, thanks, that's a good idea."

I padded up the stairs again. It seemed fitting that I should reveal my understanding of the case there…looking down on the world I was about to change forever, for so many.

"...a mingled yarn, good and ill together..."

The mackerel sky above Beulah House was losing its lustre by the time Worthington and Bud arrived to meet me in the palace room.

"Thanks for this," I said, facing both men. "Please, feel free to get comfy – I need to explain a few things, and ask for some help."

Bud settled into a chair close to the one I'd been occupying beside the smokers' table, while Worthington turned a seat from the large desk to face us.

I began, "This is an unusual case, in that I believe it began with a fit of anger but was followed by a series of coldly calculated actions, all of which have resulted in a dreadful situation. As you know, Mr. Worthington, I'm a victim profiler, and that's where I want to begin – with our original victim, Sasha Tavistock. What sort of a woman was she? She had what most would consider to be a happy, contented married life. She wanted for nothing, it seemed, and she made her mark in the worlds of PR and politics. But we also know she suffered from bulimia, which is a complex condition with roots than run deep, whatever they might be; there's often a trigger, and frequently it's a condition which begins in a person's early life. I believe I might have found several threads which became woven together to lead Sasha to suffer as she did – one of which means I have to consider the role her father played in her life, which leads us back to the so-called 'suicide note'."

Worthington leaned forward. "So-called?"

I nodded. "Yes. Let's consider what the note itself said. 'He'd have been eighty today. His shadow will never leave me. It's too late for me to try to be whatever I could have been, had he not been my father. I thought it would all end with his death. But now it seems that was a foolish hope on my part. It will never end, until I end it. So I shall. No procrastination. No more…anything. Sasha.' First of all, as I've already mentioned to Bud, I believe this was just the final part of a longer letter Sasha had written referring to a situation she had decided would now come to an end."

"But what situation?" Worthington snapped.

"I believe Sasha was being blackmailed, or threatened, by someone, and that she was about to bring the matter into the light, to remove that person's leverage. If you recall, Bud, Sasha told Julie she had something she wanted to say to the assembled group before dinner…"

Bud nodded. "She did."

I added, "And bear in mind that Sasha was a woman who felt it necessary to write things down, in notes and letters, that she wanted people to take seriously."

Worthington nibbled his bottom lip.

I continued, "My field of research – and the work I did when I consulted on Bud's cases, back in Canada – has nothing to do with apportioning blame to the victim at all; rather, it's about understanding their lives in a way that helps illuminate how they became a victim. I'm a psychologist, not a psychiatrist, which means I observe behaviors, rather than carrying out medical diagnoses – but my observations of Sasha both when I knew her many years ago, and in the brief time I spent with her here at Beulah House, as well as the information I've been able to glean about her life since then, lead me to believe she displayed what would be called psychopathic traits. I know we're all accustomed to thinking of psychopaths as only evil mass killers, but the classic traits of narcissism, lack of empathy, need for control, and absolute self-interest, are also known to be observable in many of the world's political and business leaders. We can see those traits in both Oleg Asimov and in Sasha. She, also, had the sort of personality that could easily allow her to make enemies – and I believe it was one such enemy with whom she was meeting before dinner that night, in this very room, to tell them she would have no truck with their desire to have a hold over her."

"Fascinating," said Worthington, "but could you tell me who you think that was, and why, because I still have people I need to interview downstairs."

"I think your interviews are over for now," I replied. "You see, we must begin by considering who *could* have killed Sasha. I believe that happened as the result of a violent outburst which led to Sasha being struck in the head with a cut-crystal ashtray, which also gave a glancing blow to the brass telescope causing it to pivot so it was out of position, and left a small mark on the brass, which Bud and I found earlier today. Sasha was groggy – and wasn't the type of person who would have allowed her attacker to go unpunished, so they took their chance to push her off the roof, using the only door which allowed her to fall far enough to make it look like a real suicide attempt. In her state, and remembering she wasn't a heavy woman, Sasha could have been led, steered, or even pushed, to the door, and relatively easily shoved over the rather feeble balustrade. A man or a woman could have done it."

"Which doesn't help us much, does it?" Worthington looked at his watch.

I pressed on. "Of those who are now dead – because we cannot discount any of them out of hand – who could have killed Sasha? Piers, Charles, Julie, or Sir Simon. All of them could have been here in this room, but none of them appear to have had any reason to threaten Sasha with…well, anything."

Worthington sighed. "It's a start. So, who are we left with? Renata Douglas. Felicity Sampson. John Silver. Glen Powell. Bella Asimov. Hardly a 'short' list, is it?"

"I notice you didn't include Vinnie Ryan," said Bud.

Worthington smiled. "You've seen how many cameras we have at our disposal? The CCTV coverage of this area on the evening in question leaves us in no doubt that Mr. Ryan was in a motor vehicle, and approached this address a moment or two prior to the call he made to…let's just say 'a colleague of mine'. I've known he couldn't possibly have killed Mrs. Tavistock for some time."

Bud and I shared a smile.

"And Glen is out of the frame; he sings…and I heard singing in the kitchen when Sasha died. But you did include John Silver," I said.

"Indeed," replied Worthington gravely.

"Go on, tell him," I said to my husband.

"Not John," said Bud. He looked grim. "The man's sound. Operationally and psychologically. Besides, he and I were chatting through the walls of the WCs when Sasha came off the roof. No way. Not your man."

"Bond of trust," I added, sounding as sage as I dared.

Worthington shook his head. "Mr. Anderson, of course I understand the type of trust about which you're speaking, but I have to consider two aspects: one, it can only go so far; two, it might lead you to believe you're doing the right thing by manufacturing an alibi for a man you believe incapable of killing Sasha Tavistock."

I was slightly blindsided to hear Worthington say he was suspicious about Bud's support of John, but pressed on. "Well, I believe Bud, but, instead of debating that matter, how about I outline good reasons for the three remaining people being here with Sasha that night? And for her having written such a letter to any one of them."

Worthington shrugged. "Please do."

I opened with, "Sir Simon Pendlebury shut down the investigation, and set up a smear campaign targeting me." Worthington looked theatrically puzzled. "He did so when only Sasha had died. That tells me one key thing – Sir Simon had knowledge, or at least a strong suspicion, that whoever killed Sasha was either an Asimov, or well-connected to the Asimovs. He had to act to protect the family name, and business."

"But everyone's connected to them in some way," said Worthington.

I replied, "First, let's take Felicity."

Worthington's eyebrows shot up. "Well, we know she caused the injuries which led to Mrs. Powell's death but—"

"Hear me out," I replied. "Felicity was once an Asimov and is still closely associated with the family. Indeed, Glen told me Felicity's been supported financially by Oleg since their divorce, and not in what one might call a 'normal' way. She have known something about Oleg that he didn't want shared with the world, and could have used that knowledge to get him to pay up for – well, whatever she wanted, whenever she wanted it. I have no idea what her bank accounts look like, but I've observed enough of Felicity Sampson to know this – she's exactly the sort of woman who'd not want to see a source of easy income dry up, and we know she phoned Bella and threatened her after Sasha's death. That could have been Felicity's attempt to get Bella to keep financing her lifestyle, having already failed to get Sasha to agree to do so. Felicity and Sasha could have agreed to meet here, Sasha gets her to read the letter saying she won't pay up, Felicity lashes out, and she dumps Sasha's body off the roof. She uses the end of Sasha's letter to her to throw us off the scent, then – the very next day – tries to get Bella to keep funding her."

"Well…possibly, but what about the other deaths? Are you saying she killed everyone else too? How? Why?" Worthington scratched his head, putting me in mind of Bud…who didn't seem to even notice the similar tell.

"Hang on – let's stick to Sasha's death, first," I said. "If not Felicity, it could have been Renata who came here before dinner, and things worked out the same way."

"What possible hold could she have had over Sasha?" Worthington's eyes grew round.

"The papers in Renata's bags? They've been gathered over years, and – when taken together – show beyond any doubt that Oleg Asimov's asbestos dumping operation has been anything but 'safe'. Renata's father died of mesothelioma, after having been a lorry driver for Asimov for decades. She could have put her case to Sasha, who might have refused to act, or who believed that Oleg's death would put an end to the threat."

"It's certainly a motive for there being bad blood between them…" Worthington nibbled his lip again. "But would Sir Simon take the steps he did to stop us discovering Renata had killed Sasha?"

I answered, "If he'd known what those papers could prove, he would have wanted to protect Renata; she could have gone on to kill the Asimov group's entire business future."

Worthington's brow furrowed. "Sir Simon Pendlebury was certainly a man who cared more about business, and moneymaking, than people…" He looked at me and added, "If you believe everything you read about him in the papers, and online."

I almost smiled. "Then there's Bella, a real Asimov, whom he'd also want to protect. Bud and I saw a photograph in Sasha's personal study that leads me to believe that Bella could have known about Sasha having been pregnant, and having an abortion during the school holidays, in Wales, when she was a teen. Bella could have held the threat of telling Oleg about that over Sasha…for decades. One look at Bella's order book tells me she's making almost no income from her goldsmithing, and yet her outgoings for materials and equipment are substantial. I'd put money on her sister having been financing her, against her will, for a very long time. They could have fought about that."

Bud shifted in his seat, and said, "So you're saying Bella, Renata, and Felicity, all had a potential reason for being here with Sasha that night, and for falling out with her – leading to Sasha's death, and them setting things up to look like a suicide?" I nodded. "And you think Sir Simon would have done what he did to protect any, or all, of them?" I nodded again. "But – and I know you've thought this through, Cait – what about all the other deaths? As Mr. Worthington has said, do you think the person who – maybe accidentally – killed Sasha, then went on to kill all the others too? Including Sir Simon? I mean, if you're right, he was the one who'd protected them in the first place."

I nodded. "I do. And I believe I know which one of them it was."

"What makes you think that?" Worthington's eyes glinted.

"I've put together the entire overview of who was where, when, on the day Piers died. This is critical, because, of course, his was the second death. If my theory is correct, the murderer gave themselves a chance to kill him by taking a huge, coldly calculated risk – which would fit with their character, and sense of purpose."

"I've read all the notes," said Worthington, "but Enderby hasn't pulled them together into a timeline yet. Care to fill me in?"

"Absolutely. In essence, I'm satisfied that the timeline does, in fact, bear out my suspicions that Julie's life-threatening injuries became known about by Bella, Charles, Piers, and John at the same time as each other – when Glen was informed about them, and whisked away to the hospital – and line up with the time Renata said she'd been at the offices of Tavistock and Tavistock, gathering the papers with which she later returned."

Both Worthington and Bud scratched their heads. In unison. It was almost amusing.

"Accepted. But this tells us what?" Worthington didn't sound impressed.

"Our killer will stop at nothing to protect themselves," I said. "And, if what I think happened is what actually *did* happen, one of the most tragic aspects of this entire sorry situation is that, even after Sasha's death, it could all have been stopped – if not for the sickeningly self-centered actions of not just one, but two, people."

"This involves more than one person?" Worthington's eyes narrowed.

"Sadly, yes," I replied. "But – and this is why I'm talking to just you two at this stage – we don't yet have any hard evidence that might prove guilt to a jury. There's one critical piece I believe I can work on providing, but I need to ask a few things of you, Mr. Worthington."

"I'll do whatever I can, if it's within my power," he replied.

I smiled with relief, knowing Worthington was finally on my side, and handed the man a note I'd written earlier. He read it and returned a puzzled gaze. "The missing crystal ashtray is hidden…there?" He sounded less than convinced.

"Yes," I replied. "I believe it wasn't thrown from this room; the killer couldn't run the risk of pieces of broken glass being discovered, thereby suggesting something other than suicide. It should be retrieved and examined for trace evidence to try to prove it was used to smack Sasha in the head. However, I understand such evidence might have vanished. Next, you need your people to re-examine the biological material found beneath

Sasha's fingernails, looking for traces of what I've listed for you."

Worthington nodded. "Can do. Anything else?"

I added, "When I expose the secrets each of those three women downstairs have been guarding, there could be some…strong reactions."

Worthington sighed heavily, "I don't have bodies to call upon to provide cover." The flash of frustration I saw in his eyes told me that, while he might be ready to support me, he wasn't receiving the backup he needed from on high.

"I'll be in the room," said Bud. "I'm not as young as I once was, but I've taken down the odd bad guy during my career." He managed a grim smile. "I dare say I could wrangle any of those women to the ground, if called upon to do so."

Worthington shook his head sadly. "And risk facing charges if everything goes…well, let's just say 'not quite as planned'? No, you'll do no such thing, thank you Mr. Anderson. If physical restraint needs to be applied, I or Enderby will be the ones doing the applying. She's wiry, that woman; don't let her size fool you."

I nodded, as did Bud, though he looked just a little disappointed. He said, "You have actual authority here, Worthington, but I can be a resource. In the know. Watching, and ready to be directed, as necessary."

"Quite the pair, you two," replied Worthington, nodding.

"...I speak as my understanding instructs me..."

Worthington invited us all to meet – for what would surely be the last time – in the dining room. There was a pervasive air of resignation, and it was clear Glen felt dreadfully uncomfortable having to be in the same room as Felicity.

After Worthington had left us alone in the palace room, I'd explained the entire case, as I saw it, to Bud. He'd told me I had his full support, which I'd known would be the case, because one of the many things that binds us together is a deep-seated belief that justice must prevail...even if, sometimes, we don't quite agree on what true justice is, under certain circumstances.

Worthington's tone was grave as he began. "I'm not going to say very much on this occasion. I shall leave the talking to Professor Morgan. She has approached me with a hypothesis which appears to make sense of the facts as we know them. Professor, please state your case."

I began. "I want to thank Mr. Worthington for affording me this opportunity to put forward my theory of what's happened here over the past few days. It's been a tragic time, no question about it, and everyone at this table has lost someone of...significance. Some more than others. We met as a group on Monday evening to mark the eightieth birthday of a man whose shadow hangs over us still. Now the Asimov organization is facing a challenging future, and I suspect there will be battles in the months ahead with those who might want to take advantage of its perceived weakness."

Everyone looked at Bella, who straightened her back and said, "I think I might be equal to the task. I might even surprise a few people. And, of course, my darling husband will be at my side to help me through it all." She gazed at John who gazed back. "He has a good brain. He'll make a wonderful managing director – his skill set in liaison means he's ideal for the job."

"Glad to hear the wedding's still on, John," said Vinnie, smiling.

"Me too," John replied, though he looked a little less certain about the future Bella had just painted for him.

"'There is a tide in the affairs of men, Which, taken at the flood, leads on to fortune'." My statement drew a few puzzled glances. "Shakespeare knew how to distill complex concepts into quotable phrases, didn't he? I believe Oleg Asimov was a man for whom that quote had particular resonance…he took his chances. And sometimes, I suspect, they were chances he shouldn't have taken. He built upon the great fortune he inherited, yes, but at what cost? I think Renata knows more than a little about that."

Everyone stared at Renata, whose expression didn't change. She took a deep swig from yet another water bottle.

I asked, "How soon after you were employed by the Townsend Agency did you realize the woman you were working for was the daughter of the man who owned the business for which your father had driven lorries, for many years?" Renata said nothing, but sipped at her bottle.

John looked surprised. "Really?"

I continued, "The papers you brought here, in two heavy briefcases and a backpack, have been taken into custody by the authorities, as the property of Sir Simon Pendlebury. There might be reason for them to examine them. I'm assuming such an examination would make you happy."

Renata screwed the top onto her bottle and placed it carefully on a coaster. She sighed, heavily. "Yes. Please read them, Mr. Worthington. They are the fruits of many years of listening to people at dinners, taking chances to search out contracts and other papers, putting together concrete evidence of business connections that had been hidden, or had gone unnoticed. Those papers prove that the part of the Asimov group responsible for the so-called 'secure dumping' of asbestos did so in an unsafe manner. For many years. My father died slowly, and painfully, of mesothelioma. He worked for that company. I knew…I *believed* my case would be rebuffed while Mr. Oleg Asimov lived, so I waited until his death, then brought the matter to the attention of Mrs. and Mr. Tavistock, who promised to brief Sir Simon. I believe they would have, between them, taken the appropriate actions to prevent any further use of such devastating corner-cutting. The proof is clear. It's all in those bags." Renata's voice had risen by an octave, and she grabbed for her bottle.

"We'll look into it," said Worthington. He nodded toward Enderby. Who typed frantically with her thumbs.

Renata glowed, silently. And didn't take a drink.

I pressed on, "However Oleg's 'sharp business practices' might have manifest themselves, I was delighted to learn he was at least a man who appreciated how very much young minds – and hearts – can derive from experiencing, first-hand, the power of a live production of the Bard's plays. Will the funding of the Shakespeare for schools project that your father founded and financed continue, Bella?"

Bella bestowed her most bounteous smile upon us all. "Absolutely. I even plan to expand it; put more money into the productions, to allow for additional expenditure on costumes, scenery, and so forth. That would allow an even greater number of artists to benefit."

"What an inspired idea, Bella," enthused John. "I've told you how much I was impacted by the way we used to read through the plays at school; I read Mark Anthony, in *Julius Caesar*, you know," he smiled proudly toward Bud, "so if I could get involved in that side of things I think I'd find it easier to learn about that field rather than construction and so forth. Not my forte, and sadly, not my interest. Besides, I could do the Shakespeare thing sort of on the side – while I continued with my real career."

"You'd make the perfect honest, reliable general," I said. "Maybe Vinnie's Vaseem could help you out," I said. "I'd bet he has some excellent contacts who could bring you up to speed."

Vinnie winked and gave John a thumbs-up. "Say no more, I'll get me man on it right away. Bella, your husband – for that's what he'll be by next week – will soon be on a par with…well, your first husband, before you know it."

I said, "Oh yes, Brian Quiller, theatrical designer and impresario, that's him, isn't it, Bella?"

Bella's neck flushed. "Yes, Brian's still in the business, though I'm not sure he and John would hit it off, exactly."

"Too much alike?" I made sure to keep my tone jocular.

John glanced uncertainly at Bella, who replied, "Utterly dissimilar, in every way." John's shoulders relaxed.

I continued, "This family is not unfamiliar with dissimilar parts, is it? You and Sasha were so unlike each other in many ways; the strains within such a family must have been tremendous – and they were, weren't they, Bella?"

She shrugged. "We managed to rub along."

I pounced, "More like you rubbed each other up the wrong way. Sasha worked for everything she had; you get what you want when it's given to you by those who see how poorly you're being treated by others."

Bella smiled. "People are so kind."

I chose to not rise to that bait. "Indeed; they rescue you, admire you for your yielding, soft qualities, and magnanimous nature. Whereas Sasha was dynamic, driven, overtly successful, and hired by clients because she was as tough as old boots. What most people – Julie aside, I suspect – didn't know, was that Sasha was bulimic. The root causes of bulimia are complex, but what I can tell you is this: in Sasha's case I believe her bulimia was an early-age response to not having enough control over her own life, with at least one root cause which, I believe, also offers an explanation of the ghost Felicity spoke about. Vinnie – didn't you mention something about Piers approaching the local historical society about research he felt should be available on the ghost Felicity mentioned?"

Vinnie perked up. "That I did. Piers said he'd heard the ghost himself...so it weren't just you who had first-hand experience of the weeping and the wailing, Felicity. He wanted to know why there'd never been any research done into it. But Sasha couldn't recall where she'd heard the story about the woman, though she said she'd known about the ghost since she was a child, living here back then."

Vinnie relaxed back into his seat again.

I continued, "Most helpful. Do you remember any stories about the ghost when you were growing up here, Bella?" Bella shook her head, frowning. "No, I thought not. The air vents which heat the palace room are fed by pipes which travel up the walls of the house. If someone – maybe a girl of about seventeen, let's say, a much more voluptuous version of the woman she would later become – were to be taken away by her mother to Wales to obtain an abortion during the school holidays, and who regretted that decision for the rest of her life...maybe increasing her likelihood of becoming bulimic...if that girl, now a grown woman, were to seek solace in the palace room during the night, where she could privately mourn the loss of her child, that pitiful sound could carry throughout the house, and end up being heard in some strange places."

Felicity's eyes widened, and Vinnie shifted uncomfortably in his seat, as did Glen.

I felt dreadful for poor Glen, who was looking haggard, with good reason, but knew I had to keep going. "Everyone's told me how Sasha bravely struck out on her own, as opposed to following in her father's footsteps, but she used all her father's contacts to help her to succeed. Now, to me, Oleg Asimov doesn't sound like the sort of man who'd have offered to share his contacts like that if he'd known about his firstborn daughter killing an Asimov heir. Thus, I believe she was absolutely desperate to keep that knowledge from him."

I spoke quietly when I addressed Bella. "Was it worth cutting yourself off from your father's toxicity, but having to pay the price of losing any chance of him supporting your career? To set yourself against your sister, then having to draw her back to live in this house after your mother died, to have at least one person who'd pat you on the head and tell you how very talented and clever you were?"

John shifted uncomfortably in his chair. I could see Felicity's eyes glitter with glee.

"I have no idea what you mean," said Bella. "Sasha and Piers came here because they wanted to move out of London a little way. It's quiet here – they needed to decompress at the end of their workday."

"And they needed the cash from the sale of their house to bail out the business," I said.

Renata snapped, "How did you know that?"

"You just confirmed it for me," I replied. She flushed. "But is that really why they did it? That was about the same time the Bella Zoloto brand was founded; I bet that cost a pretty penny."

Glen's voice cracked, and he glared at Felicity when he said, "What on earth has any of this got to do with Julie? Everyone knows that woman killed my wife. I don't even know why I'm here."

Glen deserved my attention, and got it. "I'm really grateful to you for agreeing to be here, Glen. It must be terribly difficult for you, and you're right, Felicity did inflict the wounds that led to your wife's death. But I thought you deserved to know why that happened."

"I do indeed," said Glen, thumping the table. "But—"

I held up my hand. "I'll explain soon, I promise. But it won't make sense unless we go back to what happened on Monday evening. We all think we know when Sasha fell from the roof – but what we really know is when her body was discovered. You see, that's the thing…no one saw Sasha fall. Not even Vinnie. She was on the ground before he arrived at Beulah House. She could have been dead for almost ten minutes before she was discovered."

Felicity bleated, "But that makes no difference, because we were all…wherever we were, for the whole time anyway."

"But were we?" I replied. "Let's pretend this is a play, and Beulah House is the set on the stage – open-fronted, facing the audience. While everyone moved away from the salon at much the same time, some would have reached their destinations sooner than others, because of exactly when they left, and exactly where they went. And maybe not everyone stayed where they began, in any case. Picture this… Sasha leaves Renata on the rear terrace and climbs the outer staircase. Piers is already in his private bathroom, so doesn't see Sasha enter then exit their bedroom, making her way up to the palace room, which I believe she did immediately. When she got there – because this was now a personal space, and personal time – she let her hair down, placing the grips from her chignon in her pocket with the intention of repining it before joining the rest of us for dinner. She'd agreed to meet someone in the palace room, but didn't want that meeting to be known about, so that's why she'd taken Renata with her out onto the terrace, as cover. Upon that person's arrival in the palace room, they read the letter she'd written to them, and they fought. I believe swinging the heavy crystal ashtray at Sasha's head was something that happened in the heat of the moment. Sasha was down, and probably close to being unconscious. For once she was vulnerable…and her attacker opened the relevant door, steered the now semi-conscious Sasha across the room, and pushed her off. Then…what then?"

"What?" Renata snapped, sitting forward in her seat, her eyes – for once – wide with an emotion…*excitement, or fear?*

"Before I answer that, Renata – you tell me this. And I need an honest answer. Did you leave the terrace behind the salon at any time when you told us you were there?"

Renata stared at the table, then looked up, tears in her eyes. "I can tell you the truth, now. I did." She hung her head in shame. "I was terribly cold, you see, so I went inside the door of the back hallway and shut it. I eventually heard all the commotion, and came around the back again, so no one would know I'd hidden away." She sniffed, loudly. "I didn't want Piers or Sir Simon to think I was unreliable, or they might not have supported my findings about the cause of my father's illness, and death. I *had* to say I'd remained where Sasha had told me to. I'm sorry I lied. I felt I had no choice – at the time."

I watched her micro-expressions like a hawk.

I addressed the ceiling. "I'm the attacker, I've pushed Sasha to her death – what now? My main aim is to be involved in the hunt for the missing Sasha. Think about it – none of us expected Vinnie to return to the house at that time. The killer would have believed we'd all nonchalantly reconvene for dinner, for Sasha's absence to be noted, and for some sort of search to ensue…with the discovery of her body in the driveway being the inevitable, though not necessarily immediate, conclusion. The killer thought they had a little time to put their hastily concocted plan into action. Not a great deal of time, of course, because they had to be back in the salon to innocently be able to comment upon Sasha's absence. So, what did they do? Well, they had to somehow get rid of the bloody ashtray, and they needed a suicide note. They were in luck, because they worked out that by dumping the first part of the letter Sasha had written to them, they had something bearing Sasha's signature that could pass as such a note."

I paused, and looked at Bella, who returned my gaze with a blank stare. "I found your order book out in your workshop, Bella. Your handwriting is extraordinarily similar to your sister's. A little more rounded, maybe…a touch more artistic, shall we say? But I bet you could write just like her, if you wanted to."

Bella smiled warmly. "I could, and often have. Sasha and I used to do each other's homework in school without the teachers being any the wiser. They all thought I was good at maths, and she was good at English – but they had no idea we were pulling the wool over their eyes."

John beamed, and said, excitedly, "So that means Bella wouldn't have needed to use part of a letter written by Sasha as a suicide note – she could have written one herself that wasn't so…vague."

Bella squeezed John's hand. "You're so clever darling, and he's right, isn't he, Cait? If it had been me, I would have written a much more convincing suicide note." She stared me down triumphantly.

I simply replied, "Yes, you could have done…but there was no writing paper in the desk in the palace room upon which anyone could have written such a note."

Bella's eyes clouded over, and Felicity shouted, "I didn't do it, either."

"No one has said that you did. Yet." All eyes turned as Worthington spoke. He smiled, broadly.

I pressed on. "One page of the letter was placed on the desk, where we were supposed to think it had been written, and I believe the killer automatically turned off the desk lamp as they left. Once they'd descended from the palace room, they had to get to where they were supposed to have been all the time…but I don't think they achieved that without being seen."

I paused, and noticed that Felicity was fiddling with her hair. "The post-mortem has shown that Charles Asimov was a habitual user of recreational drugs. I believe that you first used the pink bathroom alone that evening, Felicity, but then you went to join Charles in the blue bathroom, where you each indulged in a snort or two of cocaine."

Felicity became the center of attention; she flushed, her eyes darted around the room, and her chest began to heave. Trapped.

She stammered, "I'm not…I won't…"

"This is one time in your life when you need to be honest, Felicity." I stared her down. "Did you join Charles in the blue bathroom that evening?"

Felicity's eyes slid toward Worthington who said, "I have no interest – on this occasion – in illicit drug consumption."

Felicity gave a little nod. "I did. We did. But I…"

I shut her down. "You don't have to say anything more, Felicity – I'll tell everyone what happened. When you made your way to the blue bathroom you saw someone who had every right to be where they were, so thought nothing of it, at the time. It wasn't until after the discovery of Sasha's body, when people were recounting where they'd been at which moment, that you realized the person you saw in the upstairs hall had lied to Mr. Worthington about their whereabouts. The next morning you phoned Bella, and told her what you'd seen. Glen overheard Bella's side of that conversation, and also told me about how very generous Oleg had been to you over the years, since your divorce. I believe you attempted to blackmail Bella during that call, because it was Bella you saw in the hallway, slipping into the yellow bedroom, and you knew that – whatever else she might, or might not, have been guilty of – she'd at least lied to Mr. Worthington. But Bella rebuffed you, didn't she? She went so far as to threaten to tell everyone about your relationship with Charles…your one-time stepson. Not quite the same as Jocasta and her marriage to her son Oedipus, but close enough for there to be a scandal. And what happens to two tabloid darlings when the sharks attack? Blood in the water leads to a feeding frenzy – and eventual oblivion."

Bella looked pale. "Yes, Felicity and I spoke on the phone that morning. And we did, in fact, argue. But that's not what it was about at all. Felicity was being rude about Sasha taking her own life. That's what it was, wasn't it, Felicity? Tell them, then everything will be alright."

Felicity said nothing. I could see she was beginning to draw blood where she'd been picking at the side of her fingernails.

I continued, "Renata, remember when Bella said she'd find work for you at Bella Zoloto, because she'd never, ever, let anyone down who put the Asimov family first? Well, I'm sorry to tell you this, but I believe she spoke as she did to let Felicity know that if she kept quiet about seeing Bella in the hallway, Bella would look after her."

Renata's expression didn't change. She looked up at Bella, then Felicity. I could see a vein pulse beneath the skin of her neck. She picked up the plastic bottle from the table in front of her, and drained it. I was amazed the woman could focus, let alone sit upright; I sincerely hoped she wasn't an explosive drunk, because that was the last thing I needed to deal with. I glanced at Bud, and was delighted to see he was also keeping an eye on Renata. He and I managed to share a fleeting smile.

Beside Bud, John noticed our silent exchange, and said, "Now, hang on a minute, Cait." He kept glancing between Bud and myself, and was chewing the inside of his cheek. "I don't think I like the sound of where this might be going." He spoke quietly.

"I'm sorry, John," was all I could say, before continuing, "now let's consider what happened to Julie."

"Yes, please do," said Glen plaintively.

I pulled the golden medallion from my pocket, where I'd placed it earlier. "Have you ever seen this before, Glen?" He took it, examined it, and returned it, shaking his head. I held it up for everyone to see as I said, "I'm sorry to tell you, Glen, that this is – indirectly – what led to your wife's death."

Glen frowned. Felicity's eyes opened wide. John's hand went to his chest. Bella glanced at John, her chin lifting.

I placed the medallion on the table. "I found this in the bin under the sink in the kitchen. And I asked myself who would put something so valuable in such a place? The first answer I came up with was Julie – because, let's be honest, not a lot of other people here use the kitchen habitually, do they? For those of you who haven't seen it before it's a gold medallion with a centaur on one side, and, look, a large capital letter C on the other." I twirled the medallion.

John's eyes told me he was thinking. Hard.

"What does yours have on the back of it?" I asked him.

John glanced at Bella. "There's no real name 'John' in Russian, they have the name 'Ivan' instead. The Cyrillic for the capital letter 'I' is on the back of mine. Which looks like a backwards 'N'."

I held up the medallion. "And this isn't really a capital letter a 'C', it's the Cyrillic symbol for the first letter of the Russian version of the name 'Simon'. But, you see, Glen, Julie didn't know that, as I dare say most folks wouldn't. Remember you told me about overhearing Bella refer to 'the center' that Felicity wouldn't be getting, after all?"

Glen nodded, looking puzzled.

"Bella was referring to this centaur medallion, which she showed to Julie, telling her she'd made it for Felicity to give the Charles. Now, I know you might not want to hear this, Glen, but…"

Glen sounded wistful when he said, "Julie had a right old soft spot for Charles, she did. Nothing…you know…untoward, like. Just a soft spot."

I decided to not disabuse him of his belief that Julie's feelings for Charles hadn't extended past the "soft spot" stage, to the slightly besotted. "Yes, Glen," I replied, "and I'm afraid Bella took advantage of that soft spot. This medallion is rather like the handkerchief embroidered with strawberries that Iago used to make Othello believe Desdemona was having an affair; Bella used it as 'proof' that Felicity was trying to get her claws into Charles. I believe she also told Julie she'd witnessed Felicity creeping down from the palace room when Sasha died, thereby convincing your wife that Felicity had killed her precious Sasha. Julie threw the medallion into the rubbish under the sink – her dustbin of choice. To further bend her to her will, Bella drugged Julie – probably with cocaine or some form of speed, from Charles's stash; I have no doubt she knew he had one, and where he kept it hidden. Unused to the drug, the surge of hyperactivity Julie felt turned to anger, and paranoia. With you having told me, Glen, that one of Julie's favorite knives had already disappeared from the kitchen that morning, it's easy to believe Bella had removed the knife, which I'm certain she pressed Julie to take with her to threaten Felicity. Bella wound Julie up, drugged her, armed her, gave her several motives, and pointed her at her target. Julie did attack you when you opened your door, Felicity…"

Felicity squealed, "I know she did – I keep telling everyone she did…I really was just defending myself. She was like a madwoman. I'm so terribly, terribly sorry about what I did, Glen…it was as though she was possessed." Felicity reached her little arms across the table toward Glen, whose mouth was hanging open, tears rolling down his cheeks.

He stammered, "M-my poor old girl. She obviously wasn't in her right mind." He stared at Bella as though she were an evil apparition. Bella remained aloof.

I said quietly, "Look, it's not much help, really, but there's something you should know, Glen. You have furniture in your flat that's worth a great deal of money, to some people. Please get it looked at by a professional. Your wife is irreplaceable, I know, but you might raise enough money to be able to get yourself a nice place to live, near family, and friends. You'll need them close by, now. As I say, it's no real consolation, but you should consider it. We are all so terribly sorry for your loss."

Through his tears Glen blubbed proudly, "Always had a good eye, did Julie. Never happier than when she was poking about in junk shops."

Bud was sitting beside Glen and handed the poor man a packet of tissues from his pocket. We'd made sure before I started that he had a few. He put his arm around Glen's shoulders, and I could hear him whispering a few words of comfort.

I wanted to say so much more to Glen, but knew I had to press on. "When word reached Beulah House that Julie hadn't killed Felicity after all, Bella knew Felicity could still blackmail her, though she also knew Julie's injuries meant she wasn't able to tell anyone why she'd attacked Felicity. So, Bella decided to try to get rid of Felicity again, using the same idea, but choosing a different pair of hands to do her dirty work. This time she picked on Piers, who was already groggy from the drugs he'd been prescribed. Bella had long enough to work on him while John and Charles were otherwise engaged, and used her skills at manipulation and persuasion – honed over decades – probably telling him she'd seen Felicity in much the same circumstances as Felicity had actually seen her. Piers was befuddled, and suggestible, and, by the time she left him, he was convinced Felicity had murdered his wife. He could have easily killed you, Felicity."

Felicity's hands went to her throat, and she said quietly, "I know. He might have done." She stared at the table, only occasionally glancing toward Bella out of the corner of her eye.

I continued, "Bella had failed again – only now she was in an even worse position, because Piers might tell any number of people why he'd attacked Felicity. Bella primed Mr. Worthington to expect no more than drug-addled ramblings from Piers when he interviewed him, then made a show of going to the coach house to change her clothes. Instead, she went outside, and gained access to the upstairs via the back hallway and the servants' staircase. I can only imagine how terrifying those moments must have been for you, Bella, wondering what Piers might blurt out, so, when Worthington left, you didn't wait to shut him up. You entered Piers' room and administered a huge amount of diazepam to him…probably chased down with brandy – acting the part of concerned sister-in-law. You returned to the coach house via the servants' stairs to change your clothes, then entered the front door making a fuss about dripping wet snow all over the hallway to cement the idea in our heads that you'd been only across the courtyard. When Piers died, Bella was safe from the danger of him revealing how she'd convinced him that Felicity was Sasha's killer – but she still had to deal with Felicity's threats somehow."

"I had no idea." Felicity's voice was small, weak.

I chuckled. "Oh yes, Felicity, when you threatened Bella, you didn't just kick a hornets' nest, you stuck your head inside it. I'll be absolutely honest at this point, Bella, and tell you I don't know if you said, or did, something that gave you away to Charles, or whether, by this time, you'd realized you were finally at the point where, with just a little more luck, everything your father once had could be yours, and yours alone."

Bella said nothing, but snatched her hand from John's, and folded her arms.

"Either way, you saw Charles as just a 'thing' threatening your greater happiness and security, and all you had to do was wait until he was out cold – which he often was. You found some liquid spice in his stash, popped it into a cuppa or a drink you probably took him the next day, and off he went into his bath, where he sank beneath the water. Or – and let's imagine I'm feeling a certain level of generosity toward you – maybe I'm wrong about all that and Charles simply overdid the drugs he would have taken anyway, to find the oblivion he so clearly sought for much of his life. In a way I feel sorry for you, Bella. Your father's genetic material, and his toxic personality, infected all three of his children as they grew: Charles was an addict; Sasha a bulimic; and you are a blackmailer, and a killer. What a legacy."

John grabbed Bella's hand, though they didn't exchange a glance; Vinnie's expression was the most grim I'd ever seen – with not a hint of a gleam in his usually playful eyes; Bud was nibbling his lip…and I could see the pain in every muscle of his face. The room was absolutely silent – except for the blessed clock, ticking inexorably on the sideboard.

I was almost done – the end was in sight. "However – with Charles dead, and you now the only Asimov remaining, Bella, you took one final, deadly step to free yourself from all the chains with which your father had bound you. Sir Simon

Pendlebury had already begun to adopt a tone that made it clear he'd be telling you how to run the family businesses, so his unexpected arrival here was your chance to pop something into his tea, too. The toxicology report will tell us what it was; this time there's no prescription for diazepam, or history of drug abuse to cover your tracks. They'll work out what it was, and they'll trace it to you, because – for all your cunning and risk taking – you haven't been very good at getting rid of the evidence, have you, Bella?"

"I have no idea what you mean." Bella spoke forcefully.

I forced a polite smile. "Well, allow me to enlighten you. The ashtray with which you wounded your sister? Mr. Worthington's people have retrieved it from the rill that's been frozen since you dumped it there. All you had to do was run down the steps which can be accessed from both the yellow room and the master bedroom to drop the weapon into the water, which you believed would wash away all trace of you…and your sister. You would have checked the coast was clear, and were lucky Renata had abandoned her post on the rear terrace. But I believe Sir Simon, sitting in the darkened meeting room that night, spotted you. Maybe he knew all along you'd been somehow mixed up in Sasha's death; at least he knew you'd been lying to Mr. Worthington. He certainly shut down the investigation into your sister's death, to protect you and the businesses. And it's no wonder you dropped your mug when the blokes were out there in the garden peering at something in the grass. Thought they'd spotted the ashtray stuck in the ice, eh? You'd be amazed how well ice can preserve evidence, Bella – though, of course, because you and your twin Sasha share a DNA profile there might be a chance you could claim any trace matter found upon it is either hers, or yours. In the same way, I'm sure you believed it's impossible for anyone to prove the skin beneath your sister's fingernails is yours, not hers. However, it might be that the scrapings sent to the laboratory are imbued with an element that's specific to just you, as opposed to both you and your sister. I'm thinking of sandalwood body oil, or patchouli residue. But we'll leave that to the scientists who are, so Mr. Worthington tells me, very much looking forward to the challenge. Apparently, cases involving twins are fascinating."

John couldn't look at me. The ticking of the clock seemed to be getting louder.

I turned my attention to Felicity, who was cowering in her seat. "Unfortunately, it's not just Bella who's to blame for all this. If you'd told us about seeing Bella coming down from the palace room and entering the yellow bedroom straight away, rather than using that knowledge as a chance to enrich yourself, Felicity, then Julie, Piers, Charles, *and* Sir Simon would be alive today. That's the Sir Simon who called you 'Fliss', and whom you called 'Simon'; the Sir Simon you've been sleeping with; the Sir Simon you knew was the man who would really have control over the Asimov empire. Yes, if you'd only spoken up – instead of trying to blackmail Bella – they would all still be alive."

Felicity's tears were silent, and I still wasn't sure who they were for; I feared they were only for herself.

"I would have made the Shakespearean scheme one of the great artistic endeavors of the twenty-first century," said Bella wistfully.

John stared at her, and pulled his hand from hers. His voice was thick with emotion. "I'd have done anything for you, Bella. Anything."

"And that's a part of the problem, John," I said. "Bella has enjoyed a lifetime of achieving her goals by convincing people she's terribly unfortunate...desperately unlucky. People believe she never gets noticed enough, or loved enough. She's incredibly skilled when choosing her mark, and knowing what will make that specific person want to help her out. It's how she's always ended up getting what she wanted – without ever appearing to be needy, or grasping, or ambitious. She drips her poison constantly, so gently that no one notices, until it's too late, and they are – in the true sense of the word – enthralled by her. And her motivation? Jealousy. Always jealous of her sister. Her father's firstborn – by ten, long, world-changing minutes. John, when we were first driving here, you mentioned Chandler's manipulative female characters, which suggests to me you knew – deep within your subconscious – that something wasn't right. I think a lot of folks have probably sensed it over the years, maybe even Bella's father himself, though Bella's always done her best to keep her true self hidden. Remember when you mentioned the way Bella sometimes looked at her sister, Vinnie? It's a terrible thing, jealousy. And I believe it's what began this chain of events. Emilia said, in Othello: 'But jealous souls will not be answer'd so; They are not ever jealous for the cause, But jealous for they are jealous.'"

John shook his head. "Cait – you know I have great admiration for you, and your skills, but this time you must be wrong. Bella's just not the jealous type. I know her. You don't. Bella's not one of your academic subjects – she's a person. The woman I love." He looked toward Bella who met his gaze.

Whatever he saw in his fiancée's eyes in that instant made him draw back from her, almost imperceptibly. Had she allowed her mask to slip? Had he finally glimpsed the woman she really was? I hoped so, because until John himself understood what Bella was capable of, there would be no way for him to come back from this.

"They can't love, can they? Psychopaths." Felicity's voice was sad. "Oleg never loved me. I knew that, but it really didn't matter at the time. It was only afterwards, when it was all over, that I realized how much that had hurt me. I don't believe he loved any of his wives. The only thing that ever mattered to him was that people *thought* he loved them. The only reason he stuck it out with Sasha was because she did the fundraising for his blessed Shakespeare thing – which he felt made people look at him with admiration. And me and Charles? It was nothing. Just a dalliance. Life can be so terribly boring, and Charles understood that. For all that he said he hated his father, the two of them were both utterly self-absorbed. I don't think either of them ever loved anyone except themselves. I wondered, sometimes, if any of the Asimovs even had a heart."

"I've known a few true psychopaths in my time," said Vinnie thoughtfully. I found it interesting that Worthington didn't look surprised. "Some of them are drawn to danger. Can't feel anything unless they're on the edge of oblivion. And you're right, Felicity, there's not a drop of love in them. Nor real loyalty, neither. Except to themselves, and at all costs. Hard-hearted they are…all of them. Yes, I'd say that sums them up alright. And let me tell you, the price you have to pay when you rely upon a person like that can be…high. Too high. John, listen to me, man. You know what, and who, I'm talking about. And you know how things turned out during that operation. They can't help it. They just do it."

Renata's voice slurred a little when she said, "They don't just do it, Vinnie, they plan it, they watch it all happening. They don't care that people are damaged, get sick, and die because of what they do. Everyone's expendable to them. I hope you're not going to come up with some psychologists' mumbo-jumbo that gets the Asimov companies off in court, are you, Cait? Because that's not fair. Oleg put profit before lives. For decades. Sasha? She really did a lot of good, you know, and I believed her when she said my evidence would be used to put things right in the company, not hidden away somewhere. But as for this one killing people? She's still got a long way to go before she catches up with her father. It wasn't just my dad who developed a deadly illness; others died too – and are still dying. Who's going to help them now, with even Sir Simon gone?"

Worthington said, "Shakespeare might have written that all the lawyers should be killed, but I suggest you use them to do what they're good at, Miss Douglas."

Renata almost chuckled. "Yes, lawyers…"

I couldn't afford to get sidetracked any longer. "One of the things I wondered about was why on earth Sasha and Bella were meeting, secretly, in the palace room in any case. They're sisters, after all – they had the chance to speak in private anywhere, at any time, without it causing suspicion. But that night was special. After your mother's death, you, Bella, were the only living person who knew about Sasha's abortion…her 'lost child'. Her note to you makes sense if we believe you'd threatened her with telling your father about it while he lived; she paid, and paid, to keep you quiet. With your father gone, you no longer had that threat to hold over her, did you? Remember Sasha said she had something to tell us before we ate that night? I believe she was going to make a clean breast of it – after all, with Oleg dead, who'd worry about a teenager choosing to rid herself of an unwanted pregnancy almost forty years ago? Your leverage had vanished. You'd have to find a new way to get what you wanted."

I pulled the envelope containing the sheets of paper from Sasha's study out of my pocket. "I found it, Bella," I said. "Shall I read the full letter aloud? Then we'll all know the truth for certain, won't we?"

Bella's eyes darted to the slate clock on the sideboard.

Of course! In the dining room after Sasha's death, she'd poured herself another brandy – an unusual move for someone who'd said she didn't like the stuff. *That* was where she'd hidden the rest of the letter Sasha had written to her – behind the clock.

As I stood, and moved toward the sideboard, I said, "I knew John had stuck to you like glue since Sasha's death, and suspected you'd not had a chance to dispose of a piece of evidence that could convince a jury that my theory is, indeed, fact. Thanks for giving away where you hid it."

Bella also stood, the realization of what she'd just done clear to me; her eyes flashed with pure hatred. She turned John's face to look up at her and bent to kiss him. She spoke quietly, her voice devoid of any real emotion. "I almost loved you, you know – closest I ever got." Then she dashed out of the door leading to the rear hall, slamming it behind her.

Everyone leaped up – except Glen and Felicity, who remained glued to their seats, open-mouthed, and Renata, who I don't think could have stood if you'd paid her. Bud and Worthington pulled at the door, but it was locked.

John was up, grabbing at Bud, shouting, "Leave her alone!"

I managed to remove the envelope containing the missing parts of the letter Sasha had written from where Bella had wedged it as I called to Bud, "Use the doors to the salon – go around that way."

Bud was first out, followed by John, and Vinnie. I was just behind Worthington, and could hear Enderby saying, "Yes, I'll record your statement, Miss Sampson."

The front door was wide open when we reached the entry hall. One velvet curtain had been pulled back, the other was flapping in the breeze. There was no sign of Bella. I glanced toward the stairs. Nothing.

"Bella!" John's shout was the cry of a mortally injured wild animal. "Bella?"

"She's gone, John," said Bud, quietly.

John turned to face us, his features contorted. "What do you mean, she's gone? She wouldn't run away, out into the night like that. You're wrong about it all, Cait. I'm sure you are. You must be. Bella would fight it. In court. Besides…" He stared into the darkness. "Where would she go?"

Bella didn't scream when she jumped, but I wasn't the only one who'd never be able to forget the sound of her landing.

FRIDAY

"...one that lov'd not wisely..."

The fact that we hadn't been able to prevent Bella killing herself weighed heavily upon us all. I felt I had completely failed her victims, and even Bella herself, by not having foreseen her intentions.

Worthington had been so angry he hadn't even bothered to question any of us; he'd packed us off as soon as possible, telling us he'd follow through as necessary, but I'd left Beulah House still not certain what that meant.

With the tragic mess behind us, to the extent it ever would be, our main concern was John.

On what should have been his wedding day, he sat huddled in a blanket on a sofa in his sitting room, struggling to understand how he could have missed seeing his fiancée's true personality, but still not quite believing her capable of doing what she'd done.

He would chatter incessantly for many minutes – largely to himself, then he'd sit without saying a word – hardly breathing – for what felt like an age. Then the chattering would start all over again.

He'd been the same way all night, since we'd got him home, and now all morning, too.

I backed off after a while, because the sight of me seemed to set him off – which Bud and I agreed was understandable.

Vaseem arrived at John's house late on Friday morning. He was a big bear of a man, which I hadn't expected – given Vinnie's worked-out physique. But what really surprised me was the vitriol with which Vaseem greeted me. Vinnie tried to placate him, but it was clear he held me personally responsible for John's sorry state, and went so far as to suggest that Bud and I should leave.

We retreated to our room. It was Bud's suggestion to find out if we could pick up our rental car a day early. We found we could, so we packed, and went upstairs to tell John we were leaving.

His relief was tangible. He even seemed to rally a little.

"Sorry, old man. A lot to deal with," he said to Bud, as I tucked away the sandwiches Vinnie had insisted upon making for us to eat on our journey; I had no idea why he'd felt we might need them, but at least it gave him something to do while Vaseem was on duty beside John on the sofa, almost growling at me whenever I approached.

John's voice was thick with tears and emotion, though he forced a smile. "These chaps will see me right." He surprised me by almost chuckling. "I'd told them at work I'd be on my honeymoon for the next fortnight, so they won't miss me. No need for any of them to know what's happened…as long as Worthington sticks to his word and manages to keep it quiet. Of course, my lot being who they are, the chances are they already know all about it. Oh God, what am I going to do? I managed to get through the Lottie thing alright. But this?"

Bud spoke softly. "Is there anything I can do? Anything at all? You only have to say the word. Our friendship means a great deal to me, John, and you know Cait and I owe you so much. We'll stay, or go, as you choose."

John said nothing. Vaseem adopted a threatening stance.

Vinnie pulled us aside. "Go on with you. Between Vaseem and me, we'll take good care of him. Too many cooks, and all that. None of this was your fault, Cait. All you did was bring it out into the light. John – and Vaseem, for that matter – just have to reach the point where they can see that. And that might take a while yet. Go on now, get away with you both. We'll keep in touch."

I trusted that John knew we weren't deserting him; he had two good friends by his side, and I suspected he wouldn't mind seeing no more of me – the woman who'd revealed his bride-to-be as a psychopathic multiple murderer.

So we left. Everyone cried. All silently.

Once we'd collected the car, I was consoled by traveling the route I'd driven so often out through West London, heading for the M4. As the towers alongside the overpass disappeared into my rear-view mirror, I settled into the slow, grinding traffic pattern.

I knew Wales would offer Bud and me the healing we needed. We only had a few days there, and I was keen to visit places that had soothed me before.

It took until a necessary loo break at the Reading services for Bud to finally say, "Penny for them, Wife?" He spoke tenderly, and reached across my seat to hold my hands.

"They're worth more than that," I replied, smiling as best I could. "I can't even find the words to express how sorry I am for what John's going through at the moment. I absolutely understand that the ghosts of the Asimov family will probably follow him throughout his life; Bella's most of all. But all I can say is that I'll do everything I can to help *you* through this, because that's the only thing within my power. So, with that in mind…let's get to Wales safely, but as soon as possible, and get up early tomorrow to walk on the beach in Gower where we were married. I'll even recite my vows again, if you like – just the two of us, on the sand, beneath the cliffs, alone."

"Hmm…my memory's not as good as yours, so I might have to make mine up as I go along. As appropriate to what I've learned about you since then."

Bud laughed.

I hadn't heard him laugh for days. It sounded good. Best sound in the world.

"Börje Ulf Dyggve Anderson, I love you." We kissed.

"…exit, pursued by a bear…"

Chapter title sources

MONDAY

1 "…all the world's a stage…"
As You Like It, Act 2, Scene 7

2 "…the course of true love…"
A Midsummer Night's Dream, Act 1, Scene 1

3 "…the memory be green…"
Hamlet, Act 1, Scene 2

4 "…more than kin, and less than kind…"
Hamlet, Act 1, Scene 2

5 "…the gloomy shade of death…"
King Henry VI, Part One, Act 5, Scene 4

6 "…the stars above us…"
King Lear, Act 4, Scene 3

7 "…I come to bury Caesar…"
Julius Caesar, Act 3, Scene 2

8 "…unloose this tied-up justice…"
Measure for Measure, Act 1, Scene 3

TUESDAY

9 "…all is mortal in nature…"
As You Like It, Act 2, Scene 4

10 "…thou art wedded to calamity…"
Romeo & Juliet, Act 3, Scene 3

11 "…he that filches from me my good name…"
Othello, Act 3, Scene 3

12 "…the map of honour, truth, and loyalty…"
King Henry VI, Part Two, Act 3, Scene 1

13 "…this tiger-footed rage…"
Coriolanus, Act 3, Scene 1

14 "…the lady doth protest too much, methinks…"
Hamlet, Act 3, Scene 2

15 "…richer in your thoughts than on his tomb…"
All's Well That Ends Well, Act 1, Scene 2

16 "…we have seen better days…"
Timon of Athens, Act 4, Scene 2

17 "…leave not a rack behind…"
The Tempest, Act 4, Scene 1

WEDNESDAY

18 "…nothing either good or bad, but thinking makes it so…"
Hamlet, Act 2, Scene 2

19 "…a stage, where every man must play a part…"
The Merchant of Venice, Act 1, Scene 1

20 "…what's past is prologue…"
The Tempest, Act 2, Scene 1

21 "…to be, or not to be…"
Hamlet, Act 3, Scene 1

THURSDAY

22 "…now is the winter of our discontent…"
King Richard III, Act 1, Scene 1

23 "…all that glisters…"
The Merchant of Venice, Act 2, Scene 7

24 "…of bloody deeds and death…"
King Richard III, Act 5, Scene 3

25 "…one sin I know another doth provoke…"
Pericles, Act 1, Scene 1

26 "…such stuff as dreams are made on…"
The Tempest, Act 4, Scene 1

27 "…a mingled yarn, good and ill together…"
All's Well That Ends Well, Act 4, Scene 3

28 "…I speak as my understanding instructs me…"
The Winter's Tale, Act 1, Scene 1

FRIDAY

29 "…one that lov'd not wisely…"
Othello, Act 5, Scene 2

End "…exit, pursued by a bear…"
A Winter's Tale, Act 3, Scene 3 (stage direction)

Quotation source: The Complete Works of William Shakespeare, The Alexander Text, 1978 edition, Wm. Collins Sons & Co. Ltd.

Acknowledgements

Each time I plan to take Cait and Bud on a journey, the place they travel to is somewhere I shall, as I write, also be visiting. Therefore, writing this book has been a particular delight, because it gave me a chance to revisit London, where I lived for seventeen years. I hope you enjoyed visiting places that mean a great deal to Cait…they do to me, too. The other wonderful thing about writing fiction is to be able to conjure places that have (as in the case of the restaurant Cait and Bud visit to indulge in some delicious desserts) disappeared, in real life. Now they'll at least live on in this book.

This book has also given me a chance to play with my love of Shakespeare – a passion I developed during my time at Llwyn-y-Bryn school, in Swansea, under the tutelage of Mrs. Hammond and Mr. Lee, my two English Literature teachers during those years. Reading Shakespeare aloud is still one of my favorite things to do, and I find his use of language and storytelling to be an ongoing inspiration. I know I'm not alone in this, but at least I get a chance to acknowledge that enjoyment here.

Once again, I want to thank my ever-supportive sister, and Mum, in Wales: I speak to them on the phone every day, and they listen to me rant on about plot points, characters, storylines, and problems for months. Thanks for doing that. Also, my husband; he puts up with everything I've already listed, but also has to cope with my lack of focus on real life because I'm living in my created world for so long. Without his support and patience there'd be no books.

Thanks, too, as ever, to my editor Anna Harrisson, and to Sue Vincent, who checks my proofs; they both pulled out all the stops on this one to meet a much tighter-than-usual deadline.

Finally, there are the members of "our community" who've played a direct role in this book finding its way into your hands To my early readers (SA, JD, KA), thank you so much for helping me hone this story. To the bloggers, Facebookers, Tweeters, Instagrammers, reviewers, librarians, booksellers, organizers of online events, and festivals and conventions – thank you for doing whatever you did that helped this reader find this book.

And to you, dear reader, thanks for choosing to spend time with Cait Morgan and Bud Anderson.

About the Author

CATHY ACE was born and raised in Swansea, Wales, and now lives in British Columbia, Canada. She is the author of *The Cait Morgan Mysteries*, *The WISE Enquiries Agency Mysteries*, *The Wrong Boy*, and collections of short stories and novellas. As well as being passionate about writing crime fiction, she's also a keen gardener.

You can find out more about Cathy and her work at:
www.cathyace.com

Made in the USA
Middletown, DE
29 May 2022

66323068R00189